A Novel

Chrissy M. Dennis

THE LION CUBS

Copyright © 2012 by Chrissy M. Dennis

Printed in Canada

Word Alive Press
131 Cordite Road, Winnipeg, MB R3W 1S1
www.wordalivepress.ca

WORD ALIVE PRESS
Just Write!

Library and Archives Canada Cataloguing in Publication

Dennis, Chrissy, 1984-
    The lion cubs / Chrissy Dennis.
Includes index.
ISBN 978-1-77069-431-6
    I. Title.
PS8607.E665L56 2011   jC813'.6   C2011-907576-8

Dedicated to my loudest cheering section:
you know who you are.

"The world beneath has its own rules of relating, moral code, and
defensive strategies that are well known to midadolescents
and are tightly held secrets of their community."
~Chap Clark, *Hurt*

||||||||||||||||||||||||||||||||||||||||||||

ACKNOWLEDGEMENTS

First and foremost, a heartfelt thanks goes to my Creator: my Lord and my Rock. This journey would not have been possible without the passion, the words, and the strength He gave me to craft *The Lion Cubs*. He is in every single page I've written.

My deepest gratitude goes out to Caroline Schmidt, Jeremy Braun, Nikki Braun, Warren Benson, Evan Braun, Lori Mackay, and everyone at Word Alive Press, who believed in my message, worked with me to refine it, and released it into the world. Thank you for allowing my dream to become a reality.

So many wonderful individuals shine in the pages of *The Lion Cubs*, both directly and indirectly. Thanks to Chap Clark, whose book *Hurt* gave me a fresh understanding for the "world beneath," and a renewed awareness of a hurting generation; Child Welfare Information Gateway, the Mayo Clinic, and Youtube user "dragonabsurdum" for shedding light on situations that were beyond me; Amy Dawson, my beautiful sister and biggest fan, who guided me through some of the deepest valleys of *The Lion Cubs*; Ginger McColl, who walked this journey with me from start to finish, threw me a celebratory party (with Skittles), and supported me all the way through; Amy Day-Janz, who endured so many of my writing woes and encouraged me every day; Amanda Chalmers, my unofficial PR rep, photographer, and beautiful friend; Jennifer Poirier, for countless hours of brainstorming and editing my first few drafts; Kari Stefanidis, for editing my first few drafts and being exceptionally picky, which motivated me to strengthen my writing in ways not otherwise possible; and my parents, for who they are and all they've done.

I must also thank my two little motivators, C & N, whose constant "Shouldn't you be working on your book, Chrissy?" always kept me on track; Erin Alexis Adams, for being Lexi's namesake, and for being a great friend; Brad Peters and Christopher Stefanidis, who offered a couple of phrases of dialogue that bring the book to life in fun and quirky ways; Bailey, Brandon, Brittnee, and Richard, a group of teenagers whose insights into the world of adolescence helped shape the culture of the tunnels; Maryl Fraser, my Grade Ten teacher, who helped me find my voice and gave me a desire and passion for writing, something I am eternally grateful for; and Jacquelyn Mitchard, my favourite author, who gave me many wonderful words of encouragement and advice, spurring me on.

There are countless others who I have not the room to list who have been amazing sources of encouragement, support, and love throughout this journey. My love and thanks go out to you all.

Finally, a warm thank you goes to Dorothy Hunse, who continuously pours wisdom and love into my life. Much of this same wisdom and love saturates these pages. She is, in the truest sense, the woman I want to be when I grow up.

—Chrissy M. Dennis

CHAPTER 1

L E X I

Thursday, October 1
8:30 p.m.

Kristen was slicing at her wrists again.

But that was no surprise, at least not to fifteen-year-old Lexi.

She was slouched over a table, alone as usual, fanning a worn out book back and forth, her dark brown eyes focussed on the bloodbath three tables over.

How is anyone supposed to get anything done with all these mental cases around?

Distractions.

Turning her attention back to the faded book, she swallowed a yawn. Who cared about *Hamlet* anyway? Sure, the play was turned to the middle of Act 2, but she saw nothing but a jumble of words. That D on her last report card was well-earned.

Evenings were always a pain, especially between 8:00 and 9:00. They called it "study hour," but the last thing on Lexi's mind was homework. She hated this place, and everywhere she turned she was crudely reminded of it. The room itself was void of windows, a box of suffocating darkness. Pitiful attempts at colourful paintings were plastered all over the cold concrete walls, a failed try at disguising the chipped paint. Above her, florescent lights flickered, most of the bulbs were burnt out, and to top it all off, dead mosquito carcasses marked their final resting places in the cobwebbed corners of the room.

1

It was no wonder she found herself staring at that cutter, Kristen.

Attention, that's what everyone said; Kristen was just desperate for attention. Lexi couldn't say she really blamed the kid. In a place like this, with at least a hundred teenagers drowning in issues Kristen had probably never even *heard* about, the competition was ridiculous. Kristen would never be seen, not the way she wanted to be.

It didn't take a genius to figure out what would happen next. Any second now, a youth worker would sweep across the room and pry the razor blade away from Kristen. Kristen would flash her crisscrossed arms and wail like a banshee. The youth worker would try to shut her up, but they'd have to pull her out, probably off to some therapist on duty or Mrs. Greenwich, the grouch who thought she could run this place. Either way, Lexi wouldn't have to watch anymore—at least not for today. Kristen would try again tomorrow.

Just another typical day at Everidge Youth Centre.

Well, maybe for everyone else.

Not Lexi.

Sure, Jackie and Eddie ramming tongues down each other's throats on the far corner sofa was typical. Tristan was only a few tables over, sketching dark skulls and shadows of shotguns while his greasy black hair waterfalled over his forehead, and Molly sniffed silently to herself as she trailed out of the room, nobody bothering to follow. *That* was all typical, but tonight, Lexi had other things on her mind.

She was getting out of this dump, tonight. This place was a joke. Did they actually expect her to stick around after everything they'd put her through?

Morons. They were all morons. They acted like saints, doing these kids a favour by placing them in foster homes, but they didn't get it. Lexi would rather die than sit around like some obedient dog, waiting for them to ship her off to another battle zone.

No thanks. She had enough war wounds.

2

Her stuff was already packed, ready to be snagged at a moment's notice. She'd been waiting for her chance all day to slink away, but so far, no luck. *That* was Katrina's fault. The place was swarming with extra youth workers because of her. Lexi figured it was extra security, a safety net, all because Katrina had plowed through a bottle of aspirin last night. She was still in the hospital, probably hooked up to loud machines, tubes shoved down her throat. Now Greenwich was watching for copycats. There were eyes everywhere.

Thanks a lot, Katrina.

It was stupid, Greenwich's reasoning. If she was smart, she'd realize nobody would actually try to kill themselves just a day after Katrina tried. No, Greenwich would *expect* that.

She really didn't know anything.

Of course, they all thought *Lexi* was a suicide risk. That just showed how much *they* knew. When her social worker, Bridget, pulled her out of her last foster placement, bringing her back here, Lexi was told to wait outside Greenwich's office, but she heard everything. Seriously, did they actually think she was *deaf?*

Bridget used the term "adolescent at risk," if you could even call that a *term.* Bridget hashed out the details of foster placement number four and warned Greenwich that Lexi might "exhibit symptoms of major depression, spiralling into suicidal ideation if she isn't effectively monitored."

What did they know? She wasn't suicidal, and as if they should talk like they knew what went on at the Toffsons' anyway. They thought they had pulled her out in time. They thought they were the heroes.

It was all a matter of perspective.

She was done. She refused to be shipped off to foster family five. All she needed was a clean break, those watchful eyes distracted for just a moment. It was only a matter of time. It wasn't like any of these people actually cared about her, about *any* of them. Their job was to stand guard, be on the lookout for suspicious behaviour.

If that was true, why did they seem more concerned with finding a solution for 32-across?

Lexi opened up *Hamlet* again, nearly gagging from the smell of the musty pages touched by hundreds of other charity cases like her. When was the last time she'd owned a *new* book?

Accidentally ripping a corner of the frail page, she heard the scuffling of chairs from across the room and the booming voices of two girls. All around her, kids abandoned their homework to surround the action. Though it wasn't unusual for fights to break out in a place like this, Lexi's curiosity pulled at her, and she left her forgotten book behind.

A crowd encircled the two girls who were cursing wildly. One was yanking at the other's hair, bobbing her back and forth like a yo-yo. The shrieks were deafening!

Lexi overheard someone saying that Yasmine, the girl getting her hair pulled out, was flirting with Jackie's boyfriend. Jackie got ticked.

Obviously.

Lexi watched, her heart crawling into her throat, but not because of the brawl.

No, she was watching the youth workers. They had all dropped their knitting and cellphones and were weaving their way through the crowd. Their job now was to break up the fight.

A momentary distraction.

All eyes were turned.

Lexi's chance.

Rolling her eyes to feign boredom, she stepped out of the room, leaving the echoes of profanity behind her. Now out of sight, she made a quick dash for her room, where she reached under her bed, snatching her backpack.

The window was open; it was another humid day in Tampa, and Everidge's few windows were always open. The city's budget didn't allow for air conditioning, not for this forgotten facility.

Lucky for Lexi. The open window was her way out.

Checking over her shoulder, she tossed her bag out the

window, then wedged her skinny self through the open crack, just fitting.

Her feet found the dead grass below, and she groaned at the stench of rotting garbage nobody had bothered to put out.

Hoisting her backpack over her shoulder, she took off down the street.

She didn't look back.

She could still hear Yasmine and Jackie going at it down the street, and it wouldn't be long before they'd be split up, punished, and then forgotten. That was how it worked, and that was how Lexi knew she'd get away with this.

She'd tried running away once before, but she hadn't been careful enough. They caught her before she was halfway out the door. Greenwich even made her write lines: *I will respect this facility and all it has done for me.*

At least this time Lexi was smart enough to have a plan.

They'd notice her absence eventually; they'd do their checks before curfew and figure out they were one short. Sure, they'd look for her. Sure, they'd call the cops because they had to, but Lexi had been here long enough to know the truth.

By this time tomorrow, they would all forget about Lexi Vogan—she'd be nothing more than a forgotten soul in a faceless crowd.

CHAPTER 2

L I Z

Friday, October 2
8:17 a.m.

"Good morning, Mr. Tustin. I'm Dr. Swavier. How are you feeling?" Liz crossed the hospital room, perusing her patient's recent test results while the man lowered the magazine he'd been looking at. Liz found a seat at the elder's bedside, her exhausted blue eyes meeting his sparkling hazels. This had to be her fiftieth patient.

"Well, Doc, I gotta tell ya, I've been better." The man's wrinkles seemed to smooth themselves out when his mouth stretched into a smile. Liz, emergency room physician at St. Marcus Hospital in downtown Jacksonville, returned the gesture.

"You may not feel terrific, Mr. Tustin, but I've got good news for you. Your test results tell me that you're going to be just fine. Your heart attack was minor."

Tustin groaned.

"Minor? Good Lord, I wouldn't want to know what a big one would feel like!"

"Well, you won't have to if you make sure you take care of yourself." Liz winked and unwound the stethoscope from around her neck, sliding the cold surface down the man's hospital gown.

A chuckle caught in her throat as her patient winced. "Sorry, I know it's cold. Well, your heartbeat is strong. You'll have to follow up with your physician, but you should be able to go home today. How does that sound?"

"Like a million bucks!" The seventy-five-year-old flashed a toothless grin, warming Liz to her core. Why couldn't all patients be this easy, this kind?

"Great, is there anyone we can call for you?" She stole a glance at the man's medical chart. "Your wife is listed as your next of kin. Can we still reach her at this number?"

An awkward silence followed, and Liz felt its cold sting. A wave of guilt flood over her; she'd asked the wrong question. She'd known it as soon as she'd asked it. There was no wife.

Her stomach sank to her knees, but she forced herself to catch those hazel eyes, a familiar sadness glazing over them, a despair she knew all too well.

"Mr. Tustin, I'm sorry, I shouldn't have assumed—"

"It's alright, Doc, you didn't know." Tustin wrung his rough hands together. "My wife, Dorothy, well, she... she passed away six months ago. I guess... I guess I forgot to update my information."

Liz felt like cement was running through her veins. She couldn't move. A darkness was brewing inside of her, starting in the pit of her stomach, a darkness that could devour her if she let it. She'd been down this road before; she knew what those emotions could do to her. Pain was like that; it could smother you if you gave it a pillow.

But it was still a choice.

She opted for silence, for pretending like those feelings weren't there. She pried her eyes away, back to her notes, where she wouldn't have to look into the empty space in the old man's eyes, an emptiness she knew went deeper than the soul.

"I guess you could call my son, Murray. Murray Tustin. I can give you his number."

Liz's patient recited a phone number, and she jotted it down, eager to ignore the biting tension stirring up inside of her. Her mind was trying to go back, back to a place she was helpless to forget. This was all too close to home.

"I'll be sure someone calls your son," she said.

She turned and headed for the door, her escape, but her conscience nagged at her. No matter how heavy her own heart was, no matter how selfish she wanted to be, no matter how much she wanted to run away, she couldn't be that heartless. That wasn't fair.

God, give me strength.

"And," Liz managed an awkward smile, "I'm sorry about your wife, Mr. Tustin."

Tustin nodded. "Thanks, Doc."

Liz left the man to his own thoughts, swallowing back the pressure in her throat, the tsunami of emotion desperate to wreak havoc. The same words echoed in her skull, again and again. *My wife, Dorothy, well, she... she passed away six months ago.*

Passed away.

Gone.

"Jill, will you please call Mr. Tustin's son and tell him his father will be released today? His name and number are right here." Liz passed the receptionist Tustin's file and ducked into the staff room.

She was met with the rising aroma of fresh coffee. Thank goodness, someone had just put on a fresh pot, and Liz poured herself a generous cup, sipping it quickly, oblivious to the burning sensation numbing her tongue. She guzzled it, like always. There was never enough time in a day to take breaks.

Well, at least that was how Liz saw things.

Tustin wedging his way to the back of her mind, she hurried back to the front desk to receive a new file, still sipping the remnants of her coffee. Amber Daeling, a twenty-one-year-old girl who had just suffered a miscarriage, was waiting in ICU 5. The young adult was to be monitored for the next few hours.

My wife, Dorothy, well, she... she passed away six months ago.

It was going to be one of those days.

But not if she didn't let it.

8

Draining the rest of her coffee, antsy to get back to work, she headed toward the ICU but felt a slight tug on her arm. Gasping, she spun around to find her friend and co-worker Jenn, laughing at her.

"Easy, Liz, I'm not Freddie Krueger." Grinning, she exchanged files with Jill and motioned to the abandoned coffee cup. "What number is this?"

Liz felt her tense muscles relaxing. She'd been working with Jenn at St. Marcus since she'd started this job nearly ten years ago. Though four years her senior, Jenn was a faithful friend who was always good for a laugh and an occasional distraction from the pressures of hospital life.

"I don't know, Jenn; I stopped counting after six cups," Liz replied.

Jenn playfully rolled her eyes. "Geez Liz, good thing you drink it black, or you'd have to worry about diabetes or something."

"Thank you, Dr. Falton," Liz said with a hint of sarcasm. "When did you get here? I haven't seen you on the floor."

"That's because you're ridiculously busy, as usual. Anyway, I started about half an hour ago. When did you clock in?"

"Um, I guess around 7:00." Liz inspected her watch.

"This morning?"

"No, last night."

Jenn moaned, shaking her head. "You serious? You realize that's thirteen hours? Are you *insane*? Geez, I thought eight-hour shifts were bad." Jenn's green eyes flickered with concern. "Why all the long hours, Liz? You're *always* here when I am—"

"Oh come on, that's not true—"

"Coffee is practically a life support for you, which tells me you hardly sleep—"

"I sleep fine, Jenn; it's—"

"I've seen the schedule up in the staff room, Liz. You work eighty-hour weeks! You're gonna kill yourself." Jenn crossed her arms, allowing Liz room for a rebuttal, but Liz hardly felt like having an argument.

"Look, Jenn, it's really not as big of a deal as you're making it out to be, okay? I am *fine.*" Liz held up the file folder. "But I will *not* be fine if I don't get back to work. Last thing I want is to get fired."

She turned but felt a hand catch her elbow.

"Relax, Liz, I'm not trying to bully you into anything." Jenn's lips curved into a mischievous grin. "I'm just saying, don't you take *any* time off?"

Liz's defences rose again. "Of course I do. In fact, I have tomorrow off," she said, lifting her chin proudly.

"The *whole* day?" Jenn asked, hands on hips like she was a parent scolding her child.

A laugh escaped Liz's tight lips. *Oh Jenn.*

"Yes! The *whole* day. It's Kevin's birthday."

"That's your younger brother?" Jenn inquired.

"Yep, he's turning thirty-four, so my mother is throwing a barbeque up at her place tomorrow."

"That's good, Liz; you deserve a break." With that, Jenn patted Liz's shoulder and strode off to continue her own rounds. "See you later."

Sucking in a deep breath, Liz fought to put the conversation out of her mind as she headed to ICU 5 where Amber would be waiting, but it was no use. Liz was already dreading the weekend. *A family barbeque, a break?* The thought made her want to laugh out loud as bitterness plagued her.

Well, it wasn't Jenn's fault; how could she know about Liz's family? It wasn't like Liz was open about her personal life.

It wasn't the whole family she preferred to avoid. She loved her brothers dearly, got along great with her sisters-in-law, adored her nieces and nephews. Even her dad was a hoot, but visiting the Deston clan meant visiting her mother too.

Wanting to forget about the upcoming party, Liz stepped into a small room, where she found a young girl curled up on the bed, fetal position style, face buried in a wet pillow. Though Liz felt her heart collapsing all over again, she knew she would prefer even a day like today over any day of having to endure her mother.

CHAPTER 3

L E X I

Friday, October 2
6:26 a.m.

Lexi's legs felt like jelly, but then she'd been stuck on a bus for the last eight hours.

Her body was already feeling the effects of losing a night of sleep; her muscles were tight, her shoulders tense, her eyelids felt like there were weights hanging from them. Sure, she could have dozed off after her transfer in Orlando, there would have been time, but she didn't trust that guy four seats back who had stared her down like a piece of meat since Tampa.

She couldn't understand what it was about her that made men look. She was nothing special: 5'2", short for her age, with unruly chestnut hair she always tied back, her skin a pale shade, her eyes dark and hollow. She was too scrawny, her bones stuck out, and she was practically chestless. In her opinion, she was plain, awkward, and unattractive. Even still, she seemed to get a lot of attention.

But why did it always come from the pervs?

She was fighting back a yawn when the bus driver finally announced their arrival in Jacksonville.

'Bout time, Lexi thought as the bus screeched to a halt in a rundown bus shelter.

Cursing under her breath, Lexi struggled to ignore the stench of body odour as a crowd of people elbowed past her off the bus.

11

Annoyed, she held back until the last of the travellers stepped off. By now, Lexi figured, she should be used to not being seen.

Now the last passenger, she swung her backpack over her shoulder and hopped off the bus.

The bus shelter reeked of tar and exhaust fumes, not to mention the lingering B.O. All around her she heard motors revving, generating a deafening hum. All she could see were old buses with scratches and dings on their sides, windows blackened and side decals peeling. It felt so sketchy. She'd never been to Jacksonville; she had no idea where she was or where she was going. She was a stranger in a strange city.

Well, one thing was for sure: she *had* to get out of this shelter. It was giving her the creeps.

How was she supposed to get out of this shelter anyway? She didn't see any sign of an exit or any maps of the city. How was she supposed to get downtown?

She eased herself forward. She had to start somewhere.

She caught movement above her; there, in the blackened rafters, a group of pigeons were picking at a nest they'd been building, their droppings lining the tattered wood in an abstract splatter.

Sick...

Lexi dug through her pocket for the little money she had left. The escape from Everidge had cost her forty-five bucks, not to mention eight hours of no sleep. Now she was tired and nearly broke.

She counted seventeen dollars. *Great; if I don't find this place soon, I'm gonna starve on this kind of money.*

She'd learned about "this place" two weeks ago, when she overheard Heather and Simone talking about it after curfew in the dorm. Heather had come back that day after taking off. She'd been gone a week.

Lexi remembered their conversation clearly:

"...getting caught?" Simone had asked. Heather scoffed in response.

"Yeah right, you really that stupid? As if they even looked for me. Anyway, doesn't matter, I didn't find what I wanted," she replied.

"Where'd you go?"

"I went to Jacksonville, downtown. Took a bus in the middle of the night."

"Why?"

"Because of what's there. Haven't you heard about it? Kids like us go there all the time. Turns out some chick found these abandoned tunnels a few years back. It's where they all live."

"Who?"

"Street kids. They all live in these tunnels, and nobody bothers 'em. The cops leave 'em alone; everybody does. I figured I'd check it out."

"So, you didn't find it?"

"Of course I found it! It ain't hard to find; it's right downtown!"

"Okay, okay, but if you found it, why'd you come back?"

"Wasn't for me; it was stupid. Scroungin' for food, dealing with the crap of living on the streets. Nah, I'd rather be fed."

Maybe it wasn't for Heather, but Lexi was suddenly daydreaming about the tunnels of Jacksonville. It would mean no more Everidge. It would mean no more Greenwich.

It would mean no more foster care.

That's what put her on that bus.

Sure, she'd considered what else street life would mean—no Internet, no telephone, no shower—but Lexi didn't care, not really. How important was Facebook when you didn't have any friends?

Now, wandering through Jacksonville's bus shelter, she felt that much closer. Yes, this had to be the place for her. A place where she could disappear underground, forgotten by everyone. In all honesty, she was tired of it all, tired of being traded off between foster homes only to be messed with in some twisted way and then told, "It's going to be alright."

No, she was done with the system, done with adults, done with it all. She was on her own, like she'd been her whole life, but she didn't care.

13

She didn't care about anything.

***

Lexi found herself in an empty building, a closed-off ticket booth on one side, taped-off washrooms on the other. The place was desolate, silent.

It's too early, I guess, she figured. The people who'd been on her bus were all heading in opposite directions, but no one had come through this hallway. Realizing she was nowhere near where she needed to be, she decided to head back.

But she was stopped, by him: the same guy who'd been staring from four seats back, the middle-aged pig whose gut stuck out and whose head resembled a bowling ball. He towered over her by at least a foot, leering at her with hungry green eyes. Lexi tried to control the strangling feeling in her throat as she glared back.

"'Scuse me." She tried to sidestep him, but he followed her lead. She went for the other side, but he mirrored, blocking her. Lexi's heart was booming, and when the man grunted throatily, her insides churned.

"What's a pretty little thing like you doin' ridin' on a bus all alone in the middle of the night?" he asked in a southern drawl, the stench of tobacco fresh on his breath. "You run away from home?"

Lexi's mouth felt like paste. She tried passing again, but he was ahead of her.

"I couldn't keep my eyes off you, little girl."

When he glided toward her, Lexi stumbled backwards, her back finding the cold wall.

"Why don't you let me give you a ride? I can take you where you need to go."

Lexi sprung forward, hoping to pass him, but he snagged her arm, reeled her in, pressed her up against his body, his free hand on the small of her back, trapping her against him. He leaned in, his wet lips grazing her neck as his grip tightened.

"Come on, baby, don't make me beg."

His hot breath tickled her neck, and Lexi reacted. She swung back her foot and felt her toes collide with his shin, hard!

The scream he let out was thunderous.

His grip on her loosened, and she darted out of the building, back out onto the platform. There was no time to find her bearings; she barrelled through the crowd, terrified to look back.

"Hey, watch where you're going!"

"Stupid kid!"

"Good-for-nothing street scum!"

Lexi found herself on a main road, cars speeding along, crowds of people strolling on sidewalks. She skidded to a stop, spinning around, making sure she had lost that creeper. He was nowhere in sight, and, heaving a deep breath, Lexi began to walk quickly, voices still ringing inside her head.

Trying to shake off the tension, filter out the voices, she pressed on, but it didn't matter how much she tried to block it out, that pervert's breath still lingered in her nostrils, his slurred speech pierced her ears, his shady eyes burned in her memory.

Push it out! Push it away!

Still, it was all too familiar. That's why it bugged her; that's why it made her stomach turn so violently.

That guy was too much like Des, her last foster dad.

CHAPTER 4

L E X I

////////////////////////////////

Friday, May 8
8:45 p.m.

Five Months Ago

It was Callie's turn tonight.

That was how Des played his game.

In the bedroom she had to share, Lexi hugged her knees to her chest, staring out the window, her eyes never leaving the end of her street. She was waiting, waiting for the blue sedan to round the corner: her safety net.

But it was like staring into a black hole. Nobody was coming.

Besides, Evelyn wasn't off work until 9:00. Still, Lexi bore into that street corner as though wishful thinking itself would force Evelyn home early, just this once. If she came home early, Des would quit his game. His bedroom window was always open just a crack, just enough to hear the garage door opening, his signal that time was up. It gave him just enough time to send whichever girl he picked that night back to the girls' room, swearing her once again to secrecy. That was easy to do; there was a new threat every night, and the three foster girls had all learned the hard way that Des's threats were far from empty.

Lexi's lesson in submission came only three days after she'd arrived at the Toffsons'. Bridget dropped her off, gave her the runaround lecture about being good and respectful, and suddenly

16

Lexi was part of a new family. Neither Jaimie nor Callie, the other two foster kids, told her about Des.

That third night, while Evelyn was at work, Des asked Lexi to come to his room. She went, curious, because Des hardly said two words to her or the others. Maybe she'd done something wrong, she wondered. But when he closed the door behind her and leaned against it, wearing nothing but boxers, Lexi knew what he was doing. He nodded to his bed and ordered her to lie down and stay still. Lexi, trembling like a leaf, said no, hoping that would be enough.

It wasn't. He took a menacing step toward her, saying it again. "Lexi, lie on the bed like a good little girl."

Vomit in her mouth, she tried to run, but Des was skilled at catching his prey. She barely got his door open when his muscular arms squeezed around her middle like a boa constrictor, dragging her over to his bed. Oh, she flailed and shrieked, but for nothing. Des stripped her of her shirt, drove her down on her stomach, and strapped her bare back with his belt until there were no tears left.

She'd pleaded for mercy. She'd promised to be good. She'd begged him to stop. He did, but he didn't stop there. He kept her for an hour that first night and vowed to her that if she ever disobeyed him again or told anyone what went on behind these doors, he would drag her in there every night instead of only every third night, and worse, he would keep her longer, trying out his new "experiments."

Her lesson in submission that night was harshly learned. Callie and Jaimie knew it too.

They had no voice in this place.

***

Driving those memories away, Lexi waited for Evelyn to get home before Des decided Callie wasn't good enough for tonight and called on Lexi instead. It wouldn't be the first time; even though Des worked on a rotation system with the girls on the nights Evelyn worked, one girl a night was never enough for him.

Evelyn was clueless about Des's weird obsession with the three foster girls. She was never home in the evenings; Des had free rein.

17

Lexi felt a shiver down her spine and tried concentrating on the billowing storm clouds in the distance. Please come home, Ev. I don't want to go two nights in a row.

Once, she'd considered running away, but only until Jaimie tried two months ago. Social Services found her, brought her back to Des and Evelyn. Des was mad. He beat Jaimie so bad that night, kept her for two hours before she returned to their room, shaking and sobbing.

That was weird, because Jaimie never cried.

No, Lexi didn't dare run away. Getting caught terrified her, even more than staying here.

Lexi clenched her eyes shut when she heard a pathetic whimper through the walls. Callie begged Des to stop, but he just laughed at her.

Lexi pressed her hands against her ears, hoping to block out Callie's whimpering, the muffled screams.

No luck.

She retired from the hopeless task of watching for Evelyn and caught sight of Jaimie, head in her science textbook, bobbing her head to the music leaking through her earphones. It ticked Lexi off, the way Jaimie flaunted her MP3 player. Jaimie could escape from the noise of what went on behind those walls, but no matter how many times Lexi begged Jaimie to share, she wouldn't.

Honestly, it was as bad as having an older sister sometimes.

"Jaimie?" No harm in asking again. Callie was getting louder.

Jaimie didn't even move. She was like a zombie with those earbuds in.

"Jaimie!"

Jaimie startled, then shot Lexi a death stare.

"What?" she asked, yanking out the earphones.

"Can I listen, too? You know, use one of your earbuds? I could come over—"

"No."

No surprises there; it wasn't like Jaimie was ever nice to anyone. Most of the time, she acted like a rock.

"Hey Jaimie, what if we called Evelyn? You know, tell her one of us is sick or something? Maybe she'd come home." Lexi went back to the window.

No sedan.

"You're just afraid Callie's not gonna be good enough for him. You know he'll come for you next. Anyway, you call Evelyn, and Des will get mad. Do you really want that to happen?" The sixteen-year-old closed her science textbook and sifted through a Cosmo instead. "Just suck it up. This is life, it's the way things are. You can't change it, so just deal with it."

"Yeah, but—"

"Dude, forget about Ev! You gotta stop thinking she'll rescue us. She has no idea what he's doing."

Jaimie donned the earbuds again. Jaimie was right; Lexi couldn't deny the truth of it. She couldn't tell Evelyn any more than she could tell her social worker. Des was a monster, and he left her paralyzed with fear. The faint scars on her back, not to mention the scarring memories, were a constant reminder that she could never make him angry again.

Five minutes sped by, and Callie was suddenly silent. Lexi's heart climbed into her throat. Evelyn wouldn't be off for another ten minutes; was Des finished with Callie already?

Seconds later, Callie exploded into the room with tears pooling in her hollow eyes, stomping across the room to grab the box of matches she kept on her dresser. Lexi wanted to look away; Callie did this every time it was her turn. Even Callie's long sleeves in the middle of May couldn't disguise what Lexi and Jaimie saw every day, the shallow burns dotting her arms like chicken pox.

As the box of matches wobbled in Callie's hands, Lexi shook her head.

"Hey, don't," Lexi pleaded. "It's not worth it." How many times could she say it before Callie believed it?

Callie pulled out a match anyway.

"What do you know? I deserve this!" Callie hollered. "I'm disgusting!"

19

"You don't deserve it! None of us do! He's... he's just sick."

It was useless. Callie lit the match anyway.

As Lexi watched the dancing flame sear the skin on Callie's arm, she heard the high-pitch squeal that was Des's door, the thumping of his footsteps down the hall.

"Lexi," he called in a quiet voice. "Your turn."

Dear Journal,

Home from another exhausting day at work. Honestly, some days go by far too quickly, and others not quickly enough. Today was one of those slower ones.

I guess tomorrow I have a day off, but is it really a day off? I mean, it's Kevin's birthday party, and I'm excited to see my brothers, and the kids too, but visiting the family also means visiting my mother, and that's always an added stress. Jenn is always going on about how I overwork myself and need a day off. Yeah right; a day with my mother is more stressful than any eighty-hour week.

I don't know, maybe it won't be so bad. Mom will be busy putting the food together. Maybe I can just talk to Kevin and Craig, but knowing my mother, she won't be satisfied until she gets to visit with me. She already complains that I don't see her enough. I can't imagine why.

The last time I was up in Arlington for a visit, Mom gave me the "speech" again. You know the one I mean. She's been on this kick for two years.

"Elizabeth, you know, it's time to move on."

"Don't give up on love."

"Meet somebody, for goodness' sake."

Yep, that's my mother—always pushing me to meet another guy, fall in love, have the family I always wanted. I try and take it all with a grain of salt, but seriously!

On another note, I've been thinking a lot about what Pastor Reid said a few Sundays ago (oh yeah, I haven't been to church in a few weeks, the hospital's been giving me Sunday shifts). He talked about all things being for the good of those who love God. I can't get it out of my head. I mean, I know Scripture is the true Word of God, but I just can't help but wonder, was it good for Kurt to die?

Anyway, enough rambling and ranting, I should probably get some sleep. Tomorrow should be an interesting day.

—Liz

CHAPTER 5

L I Z

Saturday, October 3
2:30 p.m.

Thank goodness for radio, Liz thought to herself as music from the Christian station echoed in her car. If there was one thing she couldn't stand, it was silence; silence was nothing but an opportunity for your mind to wander out of control.

She was on her way to Arlington, where her parents lived, where she'd grown up. The trip usually took her a little over half an hour, and while most people enjoyed the scenic beaches along the way, she'd grown tired of them years ago. How exciting was a beach when you grew up around the corner from one?

She caught sight of herself in the rear-view, marvelling how she still looked identical to the woman of two years ago, five years ago. Her sapphire blue eyes stared back at her, her most intense feature. The rest of her, her wavy blonde hair, her high cheekbones, her 5'9" height and toned muscles, all seemed so ordinary, but Kurt always said she had the eyes of a Greek goddess.

Liz found herself humming along to the familiar songs as she wove through the little community of Arlington. She checked her watch. Well, she had hoped to take her time, but she tended to be a little pedal-heavy, and now she'd be early, as always.

Well, the earlier I arrive, she reasoned, *the earlier I can leave.*

As she turned onto Oswald Boulevard, the steady riff of a

23

guitar slowly faded away, ending one song, and another began with a melodic piano solo.

Liz's fingers tightened around the steering wheel. Only two beats in, and she recognized the old hymn. As a deep tenor belted out lyrics she'd heard a hundred times over, she suddenly felt suspended, hovering somewhere in the balance while her car drove itself. She certainly didn't feel present, because this song always transported her to another time, another place. Her stomach twisted into thick knots; memories caught up to her, threatening to take her captive.

Amazing love! How can it be, that Thou, my God, shouldst die for me?

That song was Kurt's favourite, the one he whistled every morning before work, the one he always got excited about when it was played at church.

It was the one he sang on their wedding day.

Tears gathered, blurring the road in front of her. It was still so fresh, like she could turn to the seat next to her, and there Kurt would be, singing along with a broad grin on his face.

Kurt...

She reeled herself back to reality, killing the radio.

Liz pulled her car into the long cobblestone driveway spiralling up to the cream-coloured mansion that belonged to her parents. It hadn't changed a bit, though she and her brothers had. Still, she remembered herself as the little blonde rich girl galloping up and down the driveway while her brothers chased after her.

"Come on, Lizzie, it doesn't bite or nothin'," eight-year-old Craig promised while Liz, only six, stumbled backward.

"No, it's slimy. Go away!" Liz cried out.

"It's a fwog, Wizzie," piped up four-year-old Kevin. *"Not a monster."*

"I know it's not a monster, stupid-head," Liz spat. "I just don't wanna."

Craig sighed dramatically.

24

"Okay, Lizzie, you asked for it." His mouth stretched into a toothless grin. *"Now I'm gonna make you kiss it!"*

Liz grinned to herself. Yes, there were so many wonderful memories of this place.

But then, there were those that weren't so wonderful.

Jesus, please give me strength to face today.

***

Liz wasn't surprised to find her niece and nephew already in the pool, taking turns plunging underwater to see who could hold their breath the longest. Liz smiled to herself. Lissy, only five, was a little fish, and Ricky, already ten, was the athlete, flaunting his "manly" muscles whenever he had the chance.

Then she spotted her oldest nephew, Liam, who was twelve, lounging quietly by the side of the pool, timing the younger kids with a stopwatch. So methodical, as always, just like his father.

Then there was seven-year-old Erica, the individual, off in her own little world, playing with her dolls.

They were so precious, her nieces and nephews, and she couldn't deny it was wonderful to see them again, but still, a familiar emptiness nagged at her, one that wasn't always easy to hold at bay.

"Lissy, *stop!* You keep splashing an' you're making Suzie *wet!*" Erica cried out, on the verge of a meltdown as she clung to her doll like the world would end.

"Don't yell at your sister, Erica!" There was Liz's sister-in-law Lisa, her hand twined with Kevin's. "She's just swimming. I don't understand why you won't. You told me to bring your bathing suit."

"Yeah, come on, Rica, go jump in the pool," Kevin echoed his wife.

"Nooo! Daddy, I want to play with my *dollies!*" Erica whined, fat tears gushing down her cheeks. Ricky, who had just bobbed up from under the water, heard the commotion.

"Why're you crying, Erica? Is it because you wish you could

hold your breath for," he checked Liam's stopwatch, "fifty-three seconds, like I can?"

"Ricky, stop bragging. Let your cousin be," Meghan, Liz's other sister-in-law, called over from one side of the pool, where she was sprawled out, working on her tan. Liam snickered, and Ricky defended his own honour by hauling his brother into the pool.

Liz had to laugh. Despite the empty feelings, even she couldn't deny the warmth welling up whenever she saw them smile.

"Hey, Lizzie!"

"Hey, Kev." Liz embraced her younger brother, comforted by his strong arms. "Good to see you. Happy birthday."

Kevin, with his shaggy blond hair and muscular build, looked nothing like a man celebrating his thirty-fourth birthday. Liz had to admit, she and her brothers were lucky in that department. None of them looked their age, except maybe Craig, who was starting to show signs of wrinkles. Well, he *was* the oldest, but he was convinced the wrinkles were a side effect of fathering two boys.

"How long have you been standing around, Lizzie? Weren't you gonna say hi?" Kevin asked as Lisa joined them.

"Of course I was." Liz motioned to the children. "I was just trying to figure out who those two little girls were, because they can't possibly be Erica and Lissy. They're too big!"

"Oh come on, Liz, it hasn't been *that* long since you saw them," Lisa pointed out.

Liz did the math. Her last visit had been in the summer, at least a few months ago. Well, at least she wasn't attacked with guilt trips about it, not from her brother and sister-in-law anyway.

That would come from her mother.

"Speaking of the girls, did you get their new school photos?" Lisa asked.

"Not this year's."

"Well, I brought some with me. Your mom's been harassing me about having them for a while. Just a heads-up, though. Lissy had a bit of an upset before her picture. They stupidly booked her class right after recess, and you know Lissy, hard-core into sports; she scraped up her knee something fierce." Lisa exhaled. "Well, her face is pretty blotchy in the picture; they couldn't get her to stop crying, but at least she smiled."

"That's kids for ya, ain't it?" Kevin asked with a grin as Craig and Meghan joined the group.

That's kids for ya, ain't it? As if Liz knew anything about kids. She was single, edging closer to forty, and childless. The only experience she had with kids was with her nieces and nephews and in the ER, but most of those kids were either screaming or unconscious.

"Good to see you, Busy Lizzie. How's work been treatin' you?" Craig asked as he wound his arm around Meghan's waist. Work: it was all anybody ever asked her about anymore, but she couldn't blame them. What else did she have that was worth asking about? It wasn't like she had hobbies.

Well, not anymore.

"It's been alright, I mean I—"

"Auntie Lizzie!" Suddenly Liz had a child's arms squeezing her stomach like a vise.

"Geez, Erica, let your aunt breathe," Lisa said, laughing awkwardly.

Liz swung her own arms around Erica, engulfing her. "It's alright, Lisa." She knelt before her niece. "Hey, Erica."

The girl was the spitting image of her mother, with a mass of brown hair that had the slightest hint of a curl. She looked nothing like Kevin or the rest of the Deston clan; Lissy inherited that side, with her silk blonde hair and blue eyes.

"Hi, Auntie Lizzie. Wanna play dollies with me?" Erica asked as she laced her fingers with Liz's, easing her toward the doll haven. "Suzie just had her birthday party, and Molly is having a tea party. She wants you to come."

Before Liz could form a reply, Meghan realized what was happening in the pool.

"Liam! What are you doing in the pool? Are you wearing a

bathing suit? No! Do you think clothes just grow on *trees?* Now you have nothing to wear!" Meghan treaded a warpath toward the pool, where Liam was already trying to explain and Ricky conveniently disappeared under the water.

"Sorry, Erica, maybe later. I'm going to visit with the grownups for a bit, okay?" She pinched Erica's cheek gently. There was pouting, but after a stern glare from her mother, Erica took off to the comfort of her dolls, a faint sigh escaping her lips.

"Geez, Lizzie, way to break a kid's heart." Kevin chuckled.

Liz shot him a typical big-sister frown that shut him up fast. "Listen, *buddy*, this is a big family, I want to make sure I visit with everyone. So no guilt trips." She surveyed the yard. "Anyway, where are Mom and Dad?"

"Dad had to pick up sausages for the barbeque. He forgot; you know how he is. Mom's inside cutting veggies," Craig replied, distracted by the scene unfolding at the pool as Meghan hoisted Liam from the water. The boy was drenched from head to toe, clothes hanging off him. Lissy and Ricky were snickering quietly.

"Well, I'd better get inside and help the mother," Liz said, retrieving the store-bought brownies she'd brought along. Heading through the sliding glass doors, she felt a sense of dread closing in on her as she imagined what today's conversation would hold.

CHAPTER 6

L E X I

Saturday, October 3
2:46 p.m.

Lexi's stomach felt like it was turning inside out.

It wasn't like it was the first time she'd been this hungry, but that didn't make the biting pangs in her gut any easier.

She'd been drifting through Jacksonville for a day now, a *whole* day, ever since she fled from the bus shelter yesterday morning. All she had to go on was a limited conversation; all she knew about these tunnels was that they were somewhere downtown, and after several blocks of aimless exploring she had found herself in the downtown district sometime yesterday afternoon, gawking up at the high-rise buildings. Smaller shops lined the streets. Smog and smoke invaded her nostrils as she treaded on neatly paved sidewalks, bicycles chained up, cars symmetrically parked along the curbs, lampposts erected on every corner.

Yeah, this was a city alright, but it wasn't what she was looking for.

Circles, that's what it felt like. Pointless circles.

I've been down this street already. Yeah, that grocery store looks familiar. Where are these stupid tunnels?

The rock in her stomach did nothing to boost her optimism either, but she wanted to hold off on spending the last of her money.

Yes, she wanted food, but she had to use her head. Once she found the tunnels, got herself settled, things would be different.

She hoped.

But she'd been wandering for hours now, more than a day had passed, and she hardly wanted to get stuck sleeping under another bridge tonight. A power-hungry beat cop prodding her was the last thing she wanted to wake up to again. No, she *had* to find these tunnels, tonight.

The streets were bustling with activity, people probably rushing home to their families, their computers, or whatever miserable excuses they called lives. Lexi considered asking somebody where she could find these so-called tunnels, but who was she kidding? They'd take one look at her and take off, maybe toss her a dollar bill out of sheer pity, but they wouldn't stop to help. All they cared about was themselves.

A chill travelled in from the waterfront, a brutal reminder that nighttime was sneaking upon her. Time was running out. Sure, it was Florida, and it wasn't like there'd be snow or anything, but it still got cold enough that Lexi knew she didn't want to suffer through another night without a warm place to stay.

How can I even be sure the tunnels are warm?

Stomach screaming at her, she resigned herself to the fact that she would have to eat. Thinking back, her last meal had been at Everidge, and that was two days ago.

Fumbling through her pocket, she took a quick inventory of her leftover pocket change.

Great, how far is seventeen bucks gonna fly?

Settling on a nearby McDonald's, Lexi waited in a never-ending line for a cheeseburger that cost her a couple of bucks. Her body argued fiercely; she could eat more than that, not to mention she was thirsty, but she had to save her money. The state wasn't supporting her anymore, so she'd have to take care of herself, and that meant being realistic.

By now, a dull ache throbbed in her feet, and her eyelids felt heavy. She imagined herself back at the youth centre. What would she be doing right now if she hadn't left? Probably elbowing her way through the overcrowded bathroom, fighting for a turn in the showers.

How exciting.

By now, they had probably stopped looking for her, had written her off as another delinquent runaway. What else was new?

Besides, if she had stuck around, what would have happened next? Lexi had the system down; Bridget would have moved her case up as a priority, since she was such a "risk." A few weeks more, and she'd be placed in another foster home. She couldn't imagine another one. She doubted anything could top the last one, but who knew? Maybe they'd be a family who got their kicks and giggles out of killing puppy dogs and making kids watch.

But even that seemed tame, after Des.

Lexi was dragging her feet now, the half-eaten burger dangling in her hand. She veered down a street she'd been down twice already. She was lost, but what could she do? She could keep walking, with a naive hope that she'd spot an entrance to the tunnels. She could start scoping out the city for a place to sleep for the night. Worse, she could start trekking back to Tampa, maybe even hitchhike, and face the consequences for running away, and another foster home.

Her options sucked.

As she bit into her cold cheeseburger, she realized she was being watched.

A boy, around her age, she guessed, was leaning against a wall at the mouth of a narrow alleyway across the street from her, hands stuffed into his pockets. Lexi cautiously took in his appearance: dishevelled brown hair, smudges of dirt speckling his face and arms, and rips savaging his oversized grey T-shirt.

Maybe he was watching someone else, but a quick sweep of her head revealed no one around her. He *was* looking at her, but why?

Then the boy waved her over, disappearing into the alleyway.

She'd always heard the rule about not talking to strangers,

31

but did that even count anymore? She didn't have a mom or a dad teaching her that stuff, even though the state tried placing her with frauds four different times.

So, what did you do when everyone was a stranger?

Besides, he was just a kid, like her.

Curious, she crossed the road, ducking into the dark alleyway. It dawned on her that most kids would be scared. Not Lexi. It took a lot to break her these days.

There he was, vertical with the brick wall, his eyes boring into her while his thumbs looped through his belt buckle. Even in the shadows, Lexi picked out the pale blue of his eyes.

"What are you doin' in Jacksonville?" the kid asked gruffly in a voice that didn't match the rest of him. He was no taller than she was, and scrawny to boot.

"None of your business," Lexi snapped.

The kid snorted through his nose, like he was some kind of comedian just for asking. Who did he think he was?

"Relax, stupid; I'm just trying to help." He nodded at her backpack. "I'm a logical guy. You got some baggage there, and you've been runnin' around this city like a chicken with its head cut off. Obviously, you're lost. Here, that only means one thing: you came for the tunnels."

Lexi kept her features stone-like. People were too good at reading emotions; it was better to be a rock.

Still, the kid seemed to know what he was talking about. Besides, if he knew anything about the tunnels, he was the last person Lexi wanted to tick off. She needed him, but she wouldn't let him know that. Even kids couldn't be trusted.

The kid spread his arms out, palms up. "So, did ya?" he asked, impatience booming in his voice.

"So what if I did?" Lexi crossed her arms. Better to play it safe. *Don't give anything away until you have to.*

"Well, it just so happens I *live* in those tunnels, so if you're lookin' for them, I can bring you there." He stuck out a hand. "Name's Barney."

A chuckle bubbled in Lexi's throat. "What kind of a name is Barney?" she asked.

"It's not my real name, idiot! You think any of us use our real names? Cops, social workers… yeah, they're all out there, and some of them are still looking for us. They'll all use your real name, so out here you gotta pick a street name. We don't even know each other's real names, 'cause if someone decided to rat, it'd all be over, get it? That's how we protect ourselves." He exhaled. "So, if you're coming with me, you gotta pick a name. Like I said, I'm Barney. What's your name? And don't use your real one!"

A street name? Well, she hadn't thought of that, but it made sense. If anyone from Everidge ever came to Jacksonville, though she doubted they would, they could easily ask any kid walking around if they'd seen Lexi Vogan, and she'd be toast. *"Oh yeah, she's in the tunnels; let me get her for you."* Game over.

She'd never been creative, and hobbies… what kind of hobbies did she have to go on? *Not like I used to.* She drew a blank, so she went for the first thing she could think of.

"CJ," she replied.

"CJ?" Barney asked.

Lexi nodded.

"Why CJ?"

"'Cause it's the initials of my two middle names."

Barney groaned.

"Seriously? That's not really creative, but whatever. Besides, I guess it's got a nice ring to it. But it's not as good as mine. It's from the Flintstones. You like retro cartoons?"

Lexi was getting restless. "You gonna show me these tunnels or not?"

"Maybe. You gonna give me half your burger?" the boy asked.

Defeated, Lexi handed over the half-eaten cheeseburger, and after a generous bite, Barney nodded.

"Alright." He headed toward the mouth of the alleyway. "Let's go.

CHAPTER 7

L I Z

Saturday, October 3
3:01 p.m.

The rec room was spotless, just another one of her mother's quirks. Liz could still remember all the times she'd been chastised as a child for leaving toys out when company was coming. "A clean house is a happy house," her mother would say.

Not always.

Liz crossed the spacious room, turned down the long corridor, and came out into the kitchen, where her mother was chopping onions at the island. Where Liz and her brothers looked young for their ages, their mother made up for it. Crow's feet nestled next to her blue eyes, pronounced wrinkles settling on her forehead and cheeks.

Still, Anne Deston made the most of it. She plastered herself with makeup, touched up her graying blonde curls with hair dye, and dressed fashionably. Anne always said her acquaintances at the country club were often jealous of her appearance.

Stepping into the kitchen, Liz noticed several dishes of salads and appetizers already on the go. That was typical; her mother tended to go a little overboard with get-togethers.

Clearing her throat, Liz dressed herself with a smile. "Hi, Mom."

The onions were forgotten, and when Anne saw her daughter, her eyes sparkled with excitement.

"Oh sweetheart!" Abandoning her knife, she rounded the counter to embrace Liz.

Liz felt herself tightening, anxiety settling on her. Sure, it seemed alright so far, but how long before her mother sucked her into the discussions Liz didn't want to have? How long before things grew uncomfortable, as they had a habit of doing?

Well, show a little optimism, Liz thought naively. *Maybe this time will be different.*

Anne pulled away from Liz and held her at arm's length.

Sizing me up.

"Well, let me have a look at you. I mean, after all, dear, it *has* been a couple of months," she said with a hint of disapproval. Liz decided not to say anything; it was better to avoid those traps.

"I brought brownies."

Hoping to change the subject, Liz reached for an onion and set to work.

"Well, thank you, darling." Anne joined her. "Though I already baked a batch this morning, but I doubt the children will complain. How was the drive up?"

"Fine. I was expecting traffic, but it wasn't bad. I made good time." Liz kept her focus on that onion. At least chopping vegetables would keep the two of them busy.

These moments were always the worst—the small talk, the tidbits of time where everything appeared fine. She'd been through enough of these moments to know small talk only lasted so long. And yet, it was the small talk Liz preferred; it warded off the deeper issues.

"And how's work treating you these days, Elizabeth? I suspect you've been quite busy." Again with the echo of disapproval, and why did she insist on calling her Elizabeth? She was the *only* person who did. Everyone else knew how much she hated it.

"Busy enough. I've picked up a few more hours, so it's been steady. Oh, and the hospital recently received a grant, so we'll be able to add a few more beds in the ER. We might even hire a couple of new doctors, so it shouldn't be as stressful. We're

35

all really excited to see that happen," Liz rambled, moving on to carrots.

She heard the low sigh and could feel her mother's eyes sinking into her. Liz chopped faster. In their mother's eyes, Craig could do no wrong, Kevin was the baby, and Liz got stuck with the criticism.

"Do you work *every day*?" Anne asked.

"Mostly, but you know, it's my choice. It's not like they force hours on me. I get days off every once in a while, but I try to make them Sundays so I can go to church."

Her stomach seized; she'd just charted into dark territory.

"Oh yes. The church thing," her mother muttered under her breath.

Liz resigned herself to silence. This wasn't new; it had always been a battle. Liz hadn't grown up in the church. In fact, her parents had always resisted the idea of religion, for as long as she could remember. Liz hadn't even stepped foot in a church until after she met Kurt. He'd been the one to lead her to her faith; he'd given her her first Bible, brought her to church, got down on hands and knees with her when she'd decided to follow Christ.

She'd never turn back now—it was the best decision she ever made—but ever since she had surrendered her life to Jesus, religion and God had become taboo in the Deston household. In fact, when Liz first broke the news to her parents, you would have thought it was the apocalypse from their harsh reaction. Sure, Liz and Kurt had tried getting them to understand, to bring them to faith, but to no avail. At least they came to accept it. But seriously, as if there wasn't enough animosity between her and her mother already.

"How's Dad?" Changing the subject was always a safe bet.

"Oh, you know how your father is." Anne heaved a dramatic sigh. "He doesn't know what to do with himself these days, now that he's retired. It's nice, how much he misses the business, but you know, Elizabeth, I keep telling him it's for the best. Let's be realistic; we're not getting any younger. He should welcome the break, but instead he stops by the firm at least once a day to make sure it's still running. I tell him time and time again that he did the right thing by turning the business over to Craig, but he can't let go. I bet you any amount of money when your father gets back, he and Craig will be talking business for the rest of the night. Your poor father, he seems so ready and willing to go back to work and start it all up again, but I keep telling him his old heart just isn't there anymore. You know how he is: in one ear and out the other."

Like someone else I know, thought Liz.

Liz nodded in all the right places, absently passing along the finished vegetables for salads as she listened. This was becoming a routine: her mother chatting, Liz listening, feigning interest. She had to resist the urge to check her watch.

For the next few moments, they worked in silence, Liz tossing a salad, her mother preheating the oven for the lemon meringue pie. Liz felt her body releasing some pent-up tension as time passed and her mother's silence prevailed. Maybe she'd be able to finish with the dinner preparations and duck outside with her brothers. At least when they were surrounded by the whole family, her mother kept her lectures to herself.

Suddenly, a loud belch travelled through the open window, followed by the kids' giggling.

"Well, would you just listen to them?" Anne sighed sentimentally. "They're so precious, aren't they?"

The room was closing in around Liz, the walls trapping her. Here it was. This was *always* how it started. How naive was she to think she'd actually get through a visit without her mother breathing down her neck about something?

"Oh Elizabeth, don't you think it would be absolutely *lovely* to add a couple more kids to the Deston mix?" Anne asked, flashing a sly smile while she popped the pie in the oven.

Liz went on seasoning the salad as though her mother hadn't spoken. Pressure, there was *always* that pressure to have children. Ever since Liz had married Kurt eleven years ago, Anne had constantly pestered the couple about popping out a couple of kids. At first, it was fine; after all, it seemed like *everyone* was pestering back then.

Then it became annoying. Yes, Kurt and Liz wanted children, but it wasn't a crime to decide to establish their careers first, become financially settled before adding children to their journey. But it didn't matter *how* many times she explained this to her mother; she wouldn't let it go.

When Kurt became sick, the thought of children was the farthest from their minds, but even then, her mother untactfully raised the issue, and continued to do so, even now, *after* Kurt's death. Liz didn't understand her mother on the best of days, but this was beyond comprehension.

"Can you imagine how thrilled those four would be to have a little baby to play with?" Anne asked, gliding over to the window to watch her grandchildren.

"Well, Mother, that baby will *not* be coming from me," Liz said sternly, collecting a salad bowl and gathering some napkins to bring outside.

Anne turned in time to catch her daughter trying to slink away. She clicked her tongue. "Oh, don't be like that, Elizabeth. I dislike it when you get all upset and defensive. I'm only saying that—"

"Yes, Mother, you're *always* saying." Liz stared at the medley of veggies in her bowl. It was a bad habit she'd developed over the years, averting her eyes in conversations like these. It was as though allowing herself to catch her mother's eye would unleash a monstrous rage that she wouldn't be able to keep leashed. It was easier to drift away.

"But sweetheart, don't you *want* to have children?" Anne asked, clasping her hands together in a hopeful gesture.

"I'm thirty-six, Mom. There won't be any children," she replied with as much patience as she could muster, but every word from her mother tore through her like a thousand blades. She needed to get *out* of here.

Her mother only scoffed playfully. "Oh, come now, Elizabeth, that's a ridiculous excuse. Nowadays, people are having children older and older. You know, I knew a woman who had her first child at forty-one. Yes, perhaps it's not ideal, but it's a possibility. Besides, there's always adoption."

"Mom, can we drop this? Please?"

But her mother, a leech for the last word, tilted her head to grab her daughter's attention. "Honey, have you even considered dating again?"

Liz froze, swallowing back the thousand and one things she wanted to say, but none of them would be appropriate. They would only ignite her mother's anger and ruin the whole barbeque. Liz couldn't do that to Kevin, or to the kids. Instead, she feigned a struggle with her armload of food and raced for the backyard, breathing heavily as she tried to control the gathering storm of emotions.

Why? *Why* did her mother *always* have to do this? Why was it that Liz could never come for a family visit and just *enjoy* herself? Why couldn't her mother understand how bad it hurt to hear all of this?

Liz blinked away impending tears. She couldn't cry here. She still had hours to go before she could leave.

"Lizzie?" A voice pierced through her silence. She straightened, realizing she was standing in Craig's shadow.

"Hey Craig," she managed, forcing a smile, but the typical big brother that he was, he penetrated her facade. He wasn't an idiot; he always knew when something was up.

"Mom stuff," she quietly admitted.

"Ah," Craig acknowledged. He flashed her a winning smile and punched her gently. "You know she just cares about you."

"No, she only cares about being a grandmother, which she already is, to *four* amazing kids!" She raised her hand to her head. It was still shaking. "I don't understand her, I just don't."

Craig wrapped his thick arm around Liz's shoulders and squeezed.

"Yeah, but that's Mom for you." He craned his neck to catch Liz's eye. "Besides, kiddo, you can't predict the future."

Liz stared.

"Well, I just mean you don't know what could change in life." He quieted his voice so only she could hear him. "Who knows, Lizzie? Maybe your heart will open up again someday."

CHAPTER 8

L E X I

Saturday, October 3
3:14 p.m.

"What exactly are these tunnels, anyway?" Lexi was practically jogging just to keep up with Barney's long strides. He was too busy picking flecks of lettuce out of his crooked teeth to notice she was falling behind.

"Are they *actually* tunnels, or is that, like, a metaphor?"

"A metaphor? Come on! Do you think we live in some kind of penthouse suite and just call it 'the tunnels' for kicks? No, it ain't a metaphor; they're real tunnels. I mean, nobody really knows where they came from, but everyone's got their guesses."

He detoured down a street Lexi hadn't seen before.

"Some people say the mob used 'em, you know, for an underground op or something. There's one guy who even thinks they were created by aliens, but he's a quack. You know what I say? I say they were for military experiments. Sapph knows better than me, anyway. She found the tunnels, started this whole thing up for us, you know? Her theory is that the city wanted to build a subway, like a long time ago, but I guess they just figured it wasn't a smart thing to do, you know, economically speaking, so they quit. Now there's this huge chunk of underground tunnels that were just abandoned. It's all blocked off, but people are too lazy to fill those holes back in, I guess."

"If it's blocked off, how do you get in?" Lexi asked, skepticism curdling inside her. Was this kid legit, or was he just dragging her along on some wild goose chase? She didn't have time to waste; if this turned out to be a false lead, she'd have to spend another night out on her own.

"Like I said, Sapph could tell you the story better than I could. A few years back, she found the tunnels when she was looking for a place to stay. It's all walled up, mostly, but she found the Tube—"

"The Tube?"

Barney sifted a hand through his wild hair. "The entrance to the tunnels. We call it the Tube. Well, Sapph squeezed through one day, and the rest is history, I guess."

"Why would they leave an opening?" Lexi asked.

"Look, I'm not Einstein! I don't know, maybe to let air circulate? The whole thing is kinda weird, but who cares, right? It's a place to live. Sapph found it, told other street kids about it, so I guess she became the leader. The tunnels are huge. There's a ton of us down there."

"Yeah, but it's closed off. Don't the cops kick you out?"

"Cops? Yeah right. Don't think they haven't tried, 'cause they have, but there's just too many of us. We kept comin' back, so they gave up. Now they just let us claim it for our own. Everyone in Jacksonville knows about the tunnels, and they know who lives in 'em, so they stay away. You know, unless we steal something. Then they might chase us, but never into the tunnels. It's kinda like there's an invisible barrier to the rest of the world. I think people are scared of us. It's like they think they'll catch a disease just by looking at us."

Lexi could relate to that.

"This *Sapph* person, you called her the leader," she said. "What's up with that?"

"Sapphire, actually, but that's just her street name. Like I said, she found the tunnels, so she figures that kind of makes her boss. Not everybody likes it, but most people just keep to themselves."

"I don't listen to no one."

Her companion snorted. "Yeah, I can see you and Sapph will get along just great." Sarcasm rolled off his tongue.

Lexi didn't care who this Sapphire thought she was. She answered to no one, *especially* on the streets.

They carried on in silence for a few blocks, Barney scooping dirt from under his fingernails while Lexi took mental snapshots of the city. At some point she'd have to be able to navigate on her own.

Better figure it out now, before this kid ditches.

Barney shattered the silence a moment later. "So, what's your story?"

Lexi studied the cracks in the sidewalk. "I don't got one."

"Whatever; everyone's got a story," Barney said. "Like, where'd you come from?"

What was with the third degree? Anyway, she figured she'd better be careful. She didn't know him. He could be *anybody*.

Still, he could be her ticket to the tunnels. She'd have to give him something.

"I've been all over." She kicked at a stray stone. "I was in Tampa before I came here, a group home. It was a drag, so I took off. I heard some kids talkin' about the tunnels, so I figured I'd check 'em out."

"Foster?" Barney asked.

"Yep, you?"

"Nah, I have a mom out there somewhere, but I split when she remarried. It was bad enough before the jerk showed up, but... well, she ignored me all the time. I figured, why should I stick around?" Barney awkwardly scratched his nose. "Anyway, what about you? What happened to your folks?"

"Got none."

"You must have, once."

"I guess."

"What were they like?"

"Dunno."

"How'd you end up in foster care?"

"It just happened one day."

Barney held back long enough to side-glance at Lexi, a knowing smile curling his lips. "Oh, I get it, you're one of those 'I don't want to talk about it' people. No prob. There's a lot of those here."

Thankfully, he stopped grilling her after that. The last thing she wanted was to get into the messy details of her life. It was *her* life, after all. She didn't care what anybody had to say; they didn't need to know.

Barney rounded another corner and ducked down another narrow alleyway, and that's when Lexi spotted it.

It was a rectangular hole in the ground, about four feet wide, a dirt slope curving down into it. She couldn't see into it, it was too dark, but there was no denying what this trail led to.

This had to be it—the entrance to the tunnels.

"Watch your step; it's a bit steep," Barney said. "They never finished construction, remember?"

Barney shimmied his way down the slanted pathway, and Lexi mimicked him. He was right; it *was* steep. She felt her feet sliding ahead of her, and she would have lost her balance if she hadn't caught a rough piece of wood protruding from the side of the "Tube," as Barney called it. Splinters savaged her hand as she plunged deeper into the darkness.

The slope eventually evened out, and Lexi's nostrils filled with the smell of something rotting. Mildew, maybe.

Smells like Everidge.

The creaking wooden rafters were low, but thanks to her height she barely had to crouch to avoid them. Barney, up ahead, was swallowed up by the dark abyss.

Lexi followed, keeping her distance.

A sudden thought occurred to her—what if this guy wasn't who he claimed to be? What if he was some maniac who lured girls down here? It was secluded, dark... a perfect playground for a serial rapist.

Great. So even if she tried to scream, no one would hear her. Not down here.

No matter how many times she blinked, her eyes wouldn't adjust to the sea of blackness around her. She kept up only by the shuffling of Barney's shoes in the dirt below.

"You get used to it, even in the dark." His voice echoed through the silence.

Impatient, Lexi wanted to ask how much farther they had to go, but she didn't have to.

There was a sliver of light ahead, and as Barney inched closer, Lexi could make out his silhouette.

The light came from a hole in the wall. Barney was right; it *was* small, but being the toothpick he was, he eased through without a problem. Lexi slid through after him, just as easily.

When she was in fifth grade, she'd done a science project on bear caves. She had scavenged the school library for every picture she could find of the animal's habitat, fascinated by how a bear could sleep in the stone-like structures and dark, dingy atmosphere.

That was what this place looked like—a giant cave.

Beneath her, the dirt became concrete, and all around her were stone walls like the ones she'd seen in those picture books, except these walls were splashed with the most intense murals she'd ever seen. Some depicted scenes of happiness: flowers, sunshine, clouds over water; and others spoke dark tales of death and abandonment, the darkest of a skeleton digging his own grave.

Not like the art at Everidge.

Along the rocky walls were rows of outdoor Christmas lights, lazily strung as though whoever had decorated the place didn't care. Still, it provided the dim blanket of light in the dome-shaped structure.

Where's the electricity coming from?

Well, did it really matter?

While her nostrils tickled with stale air and smoke, Lexi noticed the kids. How she hadn't heard them in the Tube, she didn't know. Maybe that thick wall acted as some kind of sound barrier. The Tube had seemed dead, but this place was crawling with activity.

There had to be more than fifty teenagers scattered throughout the place, all busy with something. In one corner, a group of junior high kids, mostly girls dressed in miniskirts and skin-tight tees, gathered around a crate, playing cards. They were roaring with laughter, cursing at each other; some even smoked while punching each other playfully.

Next to them, a few older boys in baggy jeans and ripped T-shirts huddled together, snorting something they were trying to hide. In another corner, a bunch of girls about Lexi's age were dining on a Big Mac meal. Front and centre, two guys tossed a Frisbee back and forth while a lone girl garbed completely in black took a long haul on her joint, watching. Lexi was reminded of the kids at Everidge, but it was different here; these kids didn't have to live by any rules.

Yeah, this was how it should be.

Barney gently nudged Lexi with a chuckle. "What?" he asked. "Not what you were expecting?"

"I didn't expect anything," Lexi replied with a shrug. It wasn't like she'd stayed up at night fantasizing about a place she'd never seen. All she cared about was finding a place to stay, hidden from the world, away from adults who deluded themselves thinking they knew what was best for her.

"Come on, I'll give you the grand tour," Barney said, cocking his head toward all the activity. "We call this part the Pit."

"The Pit?" Lexi arched an eyebrow. "You couldn't come up with anything better than that?"

"*I* didn't name it. Geez, I keep telling you, Sapph's the one who found them."

Barney zigzagged through the crowds of people, Lexi following. Some kids peered up, but mostly they ignored her.

They must be used to people coming in and out.

Besides, if they were anything like Lexi, they probably kept to themselves.

46

Barney was mumbling about something, but Lexi's attention had drifted. Off to one side stood a boy who was painting one of the stone walls. It was a larger mural, exploding with colour. It wasn't finished, but the mural depicted a meadow with a fierce blue sky and gigantic sun. A lifelike tree was to the kid's left. He hummed to himself as he made meticulous brushstrokes. The mural was good; maybe he had painted the other ones too.

Craning her neck, she could see he'd just finished painting a bird's nest, under the tree. She held back a groan. It was too sappy, like something out of a kid's lullaby.

He must get the snot beat out of him a lot.

"How exactly does this work?" Lexi asked, turning her attention back to Barney. "I mean, where do you sleep?"

"Oh right, I should've known you wouldn't care about military experiments."

So that's what he'd been mumbling about.

"Anyway, you sleep where you can find room."

He pointed to an opening on the opposite wall. "That's where the Combs start. Oh sorry, I mean the tunnels. Everyone's got their own spot. Sapphire's got a storage of blankets, so everyone who's new gets one. You get a candle, too. You know, for your spot. You got a lighter?"

Lexi shook her head.

"Fine, I'll spot you one. Anyway, want me to show you where there's free spots? I've been here long enough, I know where they are."

"Sure, I guess."

It was better that way, she figured, much better than accidentally claiming some other kid's spot and earning a black eye.

"Heads up," Barney said suddenly, and Lexi spotted the tall blonde girl drawing closer.

The girl could have been on some varsity basketball team, with her height. Her bleach-blonde hair dangled to her waist, and Lexi noticed its natural shine. How did she keep it so clean, living on the streets?

The blonde closed in on them, arms crossed, eyeing Lexi like she was contagious with something. Lexi already didn't like her. True, she didn't like a lot of people, but this girl just screamed control freak.

This must be Sapphire.

As though Barney could read her mind, he nodded toward the blonde. "This is Sapphire."

Figures.

Lexi scowled. If Sapphire was trying to intimidate her, she was failing miserably.

"This is CJ," Barney said, jerking his thumb at Lexi.

"*Tell* me that's not her real name," Sapphire demanded, her glare a weapon.

A chuckle rose up Barney's throat. "Of *course* it's not her real name! You think I'm an idiot? I told her to pick a street name, and that's what she picked."

Lexi bit her tongue. They were talking about her like she wasn't even there!

"Fine, you can stay, *if* you can follow the rules!" Sapphire told her. "You're on your own for food and shampoo and anything else you need or want, but money? Money is what keeps us going down here. It buys us things like candles and blankets. So, if you're up there stealing, and you get a wallet full of cash, you give me half; got it?"

Lexi couldn't help it. A snicker parted her lips.

Sapphire's eyebrow shot up. "You got a problem with that?"

"How old *are* you?" Lexi asked.

"What?"

"I said, how old are you?"

Sapphire's death glare radiated how unimpressed she was, but still she answered. "Seventeen."

"I get that I'm new here, I get that I'm younger, but I don't get why *you* get to be in charge." Lexi mirrored Sapphire's defiance. She had to lay the groundwork now. If she came over as a pushover, Sapphire would walk all over her. No, Lexi had been through enough of that in her life. Now, she was calling the shots.

"I can see we're going to have a bit of a *problem* here," Sapphire said condescendingly. She sounded like a teacher scolding a student. Lexi held back the chuckles this time.

"Come on, Sapph, give her a break. She's been wandering all day and night trying to find us," Barney said with an awkward grin.

Probably trying to lighten things up.

"Fine, but Barney, keep her in line or she's *gone.*"

Sapphire shot Lexi more dagger eyes before she stalked off toward a group of girls who were waiting for her.

Lexi followed after her tour guide, but she was still seeing red. Stealing a glance over her shoulder, she found Sapphire watching, whispering to her girlfriends. Great. Sapphire was going to be a thorn in her side; she could *feel* it already.

***

Barney found Lexi a blanket and candle, and soon she was trailing after him through the gaping hole in the wall that led to the Combs.

The only light they had to go on was from the dim bulbs in the Pit. It definitely made the Combs hard to get through. Good thing Barney seemed to know where he was going. The whole set up was like a maze, with all the corners they took and paths crisscrossing everywhere. The deeper they went, the darker it became.

It didn't take long for Lexi to see what Barney meant by kids claiming their own spots. Nestled along walls or in dingy corners, blankets were set up, a candle lit. Sometimes, a kid would be dozing. Sometimes, there were posters taped to the stone wall, mostly of bands. Sometimes, nothing. Everyone's spot was different, but it made sense; this was the closest thing to a bedroom these kids had.

"By the way," Barney said suddenly. "Don't backtalk Sapphire."

"What?"

"Well, like I said, she's kind of in charge. Nobody likes it, but you kinda learn to do what she says. She hates kids who challenge her. Seriously, she's kicked kids out before." Barney puttered down another trail.

"That's stupid! I mean, how do you *stand* it? It's not like she owns the place. Does she have a permit?" Lexi asked, tasting sarcasm in her mouth.

Barney laughed his response. "It don't matter. She found 'em; she gets to make the decisions. Just ignore her, and she'll leave you alone. But trust me, if she tells you to do something, you should probably do it. Although," he grinned at her, "that whole fifty-fifty thing with the money? I don't give her nothing. I keep it. I use the money for other things."

Lexi didn't bother asking what for.

"This is where I sleep." Barney stopped, hunching over as he reached into his pocket for a lighter. When his candle was lit, Lexi swallowed back a giggle. Posters of cartoon characters were plastered to the wall over his green woolen blanket. The characters were so old, some of them Lexi didn't even recognize.

"Geez, you weren't kidding about liking cartoons," she said.

"*Retro* cartoons, only the classics," Barney corrected her. "Anyway, let's just say I watched a lot of TV growing up."

He took her around one last bend and spread his arms out, displaying an empty corner.

"*Voila!*" he exclaimed. "What do you think? Want it?"

Lexi shrugged.

"Sure, whatever." She dropped her blanket and buckled to her knees, glad to have a place to sit.

Barney squatted down, taking her candle and lighting it. When she could make out Barney's features again, she noticed he was missing a tooth.

"Here, you can have this one." He handed Lexi his lighter. "I got another one in my crib."

"You call *this* a crib?" she asked.

"Beggars can't be choosers." He dove into his pocket again, this time revealing a Swiss Army knife. "Here."

He inched over to the wall and began scratching into the stone with his knife. Lexi had to cover her ears. It was like nails on a chalkboard.

When he was finished, Lexi hoisted her candle to reveal two lone letters scratched into the stone.

CJ

"There," Barney said. "Now it's yours."

Lexi felt a small smile stretching her lips. "Thanks."

"No problem." Something was in his hand, something she hadn't seen before.

A joint.

"Want one?" he asked, borrowing Lexi's new lighter to light up.

"Not into that," she confessed.

"Alright, cool." Barney found his feet, gave a slight nod. "Catch you later."

Lexi watched him disappear around the corner, probably heading back to his own space. She sucked in a breath, feeling a little better now that she was alone.

Settling back against the stone wall, she began biting at her knuckles. It was a bad habit of hers, and had been since she was eight years old. The kids in her class used to make fun of her, because *normal* kids chewed their fingernails, not their knuckles.

Well, since when had Lexi's life ever been normal?

The noises around her would take some getting used to; kids were fighting, laughing, chatting, crying. She felt a chill seeping through the cracks in the tunnel walls, grazing her skin, making her shiver. The air was thick with the smell of weed, and it was making her lightheaded.

She was surrounded by darkness.

And in the midst of it all, she felt like she'd finally found the one place she was supposed to be, the *only* place left for someone like her.

How sad is that?

She didn't care.

CHAPTER 9

L I Z

Saturday, October 3
10:00 p.m.

So much for leaving early.

By the time Liz could pry herself away from Erica's tea party and endure her father's lecture about car parts not being what they used to be, she didn't get out of there until nearly 9:30!

Now, half an hour later, and struggling to keep her eyes open, she finally parked her car in her driveway.

A puff of air escaped her lips.

She'd gotten through another family visit.

It was never like this when she and Kurt had visited his parents before they moved across the country to California. A visit with the Swaviers was nothing short of a good time, brimming with laughs and love and, best of all, free of guilt trips.

Liz never heaved a sigh of relief when she and Kurt returned from those visits.

Flipping on the lights in her front hallway, she groaned when she caught sight of the time. Dreading the busy day tomorrow caused her very bones to ache; church in the morning, and then another night shift.

Bed: that was what she needed right now. Not only was she physically exhausted, but her emotions were shot. Her mother's desperate laments echoed in her brain. Would there ever be a day when her mother would get off her back?

Yeah, when I have a husband and kids.

It was a battle Liz couldn't win.

Abandoning her purse near the stairs, she spotted the flashing red light on her answering machine. She exhaled loudly.

"I just wanna go to bed!" she whined to nobody in particular. She caught herself, blushing. Could she sound any more like a child?

Besides, nobody ever called her, unless the hospital was desperate or her mother needed to complain about something.

Probably complaining I left too early.

She considered ignoring it but hit the play button anyway.

"Hey Liz, it's Kathryn," the voice said.

Well, Kathryn was another story. That was one voice she didn't dread.

"You're probably working, I get it, but hey, just so you know, those of us who don't have the hectic schedules you do, mostly me, are missing you. Don't think I haven't noticed you not being in church for the last two weeks. I'm assuming you had to work, but I thought I'd call and see if you're coming tomorrow morning. I hope you can make it. We can have lunch afterwards; how's that sound? Anyway, give me a call if it's not too late. If not, hopefully I'll see you tomorrow. Bye."

A beep concluded her message. It was definitely too late to call her back now. Kathryn was an early-to-bed, early-riser kind of woman. If Liz called her now, she'd wake her for sure, and Kathryn wasn't a happy camper when her sleep was interrupted.

Liz settled on seeing Kathryn in the morning.

Guilt tugged at her for her failure to make a better effort at visiting Kathryn. Liz couldn't even *remember* the last time the two of them had gone out. Gone were the days of Kurt and Liz spending an evening with Kathryn and her husband, Brian, at least once a week, playing cards, watching movies, chatting until the wee hours of the morning. They'd all been such good friends, and Kathryn was still her best friend, but with work being so demanding, Liz hardly had time for anyone anymore, including herself.

54

Was that a legitimate excuse?

Well, at least I'll see her tomorrow.

Bed was calling her, but she had to do something first, something she'd forget if she didn't do it right away. Her memory was like that these days; work demanded so much of her mental capacity that she hardly remembered the tiny details life sometimes presented.

She scavenged her purse for four photographs, the newest school pictures of Liam, Ricky, Erica, and Lissy. Mechanically she floated into her living room, where four frames neatly decorated the mantel of her fireplace. Younger copies of her nieces and nephews stared out at her, all with the bluest of eyes. Just like their fathers, just like Liz.

She remembered her brother's voice on the day Lissy was born five years ago: *"Look, Lizzie, she's got your eyes."*

The eyes of a Greek goddess...

As Liz replaced the old photos with the new ones, her mother's voice surfaced again.

"Oh Elizabeth, don't you think it would be absolutely lovely to add a couple more kids to the Deston mix? Can you imagine how thrilled those four would be to have a little baby to play with? But sweetheart, don't you want to have children?"

Liz's eyes burned as she stared at the kids in front of her, those beautiful smiles, their bright eyes. Of *course* Liz wanted children! It was always something she and Kurt had dreamed about, but why couldn't her mother realize it wasn't going to happen? Didn't she realize how violently it ripped Liz to shreds to come home every day to pictures of children that weren't hers?

Those frames should hold shots of my son or daughter.

Did her mother actually believe she enjoyed being alone?

Kurt was dead; there would be no children. After he died, her heart had shattered, the world had stopped turning, and everything changed. Any dreams or aspirations she had for her life died with Kurt.

It doesn't matter. Why do I always let my mother get to me like this?

Massaging her temples, she killed the lights and scampered to her bedroom, hopeful that sleep would draw a shade over all these pent-up emotions.

As she readied herself for bed, she let her mind float to the hospital, counting her hours for the week, mentally calculating this week's paycheque, and imagining the patients she would have to treat tomorrow.

Only in this cloud of distraction was she finally able to drift off into a restless sleep.

CHAPTER 10

L E X I

Saturday, October 3
10:26 p.m.

Lexi lost track of time.

It was easy to do in a place like this, a dreamlike world dancing with shadows. All she had was a candle, shedding its skin a little more each hour. Nothing else hinted at the time; she *was* underground, after all. It wasn't like there was a window to watch the sunset.

For all she knew, she could have been sitting there for hours, and it didn't help that she felt like she was spinning around in some kind of alternate reality. Was it really only yesterday that she'd stepped off that bus? Was it really only hours ago that she'd run into Barney? It was all a haze, like she was watching her own life through a thin veil.

Okay, this was getting ridiculous. She couldn't just float away with her thoughts all night. No, she'd been lazy long enough; it was time to stretch her legs, maybe explore the tunnels a little more... maybe figure out what time it was.

It would be too easy to get lost in the shadows if she stayed here much longer.

Good thing she had solid hearing; the chorus of kids' voices bouncing off the walls would be coming from the Pit. All she had to do was follow it.

Navigating through the winding tunnels, she began to pick out patterns in the wall, familiar crossroads she remembered from earlier. It wasn't so bad, once you had an idea of where you were going.

Soon, the light coming from the Pit invaded the darkness of the Combs, and Lexi blinked a few times to readjust to the changed atmosphere. The Pit's activity had really died down since she had first arrived. There was hardly anyone left.

It must be getting late. Maybe they're sleeping, or at clubs, or maybe they're gettin' a fix or something.

Now that she thought about it, she didn't want to know where everyone went.

"Hey, you new?"

Lexi whirled around to find the source of the voice.

It was the mural kid, the guy who'd been painting earlier.

She shrugged. "I guess."

The boy's chocolate skin brought out his deep brown eyes. His fuzzy black hair almost resembled the straw-like nest he was painting. He wore a torn basketball jersey and denim shorts. He wasn't wearing shoes.

The kid didn't ask any follow-up questions. He returned to his art as though he often slipped back and forth between his two worlds.

Now that she was closer, Lexi was captivated by the mural's beauty. The whole thing seemed like something out of a kid's storybook, but this boy worked with ferocious intensity. His thick eyes connected with that nest as though breaking contact would make it disappear.

"It's good," Lexi mumbled, nodding at the wall.

When the boy smiled, she noticed his teeth were a shade of yellow.

"Thank you; it's always nice to have a fan." He turned back to his meadow, passion twinkling in his eyes. "I've been working on this piece for a few weeks now. I strive for perfection. I'm still not happy with the way the leaves turned out, but I still got time. I mean, it's not like I have a deadline. It *would* help if I had decent supplies, but having to give half of my hard-earned cash to Sapphire, well, I guess I can't be picky. My art would be famous if I could do things my way."

Man, the kid could talk, but he never once cocked his head to glance her way. Good thing, too; she was always awkward in conversations and tended to avoid them, but this didn't feel strange, not with his back to her.

"Sorry, man." The boy's brush dabbed at the nest's corners, casting its shadow. "Totally forgot—I'm Da Vinci. Well, obviously that's just my street name. Most people call me DV, though. How 'bout you? You pick a name yet?"

"CJ," Lexi replied.

"Well, I guess we can't all be creative, can we?" His lip curled into a smile. "Nice to meet ya. So, you're the new kid."

"You say 'kid' like *you're* ancient. I mean, how old are you?"

DV's laugh reverberated off the stone walls. "Fourteen."

"You're younger than I am, so who's the kid?" Lexi brought her arms over her chest.

Her cheeks felt warm. *Wow, Lexi, way to sound like you're six!*

DV didn't seem to notice.

"Touché." He grinned, tilting his head toward her. "So, do you like to paint?"

Lexi eased down to her knees, entranced by how gently DV dabbed black specks along the edges of his nest. "No. Like you said, we can't all be creative. I don't have an ounce of creativity in me."

"That's what *everyone* says, isn't it? 'I don't got any creativity.' Me, on the other hand? Well, I always knew I got it, but some people don't get that, you know? That's why I split. My parents were artists. Man, you should have seen their work, you couldn't take your eyes away! I wish I had half the talent they did. When they died, I got stuck with my grandparents. They didn't like the art. They thought it was a waste of time. Whatever. They actually tried telling me I wasn't *allowed* to paint, if you can believe that! I took off and never looked back. I needed to paint, you know? It's my only connection with my folks. Here, I got all the walls in this whole tunnel. Sapphire said so. Now I got me a place to stay, and I can paint as much as I want—when I want and *how* I want."

He never once lifted his paintbrush as he spoke; he was *that* focussed. How lucky was he to have an escape like that?

She could see herself getting used to this. DV didn't expect her to say anything, and she could easily slip away with each brushstroke. It was hypnotic to watch, like falling into a dream.

Maybe it could work as an escape for her, too.

***

"Hey." A voice pulled her down from the cloud she'd drifted off on. An older girl was beside her, smiling down at her.

"Uh, hi," Lexi mumbled.

Without asking if it was okay, the girl planted herself next to Lexi, stretching out her legs and linking them at the ankles.

Lexi watched her, both curious and annoyed. The newcomer stared fixedly at DV's mural for a moment, tilting her head this way and that, like she saw something in the colours nobody else could.

The girl had to be older, maybe seventeen or eighteen, with a bounty of thick red hair. Where Sapphire's hair was smooth and shimmery, this girl's hair was tangled and matted. Cheap earrings dangled from her earlobes, and around her neck was a metal cross.

"Looks good, DV." The girl was dressed with a smile that touched her green eyes. How could she be so happy? Had she forgotten where she was?

"Aw, Star, you're too kind," DV replied, traces of humility in his voice.

"No, I mean it. You're truly talented." Star shared a glance with Lexi. "I'm Star," she said, as though Lexi hadn't just heard DV say her name.

"CJ, I guess."

"Don't worry, you'll get used to your new name." Star swept an arm out toward the Pit. "So, how do you like them? The tunnels, I mean."

"They're alright," Lexi replied with a shrug. What else was she supposed to say? *"Oh, actually, they're a little small, and the smell is disgusting. Oh, and it's dark and dingy, like something out of an old horror movie, but yeah, whatever!"*

Barney was right; beggars can't be choosers.

"So, where'd you come from?" Star asked.

"Tampa."

"How was the trip?"

"Decent."

"Did you find us alright?"

"Eventually."

"Did you get a blanket and a candle already?"

"Yep."

"What about a space to sleep?"

"Yep."

Star's questions stopped, but she was still watching Lexi, as if trying to see past her brown eyes to the secrets of her soul. Though she wanted to, Lexi never lowered her own gaze. Looking away meant losing a piece of yourself. You became vulnerable, and people would walk all over you.

She wouldn't let that happen ever again.

"Well, anyway, it was nice to meet you, CJ." Star stood. "Oh, and if you ever need someone to talk to, I'm here."

That took Lexi off-guard. "Uh, what?"

"You know, if you're having a rough time, you can talk to me."

Talk? Yeah right, Lexi thought. Well, it wasn't like the girl *knew* Lexi. Lexi couldn't fault her for that.

"Thanks, but I'm not a talker," she explained, shrugging it off like it was no big deal.

Star furrowed her brow. "What do you mean?"

"I mean I don't talk, you know, about my feelings or whatever. I don't talk about 'em because I don't got any."

61

Star looked amused about something. "That's ridiculous, CJ. Everybody's got a story, and everybody's sad about something down here. You can't deny your feelings. Even though most people here pretend they're okay, they're not. Everyone's got something that just eats them up inside. So don't tell me you don't have any feelings, because that's just not true." She offered that smile again. "Sometimes it's good to have someone to listen, you know?"

"Well, thanks, but you're wasting your time with me. I don't talk." Lexi got to her feet, stealing a glance at DV, who hardly seemed to be paying attention. "I'm going up for a walk."

"I don't think that's a good idea, CJ." Star's smile was gone. "It's really late, and you're new to the city. Besides, I don't like it when people go out at night."

The girl seemed genuinely concerned, but Lexi was done taking orders from people, done having people think they knew better than her.

"Well, I'm going anyway." She caught sight of Sapphire in a far corner with a group of girls, passing a cigarette around their little circle. "Unless there's a stupid rule about that, too?"

Star had no response, and Lexi took it as her cue to book.

On her way out, she felt eyes on her. She spotted an older boy slouching against a wall on his own, garbed in black from head to toe, his greasy black hair falling over his face. He was watching her with a creepy curl on his lips.

"Maybe ol' Star is right, babycakes," the boy called, halting Lexi in her tracks. "A hot minx like yourself hittin' the streets at this time of night, all alone? Might be some pervs out there lookin' for a good time." The boy's eyes crawled over the length of her body. "Might just be a first impression, but I think you would *definitely* be a good time."

Lexi glowered at him, suppressing the uneasy feelings churning inside.

"Thanks for the advice, but I'll be fine," she snapped, turning to leave.

"Hey! Name's Slick!" he called, winking at her, his tongue like a serpent's grazing the top of his lips. "I'll be seeing you around, baby."

Lexi spun on her heels and took off, trying to control the nausea. No, no, no, she would *not* think of Des. She would *not* let herself remember how he used to call her "baby" too. She would *not* relive those nights in his dark bedroom, his eyes bobbing up and down as he made her stand cold and naked before him, just so he could "have a look."

Shut it out.

Shut it out.

Shut. It. Out.

The night sky was black, the moon was out, and the street lamps pooled light around her. Yes, it was late, the streets were practically empty, but she didn't care.

As she strolled through the deserted city, she shut everything out, crawling into the void she'd created.

She was empty.

She was numb.

She felt nothing.

Maybe she had her own escape after all.

CHAPTER 11

L I Z

Sunday, October 4
10:25 a.m.

Liz pulled into her church's parking lot with five minutes to spare. It wasn't until she was parked that she realized just how much she'd missed this place. When had she last been here, two weeks ago? It wasn't like she was a regular attendee anymore. Her work hours were too unpredictable. In August, she hadn't gone to church at all.

Well, she was here now, and that was what counted.

Stretching her face into a smile, she rose out of her car, anticipating the procession of elderly ladies who were always the first to greet her. They always came bearing hugs and shoulder pats.

This Sunday was no exception.

"Liz, it is so great to see you," a stout lady said as she patted Liz's free hand.

"Yes, dear, we have missed your presence these last few weeks," another added.

Okay, is that Ethyl, or Jean?

Liz was terrible with names.

"Thank you," she said with a smile, avoiding names altogether. "I'm glad to be back."

Engulfing both ladies in one group hug, she extracted herself long enough to join the rest of the congregants filing into the large church. Inside, Liz was met with the bellowing church organ and the quiet hum of Sunday morning chatter. Yes, this place always helped Liz feel welcome, no matter how long she'd been absent.

"Liz! You made it!"

And there was Kathryn, springing from her pew when she spotted Liz. Another reason this place was so inviting.

"Long time, no see!" Kathryn exclaimed, swallowing Liz in a tight squeeze.

"Hey Kathy."

The two friends found their seats in Kathryn's pew, where Kathryn's daughter, Nancy, tugged on Liz's hand.

"Wike my dwess, Wiz?" the child asked as she hopped in a circle. Liz noticed Kathryn cringing in her seat. It still made Liz laugh; she'd insisted on a first-name basis ever since Nancy had been old enough to talk, though Kathryn insisted her daughter needed to learn respect for her elders.

"Elder! Kathryn, come on. I'm your best friend, not a geriatric! She can call me Liz."

So she had, for the last four years. Nancy was only six but was already just like Kathryn, not only inheriting her mother's large brown eyes and thick copper hair, but also her stubborn streak.

"Nancy, yes! I *do* love your dress. Your mommy has good taste. You know, turquoise is my favourite colour." Liz squeezed Nancy's hands and let her sway her arms to and fro.

"What's turquoise?" Nancy inquired, dropping her chin to gawk at her own dress. Smiling, Liz pointed out the turquoise in Nancy's little ensemble.

Thoroughly impressed she'd learned a new colour, Nancy dove onto Kathryn's husband's lap, chatting him up a mile a minute.

Kathryn turned to Liz.

"So, I called you yesterday, but you didn't answer *or* call me back." She wore a terrible attempt at a not-impressed face. Both women succumbed to giggles.

"Yeah, I know, I heard your message when I got in last night. I was at the parents' house. Kevin's birthday. The usual, you know, a barbeque and fancy party. I got home late. I didn't want to wake you."

Kathryn sucked in her breath, held it for some added drama, then exhaled with a smile.

"Well, I guess I'll let you off the hook, since it *was* family." She paused. "Next order of business, do you have the whole day off today?"

"Yeah right." Liz scoffed. "I'm working the night shift. I clock in at three, work until three in the morning, and start again at seven."

"In the morning?" Kathryn bellowed, earning her a curious glance from the elderly couple two pews ahead. Liz almost had to bite her fingers to keep from laughing. Thank goodness the service hadn't started yet.

"Yeah, in the morning. It won't be the first time I've worked that early."

"But you realize that means you're only gonna get about two hours of sleep," Kathryn pointed out.

"It's okay, Kathryn. I've done it before. I just catch up on sleep the next day. Besides, coffee does the trick. It's really no big deal."

She flashed a wide smile, hoping it would be enough to convince her friend. But she could never pull anything over Kathryn's eyes. She shot a breath through her nose, her face radiating disapproval.

"Anyway, I like the long hours. It keeps me on my toes." Liz patted Kathryn's hand. "But I *will* have lunch with you, after the service."

"Well, alright, but I still think you work too much." Kathryn stretched her neck toward her husband. "Brian, is that alright?"

"What?" Brian asked. He'd been occupied with Nancy's loose pigtail.

"I haven't seen Liz in a while. Do you mind if I go out for lunch?" Kathryn asked. "Can you be on kid duty?"

"Sure, no problem. I'll just take Nancy to the park after we grab a bite to eat. How's that sound, kiddo?" Nancy was already making the pew squeak with her excited bouncing. Clearly, it was okay with her.

"Yay! Daddy, you can push me on the swing!" She threw her arms around Brian's neck. "Is it Sunday school yet?"

***

The worship band began the service with a round of lively tunes. Soon afterward, Nancy joined the rest of the children as they stampeded off to Sunday school downstairs. The ushers wove through the aisles, taking up the offering, and before Liz knew it, Pastor Reid was in front of the pulpit, notes in hand.

"Good morning, everyone." The pastor beamed. "What a glorious day the Lord has given us."

The congregation responded in a chorus of amens.

"Amen!" Reid opened his tattered Bible. "I want to talk about my favourite part of the Bible today, called the Sermon on the Mount. This is where we hear the most from Jesus in one sermon, and He seems to touch on almost everything, doesn't He?"

Pastor Reid was so animated when he spoke. He seemed excited, like every sermon was a burning fire inside of him, waiting to be released with a ferocious passion.

"My personal favourite part of the Sermon on the Mount happens to be today's Scripture reading. If you have your Bibles, turn to Matthew 5:4." Pastor Reid's eyes went to his Bible, and he began to read. "'Blessed are those who mourn, for they will be comforted...'"

That was when Liz shut herself off.

It wasn't completely intentional, but her heart plunged to her knees when she heard that Bible verse. *Mourn... comfort...*

She remembered Kurt, and all the suffering he'd endured during his last six months of life, the suffering *she* had endured.

The suffering she had endured after he passed away.

Kurt's face floated in her mind, her soul, an image forever stamped there, his smile so vivid. It was as though he was here. *Kurt...*

"For they will be comforted." Lord, I trust You with my whole life, and I trust the Bible, too, but I don't understand. Where is the comfort?

Why, after two years of being alone, did it still hurt?

No, she couldn't let herself do this. She wouldn't let herself fall into the "woe is me" gig. Instead, she passively sifted through a hymnal until the sermon was over.

*****

After the service, Liz inched down the aisle with the rest of the crowd, Brian, Kathryn, and Nancy close by. The pastor always extended his hand to everyone on their way out.

Liz's heart fluttered. Pastor Reid had a good eye for catching who was present and absent most Sundays. It was a small church, after all.

Sure enough, Reid caught her eye, and that was it.

"Why, look who it is!" he exclaimed as he pumped her hand. "I'm so happy to see you, Liz. You weren't here last week, were you?"

"No, I wasn't. I... missed the week before, too. Work's been busy. I've had a lot of hours." She shrugged it off. Why couldn't the rest of the world see that it wasn't a big deal?

He gave her a wink. "Well, Liz, just be sure to be gracious to yourself, understand?" His smile could brighten any room.

As Reid turned to greet Kathryn's family, Liz escaped into the sunlight, momentarily blinded by its rays.

While her vision cleared, her mind wouldn't. What was Pastor Reid talking about? What did that even mean? *"Be gracious to yourself, understand?"* Maybe it was just something pastors said. Maybe it was something he told everyone.

Or maybe not.

She sighed.

Before too long, Kathryn and her family joined her. After Kathryn blew a kiss to her family, she and Liz strolled toward Liz's car.

"Good sermon, huh? Pastor Reid never ceases to amaze me," Kathryn said conversationally. "You know, he could be one of those television evangelists. Except he'd never want the fame. He's much too humble for that."

"Oh... yeah, it was a good sermon," Liz muttered.

"Did you even hear the sermon?" Kathryn asked.

Liz felt her cheeks burning. It was like the woman had a radar for these kinds of things. Honestly, sometimes she felt like Kathryn could see right through her.

"To be honest, no." Liz bit her lip. "My mind wandered... a bit."

Kathryn stared at Liz, like she could read her deepest thoughts. "Alright, that's it, it has been far too long since you and I chatted," Kathryn decided as she and Liz hopped in the car. "Shall we go to our usual haunt?"

CHAPTER 12

L E X I

Sunday, October 4
11:42 a.m.

DV's mural is melting; the colours are shifting from a flourishing meadow to a dark forest, lonely and threatening. The nest is still there, but something is different: large eggs appear in its centre. They hatch, releasing monstrous-sized birds with matted feathers and dripping fangs. They pound their way through the tunnels, each step a rumbling earthquake. Their red eyes scavenge the Combs for prey, and when they reach Lexi's cove, all it takes is one swift movement, and they devour her whole...

She is in a dark room, blackness clawing at her from every angle. She is blind here, until a green light outlines a doorway. There is someone standing nearby, a black shadow slithering toward her, but she can't make the creature out. Fear grips her stomach... the familiarity of this haunts her, but why?

Fast as a bullet, the thing locks her arm in its hold, its touch like fire singeing her skin raw. She sees him now and she tries to scream, but no sound comes out. It's like an invisible force stripped her of vocal chords.

She is helpless.

The man yanks her. She stumbles, but he won't back down. He hoists her up and swings her onto a rough platform. She can't push herself up. The man is on top of her, pinning her, breathing fire into

70

her neck, smothering her lips with sloppy kisses that reek of beer and death...

She slips through the cracks of the platform until she hovers over the streets of Jacksonville, gazing upon a copy of herself wandering around like a lost dog...

She plummets to the concrete, only to find it has become ice water. She's drowning...

Her lungs turn inside out...

The tunnels fill her last thoughts...

Someone is calling her name...

Hey, CJ...

CJ...

"Yo, CJ, you ever gonna wake up, or what?"

Lexi woke with a start, feeling a cold sweat on her cheeks. She sucked in a breath, her memory clearing. She remembered where she was and how she got there.

Just a dream.

"Geez, I didn't think you'd *ever* wake up."

Lexi sat up, shaking off the foreboding nightmare. There was Barney, cross-legged in front of her, chomping on one of his filthy fingernails. Lexi moaned under her breath.

"Do you always hover when people sleep? Most people would consider that creepy, you know."

She twined her arm around to knead the knot in her back. *How long will it take before I get used to sleeping on concrete?*

"Sorry, I just wondered if you were ever plannin' on getting up. It's almost noon, y'know," Barney said. "Anyway, I figured I could teach you the ropes, how to survive on the streets and stuff."

Lexi swallowed a threatening yawn. Almost noon? She hadn't slept well. Kids were in and out all night—some whispered, some didn't, some couples made out, some fought, and some kids were giggling under the influence of weed.

She'd also had to deal with the dreams. They didn't make sense, and yet even the dreams seemed to make more sense than her current reality.

"I think I can handle it," Lexi replied to Barney's offer as she found her feet, brushing off the dust that had collected on her jeans.

"Dude, at least humour me. I'm gonna go out on a limb here and guess you've never been to Jacksonville. Believe me, you may *think* you can handle it, but all it takes is one wrong move, and you end up getting nabbed by the cops. Trust me, you don't want that to happen."

Impatiently, Lexi rolled her eyes. She hardly wanted to admit it, but Barney was right. What did she know about survival? She only had a few bucks left, and yeah, she'd never been to this city before.

I spent two days just looking for this place!

Okay, so maybe she did need his help, but the last thing she wanted was to look vulnerable.

"Fine, I'll humour you." She ran her fingers through her messy hair. "Lead the way."

***

On their way through the Pit, Lexi spotted Slick loitering near the Tube, his empty eyes catching her, like an animal on the hunt. She held his eyes; she didn't want to seem afraid. Guys like him fed off fear.

Lexi ignored the goosebumps erupting on her arms, and she caught up with Barney, already into the Tube.

"So, what's his story?" Lexi asked, her hands extended before her. Sure, it was the middle of the day, but the Tube was still black as night.

"Who?" Barney's voice seemed so far away.

"That guy back there," Lexi replied as they crawled up the narrow slope into the sunlight. "Slick."

"So, you met Slick, huh?"

"You could say that." As if being drooled over like a hunk of meat was a formal introduction.

"Yeah, he's... well, he keeps to himself for the most part. Nobody likes him," Barney explained.

72

"Can't imagine why."

"Don't worry; he's all talk. I mean, just listen to the name he picked for himself. He thinks he's, like, God's gift to women." Barney shrugged. "But he gets me weed, so I kinda need him around, you know?"

Lexi didn't answer.

"Anyway, let's get some breakfast. Or lunch, I guess. You hungry?"

"I guess." Honestly, she hadn't even thought about food.

"Don't worry; I'm all over this. Just follow me." Barney sifted his way through the crowd, Lexi miming him. The sidewalks were packed, people almost walking shoulder to shoulder. Lexi felt her elbows collide with a few strangers.

They reached a corner, and Barney came to a stop. His goofy grin transformed into a straight line as he grew silent, motioning for Lexi to lie low. She watched him while he gazed down the street like a secret agent. He was scoping something out, but what?

"Okay, wait here and watch carefully," he ordered.

Lexi circled, feeling exposed and suspicious, even though she hadn't done anything. Was she guilty by association? What was she even associated with?

Barney strolled by an outdoor fruit market. Nobody seemed to pay him any attention, except Lexi. She followed his every move as he doubled back toward the fruit display, sliding a hand into his pocket and rummaging through loose change or something.

What was he *doing*?

Then, like a pro, he tossed a coin into his left hand and swept up a bunch of bananas with his right.

And just like that, he strutted back to Lexi.

"Walk," he commanded.

She did.

Lexi's hands shook as she followed Barney away from the scene of the crime. Her stomach was knotting furiously as she stole nervous glances over her shoulder. Had anyone seen him? Were the cops coming? Would they be arrested?

But Barney glided along with an air of confidence.

"See? Piece of cake." Barney passed her a banana. "The trick is to pretend like you're doing something else, and they'll all think you're distracted. Then, you just pick it up and walk away. Most people don't even pay attention. And if they do, you run!"

Barney chuckled as he tore into a banana. Lexi held hers at arm's length. Her heart was doing jumping jacks, pounding into her the reality of what street life would mean. Barney stole food, and if she wanted to survive, she would have to as well.

It wasn't like she'd ever been religious or cared about what was right or wrong, but there was just something about stealing that rubbed her the wrong way.

This was what her life had come to, wasn't it? And it made sense. Of *course* she'd have to steal. How could she not have seen this coming? Had she thought the tunnels would have a gourmet kitchen?

I'm such an idiot!

"What?" Barney asked, eyeballing Lexi's uneaten banana.

"Nothin'," she replied, staring at the sidewalk.

"Oh, you're not gonna get all moral on me, are ya?"

"Give me a break!" Lexi snapped, hesitantly peeling the fruit. "But doesn't it ever bother you? You know, stealing?"

Barney shrugged, tossing his peel and going for seconds. "Nah. It's survival. If you were on a deserted island, you'd take stuff from the trees to survive."

"That's different, Barn."

Barney paused. "Is it?"

Lexi didn't want to know what he meant. She nibbled on her own banana like it would grow fangs and bite her at any minute. It was wrong, and even though it was just one banana, she felt like a criminal eating it.

***

For the next few hours, Barney gave her the grand tour of downtown Jacksonville, lecturing her on all the best places to steal. On Park Street, you could steal food from the market but not money from people's pockets, because of the crowd. Too many eyes. On Bay Street, you were safer pocketing wallets in the morning, because people were more interested in getting their coffees than watching for thieves.

Barney showed her where the second-hand thrift store was and how you could swipe clothing from the drop-off bin when nobody was on duty.

"It's better to change your clothes every now and again. The less you look like a street kid, the less you'll be noticed."

Barney told her she should wait until Donna was on duty at the bakery, because all she did was read; she'd never notice if you took a muffin or two. He also told her about Gina over at the hotdog booth, who sometimes gave out free food to street kids because she felt sorry for them. He even showed her which trashcans to avoid, because those were the ones cops loitered around, just waiting to pick up the trash of the streets.

The more she heard, the more Lexi felt sick to her stomach. This all felt so wrong, so messed up, but hadn't that always been her life? Besides, Barney tried showing her some perspective.

"I figure you're here for the same reason we're all here. Because adults suck! They messed with you, and now, here you are. Don't you think we've earned the right to take back from them? After everything they've taken from us?"

Lexi couldn't argue that logic. She'd been messed with, and *that* was the understatement of the century. She couldn't count the number of times she'd been screwed over by adults who thought they were the boss, superior, the king of their castle, or whatever. They hurt her, bad. What had she done to deserve any of it?

Maybe Barney was right; maybe she had every right to steal, as a statement about everything that had been taken from her, things she wouldn't get back, *could* never get back.

It didn't matter how much she tried to justify it. That banana still felt like it was on fire, just like her conscience.

CHAPTER 13

L I Z

Sunday, October 4
12:15 p.m.

"If you keep eating like that, you're going to have a heart attack," Liz said, pointing to the plate of greasy fish and chips in front of Kathryn, a contrast to her own spinach salad.

"Yeah, yeah, you tell me that *every* single time we come here." Kathryn made a show of pouring on extra ketchup and vinegar.

"You know, salads won't *kill* you."

"Yes, Doctor, anything you say."

The two friends were relaxing in a cozy booth at their favourite restaurant, Micky Jo's. They'd been coming here for years, and Kathryn was still ordering the same dish.

"Do you let Nancy eat food like that?" Liz asked.

"Yeah right. As if Brian would let me feed Nancy this kind of food. He's in charge of the cooking, remember?" Kathryn snorted. "I just sneak the junk after Nancy goes to bed."

"Kudos to Brian. It's important for kids to eat balanced meals."

Kathryn paused, flashing Liz a knowing smile.

"What?" Liz asked.

"That," Kathryn said, pointing her fork at Liz, "is why you would have made a great mom."

There it was again, her insides turning to ice. Any time and *every time* this came up, the same rock settled in her stomach.

Liz steeled herself, kept her face a mask. She didn't want

Kathryn to see how deeply it stung. *This is supposed to be a pleasant visit!*

Kathryn, however, wasn't stupid.

"Oh, Liz, I'm sorry." She dropped her fork and reached over to envelop Liz's free hand. "Honey, I didn't mean to hurt you."

Yes, Kathryn always could see right through Liz's facade.

"I'm fine, Kath. It's just..." What? She didn't even know. "I was at Mom's yesterday, and she harassed me about having kids. I guess when you said I'd make a good mom, it reminded me of my own mother, and... you know how she is."

It wasn't the whole truth, but it wasn't a lie either.

"Yeah." Kathryn nodded. "Your mom doesn't exactly have tact, does she?"

"Thank you! So I'm not imagining it!"

"But Liz, you do know your mom loves you, right?"

"She has a fine way of showing it."

"Well, every mother has her days." Kathryn sipped her soda. "So, what made you tune out Pastor Reid this morning?"

Liz pursed her lips. Typical Kathryn, always honing in on the very things Liz preferred to bury.

"Were you thinking about him?" Kathryn asked. "Kurt?"

Well, Liz guessed it didn't take a genius to figure that one out. Liz *was* a widow, and Reid *had* preached on mourning. The math wasn't too hard to calculate.

"Yeah," Liz admitted. She felt hot tears stinging her eyes, but no, she would not cry. She hated how vulnerable she could be when Kathryn was around. It was like the woman had some hidden emotional-control device that could shatter the walls surrounding Liz's heart in seconds. It could be exhausting.

"Honey, don't expect the pain to go away. It won't, because you loved him, and that's okay. What's *not* okay is living your life each day hoping to stop feeling altogether, just because it's easier. Liz, you love Kurt so much. You can't just shut out that part of your life. It's okay to feel. It's *not* okay to work ridiculous hours to numb the pain."

Kathryn eyed Liz with a ferocious intensity, conviction behind her eyes. Liz felt her defences rising.

"That's not what I'm doing, Kathy."

"Yeah, okay." Kathryn breathed out. "Really, Liz, you should at least take some time off. Some time for *you*."

"And do what with my life? Come on, Kathryn, I'm a single woman who works full-time."

"You could always take up painting again."

"You *know* I gave that up."

Kathryn lifted a finger. "No, you put it on the side burner. That's how I like to look at it."

"Whichever way you want to look at it, I'm not interested."

"Well, that's a shame, because you're really good." A long moment of silence passed before Kathryn spoke again. "Look, I know you quit painting when Kurt died. I know he encouraged you with it, so you think going back to it would just remind you of him, but Lizzie, be honest with yourself. Would he want you to stop?"

Liz didn't answer but instead turned her gaze out the window, a welcome distraction. Why did Kathryn always have to be right? Why did she always have to nail things right on the head? Why couldn't she understand that the last thing in the world Liz wanted to think about right now was painting?

That art studio is probably caked in layers of dust!

Kathryn was saying something more, but Liz spotted something out the window that sparked her curiosity. There were two kids—well, teenagers—coming to a stop on a corner across the road. Liz observed the teens interacting, but it didn't seem natural. Something was up. The boy, a kid with shaggy hair and loose-fitting clothing, spoke to the girl, who glanced around as he slipped away. Why did the poor girl look so frightened? Her jerky movements made her look like a criminal for just *standing* there.

"Liz, what are you looking at?" Kathryn asked, following Liz's line of sight.

Liz didn't answer; she waited as the scene unfolded. The boy nonchalantly lifted a bunch of bananas, then strolled off with a nod at the girl to follow.

Just like that, they disappeared around the corner.

Liz felt a strange feeling overcome her. It wasn't that she'd witnessed a crime. No, she'd seen stealing many times in Jacksonville; it was no secret that the Tunnel Kids were everywhere.

It was the girl who had caught Liz's attention—the scrawny, mousy-haired girl who couldn't have been more than fourteen. Something didn't sit right. That girl's eyes had widened to the size of saucers when her friend took those bananas. She'd watched as if he'd just *murdered* someone.

"Oh, those kids. I mean, you gotta feel for them, living on their own like that, fending for themselves, but I mean, come on! Could they be any more obvious about what they're doing, in broad daylight?" Kathryn sighed. "Maybe the cops ought to chase them out, you know? Put them into group homes or something, but get them out of Jacksonville. It's probably dangerous for them, and besides, there's too much theft going on. Everywhere I go, I cling to my purse like the jaws of life."

Liz was only half-listening. She couldn't get that girl out of her mind, that pitiful expression of utter dismay as she witnessed the thievery by her buddy's hand. Such a simple gesture, something every street kid had to do in order to survive, but this girl...

She just seemed so... so unsure.

Liz leaned back in her seat, surveying the street the two kids had taken off down.

"Did you see her?"

Kathryn furrowed her brow. "Who?"

"The girl."

"Sure. The kid who took off with him after he nicked the bananas."

"Did you see the look on her face?" Liz asked.

"No, why?"

"Kathryn, she didn't *like* what she was seeing. She was terrified! You should have seen her face. I mean, I've seen these kids steal before, but this kid, well, she seemed absolutely torn apart by what he did, like it was the crime of the century. I know these kids steal all the time, but that girl, she knew it was wrong."

Why am I still talking about this? Why in the world does it even bug me?

"Maybe she's new to the streets," Kathryn said with a shrug. "You know, maybe she just arrived, and they're showing her what to do."

Maybe, but that didn't make Liz feel any better.

It was strange; it was like that girl had a thread tied around Liz's heart, and she was pulling it away with her. For whatever reason, Liz's curiosity got the better of her. Where had the girl come from? What had gone so wrong in her life that she had to escape to the underground of Jacksonville? Was she running from someone? Hiding from someone? Liz had never really given any thought to these Tunnel Kids, save for their brief visits to her ER, where they were treated for drug overdoses or stab wounds. So why, all of a sudden, was her heart melting because of one girl? Why this random kid in a sea of hundreds?

"Anyway, as I was saying, Liz." Kathryn lifted an eyebrow. "Take some time off, some time for *you*."

Liz felt the corners of her mouth twitch into a small smile. "You sound like Pastor Reid. He was telling me to be 'gracious' to myself, whatever that means. I swear, you're all building an alliance against me."

"We're not," Kathryn promised. "But you should take it to heart. He's a smart guy, you know. Maybe you ought to listen to him, since you don't listen to me. Don't look at me like that, Lizzie. I'm not offended or anything, because I know you don't listen to anybody. But if you ever *do* decide to start listening to me, take my advice: take some time off and start painting."

"Now's not the time, Kathryn, but I do appreciate your concern. It means a lot." Liz paused. "How are things at the magazine?"

Liz was thankful Kathryn knew when to stop, when to read Liz's cues, and when to drop a subject. As Kathryn plowed into the details of a story she was working on for the December issue, Liz listened with eagerness, managing a silent prayer of thanksgiving for a friend who cared enough to press her but cared enough to let it go.

And that was only one of the reasons she loved Kathryn so much.

Dear Journal,

This will be quick. I'm due for work in half an hour.

I had lunch with Kathryn today. It was so great to see her. I hate the lengths of time that pass between our visits. She's looking great, as always, still smiling and still the same old Kathryn, meaning she definitely centred in on things I didn't want to talk about. She's always been this way, even when I first met her at that couple's retreat. Was that ten years ago? Wow. Anyway, I'd only known her and Brian for an hour, and she was already digging her way into my life. I love her to death, but I must admit there are times when she drives me crazy!

Oh, and the weirdest thing happened today. I still don't know why I'm making such a big deal about it. I saw these two street kids, a boy and a girl. That's not strange, I see kids like them all the time, but this time was different. The boy made the girl watch while he stole a bunch of bananas. No big deal, right? Except you should have seen the look on that poor girl's face! I don't know how else to describe it except pure agitation, terror, like she was afraid of something. It really hit me, for some reason, and it got me thinking about these Tunnel Kids a little more. I can't help but wonder where this girl came from, why she had to resort to living on the streets.

I don't know why I'm so curious. It was just strange; most of these kids are desensitized about stealing. I don't think this girl is there yet.

I have to head to work, but one quick thing: Kathryn thinks I ought to start painting again. I know I can't right now. I'm not ready to cross that threshold. Maybe I just need more time. But really, when is the *right* time for anything?

—Liz

CHAPTER 14

L E X I

Sunday, October 4
7:31 p.m.

A part of her wanted to run away again.

The air had gotten cooler by the time Barney was convinced Lexi had passed Street Life 101. As the two meandered back to the tunnels, Lexi's mind raced.

Barney had revealed the secrets of making money in a place like this; most kids panhandled or stole, but some people were talented enough to create salable merchandise. Like DV. Barney said the painter used to do portraits to make a buck here and there, but he'd given it up after too much criticism.

Other kids played guitar, if they were lucky enough to own one, and they'd play heart-wrenching ballads all day to gain some pity—pity equalled cash, sometimes. Then there were the drug dealers, like Slick. Barney said he didn't even want to know how loaded he was.

Lexi didn't want to think about the older girls who waited until after midnight before hanging out in the shadows of street corners for the older pigs who'd pay them for a few tricks.

Weighing her options, suddenly stealing didn't seem so bad.

But that wasn't the point; it still *felt* bad.

That was why she wanted to run. She'd only been here a day, and she was already losing herself.

***

"Dude, hang back; I'll just be a sec." Back in the tunnels, Lexi snapped out of her daze long enough to see Barney jogging toward the wall.

And there was Slick, rocking back and forth on his heels.

Oh good, my favourite person. Lexi grimaced.

"You got money for me, Barney boy?" Slick asked with a sharp nod at Barney's pockets.

Great, a drug exchange. That was the last thing she wanted to see. She thought about ditching, heading to her space alone, but Barney gave up his whole day for her; the least she could do was give him two minutes.

"Yeah, it's right here." Barney pulled a wad of cash from his pockets and pushed it toward Slick.

Lexi turned her attention to a small spider spinning its web above her. Still, she heard the rustling plastic and a relieved sigh from Barney.

"That's the stuff, huh, Barn?" Slick asked. "Hey, by the way, did you do her yet?"

Lexi's eyes never left that spider, but her stomach seized, nausea creeping in.

Ignore him! He's just a pig!

"No," Barney replied, irritation lacing his voice.

"Oh, come on, man! You gotta be kiddin'! You been out there all day with her, and you didn't even get laid?"

"Back off, man," Barney said carefully, heading back toward Lexi. "It ain't like that, alright?"

Thankfully, Slick shut up, but Lexi kept her face a rock so Barney would think she hadn't heard anything. It must have worked, because Barney was speechless as they strolled through the Combs in silence, Lexi already numbing herself against Slick's snide remarks.

He's just a pig. He's probably like that with all girls. It doesn't matter.

In Barney's space, he knelt to light his candle while Lexi found a spot against the cold wall. Man, it felt good to sit, and she kicked off her runners to massage her sore feet. Barney was already rolling joints by the flame. At least, that's what she guessed he was doing.

What do I know about weed?

After rolling a few, he tossed her a finished product.

"I already told you I'm not into this crap," she said, hucking it back.

"Oh, right, right. Sorry, I forgot."

"You forgot because that stuff kills brain cells." Lexi shook her head. "Anyway, drugs are stupid, so I'd rather stay away from them, thank you very much."

"Listen, ya little punk, weed is *not* a drug. It's not even *bad* for you. Don't you know they use it for medicinal purposes?" Barney asked, rolling his joints faster and faster like a pro.

"Yeah." Lexi snorted. "Except you don't have cancer."

"You don't know that!"

Lexi's eyebrows went up.

"Okay, fine, so I don't have cancer, but whatever. It's still not bad for you." He paused. "Besides, even if it were, would anybody really care?"

He had her there. He was right, and that's when it hit her—nobody would care if she started smoking weed, drinking every night, slicing her arms, throwing up her food, overdosing on heroin.

But then... nobody really cared anyway.

Except once.

Yeah, and look how well that *ended.*

By now, Barney had already lit one of his joints and was puffing away. His eyes were already starting to go red, and he was grinning like an idiot.

Realizing Barney would be in his own little world for a while, Lexi decided to take a walk, maybe ease off the bitterness creeping in. Why was she letting it get to her, anyway? It wasn't like anything Barney said wasn't true. Nobody cared about her anymore; they never had. She could kick the bucket tomorrow and nobody would be the wiser.

Screw the world. She'd rather they *didn't* remember her.

Hands shoved in pockets, she stalked through the Pit, brushing off the stabbing pains in her gut. She hadn't eaten anything since that banana.

Whatever. She wasn't ready to steal, and panhandling... well, she wasn't quite ready to be a beggar, either. All she had left was her dignity. In fact, she wondered if it was the only thing left that kept her human.

"Hey."

Lexi looked up, and there was Star with that out-of-place grin on her face.

"How was your day?" she asked conversationally.

Lexi shrugged. She wasn't in the mood for small talk. The tension was mounting. She needed to get out of here.

"I... I know the first day can be really difficult, you know, on the streets," Star said. "I remember my first day. I was a wreck, and I can remember—"

"I'm fine, really, it's no big deal," Lexi interrupted. "It's not the worst I've been through."

Star didn't say anything, but she stared Lexi down like she was trying to pierce through deeper layers, hoping to catch a small glimpse inside the shell that was Lexi. It made Lexi want to laugh.

There's nothing in there, Star. Just emptiness, so you can stop trying to find anything else.

"Anyway, I'm heading out," Lexi said. "You can stop worrying about me. I'm tough. There's probably tons of other girls down here for you to worry about."

Without waiting for Star to reply, Lexi pushed past her and tore out of the Pit, oblivious to Slick's catcall.

***

Sauntering through the streets, the moon high above her, Lexi emptied herself of believing she was hungry. The mind was a powerful tool. If she could just distract herself, at least for now, she could go longer without eating.

The longer I don't eat, the longer I don't have to steal.

She wondered how long that would last.

"Come on, Mom, can't we just go in this store?"

Lexi noticed the teenage girl up ahead, gripping a large collection of shopping bags. The girl could hardly hold them all!

"Tamara, sweetheart, aren't you getting tired of shopping? We've been at it for hours now," the mom said, relieving the girl of some of her bags.

"Please, Mom! I promise this will be the last one!"

Lexi waited as the mother considered her daughter, as if to say, *"You win again, and only because I love you so very much."*

A chill ran down Lexi's spine.

"Alright, last one." The mother held the door for the excited girl, and the two disappeared into a small boutique.

Lexi stood frozen on the sidewalk. It was so familiar, but it was all so distant now. Had it been a dream? No, it was real. Hilary *did* exist, once upon a time.

In fact, maybe the reason Hilary felt so surreal was because Hilary was the only good thing Lexi's life had ever held.

CHAPTER 15

L E X I

Saturday, July 12
1:40 p.m.

ONE YEAR, THREE MONTHS AGO

*"I just don't get why I have to get a whole new outfit. I
have clothes," Lexi whined, dawdling after Hilary through the
department store.*

*Hilary turned around, her long dark hair falling over her
shoulder as she smiled warmly at Lexi.*

*"Honey, it's your first date! If you're not going to make a big
deal about it, then I have to. Getting a new outfit is good luck."
She lifted a lavender blouse off a rack, holding it against Lexi, who
made a face.*

*"Besides, I don't think Zack is even gonna care what I wear."
She snatched the blouse from Hilary, hanging it up again. "Anyway,
I don't see anything I like."*

*"That's because you aren't looking, which is exactly why I'm
here." With a cheesy grin, Hilary took Lexi's hand and lured her
deeper into the store.*

*Three months. Lexi had counted it a couple of days ago; she'd
been living with Jared and Hilary for three months now, and life
was slowly becoming easier, something she wasn't sure would ever
happen.*

When she'd first met the Notts, she hadn't wanted to be placed with them. She'd just been pulled out of another horrible foster situation, after all. She didn't trust anyone, but Bridget, her social worker, told her that the Notts were nice people.

Yeah, that was the problem. They all *started out nice.*

But the Notts were different.

Lexi didn't see much of Jared, who worked crazy hours. He was always at the office, meeting with clients or attending court. He stayed late at the office a lot, but Hilary, who worked part-time at a daycare, was always around when Lexi got home from school and on weekends. It was always the two of them, Hilary and Lexi.

At first, Hilary's steady presence felt awkward, something Lexi hadn't experienced before, but soon Lexi began to enjoy the company. Sure, it was a huge change from what she was used to, but Hilary helped her with her homework, drove her to school, went to the parent-teacher conferences, even took her shopping. It had only been three months, but Lexi was having the time of her life.

"What about this one?" Hilary displayed a green tank top with a scoop neck. Lexi shook her head. Hilary had such a different way of looking at things, not like anybody Lexi had ever met before. Yeah, it was Lexi's first date, but it really wasn't that big of a deal—not to her, anyway. She had met Zack on her first day of school. He'd offered to show her to all her classes, they'd spent their lunch hours together, and later they'd learned they lived down the street from one another. When school let out in June, they started spending more time together. It wasn't anything special, mostly just walking by the beach or getting ice cream. It took her by complete surprise when he asked her on a date... like, an actual date!

Well, as soon as Hilary found out about it, it was only a matter of seconds before she suggested a shopping trip.

"Lex, at least try to keep an open mind," Hilary said, as she rummaged through a sale rack. "You don't like anything here, because you don't see it as a big deal. I get that, but come on! Try and be at least a little excited about it. You only get one first date."

"I don't get what makes this any different than Zack and me—"

"Zack and I."

"Sorry. I don't get what makes this any different than when we have ice cream on the beach. Now there's all this pressure, because I know he likes me, you know, in that way. What if this ruins our friendship? I mean, I really like Zack, but I thought we were friends. Like, what if we go out, and it's the worst date in the history of all dates, and we end up hating each other? What if he doesn't ask me out again? What if he never talks to me again? Then life is gonna get super awkward. I won't have Zack as a friend anymore, and school is gonna be unbearable in the fall."

"Honey, it's just your first date. Don't be so paranoid." Hilary placed a hand on Lexi's shoulder. "You are going to have plenty of dates in your future, especially for a girl as gorgeous, smart, and funny as you are."

Lexi distracted herself with the sleeve of a display cardigan. "Yeah, sure. Whatever," she mumbled, rolling her eyes. Hilary was always saying stuff like that, telling Lexi how great and talented she was. Lexi never believed her.

As though she could sense this, Hilary took Lexi's chin in her hand and lifted her face so their eyes met.

"Hey, I don't just say these things because I like the sound of my own voice, kapeesh?" Hilary asked, a serious look on her face. "I know you're not used to hearing it, but I mean it, Lex. A girl like you—you'll go far in life."

With a wink, Hilary turned to sift through more outfits. Lexi trailed after her with a huff.

"Anyway, I don't even know what I should get, because I don't know where we're going," Lexi said. "Zack said he would figure something out, but he doesn't know either. If I don't know where we're going, how am I supposed to know what to wear?"

Hilary bit her lip, like she always did when she was thinking. She donned the same look during their homework sessions too. It made Lexi laugh, especially because half the time Hilary didn't even realize she was doing it.

"Well, the best thing to do in situations like that is go for something kind of casual, but kind of dressy. That way, you're not overdoing it, but you'll still look great." Hilary directed Lexi away from the leftover prom dresses. "Besides, chances are good Zack won't be taking you to a five-star restaurant."

"He might!" Lexi exclaimed.

"You're fourteen, kiddo! He probably doesn't make that kind of money on his paper route," Hilary said. Lexi had to giggle.

"Okay, seriously, we've got to get down to business!" Hilary picked out a purple tank top, made of silk. "How 'bout this?"

Lexi shook her head.

"Why not? What's wrong with it?" Hilary's hand was on her hip.

"I hate purple."

"What?" Hilary's eyes widened. "Now, come on, that can't be true. You wore purple at your piano recital in June, didn't you?"

Lexi felt her cheeks getting hot. She cleared her throat.

"Uh, I only wore that sweater because, um, you and Jared got it for my birthday." She stared at the floor, avoiding Hilary's eye, but Hilary only laughed.

"Well fine, then!" she said with a smile. "Okay, no purple. Do you have any problems with turquoise that I should know about?"

Lexi didn't, and soon her arms were piled high with several outfits Hilary wanted her to try on, forcing her into the nearest change room.

***

"No, not that one; it doesn't do your figure any justice at all."

***

"Oooh, yes! I love that!" Hilary exclaimed.
"It's too frilly."
Hilary groaned.

***

"Definitely not, there is no way I'm letting you leave the house like that!"

***

"Yes, oh Lexi, it's beautiful!"
"It's an old lady's shirt!"
"Oh for goodness' sake!"

***

Finally, they settled on a sleek black button-up top with a new pair of classy jeans. Hilary even bought her new shoes that had a bit of a heel, which she told Lexi she'd need to practice walking around the house in.

"Well, you don't want to fall on your first date, do you?"

After they paid, they left the department store, Lexi carrying her new outfit.

As Hilary unlocked the car door, she shot Lexi a wink and tapped her on the nose. "Hey, Zack's gonna be nuts not to ask you out again."

CHAPTER 16

L E X I

Sunday, October 4
11:45 p.m.

It was late when Lexi got back; she must have wandered the streets for hours, though it hardly felt like it. Mostly, she couldn't even remember where she'd been. She felt so mechanical, her mind elsewhere while her body moved robotically with no real destination.

Now, tucked away in her haven deep in the Combs, Lexi longed for sleep but found herself wide awake. Her mind was buzzing with memories. She hated it, *hated* it, when something triggered her past. She hated how easy it was to slip through the cracks of the here and now, collapsing into vivid memories that would never leave her. She wished she could just forget—forget Des, forget Hilary, forget *all* of them—but they were always with her, like weights tethered to her ankles, pulling her underwater.

She reached for her backpack, tearing it open and digging around for the one thing she had thought about leaving behind. Why she'd decided to grab it last minute, she wasn't sure. It was useless, wasn't it? It didn't mean anything, not anymore.

There it was, just as she remembered it: a small envelope with nothing but the tiny written name "Lexi Vogan" and the address at Everidge. She'd read this letter so many times, she could probably quote it line by line, but every time she read it, it stabbed at her like a sharpened sword. The name on the return address was

"Hilary Nott," and it was written three months after the Notts had kicked her out.

Sliding the thin paper out of the tattered envelope, she read it again.

Lexi, I've been trying to talk to you for a few months now, but whenever I call Bridget tells me you don't want to talk to me. I understand you must be very upset about everything that happened, but I hope you will read this letter and hear what I would like to say to you.

Sweetheart, please know that I don't regret any of the time we spent together, and know that I'm genuinely sorry for sending you away. Having you here was a rewarding experience, and I'm filled with wonderful memories. I hope one day you can understand why Jared and I came to our difficult decision. With a baby on the way, we couldn't give you the proper attention. It just would have been too hard, and unfair.

I know you were hurt, and you need to know I would never intentionally hurt you. You are a special girl with raw talent and a good heart. I truly wish you all the best, and I will always love you. I hope one day that you will be able to forgive me.

All the best,
—Hilary

Lexi clenched the letter tight in her hand. She didn't care. Why *should* she? They hadn't cared about her, so it didn't matter what that letter said. Lexi had been nothing but a means to an end, a second choice, unwanted. She didn't care *how* genuine the letter seemed. She didn't care *how* sorry Hilary seemed, *how* much they said they would always love her. Lexi knew better. She'd been through enough in her life to know how things worked. Nobody really cared about anybody else; it was all a show. Behind closed doors was a different story. Hilary may have been different, but that was all an act too. It *had* to be.

"Hey, Ceej."

Lexi looked up in time to see Barney plop himself down on the concrete floor. He looked wiped! His head was swaying, his eyelids were drooping, and he wouldn't stop yawning.

"Geez, Barn, if you're tired, go to sleep," Lexi said.

"Yeah, yeah, I'm headin'." He saw the letter as Lexi played with it in her hands. "What's that?"

"A letter."

"Well, *duh!*" Barney chuckled softly. "Who's it from?"

Lexi shrugged. "Nobody important, just a foster family I stayed with."

Nobody important. Nobody important. Nobody important.

"Oh." Barney cleared his throat. "So… didn't work out?"

Lexi scoffed, eyes on the ceiling. "Do they ever?"

Barney was quiet. Lexi counted the cobwebs decorating the corners. *Sixteen… seventeen…*

"So, like, what happened?" Barney asked, breaking the silence.

Lexi shrugged again. "Nothing. I was there for nine months. They wanted kids, they couldn't get pregnant, so they did the foster thing. Long story short, they got pregnant and they ditched me. The end."

Absorbed in her own bitterness, she impulsively shredded Hilary's letter, her expression like ice.

She didn't care. She wouldn't *let* herself care.

"Well, what's with the letter then? I mean, if they ditched you, why'd they bother writing a letter?" Barney's mouth stretched into another yawn. He was probably burning out from the weed.

"She wrote it. The foster mom. She tried keepin' in touch with me after they made me leave. Nine months, and they threw me out like it didn't matter, so whatever, I never wrote her back. She can keep her stupid baby and perfect family. I don't need it!"

She took one of the ripped pieces of the letter and held it over the candle's flame, watching as it slowly caught fire.

"I'm sorry," Barney said. Lexi peeked up and caught a look she hadn't seen on him before. He looked genuinely concerned, almost sad for her. Lexi couldn't take it.

"Why? I told you, I don't care! You said it yourself, Barney. All *they* do is take from us. They don't care, and if that's true, then why should I?"

Barney didn't say anything right away. He stared at the flame like he was thinking about something.

"Yeah." He stood, clearing his throat. "I guess you're right."

With a final wave, he left her alone.

Lexi watched him go. Had she said something to set him off about something? What was going through his mind? He never said anything about his life before the streets, only that his mother had ignored him because of the new boyfriend, but Lexi was beginning to wonder if there was more to Barney than he let on. Maybe he was more like her than she realized. Maybe that was why she was okay with him hanging around all the time, because he got it somehow.

Curling up on her blanket, she puffed out the candle and stared into the darkness. She focussed on voiding herself of all the memories, all the emotions, because she knew if she let them grab hold of her, even for a second, they would destroy her.

Dear Journal,
I'm exhausted, heading to bed. Nothing to say, really, I just worked another twelve-hour shift today. Will catch up on writing another day.
—Liz

Dear Journal,
A kid was rushed to the ER tonight because he swallowed a nickel. Thank goodness he was okay, but seriously, what kind of parent lets something like that happen?
—Liz

Dear Journal,
I worked again today. What else is new? Maybe soon I'll have time to write more than three sentences.
—Liz

Dear Journal,
Nightshift tonight, and I just know it's going to be busy. Jenn has the night off, so it's just me and Geoffrey, since Edward's off sick. It's going to be crazy, and I have to work tomorrow, too. I wouldn't be surprised if it's a while before I write in here. Life is hard to keep up with sometimes.
—Liz

CHAPTER 17

L I Z

///////////////////////////////////

Friday, October 9
7:24 a.m.

It never failed.

No matter how late Liz worked the night before, she never slept in. It was like her body ignored logic altogether, ignored all the signals that screamed, *Hello! I've had four hours of sleep. Cut me some slack here.*

That was why Liz was up at such an unholy hour that Friday morning, though she wasn't expected at the hospital until 2:00 p.m.

That was always the case on mornings like this... she had hours of empty time to kill.

Dragging herself to the kitchen, she put on a pot of coffee, dumping in extra grounds for an added boost. Four hours of sleep wouldn't get her very far. While she waited, she booted up her computer, its gentle *whrrr* a lullaby in the thick silence.

Blinking the sleep from her eyes, she checked her emails. Mostly junk, as usual, except for the stand-alone message from her mother.

Elizabeth, I decided to email instead of call, so you can respond in your own time. I know you're busy, but you know, I was hoping we could get together again sometime soon. Don't take it so personally, what I say about having children of your own. Craig spoke with me later and thought I may have overdone it with you, but Elizabeth, you know, you've always been a little sensitive about things.

Great.

Terrific.

Just what I need.

Bubbles of tension bloated inside of her, and Liz felt anxious to release it—fast. The last thing she wanted was for these feelings to nag at her all day. Forgetting about the brewing coffee, she flew upstairs, pulled on some sweats, and headed for her basement, where Kurt had built a small gym about five years ago. He had been all gung-ho about it at the time, convinced it was the ultimate motivation to get fit.

"*You know, if I actually have a gym, I'll use it!*"

Well, that lasted a week.

Now, Liz used it for moments like these, when she needed to blow off steam.

What was it about her mother that crawled under her skin and wriggled around uncomfortably? Why was it that even a simple email could irritate Liz for days?

It's because she says things I don't want to hear!

Liz blasted the radio and ran an hour on the treadmill.

***

Yes. It always did the trick.

Stepping off the treadmill, dripping with sweat, she already felt her muscles relaxing, and she forgot all about her mother.

For now, anyway.

She silenced the radio and spiraled back up through her house, eager to hit the shower. She still had a few hours to kill before heading off to work, but at least her mind was clear.

That was, until she passed the art studio.

It was like a magnetic reaction any time she passed this room. She always stopped, felt its pull.

100

But when was the last time she'd even been *in* there?

She couldn't remember.

Hesitantly, she crossed the threshold separating her from her art. It was all unfamiliar territory. Two years was a long time, after all. The room had a ghost-like ambience. It sent shivers down her spine.

Well, she'd been right about the dust; it was caked on *everything.* She really should get in here and clean. She was positive she even spotted a few cobwebs interlacing stacked canvases.

Once upon a time, she could navigate this room in complete darkness, hopping over buckets of paint, avoiding her hanging models. She could even point in any direction and tell you which piece hung there.

Now, it was like stepping through a labyrinth, a jungle of uncertainty. Even the paintings seemed surreal, like someone else had painted them.

To her right, she met the deep azure eyes of an infant Lissy, in a portrait Liz had painted the day after Lissy was born. To her left was a landscape of Niagara Falls, where she and Kurt had spent their honeymoon. Straight ahead was a watercolour of Jesus on the cross, head tilted upward as Heaven opened up. The walls were plastered in art, all tagged with the "EADS" she signed all her work with. Elizabeth Anne Deston Swavier. She'd always been a fan of long names.

Her hand grazed her work easel, caressing its smooth wood, the smell of paint still strong. She picked up a lonely paintbrush, cradled it as though no time had passed at all. It felt so natural, like riding a bike.

Some things couldn't be unlearned.

"You could always take up painting again," Kathryn had told her. *"Look, I know you quit painting when Kurt died. I know he encouraged you with it, so you think going back to it would just remind you of him, but Lizzie, be honest with yourself. Would he want you to stop?"*

Kathryn was right. All of this—her art, her talent, everywhere she looked in the abandoned room—Kurt was a part of it. Every painting told a story, and Kurt was a part of every story. Maybe that *was* why she couldn't paint. Her inspiration was gone.

He had encouraged her art more than anyone ever had. As a child, her teachers had praised her, told her she had a gift, but her parents were insistent that art wouldn't take her anywhere in life, so she stopped pursuing it.

Until Kurt.

When he had accidentally stumbled across an old sketch of hers, he'd been blown away. Encouraged, Liz began painting again, and Kurt visited her studio several times a day, complimenting her work, lifting her up with such heartfelt praise whenever she felt inadequate.

"Hon, you always think your art sucks. Always! Then you finish it, and you say 'I'm happy with how it turned out.' Give yourself some credit, and for crying out loud, finish it first."

But that was Kurt. Full of laughs and full of wisdom.

"Come on, Pix, don't give up. Sure, it only looks like… a kind of blob right now, but I know you've got a bigger vision for this!"

"Well, I did, but it's not turning out anything like I imagined it would."

"That's because it's not finished yet."

"That's not *why."*

"I guarantee you, if you follow through and finish it, you'll be happy with it."

"Is that a bet?"

"Sure. Winner gets a backrub."

"Well, that's hardly fair. You suck at backrubs, love."

"Ah, but you're assuming you'll win the bet. You won't."

"I doubt I'm even going to finish it."

"Oh, come on, Liz. You have to." Kurt paused, tilting his head. *"You know what it needs?"*

"What?"

"It needs more pink."

A smile stretched out Liz's lips, and she almost forgot she was alone in the old studio.

That was Kurt's joke.

It needs more pink.

He only brought it up to tease her; he knew she *hated* pink with a lurid passion and preferred to avoid it like the plague, but Kurt still suggested pink every time, just because it made Liz laugh.

Kurt was like that.

Liz waded deeper into the abyss, accidentally kicking over a canvas that lay forgotten against her supply cabinet. Kneeling, she rescued the painting and recognized it immediately.

It was the only piece in her whole studio she hadn't finished.

There was hardly anything on the canvas, just a few brush strokes over rough pencil lines, but the vision she'd had for it was as fresh in her mind as it had been the day she had thought of it. It was a piece she had been particularly excited about.

She'd been planning to call it *The Lion Cubs*.

"Cubs? Like, baby lions? Why would you pick the babies when you could paint the big lion, the alpha lion? Now they're awesome!" Kurt said.

"I like the cubs," Liz replied. *"I was watching a documentary on Africa, and there was a bit about lions and their young. Did you know lions are born blind?"*

Kurt flashed his winning smile. "I did not."

"Well, they are, wise guy. Being blind makes them totally and utterly helpless, dependent on their mother for survival. The mother moves them around to get rid of their scent. Otherwise, they're easy targets."

"Still not seeing why you want to paint them, hon..."

"Because it kind of represents my own life. You know, I was born blind, until you showed me who God was." Liz smiled. *"Then He claimed me as His own child and protected me."*

A fat tear tickled Liz's mouth, and she impatiently swept it away. This was a mistake, coming in here. What had she expected?

No, she would never paint again. *The Lion Cubs* would never be finished. It would sit there, untouched, until the day she died, because she never wanted to lay eyes on that canvas again.

It was the last piece she'd worked on before Kurt went into the hospital for the last time.

The smell of brewed coffee suddenly alerted her senses, pulling her out of the fog she'd stepped into. Like an alarm had gone off in her mind, she fled from the studio, desperate to leave the memories behind, forgotten to collect dust, just like the unfinished painting.

CHAPTER 18

L E X I

Friday, October 9
1:36 p.m.

Eggs. Now, DV was working on eggs.

Lexi spent a lot of her time in the Pit these days, mostly in DV's corner, watching the young artist work on his mural. They hardly ever said two words to each other; maybe that was why Lexi hung around. It passed the time, it was mindless, and nobody really bothered her.

Watching him paint was captivating, and it never once got boring. It was like, by miming his soft brush strokes with her eyes, she could disappear into another world completely, one where you weren't sentenced to digging through trashcans for food because you were too good to steal, a world where you didn't have to curl up tight at night so you didn't freeze because, Florida or not, it still got cold—especially down here.

Street life was rough, but she tried to remember how much worse it could be. Foster family five could have psychopathic murderers, for all she knew.

At least she had access to a shower. She knew a lot of the street kids didn't, and it was obvious. When they passed, a distinct smell rolled off them. No, Lexi vowed she would never stink, no matter *what* she had to do.

Luckily, Barney had an older buddy with his own place. The guy was never home, and he always left a key under his mat, so it was easy to slip in, shower, and slip out. Barney said the guy didn't care. He used to live on the streets; he knew the drill and told Barney to come anytime. Barney thought it only fair to extend the invite.

She'd been twice this week already and had made a trip to the thrift store after midnight last night to pick out some new clothes from the donation bin. Well, *that* wasn't really stealing; these clothes were rejects, just like her.

Now sporting a pair of ripped jeans, a black T-shirt, and a red hoodie that was way too big on her, she hardly recognized herself. It all felt so surreal, wearing someone else's clothes, using someone else's shower.

It had only been a week, but she was already forgetting who she was.

***

"So, CJ, you been here a week already." DV broke through the silence.

"Six days, actually," Lexi corrected, nibbling thoughtfully on a turkey sandwich.

"Whatever." DV switched brushes. "So, you all, like, chillaxin' and stuff? Havin' a good time?"

"Sure." Lexi shrugged. "It's alright."

DV snorted. "Oh come on, even *you* can't convince me! Girl, it took me, like, three months to get over the crap I came from. Livin' on the streets don't numb you from the pain, man."

"Don't mean nothin' to me. It's been working out alright," Lexi explained, shoving a piece of crust into her mouth.

"You are a shell, woman!"

"What's that supposed to mean?"

"Listen, chickie." DV turned to face her this time. "I've been here a while, and I've seen girls come and go, and all of them, every single one of them, cried at least once. You know, mournin' over whatever they left behind or whatever left *them* behind. You trackin'?"

Lexi didn't answer.

"But you, girl, you just do your own thing. You kinda remind me of a robot. It's all in your face; it never changes, not really."

Lexi listened, with a growing curiosity about the boy who did nothing but paint. He sounded so wise, like some kind of ninja sensei. It was easy for Lexi to forget the kid was a year younger than her.

Anyway, what he was saying was bogus.

"DV, you notice the *strangest* things about people," she said with a chuckle.

"It's the artist eye. I gotta say, it's a gift. I see inside people," he bragged. "Anyway, man, I'm just sayin', you might wanna loosen up a little. You know, let yourself be human instead of a cyborg. Street life makes too many people hard, shut off. I'd hate to see what it could do to someone who's already there."

Hard? Shut off? So what if she was? Whose business was it but hers? What did *he* know anyway?

Whatever; he was just talking. Maybe he said the same thing to every new kid. Maybe he didn't even know what he was saying.

"CJ!" Before she knew it, Barney trapped Lexi in a quick headlock, then eyed her sandwich with a hearty laugh. "Come on, man, you holdin' out on me?"

She elbowed him in the stomach for good measure, sending him groaning to his knees.

"You're a dork, Barn," she said, forking over the rest of her sandwich. DV had already eaten half, leaving Lexi with an empty feeling in her gut. Still, she wouldn't complain. Barney deserved it; he'd been really decent this week. He hardly left her side, and she guessed that made him a friend. He'd already shown her the ropes (though she didn't stick to them), but more than that, now that she was taking care of herself, he still stuck around— and man, did they hear about it. Rumours were already floating around about Barney and CJ hooking up. That was all it was: a rumour, and both Barney and Lexi were quick to squash it every chance they got. Lexi wasn't even remotely interested in Barney that way, and she was sure he felt the same way.

"So how'd ya land the sandwich?" Barney hoovered his piece whole. "Did you steal it?" For a second, he almost looked proud. Yeah, he'd been on her back about stealing all week, but she never once gave in.

"Nope. I found some loose change, so I bought it," Lexi said, brushing the crumbs off her new pants.

"Ceej, you can't expect luck to be on your side all the time. You know, you're gonna *have* to steal eventually." Barney paused. "Or you could do what I do. Asking people for money isn't that bad, ya know?"

"Nah, I don't wanna deal with people," Lexi replied with a shrug. "Anyway, I've been okay so far."

"Yeah, only 'cause you never eat. Man, don't give me that look, I watch you. You probably eat, like, one thing a day, if you're *lucky.* I swear, you're already losing weight!"

Lexi raised an eyebrow. "What, are you checkin' me out or something?" she asked with a sarcastic grin.

Barney snorted and pushed her over. "No. It's just, you're already like a stick. Don't push it. You'll disappear."

"Yeah, *you* should talk." She stood, pointing out Barney's scrawny arms. "Anyway, I'm heading up to find some money. If I do, I'll take you to McDonald's, deal?"

"Sure, but I ain't gettin' my hopes up." Barney rose. "Oh hey, before you go, will you come with me first?"

"Where?"

"I have to get my stash from Slick, but he ain't here. He's probably in his space."

"Why do you need me to go?"

"I don't." Barney ducked his head sheepishly. "But, like, Slick is kind of... creepy, you know?"

"Really."

"I just hate going alone. His place is, like, in the furthest corner of the Combs. It's dark and really isolated and stuff. Nobody likes to go there, 'cause Slick, well, he's just so..."

"Yeah, I know." Lexi sighed. "I'll go."

He didn't need to explain. Slick was a pig and an all-around jerk. Why would anyone go there willingly?

Barney smiled gratefully as they said bye to DV and headed into the Combs.

They passed Barney's space, passed Lexi's space, where she abandoned her oversized hoodie. It was way too warm to be wearing it.

Then they kept going, and going, deeper and deeper. Lexi hadn't done any exploring of the Combs past her space, but she hadn't realized they were *this* big. She distantly wondered if the tunnels covered the entire city of Jacksonville.

Barney wasn't kidding. Wherever Slick was, he *was* far in. Barney led her down many paths, around countless corners. At least *he* knew where he was going; it would be so easy to get lost this far in.

"You know, Barn, if you don't like going to Slick's, you should just stop smokin' weed. That would solve all your problems," Lexi said.

"What, and not get high?" Barney scoffed. "No way! And man, you gotta stop tryin' to get me to quit. It's not gonna happen, and like I keep telling you, it's no big deal."

"Whatever." Lexi sighed. She was feeling uneasy as she bit at her knuckles. They'd been walking for ages now; why did Slick insist on housing himself so far away?

Well, that was a stupid question. It *was* Slick. As if anything he did made sense.

After what seemed like an eternity of stumbling through darkness, they came to a wall. At first, Lexi thought Barney had hit a dead end, lost his way, but then she caught sight of the sliver of light snaking down the side of the stone. *Slick's place must be in there.*

Weird. His space wasn't out in the open like the rest of theirs. He was the king of his own castle.

Barney inched toward the edge of the wall and wiggled through a wide crack. Lexi squeezed in after him and found

109

herself in a small opening. It was eerie, like an abandoned cave. An old-fashioned lantern provided the dim lighting, a black shag carpet clothed the floor, and that was it. There was nothing to hint at Slick's personality.

What personality?

Still, standing there gave her the creeps. She felt like a fly caught up in a spider's web.

And there was Slick, hovering in a far corner, smoking a joint of his own when he saw he had company. Lexi didn't move, didn't show any signs of disgust as his eyes cruised along her body.

"Nice." He sprang forward until he was only inches from Lexi, gawking at her with black eyes. She could smell the weed on him.

"So, Barn." Slick circled Lexi. "Did you bring me something to play with in exchange for your weed this time?"

"Screw off, man!" Barney yelled, pushing Slick. "I got your money."

Slick took the wad of bills, made a show of counting it while staring hungrily at Lexi.

"Too bad," he said. "A little roll in the hay would've made my day."

"You're sick," Lexi growled, clenching her fists.

"Girls like that, doll." He flashed his viper's tongue. "Girls like the bad boys. You should stop by sometime, let me show you what a real man can do. Not like cartoon boy over here."

Lexi looked away; she wouldn't give him the satisfaction of a conversation.

Slick backed off, tossing Barney a small baggie from his own pocket. The exchange complete, Barney guided Lexi through the crack in the wall.

"No?" Slick's voice boomed off the walls. "Well, maybe next time, hot lips. Now you know where to find me."

"Don't count on it, perv," Lexi muttered under her breath.

"What?" Barney asked as they wound their way back through the Combs.

110

"Nothin'."

"Look, I'm sorry, CJ. I shouldn't have asked you to come. I mean, I know he's a pig, but I shouldn't have—"

"Forget about it, Barn," Lexi replied, staring into the heavy darkness. "I've heard worse."

CHAPTER 19

L I Z

//////////////////////////////////

Friday, October 9
1:47 p.m.

Liz ordered her third coffee of the day.

The coffee at Eva's Espresso was much stronger than the blend she tried pulling off at home, and the stuff at work... well, it tasted like swamp water. That was why Liz always chose to stop at Eva's before a shift, to guzzle down a cup of the world's best coffee.

The sun was high in the sky, the humidity low. It was a perfect day to sit in the outdoor café with a large cup of coffee and a copy of today's newspaper.

A motorcycle crash in the east end of the city. Dead.

The Jaguars were playing the Seahawks on Sunday. Well, Craig would be thrilled; he was convinced the Jags would make the playoffs this year. Liz, on the other hand, knew nothing about football.

There was an article on global warming, a headline about a bank robbery, and a three-page feature about a high school basketball player who had received a full sports scholarship at an Ivy League school.

Liz sighed.

Another typical day in Jacksonville.

CHAPTER 20

L E X I

//

Friday, October 9
1:49 p.m.

Lexi's eyes trailed along the edges of the sidewalk as she dawdled along. That was where loose coins ended up, kicked aside by the crowd.

So far, no luck. It usually took Lexi the better part of a day to scavenge enough money for food. It was all about patience, which she was coming to realize she had very little of. Still, if it was a choice between this or stealing, patience came out the winner, hands down.

Besides, she'd only been up here for ten minutes. Before she'd left Barney to his fresh stash, he kept asking her if she was okay.

Yeah, she was fine, wasn't she? Who cared what Slick had to say? It wasn't like she'd never heard it before, right? She should be immune to it by now.

But there was Des, a voice floating in her consciousness, a voice she couldn't forget, no matter how much she wanted to.

"Do what I tell you, Lexi. You don't want to make me mad, do ya? Good girl."

She thought she might vomit. Those memories were branded in her mind, stamped there for life. His voice still rang in her skull as though he was just around the corner, waiting for her.

"Lexi, your turn."

But then there was another sound, a sound that smothered

Des's callous voice, a sound that pulled her out of her prison of nightmares.

The familiar tickling of ivory keys.

A piano.

The melody settled upon her, calming her from the inside out. It was distant and she could barely make it out, but it was enough.

She needed to find the source of the music.

It was like she had a built-in radar; the ballad was coming from the external speakers above Ed's Music Shop across the street. Racks of CDs were set up outside. Ed must be having a sale.

Checking for cars, Lexi raced across the street, where the classical piece came to life around her. She recognized it immediately. In fact, she'd played *Moonlight Sonata* for her last recital.

Her last recital... that all felt like a million years ago. When was the last time she had even *touched* a piano?

Lexi loitered under the speakers, letting the music swell up inside of her as she perused the CDs. She tuned out Barney's nagging voice in her head: *"Never stop to look at anything! People always expect the worst from us."*

She didn't care; she was *just* listening. There was no crime in that. Beethoven had been her favourite; he *was* her favourite. She couldn't just walk away. It would be like knocking the wind out of her.

Unconsciously, Lexi delicately fluttered her fingers as the piece moved into the allegretto. The notes came back to her like they'd never left. She had to fight from humming along.

"Hey!" an ugly voice polluted the beauty. She looked up, and there was Ed, stalking toward her, a scowl on his face. Lexi's heart leapt into her throat as she backed away.

"How many times do I gotta tell you street kids to quit stealin' my stuff!" Ed screamed.

"I–I didn't take nothin', I was just—"

"Don't give me that crap. I saw you. Give it back!"

114

Ed moved in for the kill. Lexi, with no other choice, ran.

"Hey, get back here!"

She could hear his heavy boots pounding along behind her. He was chasing her!

She sped up, thoughts racing just as fast. It wasn't fair; she couldn't even stop to reason with the guy. She *hadn't* taken anything, but she could tell that to Ed until she was blue in the face; it wouldn't make any difference.

Barney was right. People would always assume the worst.

She ducked into an alleyway, hoping to exit out onto another street.

No luck. It was a dead end. There was nothing but a high fence, towering at least fifteen feet over her.

"Get back here! I'm gonna call the cops!"

Ed charged.

Breathing heavily, Lexi clawed at the fence, climbed it quickly, and hurled herself over.

CHAPTER 21

L I Z

Friday, October 9
1:50 p.m.

Liz contemplated ordering a second cup, but after a quick check of the time, she decided to get a move on. Sure, the hospital was seconds away—minutes, if you walked—but there was a lineup at Eva's counter.

Too bad. I'll have to settle for the swamp's brand at work.

Leaving the newspaper on the table, she rose to her feet.

That was when something caught her eye.

Across the street, there was a fenced-off alleyway, but something was happening on the other side of the wire fence. Liz shaded her eyes from the sun in hopes of getting a better look.

Someone was running, a small figure with a mane of brown hair, a black T-shirt, and baggy jeans. She was running right toward the fence.

Why is she running? What's she running from?

Liz gawked as the girl climbed the fence like a pro, throwing herself over and colliding with a heavy *thud* Liz could hear all the way from where she stood. Liz grimaced. That fence had to be fifteen feet high!

The kid wasn't moving, and an uneasy feeling settled in Liz's gut until a gruff old man on the other side pressed his pudgy face up against the fence. The girl shifted away.

"Next time I see you, I'm calling the cops!" the man yelled, followed by a long chain of swears before stalking off.

Liz swallowed, her eyes fixed on the lump of kid that lay there, barely moving. People rushed past her, too busy with their own lives to take notice. Did they even see her? How could they not stop? The girl was obviously hurt!

As the girl slowly sat up and cradled her wrist tenderly, Liz couldn't take it anymore. She'd be late, but that girl could be seriously injured. She might have broken a bone, and *nobody* was stopping.

If nobody's going to help her, I will.

CHAPTER 22

L E X I

Friday, October 9
1:51 p.m.

Lexi's plan had been to climb down the other side of the fence, not fall over.

But fall she did.

She crashed hard on her side, crushing her arm under her body. She was sure something in her wrist gave; pain shot through her arm like a bullet. She had to clamp her mouth shut so she wouldn't cry out.

Ed caught up to the fence and shot her a death glare through the wire barrier. Lexi inched away from the fence; if he climbed it, she'd have to jet, *fast*, but he didn't. Instead, he swore at her before leaving her like a pile of trash.

Well, at least he wasn't chasing her anymore.

Lexi gingerly hoisted herself up, pressed her back up against the fence as she clung tightly to her wrist. She tried moving it, but that only made it feel like a bunch of knives were piercing her skin from inside. She'd broken it; she *must* have. Why else would it hurt so badly?

I shouldn't have stopped at Ed's. I should have just kept walking. Why didn't I listen to Barney?

She hugged her wrist to her chest, as if that would make it all better. It didn't, but at least she wasn't moving it. Moving it was torture.

118

What am I supposed to do now?

Closing her eyes, she tried to direct her attention elsewhere, on anything but the throbbing pain: the steady rush of cars speeding by, the gnawing hunger in her belly, the beautiful and perfect melody of Beethoven's *Moonlight Sonata*.

Nothing worked. It was still sore.

"Way to go, Lexi!" she said to herself, ignoring the flock of people who sped past her like she wasn't even there.

She was invisible, just like she always had been and always would be. Why would she expect anything else?

"Hey, you okay?"

Some kid probably fell and hurt his knee. At least his mother had the decency to make sure he was alright. Whatever; she didn't care. She kept her eyes shut and concentrated on breathing.

"Are you okay?" The voice was louder this time, and it wasn't until Lexi felt a gentle finger touch her shoulder that she startled, her eyes popping open, to find a woman standing over her.

She was wearing hospital scrubs, her long blonde hair was tied back into a loose ponytail, and she was staring at Lexi's arm. Had she seen her fall?

Great.

"I'm fine," Lexi lied. "No big deal."

Maybe the woman would leave now.

No such luck.

Instead, the stranger knelt before Lexi, nodding at her wrist.

"Can you move it?" she asked quietly.

"Of *course* I can move it!" She hardly wanted to be rude, but if she had learned anything from Everidge, it was that backtalk made adults angry, and they almost always left you alone.

So what was wrong with this woman? Why was she still here?

When Lexi stole a peek, the woman was actually *smiling* at her!

"Alright," she said, pointing to Lexi's wrist. "So, move it."

She didn't say it like she was mad or anything. It was like she knew Lexi was lying. Well, the last thing Lexi wanted was to be proven wrong!

But she had no choice. Lexi wouldn't move her arm; it hurt too much.

The woman slid a little closer, and Lexi instinctively shrunk back. The woman seemed to notice the gesture and froze.

"Do you mind if I take a look at it?" she asked. "I'm a doctor."

That would explain the hospital scrubs.

Still, Lexi didn't want anyone touching her, especially her wrist. Besides, letting this stranger check her wrist would be like surrendering something, admitting defeat, and *that* would make her vulnerable.

That couldn't happen.

Like she could read Lexi's thoughts, the doctor offered a small smile.

"Listen, I'm not going to hurt you. I just want to help. Cross my heart," she said quietly.

Lexi swallowed. What was she supposed to do? No, she didn't *want* this woman to help her, but she weighed her options. If she was a doctor, she'd know what was wrong with it, and maybe even fix it. Her other option was, what? If it actually was broken, what would she do?

Besides, the pain was unbearable. Even if the only thing this doctor could do was stop it from hurting, it'd be worth it.

Sighing, she released her wrist.

The woman waited a second before carefully taking Lexi's arm in her hands. Lexi winced as the woman moved it up and down, rotated it, felt along the bones. It killed, but Lexi couldn't deny that the woman was gentle. Still, she had to bite her lip so she wouldn't make any stupid sounds. The last thing she needed was to appear weaker than she already was.

"I think it's a sprain," the woman explained, letting go. "I can't know for sure without seeing X-rays, though."

Lexi sighed, pulling her arm to her chest.

"Listen, I'm on my way to work. I just work down the street, at the hospital. If you want, I could take you over."

Okay. Lexi had let this go on long enough. She jumped to her feet, ignoring the twinge of pain it caused her.

The woman rose as well, staring at Lexi curiously.

"No, I'm fine," Lexi managed through clenched teeth. "It'll go away, on its own."

The woman smiled again.

"Maybe," she said. "But the more you move it, the worse it's going to be. Come on. Why don't you just let me take you in? It's on my way; I'm going anyway. I promise it will all be quick."

Promises. Lexi knew how well adults kept promises.

"No, I'm not going to the hospital. I'm—"

What, a street kid? Yeah, as if she wanted to make that information public.

"I'm not going to the hospital."

The woman didn't seem happy about it. Not mad, but like she was disappointed.

And she *still* wasn't leaving.

"Okay, tell you what," the woman said. "Your arm needs to be immobilized… that means it shouldn't move. Sometimes that means we put a cast on it, but you don't want to go to the hospital. I have a kit in my car. Will you at least let me wrap it for you?"

Lexi exhaled. She thought about Barney, wished he was here. He'd tell her what to do. If it all turned out to be a trap, he'd get her out of it. She was lost; without her guide to street life by her side, she'd have to make a choice on her own.

Swallowing whatever dignity she thought she might have had left, she agreed.

CHAPTER 23

L I Z

Friday, October 9
1:56 p.m.

What am I doing?

The same question raced through Liz's mind as she jogged toward her car, alone. The girl was hesitant to go with Liz, and Liz couldn't say she really blamed her. She went for the kit herself, promising she'd be right back.

Lexi. That was her name. No, the girl hadn't told her that, but Liz heard her cursing herself after her fall. *"Way to go, Lexi."*

So the face finally had a name.

That was the strangest thing about all of this: *who* the kid happened to be. Yes, Liz saw the kid collapse over that fence, but she hadn't recognized her until they were face to face. When that girl looked up, Liz knew her in a heartbeat. It was the same kid she'd seen a week ago, the kid who'd been bent out of shape over a banana, the kid who hardly seemed to fit into this street-life puzzle.

Lexi.

Liz was never one to believe in coincidences, not even before she became a Christian. Now, she believed everything that happened was divinely orchestrated. Nothing happened by chance.

So then, was it an accident that the same kid Liz had felt

compassion for a week earlier just *happened* to sprain her wrist across the street from her?

Liz wasn't sure, but here she was.

The other thought crossing Liz's mind was whether or not Lexi would still be waiting by that fence when Liz went back. What was to keep the girl from taking off? Maybe Lexi had agreed just so she could book it back to the tunnels before Liz returned, if that was where she lived.

Well, Liz had to take that chance. If Lexi was still there, Liz had to help her.

And she still kept coming back to that same question: *What am I doing?*

Jesus would do it in a heartbeat. Even Kurt would have been eager, but why did Liz feel the need to help? Liz, who'd been so caught up in her own life and work schedule for the past two years that she had forgotten to drop her best friend a line more times than she could count.

So why a complete stranger? Kathryn's attitude toward the Tunnel Kids was one of disdain, intolerance, and, Liz had to admit, so was hers.

Until Lexi.

So what made Lexi different?

Still, she was definitely curious about the tunnel girl, and had been ever since she first spotted her. For a week now, the stranger had floated into Liz's mind anytime a teen came into the ER, whenever she spotted other street kids in the crowd, even when Jenn spoke of her teenage daughter.

Maybe Kathryn was right. Maybe Lexi was a newcomer to the streets of Jacksonville. If that was true, Lexi would have only been here about a week or so.

I wonder how life on the streets is taking its toll on her.

Even if this wasn't a coincidence, what did it mean? Was she supposed to do something? Grab this opportunity to… what? Save this kid from the streets? Was that even Liz's job?

She didn't have all the answers. No, she didn't have *any*

answers. For now, all she could do was dial a quick call to the hospital, tell them she'd be late, grab the medical kit she always kept in her car, and help Lexi the one way she knew how.

CHAPTER 24

L E X I

Friday, October 9
2:13 p.m.

Lexi waited, cross-legged against the wire fence, nibbling away at her knuckles, tasting the blood from the fresh wounds. That doctor woman had gone to her car to get a first aid kit or something, promising she'd be right back.

Promises... she probably just jumped in her car and drove off, she thought bitterly.

What Lexi couldn't figure out was why *she* hadn't run off. Yeah, her arm was still throbbing in the worst way, but was sitting here out in the open worth the risks? Besides, this was an adult! How long before that doctor realized she was dealing with a street kid?

Or... has she already?

Not to mention the nagging reality that Sapphire was going to wring her neck if she ever found out. Anyone from the tunnels could have already seen her with that doctor; she was a sitting duck, and by now Sapphire could already be plotting the quickest way to kill her.

Whatever. Truth be told, Lexi couldn't care less. As far as she was concerned, Sapphire owned no one, especially not Lexi.

Let her find out. I don't care anymore.

Sapphire was the last thing she had to worry about. How could Lexi even be sure the doctor hadn't already called the cops, or Social Services? What if they were already on their way? At least she hadn't given the doctor her name. A safety net.

She might be able to lie her way out of it. If that didn't work, she'd run, because as long as she could help it, she was *not* going back to Everidge. She was done with foster homes.

So why stick around? The risks weren't worth it, were they?

But the thought of trying to bend her arm in any way made her nauseous. Maybe the pain wouldn't be so bad if it was all wrapped up. She didn't know... *she* wasn't the doctor.

Leaning back, dizzy from the sharp pain, she thought of Suzie, a little girl she'd once known. A foster sister, younger, who'd once broken her arm.

Was Suzie in this much pain? Did it hurt worse?

Steady footsteps growing closer brought Lexi back to her senses.

So, the doctor had come back after all.

"Sorry I took so long," the woman apologized. She sounded like she'd been running. "I just had to make a quick call to the hospital, to let them know I'd be a little late."

Kneeling again, she signalled for Lexi's wrist, and, wincing slightly, Lexi eased it into the doctor's ready hands.

"Does it hurt if I do this?" The woman gently squeezed.

A blinding jolt of pain!

"Yes!" Lexi cried.

"Okay, I'm sorry." She actually sounded like she was. "You really did a number on your wrist. What I'll do is wrap it with a wrist splint. You should keep that on for a week, just to make sure it has a chance to heal."

Great, Lexi thought, wishing she could go back in time and never stop at that stupid music store.

As the doctor rummaged through her kit, Lexi thought about Barney. How long had she been gone? Would he go out looking for her?

Don't come looking for me, Barn, she thought. *You'd smack me for being so stupid.*

The doctor gently took Lexi's wrist again, cradling it carefully. Lexi dug her teeth into her bottom lip, numbing out the pain.

"Just tell me if anything I do hurts, okay, Lexi?"

Lexi froze!

How?

How did she know her *name?*

Rule #1: Don't let *anyone* know your real name. Especially adults.

Think back!

Lexi knew she hadn't said her name. In fact, she was a hundred percent positive the doctor hadn't even *asked* for it, so how could she know? Was there a missing child poster plastered somewhere? Had the doctor seen her on the news? Was Bridget in Jacksonville, scoping her out?

Busted, she was absolutely *busted.* She felt sick.

I'm so screwed!

As though the doctor could read her thoughts again, she offered a smile.

"I heard you say your name when I found you by the fence. I believe your exact words were, 'Way to go, Lexi.' I guess you were talking to yourself. Nobody else was around."

Lexi sighed.

"I just keep screwing myself over," she muttered to herself. That was it. Her name was on the table. She couldn't be any more exposed. She might as well have bought her own ticket back to Everidge.

"Well, I'm Liz," the doctor said. "It's only fair for you to know my name if I know yours, right?"

Lexi didn't answer. What was this Liz person doing? Was she only being helpful so she could gain more information, gather enough evidence to report her to Social Services, have Lexi shipped off to another foster hell?

Well, even if she did have a sprained wrist, she wouldn't let them take her *that* easily.

Liz gently rotated Lexi's wrist upright, carefully wiggling her fingers before her blue eyes fell upon the small purple scar in the shape of a circle that rested in the nook of Lexi's wrist. Lexi held her guard. She wasn't telling her anything that could easily implicate her, but Liz would still ask.

They *always* asked.

"How did you get that?" Liz let her finger touch the blemish. Lexi would have pulled away, but her arm wouldn't thank her too kindly for that.

"I was eleven," she replied simply. Of course there was more to it than that, but she wasn't telling.

Maybe Liz picked up on that, because she didn't press. Instead, she hunkered down to work on wrapping Lexi's wrist. It hurt, all this moving around, and yeah, Liz was being careful, but still.

Lexi concentrated on a seagull chasing after a runaway potato chip.

"So, is there anyone I can call for you?" Liz asked.

"What?"

"Well, when minors come into the hospital with an injury, kids under eighteen, we're required to contact a legal guardian, a parent. I know we're not at the hospital, but I still feel like I should call someone," Liz explained, meeting Lexi's worried gaze.

I'll have to lie.

Lexi relaxed her face and shrugged casually.

"Oh, well, you don't have to worry, then, 'cause I'm eighteen."

She was shocked when Liz just chuckled.

"Yeah right," she said calmly, still smiling. "No offense, sweetheart, but you don't look a *day* over fourteen."

Lexi wanted to swear. It wasn't fair! Girls her age who looked ten years older got away with *everything.*

"So why don't you try telling me how old you really are," Liz said in a soft voice.

Lexi huffed.

"Fifteen," she replied, following the seagull again. What was the point in dragging out this lie, anyway?

128

"I guess that means I was wrong." Liz continued wrapping Lexi's wrist, gently. "So, where are your parents? Is there a number I can reach them at? I have my cell with me."

Lexi shook her head.

"No," she said simply, shrugging because it didn't matter. "They've been dead for two years."

There was the usual silence. The news always seemed to bother others more than it bothered her.

"I'm sorry, Lexi," the doctor said quietly, staring at her with what looked like sincere concern.

Lexi shook her head. "Whatever." She paused. "It's no big deal."

"Sure it is."

"Are you done yet?"

"Almost." It was Liz's turn to pause. "Is there someone else I can call for you? A guardian, a brother or sister?"

"Nope," Lexi replied quickly. "I'm on my own."

Liz looked up again and cocked an eyebrow.

"Does 'on my own' mean you're living in the tunnels?" she asked.

That caught Lexi off-guard. She hadn't expected *that* question.

Well, as if she was going to disclose her address to this stranger. That was where she drew the line.

"Listen, you don't have to worry. I'm not telling anybody anything. I know you don't trust me, I get that, but like I said, I'm not saying anything."

Liz released Lexi's arm, tightly wound up in a tight bandage, all finished.

"I think you sprained it pretty badly. I work at St. Marcus, just up the street there." Liz pointed. "If you're around in a week, would you stop by? I'll check it out, make sure it's healed okay. If it hasn't, you might need an actual cast."

"I'm not going to the hospital," Lexi said.

"You don't have to. Just ask for me. I'll meet you outside." Liz paused. "You don't want it to get worse."

129

"Maybe." Lexi jumped up, mouthed a quick thank you, and turned to leave.

"Hey," Liz called out.

Lexi craned her neck to see Liz standing there, looking helpless for some reason.

"Be careful," Liz said quietly. "I don't know anything about street life, but... well, you're just a kid."

Not knowing what else to say, Lexi shrugged. "I can deal," she said.

With that, she took off down the street, leaving the doctor behind.

She lifted her arm. Well, she could still move it a little, but it still hurt.

Her mind was running ahead of her. She wondered what Barney would say. She wondered what *Sapphire* would say. Maybe she'd be able to hide it from her, wear baggy sweaters over the evidence. Maybe...

She wondered why Liz hadn't called the cops, even though she'd figured out she was a street kid. In fact, there were a lot of things Lexi was beginning to wonder about Liz. Like, why had she come over in the first place? Why had she offered to help her? Why was she so gentle, why did she ask so many questions if she wasn't going to report her? Why did she want her to go to the hospital next week?

Well, the world had never made sense to Lexi before, so why should it now?

CHAPTER 25

L E X I

////////////////////////////////////

Thursday, February 28
6:17 p.m.

One Year, Eight Months Ago

Lexi was the only one in the car who wasn't crying.

She could understand the waterfalls from little Suzie's eyes, who clung to Lexi like the jaws of life, nestling into her. Suzie was allowed to cry—she was the one who'd been hurt—but Shelley, who was actually choking on her strangled sobs... well, she was supposed to be the mother, the strong one. But no, her hands trembled on the steering wheel. She was rattled, and why shouldn't she be, after what had happened?

Lexi guessed that made her the strong one, for now. Maybe that was why Suzie had flat-out refused to let anyone take her from Lexi's arms back at the house. Really, that was the only reason Shelley had let her come along. If Shelley could have it her way, it would be just her and Suzie; more kids meant a greater threat that the truth would come out. But Shelley didn't really have a choice, because Suzie had shrieked like a banshee until Lexi got in the car.

That was only a few minutes ago, but it felt like hours. Still, it didn't matter how much time went by; Lexi knew she would never

131

be able to erase from her memory all that had gone down this evening.

Lexi and Kyla had been looking through one of Shelley's People *magazines in the quiet haven of their bedroom.*

That's what was weird about today; it was too quiet.

Especially for an evening Ray was home.

Lexi and Kyla got along decently, probably because they were the oldest two and the only fosters. The three younger kids belonged to the Norwoods. Kyla had been with the family seven months before Lexi showed up, and the day Lexi was dropped off, once the two were alone, Kyla warned her about Ray. Lexi didn't sleep for two nights. Well, at least she'd gotten through a week before Ray started beating her, too.

Sure, they were all struggling to survive the waking nightmare now, but at least Lexi had Kyla. Kyla got it, like Lexi did; they knew what it was like to be dumped like trash and shoved into the first foster home that would take you.

Kyla was a year older than Lexi, who hadn't turned fourteen yet, but her birthday was fast approaching. Not that Lexi expected any kind of birthday celebration. Last month was Kyla's fifteenth birthday, but nobody said or did anything. Except Suzie, who gave Kyla a little card speckled with colourful butterflies she'd made, because Suzie was like that. Luckily, Ray never found out about that. He wouldn't have liked it.

That was how Ray was.

Shelley was nice enough, but it hardly mattered. Ray was the one in charge, and Shelley stood frozen in his shadow. She hardly spoke to Kyla and Lexi unless Ray was out. If Ray thought Shelley was getting too chummy with the "foster freaks," he'd get angry.

And nobody wanted that to happen.

***

The girls had just been flipping over to a centrefold on Brad Pitt and Angelina Jolie when it happened.

It started with the stomping.

Ray.

You always knew when to make yourself scarce; there were signals. Ray would thunder through the house with his old military boots on, like he was on the prowl for an outlet, someone to get mad at. Not like he needed an excuse; he was mad all the time.

Especially when he was drinking. That was another signal.

Shelley wasn't home, so Ray was scoping out one of the kids to unleash his rage on. Lexi hoped with all her might that he didn't go after the younger kids; she hated it when he went after them. For all the times she'd been thrown into a wall, belted in the gut, backhanded or strapped with his belt, she'd take it if it meant he'd leave the younger ones alone.

Suddenly, a quiet little whimper of a cry carried through the house to Lexi's ears.

Ray was going after Suzie.

Suzie was six, a spunky little girl who was skilled at dodging Ray because she was so tiny and could squeeze into the smallest of hiding places. It meant more beatings for the older kids, but Lexi would take it for Suzie any day of the week.

Kyla sifted through that magazine as though she couldn't even hear the drunken earthquake that was Ray. Then there was Lexi, whose heart was doing flips. Even though she couldn't make out what Ray was yelling about, she could still hear Suzie's sobs getting louder until they were replaced with a thump, a crash, and an ear-piercing screech that shook Lexi to her core. It was enough to send her bolting from her room toward the desperate pleas for help.

It hit her, then, that running toward the chaos could mean having to endure Ray's wrath, but Suzie sounded hurt, really *hurt, and Lexi couldn't just sit there and pretend like Suzie was alright. Nobody who screamed like that was alright.*

And there was Suzie, in the living room, sprawled out on her back as fat tears spouted from the corners of her eyes. She choked on air as she struggled to breathe. Lexi's stomach seized when she noticed Suzie's left arm. Something was wrong with it; it wasn't... straight.

"Oh…" Lexi felt sick but dropped next to Suzie, while Ray grumbled incoherently, grabbing another beer before storming out of the house.

"Wexi, it hurts, ow, ow, ow!" Suzie shrieked while Lexi's heart was clawing its way out of her chest.

She had to think fast. Shelley wasn't here, and Suzie was in trouble. What was she going to do?

"Kyla!" Lexi called, and in seconds Kyla hovered over them, her black hair falling over her eyes as she stared at Suzie.

"Oh my g—"

"Call Shelley!" Lexi ordered. "Tell her to come home now!"

Kyla sprang to life, fleeing from the room while Lexi carefully gathered Suzie in her arms. The little girl buried her face into Lexi's shoulder.

"I was bad, Wexi. Daddy did this to me because I was soooo bad," Suzie wailed, her long dirty blonde hair cemented to her face.

"No, you weren't, Sue. You're never bad." Lexi heard Kyla's panicked voice in the next room, begging Shelley to get home, fast. That was when the other two kids appeared in the doorway.

Twelve-year-old Melanie started to cry while Caleb, who was ten, fell next to Suzie and Lexi, touching Suzie's hair, his facial features pure ice. His face never changed, not even when Ray was pounding on him. That was something Lexi knew she needed to work on; if you acted like you didn't feel anything, it made life easier.

"What happened to Suzie?" Melanie asked from the doorway, tears streaming down her pale cheeks. Maybe the girl was only a year and a bit younger than Lexi, but sometimes she seemed so much younger, shadowing Kyla and Lexi like a little kid desperate for someone to look out for her. Well, they weren't heroes in any sense; Ray still went after Melanie.

"You know what happened to Suzie," Lexi said.

Lexi tried to keep Suzie still. She didn't know much about broken arms, but if that's what was wrong, Lexi didn't think moving it was a good idea.

"Shelley's on her way," Kyla announced, and nobody said anything else. All they could do was wait, and hope Shelley got home before Ray did.

***

A couple of hours later, stuck in a packed hospital waiting room, Lexi was furious that a doctor hadn't seen Suzie yet. Didn't they know the pain the kid was in? Maybe Suzie wasn't screaming anymore, but she was still crying silently in Lexi's lap. Shelley, on the other hand, was a basket case, biting whatever nails she had left, stealing obsessive glances toward the entrance, as if Ray would dare show his face here.

Lexi didn't understand why Shelley was so nervous. Nobody would know what happened, not unless somebody said something. Oh, Lexi wanted to; in fact, she'd considered it on more than one occasion. Ray's threats were brutal. He'd always warned them if they ever said anything, they'd be sorry, but holding Suzie like this, her arm dangling helplessly at her side, without any tears left... well, it wasn't right. None of it was right.

Between Suzie's sniffles, Shelley leaned over toward the girls, lowering her head to their level, enough to whisper without being overheard.

"Neither of you say anything, alright?" Her voice still trembled. "Just... let me do all the talking. Suzie, don't tattle on Daddy, okay? We'll... we'll just say you were riding your bike, and you fell down."

Yeah right. Kids get cuts and scrapes when they fall off their bikes. Where were those?

Suzie nodded helplessly. After all, she was just a little girl who wanted to please her mommy. Lexi had no mother, she had nobody to please, but Shelley's wide eyes bore into her, pleading until she cradled the back of Lexi's head, pulling her close so only she could hear.

"Please, Lexi." Her breathing was heavy. "You know what he'll do."

In the end, that was why Lexi kept her mouth shut.

After Lexi talked Suzie into going for X-rays with her mother, she sat alone in the waiting room. She felt like crying, but no, she wouldn't. She had to be strong, for Suzie.

She thought of Ray, of all the hidden bruises that were a map all over her body: a bruise for each time he decided to get angry.

It was bad enough he hurt all of them.

But Suzie was only six.

CHAPTER 26

L I Z

Friday, October 9
2:42 p.m.

Had she done the right thing?

Liz wasn't sure, but it plagued her.

That girl, Lexi, had all but admitted to living on the streets.

So why did I just let her walk away?

Maybe she should have done more. Maybe that was why guilt was eating her up inside.

Should I have called someone? Should I have tried to convince her how dangerous it is for a girl her age to be living there?

She wasn't sure, but it was killing her. There must have been *something* she could have done.

Or maybe not. If Lexi was on the streets by choice, she wouldn't exactly be eager for help. What could Liz have done: tie her to the car door until Social Services came and dragged the poor child away?

No, Liz couldn't have done that.

Still, the thought of a young girl who was nothing but skin and bones, frail and pale, retreating into an underground world where kids ran wild, starved, and dabbled in things Liz didn't even want to think about... well, it was enough to make her sick with worry.

For now, she'd have to concentrate on work. She was already behind schedule.

Finishing up with her first patient, she ducked into the staff room, where she poured herself a cup of coffee. It had already been too long of a day. Liz welcomed the caffeine.

"You look like you've had a rough start."

It was Jenn.

Liz smiled. "Something like that."

"Is that why you were late?" Jenn wanted to know, draining the remnants from the coffee pot into her own mug.

"Not really." Liz paused. Everything was still so fresh in her mind. "I helped this kid who fell and hurt her wrist."

"Was she okay?"

"It was a pretty bad sprain. I wrapped it up for her, but I think it should've been casted."

"Why didn't she come for X-rays?"

"She didn't want to go to the hospital." Liz felt guilty again, like she was breaking the girl's confidence. "I think… I think she lives in those tunnels."

"Ah," Jenn said casually. "Tunnel Kid."

She acted like she didn't care.

"Doesn't it bother you at all?" Liz asked, her voice rising. "There are all these *kids* who live underground without parents, without any direction, without a future, because nobody loves them or cares about their well-being. It seems like everybody would rather forget they're even here."

As if she had any right to talk. She was just as guilty. *Before Lexi, I ignored them just like everybody else.*

"Whoa, Liz, calm down. These kids are everywhere, and they have been for a while. I don't know what's got you so upset all of a sudden. I've never heard you this passionate about anything, at least not since…" Jenn trailed off. "Look, in all honesty, it doesn't bother me, because you accept it as the way things are. Over time, you *do* forget they're there."

"It just seems so wrong. I can't believe we've let ourselves just forget them like that, like they don't matter." Liz huffed.

God, where is all this coming from?

138

"Look, what you did was real nice, even Christian-like, I guess, so kudos to you." Jenn placed a hand on her friend's arm. "But Liz, you gotta let it go. She's got her life, and you've got yours. She's one kid, one out of hundreds. It doesn't matter."

It doesn't matter? No, Liz couldn't accept that. Sure, Liz was guilty of turning away whenever she saw a Tunnel Kid, and every now and then she'd toss a panhandler a quarter or dollar bill, but she'd never given them the time of day. In fact, she'd barely even *spoken* to one. Why in the world should Lexi be any different?

Liz didn't know, but somehow she was.

And maybe that was why Liz found herself worrying like crazy about what Lexi was going back to.

CHAPTER 27

L E X I

Friday, October 9
2:47 p.m.

"So, did you find any change? Man, I hope so 'cause I'm really craving a cheesebur—" Barney's eyes fell upon Lexi's arm. "Oh."

Thirty seconds in the Pit, and Barney knew. No, you couldn't pull the wool over his eyes.

Lexi shrugged it off.

"No cheeseburger, Barn. Sorry." She motioned to her wrist. "I was a little busy."

Yeah, a little busy being an idiot!

Without missing a beat, Barney snagged her good arm and drew her to the side of the Pit, away from curious ears.

"What happened?" he hissed.

"In a nutshell," Lexi began, "I was just checking out some music at Ed's. He thought the worst and chased me off. So I jumped a fence, and... well, I guess I sprained my wrist."

"You stopped to check out music?"

"I didn't say it was a *smart* thing to do."

Barney sighed, glaring down at the neatly wrapped wrist. "Did you do that yourself?"

"No, where would I have gotten the stuff? Besides, as if I know anything about wrapping sprains."

"Okay, then how'd you get it?"

"Just some doctor walkin' by. She saw me lying there, so she gave me this, wrapped it for me." She caught the look of disapproval from her friend and huffed impatiently. "Come on, Barn, what would *you* have done?"

"Okay, okay, easy Ceej." He laughed. "Be prepared though, man, 'cause Sapph's gonna *kill* you! You know how she is about, well, everything."

Lexi shrugged. She didn't care.

"I'll deal," she replied. "Just bury me somewhere nice."

Besides, Sapphire didn't have to find out. If Lexi could just get to her space, she could pull on her baggy sweater, hide the evidence.

No such luck. Sapphire was already looking their way.

And she was looking right at Lexi's arm.

"Be cool," Barney warned.

"Whatever."

Sapphire glared Lexi down like a wild animal, stalking over until she was only inches from Lexi's face, her arms tightly crossed. Lexi thought if the girl could breathe fire, there'd be smoke seeping from her nostrils.

Sapphire nodded sharply at the bandage. "What happened?"

"Just a sprain, but thanks for your concern," Lexi retorted.

"Who did it?"

"Well, it was a combination of a fence and a sidewalk—"

"Who wrapped the *wrist?*"

"A doctor."

Sapphire seethed. "Are you stupid? The hospital?" she asked, her voice loud enough for several people to turn. "Look, I get that you're new, but really, use some common sense! Don't you know the kinds of questions they *ask* at hospitals?"

"For your information, I didn't go to the hospital." Lexi glowered. "The hospital came to me."

"So, you let some stranger do it? Are you insane?"

"Excuse me, but I couldn't move it. As if I had a choice."

"There *are* no choices! You tell me, and I decide what to do!"

Sapphire screamed, stomping forward. She was so close, Lexi could feel her hot breath on her face.

"Actually, *I* make my own decisions. Besides, this is my arm we're talking about, not yours," Lexi snapped. Barney was desperately whispering words of caution to her, but she ignored him.

"You could have exposed us! Don't you get it? That person could have followed you back here, called the cops. That could have been *it* for us! I've worked too long and too hard to keep this place going, and I'm not about to let some whiny little *kid* ruin that!"

Sapphire was screaming in Lexi's face, but she took it without flinching a muscle. She was just as determined, glaring at her rival with fierce defiance.

"If the cops wanted this place shut down, they would have done it already," Lexi said.

"You don't get it!" Sapphire yelled. "You don't know what it's been like!"

"What don't I get? That you're a power-hungry control freak who gets off on bossin' people around? No, I got that!"

Her vision blurred when Sapphire backhanded her across the face.

It took two seconds, enough time for Lexi to blink, touch her cheek, and feel its fresh sting. Enough time to look up and catch Sapphire *smiling*.

Then, Lexi jumped her.

They collided hard, and Lexi was only partly conscious of the circle of kids closing in on them.

Let them watch. Sapphire isn't getting away with hitting me.

Lexi shifted her way on top of Sapphire, throwing balled-up fists with her right hand. She kept her left, the sprained wrist, tight to her chest, for protection, but little good that did.

Sapphire was tough.

She was like a snake with all her squirming, and it was only seconds before she delivered a harsh blow that sent Lexi rolling.

Before Lexi could reorient herself, Sapphire plunged onto her back, twining her fingers in her hair, yanking back hard.

Teeth clenched, Lexi felt her eyes water. The anger fuelling her intensified, adrenaline pumping in her blood. She stretched her arm back and dug her nails deep into Sapphire's forearm.

Shrieking, Sapphire recoiled, giving Lexi enough time to find her feet before dodging a few more blows. But one didn't miss its mark; it hit Lexi. She felt warm blood trickle down her chin.

Red dots blurring her vision, she charged. Blind with hot rage, she threw her sprained wrist forward.

But Sapphire caught it, gripping it tightly before twisting it enough to drive Lexi to her knees.

The pain shot through her like a thousand little needles. It was nauseating, but time didn't stop. Sapphire was still trying to hit her.

Lexi went to throw another punch, but that was when Barney's hands clamped around her middle, reeling her back.

"Okay, quit it, you two!" he yelled, wedging himself between the two opponents. He looked to Lexi. "Let's just go."

Lexi gasped for air, feeling her blood boil as she glowered at Sapphire, who was brushing dust from her pants.

"Come on, CJ." Barney's gentle hand took her arm, easing her toward the Combs as the crowd dispersed.

Sapphire called after them. "You better keep a tight leash on that girlfriend of yours, Barney, or she's *gone!*"

Infuriated, Lexi struggled against Barney, driven by her urge to attack her rival from behind, but Barney wasn't letting go. He was a lot stronger than she would have guessed.

***

Once they were alone in the Combs, Lexi pried her arm away from him.

"Who does she think she is? She doesn't own this stupid place! She's not the boss of *anyone*! This is *my* life!" Lexi screamed, her voice an echo lost in the abyss.

Barney exhaled. "Let it go, CJ. She's got an ego the size of a bull. Everyone knows it. You can't let it get to you." He shrugged. "Besides, she's had a brutal past."

"Am I supposed to have pity on her for having a brutal past?" Lexi asked, scoffing. As if having a bad life was a legit excuse for being a jerk. *Everyone* in these tunnels came from something. Why else would they be here?

"Come on, her dad was a boozer, and an angry one, too. I guess he was pretty violent, so she ran away," Barney said, though Lexi hadn't asked.

"Sorry, but she gets no sympathy from me." Lexi shook her head, still edgy. "I've already been through all that, and more! Once, I had to help my little foster sister because her dad broke her arm. So don't talk to me about her having a bad past. It's no excuse!"

Barney, with an awkward grin, rubbed his chin.

"Okay, you're mad, I get it." He paused. "Let's see, how can I cheer you up? Oh, I got it!"

***

For the next hour, Barney held Lexi's arm still, sketching retro cartoon characters into the fabric wrapped around her arm. They looked ridiculous, especially with the marker soaking through, smudging everything. Besides, he was no artist.

But that didn't matter. It didn't even matter that her arm hurt like crazy, because after each drawing, they laughed like idiots. Scooby-Doo looked more like a hot dog with legs, and his attempt at Bugs Bunny resembled a mutant octopus, but Barney only wanted cheer her up, so she guessed it was working. Barney was like that, and even though Lexi wasn't big on admitting these things out loud, he was the closest thing to a friend she had right now.

Dear Journal,

Something happened today, something I'm still not sure about.

I saw this young girl hop a fence and land so badly that she managed to sprain her wrist. I was already running late, but I went over to see if she was okay. I knew I couldn't just leave her there. What kind of person would that make me?

Well, you'll never guess who it was. It was the same kid I saw last weekend, the one with the bananas. Small world? Well, that's just it. I don't believe in coincidences, so I'm not sure what to make of it.

Her name is Lexi.

I don't think she was too happy when she realized I knew her name. Maybe there are certain rules for these kids. Maybe not giving out names is part of that. I don't know.

I tried to get her to the hospital for X-rays, but she was stubborn. At least she let me wrap it. Thank goodness I keep a kit in my car.

I've never met a more non-responsive human being in my life. She didn't seem to care about anything. She sat like a rock through it all, staring off into space. She was just so evasive. She didn't want to tell me anything.

The worst part was when I asked about her parents. I wasn't trying to be nosy, and part of me already knew there wouldn't be parents involved if she was living on the streets. But I had to ask.

She told me her parents were dead, but it was *how* she told me. It was so strange. She spoke of their death like it was nothing and even said, "It's no big deal." This struck a chord in me, and I guess it got me thinking: what could have happened to this girl to make her so cold toward everything, to make her not care about anything?

One thing's for sure: my attitude toward these Tunnel Kids is changing. I don't understand why this one girl tugs on me so fiercely. I've known about the tunnels for a long time, and I've known about the street kids just as long and never gave it a second thought, so why now? Why Lexi? Why am I so worried about her? Why am I wondering if she's okay? Why do I even care?

—Liz

CHAPTER 28

L E X I

Friday, October 9
11:59 p.m.

At least her lip stopped bleeding.

Now that Lexi was in her space, alone, her body was hit with a tidal wave of exhaustion. But with hundreds of stray thoughts rattling around in her head, and her wrist heavy with a stinging pain that made her eyes water, sleep was impossible. It didn't matter how much she tried not to move; the wrist still hurt.

It was worse now, thanks to Sapphire, and that was only one of the reasons Lexi wanted to jump her in her sleep, sprain *her* wrist, maybe even break it—but Lexi was smarter than that. As stupid as it was, the ugly truth was that Sapphire had gained a reputation as the tunnels' owner. She *could* decide whether Lexi stayed or not, and with no other place to go, Lexi would have to suffer in silence under Sapphire's tyranny.

Frig, when's it gonna quit hurting?

What had that doctor said? *"If you're around in a week, would you stop by? I'll check it out, make sure it's healed okay."* Well, Lexi hardly knew whether or not she'd go, but she did know Sapphire would freak if she found out Lexi was even considering it.

She'd probably smother me in my sleep.

Lexi knew going to the hospital would be risky, in more ways than one. First, there were cops to worry about, not to mention

Social Services, and she would somehow have to get there and back without Sapphire's suspicion.

And she's already suspicious. Great.

It hardly seemed doable, but it was late; she wasn't thinking straight, and besides, Barney would help her out. He always knew what to do.

"There you are," a voice interrupted Lexi's thoughts. "I've been looking for you."

Lexi lifted her eyes to see Star stepping into the candlelight, crouching to grab a seat.

"I heard about your wrist," Star said. "I wanted to see how you're doing."

Lexi scoffed, displaying her damaged arm.

"Peachy," she replied, a smirk crossing her lips.

She was surprised to see Star; the older girl had been busy with other things all week. That was fine. Sometimes Star was a little too overprotective.

"So," Star said, nodding at Lexi's arm with a hint of a smile. "Does it hurt?"

Lexi laughed. "Yeah."

"I thought you might say that." Star dug into her jeans' pocket and pulled out a couple of pills. "Aspirin. I try to keep a bunch on hand, you know, just in case."

"Thanks," Lexi said, swallowing them without any water.

"Wow," Star said, grazing her fingers along her own lip. "Sapphire really clocked you one."

"Yeah, well, she wouldn't have gotten away with it if *both* my arms were working," Lexi growled.

"I bet." Star paused. "So, what happened? I want to hear everything."

"Why?"

Star shrugged with that smile of hers. "Just curious."

Well, there wasn't any harm in that, was there?

Lexi recalled the day's events, from Ed's Music Shop to collapsing over the fence. She left out the part about Liz on purpose.

"That wasn't very nice of Ed, but he's a greedy man." Star leaned in, a curious glaze over her eyes. "Did you wrap up your own arm?"

Lexi chewed on her lip. She could easily lie; it wasn't like she had a problem with lying. Sometimes you had to do what was necessary to survive.

But then, what was the danger in telling Star about Liz?

"Well no," Lexi replied. "This random lady came over. I guess she saw me fall. She was a doctor, so she offered to take me to the hospital. I didn't go, obviously, but she thought it should be casted. Instead, she did this."

"Really?" Suddenly, Star seemed very interested. "Tell me about her!"

Weird, the things Star found fascinating.

"Um, well, her name was Liz. I don't really know why she told me that." That was a lie. She'd told Lexi her name because it was only fair.

"And she's a *doctor?* That's awesome! What else did she do?"
Why all the questions?

"Uh, she asked, like, a thousand questions while she was putting this on." Lexi raised her arm. "But she didn't makes any calls or tell anybody I was from the tunnels. I didn't tell her anything, but I think she figured it out."

"How?"

"I don't know!" That was a lie, too. All those questions Liz asked about her parents, about who to call, about staying safe in the tunnels... yeah, it didn't take a genius to figure it out.

Oddly enough, Liz hadn't done anything about it.

"So she didn't report you, even though you were obviously a runaway." Star smiled. "Sounds like divine intervention."

"What?"

"Come on, CJ, you've been here a week. You know most people walk right past us... it's like they don't see us. Why? Probably because they don't care, and that's okay, it's their life, but this Liz person, she stopped what she was doing *just* to see if you were

149

okay." Star was absolutely glowing. "God was smiling on you today."

Lexi snorted. "Come on! You don't believe in God, do you?"

Star wasn't laughing.

"Yeah, I do," she replied. "Sometimes, it's all I have to fall back on. In fact, that's how I picked my name. My street name, I mean. You know the Christmas story? Not the one about Santa Claus. When Jesus was born, there was a star in the sky that showed the way to the manger where Jesus was. Well, it's kind of like that for me; Jesus points the way in my life, in everything I do."

Lexi listened, out of respect, but still shook her head.

"No offense, but how can you believe in a God who lets kids like us live on the streets without food or good shelter?"

"Well, sometimes, when it seems like God is most absent, He's actually most present," Star replied with a strange sort of confidence Lexi didn't understand. "His ways aren't always clear, but His love is. That never changes, no matter who you are or how messed up your life is."

"What's your story, then? I mean, your life couldn't have been *that* bad if you're naive enough to believe in God," Lexi said before thinking.

When Star's eyes glistened with a veil of tears, Lexi felt a pang of guilt.

"My dad left when I was two, and I never heard from him again. I found out later he was dead. He died when I was twelve. I don't even remember him, so it was always just me and Mom. Things were fine, you know, unless she forgot to take her pills. Then, she'd just sleep all day and cry all night. I couldn't get close to her when she had her lows. It was easier for her to pretend she didn't have a daughter those days."

Star paused to swallow.

Probably trying not to cry, Lexi guessed.

"One day, she got so low, I guess she couldn't take it anymore. She... she swallowed a bottle of pills. The doctors... well, they couldn't save her. I was sixteen, with no relatives, so I came here.

There wasn't anywhere else to go." Star was staring at the candle's flame, lost in its dance.

Lexi felt like such a jerk for claiming Star's life must have been easy just because she believed in God. Whether or not Lexi understood it, what right did she have to say something like that?

"I'm sorry," she said awkwardly, scratching her head. "That really sucks."

Silence followed. Lexi wondered if she should say more. She was so bad at this.

"God's still good, though." Star met Lexi's eyes. "Maybe you don't believe that, but I do, and I hope you will too, one day. He's kept me alive, and He gave me a new attitude about life. I believe He's called me to the tunnels for a purpose: to help out younger kids. I mean, none of us have parents, not really. Someone's gotta look out for them, and I'm eighteen. Sure, I could get a job, start my own life, but I get the feeling God needs me here, so I stay."

Lexi tried to wrap her mind around it. It didn't make sense. Why would anybody choose to stay in these dark and dingy tunnels just because they thought God wanted them to?

"So, what about you, CJ?" Star asked, shifting gears. "Why are you here? What happened to you?"

Lexi's stomach turned. It was one thing telling Star about meeting Liz and getting her arm fixed up, but it was something else entirely to share her life story. Maybe Star was okay with reliving her own past, but Lexi wasn't.

"Nothing *happened* to me," Lexi lied. "I just ended up here, end of story." She knew how it sounded, but right now, she didn't care. She had come to the streets to get away from that crap, not so it could resurface every chance it got.

She could feel Star's penetrating gaze upon her, so Lexi distracted herself by tracing her fingernail along the marker lines on her makeshift cast.

"CJ, why don't you talk to anybody?" Star finally asked. "You know, it's not good to shut yourself off from the world."

"Yeah, well, it's not good to talk to people either. You only end up getting hurt!" Lexi snapped. "It's better to keep to yourself. Maybe that kind of life doesn't work for you, but it does for me."

Star seemed out of things to say, and Lexi was glad. Maybe it was Star's desire to be a mom to the younger, forgotten kids, but Lexi wasn't interested. She didn't need anybody. She'd already survived fifteen years on her own.

Star gave a small nod before scrambling to her feet, then leaned forward to drop something into Lexi's palm. It was more aspirin.

"For later," she said, turning to leave. She held back for a second, sucking in a deep breath. "I used to be like that, too, CJ, shut off from the world, cold. I stopped caring. After my mom died, I didn't trust anybody. I shut out anyone who tried talking to me, anyone who tried to get close. All it does is make you cold and less human."

Lexi looked away, pretending she wasn't interested.

"If you don't let anybody in, you could lose yourself completely." Star headed off. "I wouldn't want to see that happen."

When Star was swallowed up in the darkness, Lexi cuddled her blankets closer, puffing out her candle, her thoughts wild. Star believed there was a God who had all the answers—she was *nothing* like Lexi. For her, the truth was here, on this cold floor, with this sprained arm and bloody lip. The truth was the sick past Lexi was desperate to forget. The truth was that Lexi couldn't hardly care less whether she was human or not. She didn't care about anything, because nothing cared about her. That was how the world worked, and that was how it would *always* work. Life wasn't a fairy tale.

Whatever, Lexi thought. That was just how Star lived her life. Lexi had her own life to worry about, her own survival to consider.

Nothing else mattered. It never had before, so why should it now?

152

CHAPTER 29

L I Z

Saturday, October 10
12:16 p.m.

"Liz, are you *sure* it was the same kid you saw last weekend?" Kathryn asked as she dipped a french fry into a mountain of ketchup. This time, Liz didn't criticize Kathryn's menu choice; it was the day after her run-in with Lexi, and, having an afternoon off, she took advantage of treating Kathryn to lunch, eager to relay her story.

"I'm sure," Liz said. "I couldn't forget that face even if I tried."

"And you happened to come across her breaking her wrist?"

"Spraining it, actually, but yes. I wanted to take her to the hospital, but she wouldn't go, so I wrapped it myself." Liz sighed. "Kathy, I can't explain it. I must be losing my mind, but I just felt so scared for her. The last thing I wanted to do was let her go, especially knowing full well where she was going. I couldn't even sleep last night, because I kept imagining the worst. I don't know anything about these tunnels. How can I know she's safe down there? And the most frustrating part of all is that I don't know why I feel like this in the first place."

It was true. Her feelings were driving her nuts! Last night, any time she'd started to doze off, her mind rebounded back to Lexi. She was haunted all night by mental snapshots of the girl trapped in some underground prison, dark and abandoned, without food or anything to keep her warm. And what about Lexi's arm? Was she taking care of herself? Was she keeping it still, dry? Was she in pain? Was she safe?

Did anybody care?

She almost forgot Kathryn was across the table.

"Liz, are you sure this girl is from the tunnels? I mean, maybe what we saw last weekend had nothing to do with homeless teenagers. Maybe that girl's pal is just a kleptomaniac."

"No, I'm sure she's a street kid. I asked her about her parents. She told me they were dead, that she was on her own, and when I asked her if she was from the tunnels, she clammed up." It was still so vivid, like it had happened only moments ago. "You should have seen her. The poor girl was just so *cold*. She just... it was like she didn't care about anything. Kath, she's been through real horrors; I could see it in her eyes, and it just broke my heart." Liz didn't blink, hoping to dry out the threatening tears. What in the world was wrong with her?

Across from her, Kathryn smiled knowingly. "Well, that I can relate to," she said quietly. "I see that same pain in your eyes all the time."

Liz's throat constricted. That was just like Kathryn, always backing Liz into a corner when it came to her own feelings.

"I didn't come here to talk about me," Liz said simply.

"I know," Kathryn replied. "You never do."

Liz focussed on stirring her salad.

"Okay, look, I think it's great you helped this kid out, and it's nice you're thinking about her, but can I be the voice of reason?" Kathryn didn't give Liz a chance to answer. "There are tons of kids like her out there, and maybe you don't want to hear this, but you probably won't see her again. I'm sure these kids have rules, you know? Common sense stuff, like, any interaction with adults is just stupid. Interaction with adults endangers their status, their independence, their safety. For them, we're the enemy. I mean, from what *I* hear, they don't even use their real names."

"But I *know* her real name. I heard her say it," Liz replied defensively. "I know it was her real name, because she went as white as a sheet when I used it."

"Liz, I know this is tugging at you, and maybe God's placed it on your heart so you can pray for her, but maybe that's where it's supposed to end," Kathryn said quietly. "You can't fix this problem. These kids come from all kinds of messed-up situations. They all have a history: runaways, dead or abusive parents, foster care."

"Her parents *are* dead, but I think there's more to it than just that. There was a cigarette burn on her wrist. My guess is it was either self-inflicted, or... or someone did it to her." The thought of someone intentionally driving a lit cigarette into a child's wrist was just evil, and it made Liz sick!

"She's one kid." Kathryn must have seen the hurt in Liz's eyes. "I'm not trying to be unsympathetic, but I want you to be realistic, and I don't want to see you hurt. It's nice that you care about her, and I'm sure prayers on her behalf would be helpful, but maybe you were just having an emotional day."

An emotional day? Is that all it was?

Maybe Kathryn was right. Was this girl placed on her heart just so she could pray for her? Was that all? Liz believed in the power of prayer, but the tug on her heart was so intense. Would praying for Lexi ease that?

There were too many questions and not enough answers. Too many feelings and not enough logic. She hadn't cared this much about anything since... well, since Kurt. After he'd passed away, her passion for everything melted into a grey existence.

So why now? Why, after two years, was her heart beginning to melt?

And why, out of hundreds of homeless kids wandering the streets of Jacksonville, was her heart melting for a teenage girl with a sprained wrist?

If there was a connection, Liz didn't see it.

CHAPTER 30

L E X I

Sunday, October 11
10:53 p.m.

"Do you think they can tap into wireless on the moon?"

Lexi caught sight of the curl in Barney's lip under the soft moonlight while he stared thoughtfully at the sky.

"Barn?" she asked. "You high?"

He giggled. "Yeah, a little."

It was late, and the two were flat on their backs on the damp grass of a baseball field, stargazing, because neither of them felt like returning to the place they allegedly called "home."

It was two days after Lexi's fall, and her arm was finally starting to lay off on the pain a little, at least enough that she could sleep. Barney was constantly adding more cartoon characters to her bandage, complaining he was running out of room. He even recommended that she sprain her other wrist so he'd have more space to work with. "Astro's only the size of a penny!" he'd complain. It didn't matter how many times she reminded him that it was probably coming off in a week; he still insisted on occupying every blank space.

She wasn't complaining. Every time she spotted the goofy drawings, she had to smile.

"Hey, Ceej?" Barney asked, his fingers meticulously picking away at the grass beside him. "Can I ask you something?"

"Yeah," Lexi replied, curious. Barney was hardly ever serious about anything.

"Well, the other night, I, uh, I heard you and Star talking."

"You were eavesdropping?"

"No! Come on, give me a break! I live around the corner from you, and tunnels echo! Besides, it's not like you two were exactly whispering!" Barney snapped. "Anyway, I heard you tell her about that doctor who stopped to help you."

"I told you about that!"

"You didn't tell me you *talked* to her, that you knew her name, that she didn't rat you out."

So much for keeping that a secret. Why had she told Star in the first place?

"It's not a big deal," Lexi said, frustrated.

"Yeah, but why didn't you tell me?" Barney asked. "I mean, I thought we were cool like that."

"I don't know," Lexi admitted. "It's not that I didn't *want* to tell you, I just... I don't know, maybe I just figured you'd think I was an idiot, you know, for talking to an adult, for not just leaving. I mean, it *was* pretty stupid."

When Barney didn't say anything, Lexi felt guilty. Had she hurt his feelings, like *actually* hurt his feelings, by not telling him about Liz? Honestly, she could be so socially awkward sometimes!

"Nah, you're not an idiot," Barney finally said, smirking sideways at her. "Absentminded? Yes. Maybe even a little psychotic, but not an idiot."

He rumbled with laughter, and Lexi smacked him with her strong hand. He raised his hands defensively, still snickering.

"Okay, okay, I'm kiddin', I'm kiddin'!"

They chuckled for a while, but it wasn't long before silence consumed them, each held captive by their own thoughts. Lexi didn't know where Barney's thoughts went, but hers tiptoed back to the night Star had brought her aspirin. Truthfully, their conversation was still as fresh as it had been that night.

157

Lexi had struggled to puzzle out this whole believing-in-God thing, to make all the pieces fit. From the little she knew, it seemed people spoke of God as this loving Person who lived in the sky. Well, Lexi didn't know much about love, but letting someone live on the streets without food or people who cared didn't seem like love to her.

But why did Star believe it?

"What're you thinkin' about, CJ?" Barney asked suddenly. "You look like you're on another planet."

Lexi breathed out, settling her head in the crook of her arm. "Do you believe in God, Barney?"

"Huh?"

"God," Lexi replied, gazing into the endless night sky. "Do you believe He's up there?"

"Man, I don't know." Barney exhaled slowly, probably not having expected a question like that.

Well, Lexi hadn't expected to ask it, but there it was.

"I guess I'm agnostic," Barney continued.

Lexi furrowed her brow. "What does *that* mean?"

"Seriously? Didn't you learn anything in school?"

"I quit tryin' two years ago!" Lexi huffed. "I used to be a straight-A student, thank you very much. I just gave up. Honestly, what good is school anyway?"

"Okay, easy." Barney smiled. "Anyway, being agnostic is, like, being in the middle, I guess. You kinda believe in God, but you kinda don't. I guess you just don't care either way, or you just don't know. So I don't know whether I believe in Him or not. Maybe." He shrugged. "So, do you?"

Lexi shook her head. "Neither of my parents believed in God, that's for sure," she said. "Even in my foster homes, nobody had anything to do with Him. So, I never went to church. I only heard about God at school, maybe on a billboard, but never at home."

Barney was silent for a moment before he turned and raised an eyebrow at her. "Wow," he said.

"What?"

"I just never heard you talk about your family before." His mouth eased into a wide grin. "Finally you open up!"

"I'm *not* opening up. Don't get all weird on me!" She paused. "Anyway, if God *does* exist, I wanna know how a God who is supposed to be loving lets bad stuff happen. There's way too much suffering, so if He *is* real, is He just ticked off at us all? Like maybe we did something to make Him really mad—"

"Or maybe you're just bitter," Barney interrupted.

"Are you *defending* God?"

"Maybe. I told you, I don't know what I believe, but I don't think you have any right to assume what He's like either way, especially when you just said you never learned anything about Him growing up."

"So?"

"So, I'm just saying you don't have enough facts, and you know what I think? I think you're just looking for someone to blame."

"Well then," Lexi said. "Who do you blame for where we ended up?"

"I don't know. Society maybe," Barney replied with a wide yawn. "You know, everyone who stopped caring about family. It's just not important to anybody anymore; nobody values it. Maybe that's why everything's so screwed up."

"Values." She rolled her eyes. "Overrated."

"No, they aren't," Barney argued. "Maybe to you, but you don't care about anything."

"Well, why should I?"

Why should I? Flashes of the last four foster homes floated in her mind, flashes of her mother and father, flashes of every one of the fifteen years she'd managed to survive.

God.

If God existed, He hated her.

"Everything just screws you over in the end," she muttered.

Barney caught her eye and shot her a corny grin. "Well, that's the spirit."

Dear Journal,

It's been three days since I met Lexi, and every day I drive to work, I find myself searching for her face in the crowd. I need to know she's okay. You hear so many stories about kids on the street who die of starvation, are killed in gang fights, overdose on heroin, and now that these stories have a face, I'm paranoid.

I've thought about what Kathryn told me. Maybe I *won't* see Lexi again. She could easily remove that splint herself, but I want to make sure she's okay. I know it's only been three days and I told her a week, but what if she doesn't remember? What if she doesn't come to find me? Is that why I'm looking for her? Maybe I feel like I need to remind her. She's just a child, after all. She doesn't have a mother to remind her to take care of herself.

But why do *I* feel the need for her to come back? What will it accomplish? If she doesn't need me to take it off, what am I expecting? Do I actually think she'll tell me more about her life, where she comes from, what she's feeling? Why would she talk to me? I'm just a doctor, and worse, I'm an adult. The last person she's going to trust is me.

Even if she did, what could I do about it? Kathryn's right; I can't fix her life.

On a separate note, Mom emailed today. She wants me to visit this weekend. Everyone will be there. Mom's planned a pool party for the kids. I haven't responded yet, but I already know I'm not going. I'm tired of playing the charade all the time. I'm tired of putting on a false smile and pretending like everything's perfect so Mom won't bother me. It's exhausting.

I wonder what Lexi's mother was like before she died...

I'd better get to work.

—Liz

CHAPTER 31

L E X I

Thursday, October 15
10:49 a.m.

Lexi was having a terrible few days.

Maybe it was bad luck, or maybe she wasn't trying hard enough, but she hadn't been able to scrounge up enough change for a meal in three days. The gnawing emptiness sat like a rock in her belly.

Lexi considered stealing, but only for a few seconds. No, it didn't matter how hungry she was, she couldn't do it. She just *couldn't*. It just had to happen once and she'd lose herself forever.

Star was fulfilling her unofficial title as den mother, asking questions like "When was the last time you ate, CJ?" and "You're as white as a sheet, CJ. What did you eat today?" Lexi lied, though Star didn't seem to buy it. Now Lexi spent most of her time on the streets, even if it was just to avoid Star's lectures about the importance of eating.

Well, it wasn't like Lexi didn't *want* to eat. She wasn't like those girls who moped in front of the mirror all day, analyzing every curve and pound. She couldn't care less about calories. In fact, she'd *never* cared about her weight. She'd always been tiny. Besides, it didn't count as an eating disorder if you were a street kid—not for her, anyway.

***

It was raining that Thursday morning, and Lexi was shuffling down a busy street, on the prowl for loose change. So far, nothing. What else was new?

She was careful to keep her sprained arm tucked inside the new sweater she'd taken from the charity bin last night, large enough to tightly gather the sleeves in her hands, guarding her arm against the rain. She didn't want the bandage getting wet; Barney would be devastated if his cartoon characters melted into puddles of ink.

Well, it didn't really matter. Tomorrow was Friday, a week since she had her arm wrapped.

That Liz person had told her she'd check it out if she went to the hospital and asked for her. Lexi was still on the fence about it. What if that doctor already had Social Services waiting by the door? Sure, Liz had said she wouldn't say anything to anyone, but what if that was a lie? Adults didn't care about telling the truth. In fact, Lexi didn't know a single one who'd ever been completely honest with her. That was just how they rolled.

How did Lexi know she could trust Liz?

Bored and frustrated, Lexi plopped down on the steps of the old library, knuckling her eyes as she considered the situation. It wasn't like this was a real cast. She hardly needed a doctor to take it off, but after Sapphire yanked on it... well, Lexi was sure she'd gone and made it worse. What if it was broken now? If it was, she really should have a doctor take a look.

Besides, Liz *had* said she'd meet her outside; it wasn't like Lexi actually had to go into the hospital. Not for long, anyway.

There were so many risks to consider, and Liz was *still* an adult.

Lexi felt a headache coming on.

"Penny for your thoughts, Ceej?"

Barney hopped up the steps, planting himself down beside her.

"Nothin', I was just thinking." She raised her arm. "It'll be a week tomorrow. That doctor told me to find her, you know, to make sure it's still okay."

"Does that mean you're going to the hospital?"

"Not *in* the hospital! Besides, I wanna make sure Sapphire didn't screw it up any more than it already was!"

"Man, CJ, take a chill pill. I never said you shouldn't." He shrugged. "I think you *should* go. Knowing your luck, it's probably broken."

"Tell me about it," Lexi replied.

"Anyway, if you do go, we gotta make sure Sapph doesn't find out."

"Yeah, I know. It's not like she follows me around, but just in case, we need a plan."

"Don't worry, I'll help you out. I'm a genius when it comes to master plans." Barney's lip curled. "Besides, the last thing you want is another bloody lip."

Lexi's finger instinctively went up to touch her lip. It was still a little puffy from Sapphire's blow.

"Trust me, if she ever tries hittin' me again, she won't get off as easy as last time," she said as the clouds parted and it began to pour harder. Lexi grumbled under her breath, donning her hood.

"Come on," Barney said, hoisting himself up. "I'm heading over to Ben's for a shower. You should come with. If you're gonna go to the hospital tomorrow, you should look clean, just in case anybody else sees you."

Barney had a good point, but she hated going to that empty apartment. Besides, it took them forty-five minutes just to get there by foot.

But showers made her feel less like a street kid.

In the end, that was why she went with Barney. It was one thing to be starving, but it was something else to be starving *and* dirty.

Dear Journal,

I'm heading to bed, early shift tomorrow.

Tomorrow will be a week since I met Lexi and told her to come find me. I can't help but wonder if she'll come.

—Liz

CHAPTER 32

LEXI

Friday, October 16
3:12 p.m.

"So, you're *sure* you know the plan?" Barney asked while Lexi fought with a hairbrush through the jungle that was her hair.

"Barney, I'm not *that* big an idiot," she replied, irritated with her tangles. "We already went over it, and besides, it's not much of a plan."

"Hey, I'm just making sure! Sapphire can't know you're going down to the hospital today. She'd *kill* you."

"As if I'd let her kill me." Lexi threw down her brush, giving up. Who cared about neat hair anyway? "Besides, she'll never know, because you're my alibi. If she asks where I'm at, tell her I went to find food."

"Which reminds me." Barney reached back and pulled out a pair of crunched-up granola bars from his back pocket. "I swiped these earlier. Keep 'em with you, so if Sapphire asks, you have proof."

"Thanks." Lexi crammed the bars into her own pocket. "Don't forget, you have to stick around here and keep an eye out for Sapphire. If she leaves the Pit, follow her. If she heads for the hospital, distract her. If she—"

"Man, CJ, you're insulting! I came up with this plan, in case you forgot."

Well, that was true, and though it seemed simple enough, Lexi was grateful she'd have one less thing to worry about on her venture to the hospital. Barney wouldn't let Sapphire out of his sight for a second.

As they stepped into the Pit, Barney quieted his voice to a whisper. "You sure you don't want me to come with you?" he asked. "I mean, we could always get DV or Star to watch out for Sapph."

Lexi hesitated. Of *course* she wanted him to go with her. Barney's presence would make her feel a whole lot safer, but it just wasn't smart, simple as that. As selfish as she wanted to be, she couldn't put Barney in that position.

"Yeah, I'm good, but thanks." She paused. "Besides, it's better if it's just me, you know, in case it *is* a trap. At least it would only be me going down."

"If you *do* get caught, I'm your one phone call!"

"Barn, you don't have a phone."

"Just be careful." Barney lowered his voice again. "And don't be long, okay? Find me as soon as you get back."

"Got it." Lexi faked a smile. "See you later."

She crossed the Pit alone, already feeling the weight of uncertainty on her shoulders. *Is this really such a good idea? Maybe I should just forget the whole thing. I could just—*

"Hey Sexy."

Lexi's skin prickled, and there, lurking in the shadows, was Slick, his dark eyes sizing her up, again.

"Y'know, I don't think any less of you with that crap on your arm." His lip curled. "Not interested in your arms anyway, if you catch my drift."

"You're sick," Lexi muttered.

"I was watchin' last week when you jumped Sapph."

"Good for you." Lexi made for the Tube.

"Hey, you don't know what you're missing!" Slick called after her. "There's nothin' that turns me on more than a girl who likes to fight."

Lexi kept her mouth glued shut, holding a steady pace as she ditched the Pit. A million insults floated in her mind, snarls of rage dancing on the tip of her tongue, but she held it all at bay.

167

As she waddled through the Tube's darkness, she willed Slick into the furthest crevice of her mind.

Right now, she had more important things to worry about.

CHAPTER 33

L I Z

//////////////////////////////////

Friday, October 16
3:30 p.m.

Liz glanced at her watch for the fourth time that hour. It was already the middle of the afternoon, nearing the end of her shift, and there still wasn't any sign of Lexi.

Maybe it was ridiculous to expect the girl to come today. Liz had told Lexi to come back in a week, but not *exactly* a week. Lexi could still show up tomorrow, or the next day, or even next week. She was just a kid, after all. Her life probably didn't revolve around schedules the way Liz's did.

Still, Liz checked out the doors each time she dropped off a chart or poured another cup of coffee. Her eyes scanned the waiting area for the small girl with messy brown hair and a bandaged wrist.

So far, nothing.

Maybe Kathryn was right. Lexi might not come at all.

Would it really matter if she didn't?

The answer to her question came quickly. Yes, it *would* matter.

Great, right back to square one.

Liz had an hour and a half left to go. What would happen if Lexi showed up after 5:00? "Just ask for me," she'd told her. What would Lexi do if Liz wasn't there? Would she let someone else take a look at her wrist? Would someone else report her? Shouldn't *she* report her?

169

Liz wanted to scream in frustration.

***

"Well, Mr. Morris, the good news is you'll only need about six stitches," Liz said to the middle-aged man who clamped down on his finger with a cloth saturated with his own blood. "But I think you'll have to leave the cooking to your wife."

The man chuckled, his face as pale as the room's walls.

"Who would have thought chopping carrots would be such a task?" he asked with an awkward grin. Smiling, Liz busied herself with arranging her equipment, gently reminding her patient to keep applying pressure to his wound.

Just as she was ready to clean out the patient's open wound, a knock on the door interrupted her.

That was strange. Nobody interrupted a doctor unless it was important.

"Excuse me a minute," Liz said absently, excusing herself long enough to peek outside.

It was Jill.

"Sorry, I know you're with a patient right now," Jill explained, quite flustered. "But I've got this teenage girl out here who's asking specifically for you. She won't give me her name. I tried telling her she has to wait for a doctor just like everyone else, but she insists it has to be you. I don't—"

"It's okay, Jill. I know her." The sick worry in Liz's stomach melted away; Lexi had come. "Tell her I'll meet her outside."

Silence.

"Outside?" Jill's eyes sparkled with confusion, and why shouldn't she be confused? It wasn't every day that a doctor met her patients outside the hospital.

"Yes. Thanks, Jill."

Quietly clicking the door shut, Liz went to work stitching up Mr. Morris's finger, all the while offering up a silent prayer of thanksgiving to God for Lexi's safe return.

CHAPTER 34

L E X I

/////////////////////////////

Friday, October 16
3:37 p.m.

Lexi was freaking out, absolutely freaking out! She felt like a mouse near a trap; any minute now, the trap would spring and Lexi would be screwed. Why had she come here in the first place? Why was she waiting around? What was she *doing*?

Maybe this had been a bad idea after all.

In fact, she *knew* it was a bad idea.

So why am I still here?

Good question.

Pacing a tight circle outside the giant hospital, she kept her eyes peeled. For what, she wasn't sure, but she felt so uneasy. The lack of control over her situation, the uncertainty of what would burst through those doors, was killing her.

All she needed was for Liz to confirm that her arm was, in fact, healing, and not broken. Then she could book it, head back to the one place she could hide.

But what if that wasn't the doctor's plan?

What if all this was a ruse to back Lexi into a corner? What if it *was* a trap? What if the cops were already on their way? What if they were already here?

She should have brought Barney after all.

CHAPTER 35

L I Z

Friday, October 16
3:38 p.m.

The first thing Liz noticed when she stepped outside was Lexi pacing a fierce trail a few feet away. Liz felt her heart skip a beat; Lexi was here, safe. All the worry and anxiety tethered to her for the last week fell away at the sight of the teen.

Thank you, Lord.

But something wasn't right. Yes, Lexi was all in one piece, safe and sound, but the poor girl seemed frantic. Her chocolate eyes were as wide as saucers, her teeth gnawing away at her knuckles, and she was still pacing.

She must not have heard the door open.

Well, it was now or never.

"Hello, Lexi," Liz said softly, stepping toward Lexi cautiously.

The girl spun around at lightning speed, and the next things Liz noticed were a purple bruise splotched across Lexi's right cheek and what appeared to be a healing split lip.

Her heart sunk as her mind went reeling. What could have happened? She wanted to ask, she wanted to know *exactly* what happened, she *needed* to know if someone down in those dangerous tunnels had hurt the girl, and why.

One step at a time.

"Hey," Lexi said coldly, dropping her hand, only to shove it into her pocket. Yes, there was definitely a different air about her today. The girl's voice almost shook with her quiet greeting, even if she *was* trying to come across as cool. Liz noted the difference; last time, Lexi had been so nonchalant, shut off.

Today, she was nervous about something.

"You okay?" Liz asked casually. She was genuinely concerned, but she couldn't help but wonder if Lexi doubted her motives. *I probably sound like a broken record.*

Lexi wouldn't meet her eyes. "Yeah," she muttered.

Okay, so Lexi wasn't interested in making small talk. She probably just wanted to get this over with.

Liz stole a peek at Lexi's bandage and found it plastered in sketches. Cartoon characters, she guessed. It was hard to tell; they looked more like little smudges than art.

"I like the drawings," she said. "Did you do them yourself?"

Lexi cradled her arm, her own eyes lingering on the pictures. She shook her head.

"No, I have a buddy who's into cartoons and stuff. He did 'em," she replied quietly, so quiet, in fact, that Liz hardly heard her.

Liz couldn't help herself. The corners of her lips crept into a smile as peace settled over her. Somewhere out there, Lexi had a friend who at least cared enough to cheer her up.

That warmed Liz to her very core.

"Well, I think they're pretty great." Liz pointed to a bench. "Do you want to sit?"

Lexi did, and the next thing Liz noticed was how loose-fitting the girl's jeans were. She'd never been big on noticing these kinds of things, and she couldn't be a hundred percent sure, but those jeans looked identical to the ones Lexi had been wearing last week, only much baggier.

Was she eating properly?

One step at a time, she reminded herself.

Liz eased herself down next to Lexi, consciously leaving enough space between them for good measure.

Better if she feels comfortable.

"So, how have you been this week?" Liz asked conversationally, curious how guarded Lexi would be this time. She had been so closed off before; how long would she have to live on the streets before shutting down entirely?

In that same nonchalant voice Liz remembered so vividly, Lexi spoke. "Fine," she replied simply. "It still hurts. My arm, I mean, but whatever."

Liz furrowed her brow. "It should be feeling better by now. Did you bang it on something?"

Lexi clammed right up, eyes connecting with the ground like a magnet. Liz watched, imagining a shell around the girl, a shell she was trying to hide in.

"What happened to your cheek?" Liz asked. She had a hunch it was all connected: her sore arm, the bruises.

Lexi's finger went up to graze the bruise, but she shrugged like it didn't matter. "Let's just say I wasn't someone's favourite person last week," Lexi replied in that soft-spoken voice, with a slight roll of the eyes.

"Somebody did that to you?"

Lexi nodded.

"And your arm. Is that why it still hurts?" Liz asked. "Did someone pull on it?"

Another nod.

Liz controlled her breathing, internalizing her own anger toward whoever had hurt this child. Her focus right now had to be on Lexi.

"That's not good," she said quietly. "You must have been in a lot of pain."

"No big deal." Lexi lifted her eyes, finally meeting Liz's. "It's okay, though, isn't it? I mean, can I take this thing off?"

"Maybe. Can I take a look?" Liz needed to be sure the bone hadn't been broken in the past week, especially if someone had yanked on it.

"Try not to move," she said, cradling Lexi's arm in her hand. "Tell me if this hurts."

She gently rotated Lexi's arm in a few directions. Lexi winced but admitted it only hurt a little.

"That's good," Liz said. "If it was broken, you'd be a little more vocal about it. I can take this off for you, but you're going to have to promise me you'll be *really* careful."

"I will," Lexi answered quickly. Liz had to refrain from chuckling. The poor girl was obviously relieved.

Liz carefully unwrapped the bandage. The last thing she wanted to do was hurt the young girl. Quite obviously, she'd been through enough.

Every few seconds, Liz peered up to check on her patient, but Lexi was too busy staring off into nothingness to take any notice. She seemed so far away, so unreachable, so lost.

"Can I ask you a question?" Liz asked, her attention focussed on Lexi's arm. She didn't even know if Lexi turned her head. "How long have you been living on the streets?"

Her question was met with stubborn silence, and Liz glanced up just long enough to catch Lexi staring at her with fierce eyes. Shell or not, Liz could see past the facade; Lexi was terrified.

"Hey, whether you believe me or not, I'm not gonna report you." She smiled empathetically. "You don't have to tell me anything specific. I'm not going to ask you for your last name or anything like that. Believe me, I'm not out to get you."

Still, Lexi didn't budge. Liz couldn't help but wonder, *Have I gone too far, asked too many questions?* Maybe she should have been a little more conscious of Lexi's comfort levels. She was already frightened coming here, that much was obvious.

I should have known better than to push; I should have—

"Two weeks," Lexi said suddenly, quietly. "I've been here two weeks."

Liz met Lexi's eyes. Kathryn had been right after all. Lexi *was* new to the streets.

"What brought you here?" she asked. Every question she asked now was risky; digging any deeper might make Lexi uncomfortable, but then, she'd answered her first question.

Maybe she would say more.

"Doesn't matter," Lexi said, shifting nervously. "This is my life now. I'm okay with that."

"Pardon my saying so, but you're awfully thin," Liz pointed out. "Are you eating enough?"

"Sure," Lexi said with a casual shrug.

Funny, she wouldn't look Liz in the eye.

"Maybe I'm just crazy, but your clothes don't really seem to fit you." She pointed to Lexi's jeans.

"I like loose clothes."

"I don't remember them being that baggy last week when you were—"

"I'm *fine*," Lexi said loudly, arching an eyebrow. "Is this almost finished?"

Liz sighed, nodding without a word as she unwound the last of the tensor bandage, leaving Lexi's arm bare and moist with a layer of sweat. Flecks of black marker were scattered across her arm where the cartoon drawings had leaked through.

"All finished," Liz said quietly, and without missing a beat Lexi shot up, heading down the street.

"Do you want a sling?" Liz called. "For your arm?"

Lexi shook her head. "No, I'm good," she replied flatly. "Can I go?"

Liz stared after the young girl, the same sense of helplessness she'd felt the week before showering over her. She didn't want her to leave like this, but what could she do? She couldn't force Lexi to stay, and the girl clearly wanted to leave.

Defeated, Liz could only nod. "Yes, you're good to go," she said, forcing a smile. "Just, you know, take care of yourself, okay?"

Lexi hesitated for only a second before narrowing her eyebrows suspiciously. "No offense, but why do you care, anyway?"

It wasn't rude, but it was a genuine question, one that caught Liz off-guard. She was speechless; what could she say? How could she answer a question like that? After all, she'd been asking herself the same thing all week and hadn't come up with anything that made a morsel of sense.

"Well, thanks for the help," Lexi said quickly.

The girl darted off, leaving Liz to watch with thick tears pooling in her eyes and nothing but a prayer on her lips for the girl she was helpless to save.

CHAPTER 36

L E X I

////////////////////////////////

Friday, October 16
4:01 p.m.

Her arm felt so weird, so exposed without that splint.

After all, she'd been stuck with it for a week, stuck being careful not to move it too much or get it wet—and now it was free.

It had all happened so fast.

Lexi's mind still wrestled with her visit with Liz as she dawdled toward the tunnels. None of it made any sense, what went down at the hospital. That doctor was *still* asking questions—questions about her life, why she was here, whether or not she was taking care of herself—and yet there was still no sign of the police or Social Services. Liz had promised on both occasions not to say anything to anyone, and Lexi had to admit, she'd come through so far.

It puzzled Lexi. Why would Liz ask all those questions if she wasn't going to turn her in? Was she seriously just interested?

No. She can't be. There has to be somethin' else going on here.

Maybe it didn't matter. It wasn't like she'd ever see that doctor again.

***

Sure enough, loyal as ever, Barney was loitering at the mouth of the Tube, waiting for Lexi.

"Hey, Barn," she greeted.

"Alright, it's not broken!" he exclaimed, grinning at her bare arm. "And you're here. Any trouble?"

Lexi shook her head. "Nah, she just took it off. No cops or nothing."

"Same doc as last time?"

Lexi nodded.

"So, like, does it still hurt?" Barney asked, his hand all claw-like, inching toward her. "Like what if I did this?"

Lexi smacked his hand away.

"Cut it out, Barn, I'm supposed to be careful! It's not even really healed all the way because of Sapphire, so don't touch it!"

She held her arm close. Sure, the pain had eased up a lot since last Friday, but a slight ache still pulsed through her arm, especially if she jerked it around too much.

Barney sputtered a laugh. "Hey, relax, I'm not gonna do anything stupid. Geez, I'm not *Sapphire*." He raised his hands in surrender. "Come on, you know I'd never hurt you on purpose or anything."

Lexi simply nodded. He didn't have to tell her that. She already knew.

"So, what's that doc's name again?" he asked.

"Liz."

"I'm guessing that's short for Elizabeth?"

"I dunno. We didn't swap life stories or anything!" Lexi sighed. "Anyway, it was weird. She even remembered *my* name."

Of course, she left out the part that Liz knew her *real* name, not her street name. It was okay telling Barney some things, but if he knew somebody out there knew her *actual* name, he'd be less than thrilled.

"Well, come on, it's probably not every day a doctor finds random patients on the streets because they were stupid enough to jump a fence and break their wrist," Barney said.

"It was a sprain!"

"Oh, whatever. Did she ask questions, like last time?"

"Yeah." Lexi picked at a stray thread on her sweater. "It was kind of annoying. She kept asking if I was eating. I don't even get why she cared. She's just some random doctor, and I'm just some random kid. What does she care if I starve or not?"

"Well, dude, you *aren't* eating. Come on, don't give me that look. I may be a stoner, but I'm not an idiot!"

Lexi rolled her eyes.

"All I'm saying is that you shouldn't be a moron about eating just 'cause you're too good to steal." Barney lifted an eyebrow. "I mean, I get that stealing isn't right, but I'm not gonna go starvin' myself over it."

Lexi didn't say anything; she was tired of hearing it. Star was already fussing over her, Liz had just finished giving her the third degree, and now Barney? No, she was spent. Besides, all this chatter about not eating was a cruel reminder of the gnawing hunger that was getting worse with every hour.

They kept their voices at a quiet pitch as they crossed the Pit, but it didn't matter. As expected, Sapphire spotted them, saw the bare arm, and like a wild animal pounced across the chasm, folding her arms tight. Lexi was tempted to laugh out loud. How many kids living here were actually intimidated by Sapphire?

"Where's your cast thing?" Sapphire asked with high eyebrows. It didn't take a genius to figure out she was just *waiting* for Lexi to say at the hospital; Sapphire was desperate for any excuse to jump her.

Well, not this time.

"Some garbage can," Lexi replied. "It's not that hard to figure out. You just unwrap the stupid thing." She knew it sounded convincing enough; she'd had to lie her way out of some pretty brutal situations before.

But Sapphire was still suspicious, staring Lexi down as if scoping out the loophole that would unravel her lie at the seams.

That was when Barney decided to step in.

"You should have seen her, Sapph," he said with a hearty

laugh. "She may be actin' all cool, like it was no big deal, but man, she bawled like a baby when she took it off."

Lexi clamped down on her tongue, restraining herself from beating the crap out of him. Instead, she glared at the dirt floor, hoping Sapphire would take her red cheeks as embarrassment, not all-out rage.

Sapphire smirked, obviously pleased with this piece of information, and with a flip of her blonde locks she bounced back to her corner of friends.

Once Lexi was convinced Sapphire's attention was diverted, she elbowed Barney hard in the ribs.

"Wow, thanks for makin' me out to be a wuss, Barney!" she hissed through clenched teeth.

"Hey! She wasn't buying your story. I had to say *something*. Instead of beating on me, you should be thanking me. Adding that bit about you freaking out was enough to bring her satisfaction, enough to leave us alone." Barney shrugged. "Face it, she hates you!"

"Really?" Lexi asked. "I hadn't noticed."

Dear Journal,

She came back. Lexi came to the hospital and met me outside, just like I asked her to. Now I'm right back where I started, feeling conflicted about my role in all this.

I came so close to breaking right down in front of her today. She told me all sorts of things, and each word tore a piece out of my heart. She had a bruise on her face, and her arm wasn't even completely healed. When I asked her about it, she told me someone had done it to her. It makes me so angry; I can't believe someone would intentionally hurt her! It made me want to go out there and find whoever did this and show them I mean business.

I don't think she's eating, either, and that just kills me. She wouldn't admit it, but you just have to look at her. She's wasting away, and she's already tiny to begin with.

I don't understand. Where did all this sudden overprotectiveness come from? Why is it that I just want to chase after her when she leaves, keep her from going back there? She's not safe there. She's been there for two weeks, and in that time she's sprained her wrist, gotten into a fight, and stopped eating. That's no place for a fifteen-year-old.

Kathryn says I need to pray for her, and I have been, but is that all I'm supposed to do? Is there something else I'm missing?

The hardest thing was watching her leave, having absolutely no idea when or even if I'll see her again. I don't know if our paths will cross. I don't know if they're meant to. I guess only God can know that.

Father, You control the universe, and You watch

over each of Your children. I know that, and even though I can't know where Lexi is tonight or how she's doing, You do, and so I have to release her to You. She's hurting, God, and I know You know that, so please help her in whatever way she needs help. Show me why I feel this way, why I feel so helpless, why it scares me to death to imagine what could happen to her out there. In the meantime, protect Lexi. She's Your child.

Amen.

—Liz

CHAPTER 37

L E X I

Saturday, October 17
12:49 p.m.

"Your arm doin' okay, girl?"

Once again, Lexi was lost in DV's mural, mesmerized by the story his art was beginning to tell. Next to his nest of perfect eggs DV was methodically bringing to life a group of baby birds: tiny sparrows with fluffy brown feathers and beady black eyes. They seemed so real, so lifelike. DV would be famous one day, Lexi was sure of that.

"Yo, CJ!"

"What?"

"Didn't you hear me?" DV chuckled. "I *said,* how's your arm doin'?"

"Oh." Lexi considered her wrist. "Still a little sore, but it'll be fine. It hasn't been the worst thing."

"So what *has* been?" DV's voice was laced with the same condescending tone he used every time he tried to burrow deeper into Lexi's world. Ever since he'd called her a robot, he'd been convinced she was burying pent-up feelings under layers of rock-hard numbness.

Well, what did he know?

"Your mural's looking great, DV," Lexi said.

"Way to change the subject. See what I mean? You're a shell."

"Oh, whatever!" Lexi flung an empty pop can at his back, and he erupted with giggles.

"Okay, okay, no need resortin' to violence." DV swished his dirty paintbrush in a cup of clean water. "Seriously, girl, you don't let nothin' faze you. Man, last week when you came in with that arm all messed up, I actually thought Sapphire was gonna kill you, but you back-talked her like you didn't care *what* she'd do."

"That's 'cause I *don't* care what she does." Lexi huffed. "And anyway, thanks to Sapphire, my arm's not even fully healed. Now I gotta be more careful."

"Well, it could be worse." DV shrugged. "You could be a lefty."

Lexi laughed quietly, and DV whipped around to direct his brush at her. "Aha! See that?" he asked, grinning widely. "You *do* have feelings."

"Who has feelings?" Barney interrupted, joining in by dropping to his knees next to Lexi.

"Rock Girl over here," DV chimed, returning to his birds.

Lexi ignored him. "Where you been?" she asked while Barney rummaged through his oversized pockets.

"Check it out; I brought you somethin'." He pulled out his prize: half of a tuna sandwich, wrapped in cellophane. Before Lexi could say anything, he tossed it at her.

"Where'd you get this?" she asked with a raised eyebrow.

"I was really lucky!" Barney's eyes lit up. "Get this! I was walking by the Patio—you know, that outdoor café? Anyway, there was a woman sitting at a table by herself, and she had a sandwich. I thought, *No big deal*, but then she went to grab something from her purse. Talk about opportunity. She never even *saw* me! I just nicked it right off the table and jetted!"

Barney was absolutely glowing with pride. Lexi, on the other hand, felt guilty. "It's okay; I already ate," she lied.

"You're such a liar. Just eat the sandwich."

Even holding the sandwich felt wrong; Barney had already done enough for her these past two weeks. Why should he have to starve because she was having a bad week?

But Barney wasn't taking no for an answer. "You're wasting away, so eat it, before I make you!"

Defeated, she kept the sandwich in the end, but only because the crumbs speckling Barney's face told her he'd at least eaten the other half.

Tearing her own half into two, she handed one to DV, who accepted it with a grin. He politely nibbled on his portion, but Lexi's half was gone in seconds.

"Yeah, *sure* you're eating alright!" Barney exclaimed with a snort. "The way you just hoovered that sandwich, you'd think you hadn't eaten in days!"

Lexi shrugged, brushing the crumbs from her lips. He might have been right, but she'd already lost count of how long it had been.

"No offence, Ceej, but you gotta get over your stealin' issues or you're gonna disappear," Barney said.

"Back off, man," DV piped up, still honing in on his masterpiece, sandwich poised in one hand. "Let her keep her morals. It makes her a good person."

Thank you, DV, Lexi thought, raising an eyebrow at Barney. He looked about ready to protest, but they were interrupted by shouting.

The three of them exchanged glances, then rose to scope out where it was coming from. Lexi wasn't surprised to be joined by several other curious stragglers; any sign of fighting was a means of free entertainment down here.

It didn't take them long to figure out who was doing the shouting; they were loud enough to wake the dead.

"I don't care who you think you are!" Sapphire shrieked. "You can't just take stuff from the stash without asking! Those blankets and candles are for new people, and the money? That's for supplies! You can't just take whatever you want, whenever you want!"

Slick casually cocked an eyebrow, arms crossed across his broad chest.

"Actually, doll, I *can*," he said nonchalantly. "Unlike the rest of these little puppets of yours, I don't listen to you. I don't listen to no one, *especially* women."

Lexi felt her own stomach seize as Slick inched toward Sapphire, eyeing her the same way he eyed Lexi.

Her skin crawled.

"I don't care about your sick attitude toward women, and I don't care what you think about me, either!" Sapphire narrowed her eyebrows. "But you *will* listen to the rules, or you're gone!"

Slick glared at her for an excruciating moment, silence closing the gap between them. Sapphire stared back with fierce defiance, and Lexi wondered if that was the end of it.

But then Slick shot forward, raising his hand to Sapphire's chest and slamming her violently into the concrete wall behind her. The impact echoed throughout the whole Pit.

Trapping her up against the wall, Slick leaned in until his face was only an inch away from hers. Sapphire watched him with trembling lips, her hands clasped around his arm, trying to push him away. Lexi stole a nervous peek around her; nobody wanted to get involved. Nobody even *moved*.

"Babe, I do what *I* want, and I do it *when* I want," Slick hissed. "And you of all people don't tell me what to do. I'll make sure you learn this very quickly."

Sapphire had no witty response this time. Lexi could see her hands trembling around Slick's hold.

Having had the last word, Slick struck Sapphire hard across the face, sending her to her knees.

The crowd scattered like sheep as Slick slunk away. Lexi, however, refused to move, and as he passed her, she bore into him with eyes of fire. She would *not* scramble out of his way like a dog with its tail between its legs. No, she would never let him think she was afraid of him.

He came to a halt and considered her for a second, staring back at her with those empty eyes. Lexi held her ground. Was he still in a power-hungry kind of mood? Would he hit her, too? Well, let him. She wasn't backing down.

But nothing happened. He just took off.

Lexi watched after him before she spotted Sapphire slowly stumbling to her feet, masking her cheek with her hand. She stole a nervous glance around, but nobody would meet her eye.

Maybe that was what Sapphire wanted. Sometimes it was easier dealing with things on your own. Her eyes wet, she strayed toward the Combs, nobody following after her.

"I hate that guy," Lexi said through clenched teeth. "Even if it *is* Sapphire he went after, I hate him. He's such a jerk!"

Barney snorted. "Well, yeah! I mean, we *are* talking about the same Slick, aren't we?"

***

They ended up back in DV's corner, and the Pit's activity bustled on like nothing had happened. Still, Lexi was stuck thinking of Sapphire, camping out in her space, probably dabbing makeup over the bruise. Against her better judgment, Lexi felt a slight pang of pity for Sapph, even if it *was* the same girl who'd given her the bruise on her own cheek. What Slick had done was just low.

Lexi hated Sapphire. She'd hated her since the beginning, but right now she hated Slick even more.

CHAPTER 38

L I Z

Sunday, October 18
12:11 p.m.

"Oh, what a gorgeous day, isn't it?" Kathryn asked as she, Brian, and Nancy joined Liz in the parking lot after church. "I think we just might have to take Miss Nancy to the pool today."

Liz watched with a warm smile as Kathryn's news set Nancy on a jumping spree. The girl yanked on her dad's hand and begged to wear her purple bathing suit, because the blue one wasn't pretty enough.

Kids.

"I'm gonna get the diva in the car," Brian said, hoisting the six-year-old into his arms. "And I'll get the AC going."

Kathryn smiled after them.

"That kid is crazy, but I love her," she said, turning her attention to Liz. "So, what did you do yesterday?"

"Nothing special. Actually, it was pretty unproductive, besides work," Liz recalled. "Oh! The weirdest thing happened to me at lunch, though. I went over to the Patio before work for some chow, and when I turned to grab my cell from my purse, I looked up, and my sandwich was gone! I mean, I couldn't have looked away for more than two seconds."

Kathryn rolled her eyes knowingly. "Street kids," she said casually. "Can't turn your back for any length of time."

Street kids.

189

Lexi.

Did the kid who took her sandwich know Lexi?

Liz decided against filling Kathryn in on Lexi's return on Friday. It was no secret how Kathryn felt about the Tunnel Kids, and she'd voiced her disapproval about Liz's desire to help the street girl from the start. No, for now it was better to keep Lexi under wraps. Liz loved Kathryn to death, but her closest friend just didn't understand.

But then, neither did Liz. Not really.

They were interrupted by the wailing of a horn.

Liz caught sight of Nancy gleefully whacking the horn inside the car while Brian roared with laughter.

"They're playing my song," Kathryn said with a contented sigh. "Call me sometime, okay, Lizzie? And for goodness' sake, take care of yourself!"

***

Relieved by the rush of cool air that greeted her when she got home, Liz set down her bag of takeout and checked her messages.

There was one from her mother.

"Hello, Elizabeth, please give me a call when you get this message. Goodbye."

Typical. Her mother's messages were always short, sweet, and to the point. She was never one to beat around the bush; she always said, why bother wasting breath on a recording when she could carry on an actual conversation?

Sighing, Liz cradled her cordless phone with her into the kitchen and dished out her Chinese food. The last thing she felt like doing was talking to her mother, but she'd already missed the pool party. According to her mother, that counted as *two* strikes. She'd better return the call.

"Hello, Mother, you called?"

"Oh hello, Elizabeth! I was hoping you would call me back today. How are you, dear?" Anne asked in her usual high-pitched squeal.

"Great," Liz lied. "How was the party?"

"Oh, well, the children had a fantastic time. Lissy's *diving* now!" Her mother paused. "But you know, the company just wasn't the same without you. You really ought to have been there."

Precisely the reason why Liz hadn't wanted to call. She'd known her mother would lay the guilt trip on extra thick.

Why did I bring up the party in the first place?

"Yeah, I know. I'm sorry, Mom. I had to work yesterday," Liz replied, popping a chicken ball into her mouth. Food was supposed to be comforting, right?

"Well, dear, do you want to know what *I* think?" Anne asked.

Not particularly.

"I think you're working too hard."

"I told you, Mom, I enjoy it." Liz eased her eyes closed, trying to simmer down the boiling tension inside. "It gives me something to do."

"Oh, Elizabeth, there is tons to do! You know, I don't work at all, and I find so much to do with my time. I bake, I sew, I redecorate, and I get to see more of my wonderful family."

"Yes, well, that's what works for you," Liz pointed out. "I prefer to work."

She was met with silence.

Silence was always a bad sign.

"Yes, dear," Anne said disapprovingly. "That's your way of coping."

"Oh Mother, not *now*!" Liz exclaimed, grabbing a fistful of hair. A headache was brewing, and she fought off every urge to end the call. "Can we please just have a normal conversation that doesn't include you criticizing how I live my life?"

She knew that hit a nerve, because there was the dreaded silence again. Part of Liz felt guilty, but if there was one thing she'd learned over the years, it was to nip her mother in the bud before she went too far.

"Alright, dear," Anne said, sighing dramatically. "Tell me how your week has been *other* than work."

The only thing that came to Liz's mind was Lexi.

"Well, I ran into this girl last weekend," Liz started, remembering it like it had happened yesterday. "A girl from the tunnels. She hurt her wrist, so I wrapped it up for her, and—"

"One of those street ruffians?" Anne asked, a disapproving edge to her voice. "Did she mug you? Did you check your purse afterwards? Was she on drugs?"

"Mom!" Liz exclaimed defensively. "Why would you think that?"

"Elizabeth, they're all the same, those young hooligans. I've never approved of you living downtown. You're too close to their little abode. *Anything* could happen."

"They've never bothered me before." Liz sighed impatiently, rubbing her temples. "Besides, I don't think this girl is trouble. I think she's hurting."

"No, Elizabeth," Anne said seriously. "*You're* hurting."

"Mother, this isn't about me!" Liz felt like pounding the table. "There are lots of people in this world who are hurting."

Silence again.

"Yes," Anne replied. "But they aren't *my* daughter."

CHAPTER 39

L E X I

Monday, October 19
10:14 a.m.

"Mmmm," Barney said after a long drag of weed. "Now all we need is some breakfast."

Lexi rolled her eyes. It was Monday morning, and she and Barney were scavenging in the downtown district, in search of food. Barney wasn't really taking it seriously, though. He was too caught up in his own little world.

"I hate it when you smoke that crap!" Lexi exclaimed, still scanning the sidewalks for loose change.

"Oh, come on, man. Lighten up." He caught Lexi's eye. "Okay, fine, *maybe* I'll consider quitting."

Lexi knew he wouldn't.

"Good," she said anyway. "You're probably giving me a high with all your smoke."

"It's cool, huh?"

He shut up fast when Lexi shot him a cold glare.

"Anyway, think of all the money you'd save if you quit," Lexi continued.

"Bonus!" Barney yelled suddenly, ignoring Lexi entirely as he bent over to collect a five-dollar bill. "It's our lucky day!"

"*Your* lucky day," Lexi said flatly. "I never find anything."

Before Lexi could say more, Barney took off toward the nearby coffee shop. A few minutes later, he scrambled back toward her, parading two large coffees and a chocolate doughnut.

"Here." Barney thrust one of the coffees into Lexi's hand. "For you."

"Uh, hello! I don't drink coffee."

"You do now," Barney said, handing her half the doughnut. "Come on, CJ, it'll give you energy. It's not like you're getting any from food, since you're too *good* to eat."

Lexi narrowed her eyebrows but sipped the coffee anyway. It was bitter and disgusting. It took all her willpower not to spew it out.

"You'll get used to it," Barney said, shoving his half of the doughnut into his mouth.

Doubt it.

They wove back through the crowd, heading toward the tunnels as Lexi took small sips of the coffee, grimacing with every mouthful. She didn't care what Barney said; she would *never* enjoy this.

But she couldn't deny he was only trying to look out for her.

As they strolled by Ed's Music Shop, Lexi felt her chest tighten. She hadn't come down this street since she'd been chased off.

She kept her eyes peeled, but there was no sign of Ed.

Probably has the day off, Lexi thought, relieved. Sure, the guy might not even remember her, but she remembered *him.* He was the one responsible for her sprained wrist.

And suddenly, she was serenaded with the same peaceful sound that had held her captive the last time. The piano ballad surrounded her, swept her away from this place, entranced her. She was captivated… and frozen. Just like last time, she recognized the piece immediately; it was *Brahms' Lullaby*, the very piece she'd promised herself she'd learn one day but never did.

There'd never been the chance.

"Dude, now what?" Barney asked, realizing Lexi was falling behind.

Lexi held up her hand. "Shut up, man! I'm listening!"

"To what?" Barney asked, puckering his brow with a glance around. "What, to this crap?"

Lexi shot him a look.

"Oh come on!" Barney rolled his eyes. "Give me Eminem over this any day."

Lexi ignored him. The piece was just ending.

"Geez, CJ, I'm learning more about you every day." Barney stalked off, holding back a little until Lexi followed. "How can you even *like* that kind of music?"

Lexi shrugged, disappointed to hear the distant melody fade as they moved on. "I used to play," she replied.

"Play what?" Barney asked. "Violin?"

"That was a piano, Barn."

"Well, what do you mean you *used* to?"

"It used to be a part of my life," Lexi replied coldly. "Guess I stopped caring about that, too."

Barney came to a halt in the middle of the sidewalk, staring after her. Lexi turned to find him arching an eyebrow at her.

"What?" she asked.

"You know," Barney replied knowingly, "all this 'not caring'? It's startin' to sound a lot like caring."

Lexi didn't say anything, because Barney didn't know what he was talking about. He was wrong; she didn't care about anything. She didn't care that she hadn't touched a piano since Hilary kicked her out a year before. She didn't care that she lived on the streets with nothing in her stomach but half a doughnut and the coffee she was gagging on. She didn't care about any of these things, because caring meant having to deal with the emptiness she ignored every time she even *heard* the sound of a piano.

Caring meant hurting.

So, it was better not to care.

Dear Journal,

I don't understand why everybody hates these poor Tunnel Kids. I don't get why everybody just passes them like they don't exist. Everybody avoids them like the plague.

Somehow, Lexi changed that for me. Now I pass these kids on the streets and I feel for them, because I know they all have a story, just like Lexi. They've all been hurt, somehow.

I don't know what it is about Lexi that changed it all for me. I've been trying to figure it out for days now. I only wish God would give me some answers before I go insane.

—Liz

CHAPTER 40

L E X I

Tuesday, October 20
10:07 a.m.

Lexi was flat on her back, staring up at the mould that was festering all over the rafters. Distracted as she was with the growing rot, she hardly noticed her candle nearing the end of its life. Well, that was easy to do when it had been burning all night long.

She knew because she hadn't slept, not even a little.

It was all because of her stomach. Throughout the night, and even now, it felt like it was under attack. She imagined little soldiers with arrows nocked, hiding in little bushes until they simultaneously fired without mercy at her empty gut. Well, that was how it *felt.*

It didn't help, either, that her throat was parched, her lips were like rubber, and her head seemed to spin constantly. She wasn't an idiot; she knew it was because she wasn't eating, at least not the way she should be. A quarter of a sandwich here and half a doughnut there did nothing, and her body was rebelling.

Lexi hated it, hated Jacksonville for deeming her unlucky in her search for cash, hated her body for being such a wuss. In fact, she was pretty sure she hated *everything.*

She rolled over onto her stomach, but that didn't help matters any, so she sat up. Just as useless. This was *all* useless. She could die down here and nobody would even notice. They'd just hop over her body like an obstacle.

197

Well, whatever! Maybe she didn't *want* anyone to notice.

"Hey Ceej, you up?" Barney's voice rang through the silent tunnels. Lexi closed her eyes; she didn't want to see anybody, not even Barney, not when she felt so agitated, so *hungry*.

He showed up anyway.

"Look, man! I found another sandwich." He paused. "Well, I *stole* another sandwich, but you get the idea. Wanna split it?"

Yes, she wanted to, more than *anything*, but she'd already made an important decision somewhere in the middle of the night. Barney had been nothing but helpful over the past couple of weeks, sharing his food here and there, all because she refused to steal, but now, the unfairness of the situation glared fiercely at her. Each and every one of the kids who called these tunnels home were forced to fend for themselves, find their own food, keep themselves alive.

No, Lexi couldn't let Barney take care of her, not anymore. He needed to take care of himself. She'd already decided not to take anything else from Barney, no matter how badly her stomach screamed for that sandwich.

"No thanks," she finally said, faking a smile. "I already had breakfast."

Truth was, she hadn't even moved from this spot since yesterday.

"How'd you score that?" Barney asked, doubt written all over him.

"Got up early, went to the market, stole some fruit," Lexi lied. "I've been thinking. It's pretty stupid not to steal, especially out here. So, I decided to turn over a new leaf, I guess. And you were right; it's really not that bad."

She wondered how convincing she sounded. Her voice seemed so far away, her head swimming with pressure, her gut caving in on itself.

"Well, finally!" Barney exclaimed, extending his hand for a high-five. Lexi slapped it half-heartedly but managed a grin for good measure. "See? I knew you had it in you."

With that, Barney began to tear into his sandwich.

Something lurched inside Lexi's stomach. Okay, this was getting to be unbearable. Maybe standing would help.

It didn't.

The dizziness came back with an awful vengeance. Blinking a couple of times to clear her vision, she headed for the Pit.

"Where're you goin'?" Barney asked with a mouthful of ham.

"Goin' to start scoping out some lunch," Lexi replied coldly. "Catch ya later."

Manoeuvring her way through the dark Combs wasn't easy with a light head and a tummy cramp. All she wanted to do was go back to her space and lie there until the pain eased up.

But the pain wouldn't ease up; that was the problem. It wouldn't get any better unless she found something to eat. Maybe she'd be lucky and score a half-eaten cheeseburger from some garbage can.

She wasn't beyond that, not anymore.

Once, when Lexi had been with the Norwoods, she'd gone a whole day without eating. Ray was home, planted in front of the television all day long, chugging back beer after beer, cursing at whatever was on the TV, smashing beer bottles here and there. Lexi and Kyla had snuck down the hall early that morning, rounded up Melanie, Caleb, and Suzie, and brought them back to their own room without a peep. Shelley was working a double shift, an overnight, and the kids had all seen Ray drunk enough times to know you stayed out of his way if you were smart.

So the five of them spent the day in that small bedroom, barricading the door with both beds to keep Ray out. Oh, he'd tried getting in, tried knocking the door down, cursed up a wild storm, but it didn't work.

As much as they all tried to keep themselves busy, hunger became a problem, but nobody dared venture out for food. They spent the whole day and night in that room, finally grabbing some breakfast the next morning, when Ray was passed out on the couch.

A day without food.

Lexi couldn't even remember the last time she'd had an actual meal.

Funny how life could change.

She stumbled through the Pit, eager to reach the streets, even just for the sun to hit her face. Maybe some fresh air would help. Even if she could find some water, she'd be okay, at least for another few hours. Maybe—

"Hey, sexy!" Slick's dark voice was like nails on a chalkboard. "How's the arm?"

She turned.

He wasn't looking at her arm.

"It's fine," Lexi said numbly, biting her tongue as she moved on.

"Come on, doll, where you goin'?" he called after her. "What's the matter, you got better things to do than talk to me?" His voice was a booming thunder. The edge in his voice sounded a lot like it had the day he attacked Sapphire.

Well, screw him! Lexi's irritation was already bubbling over. She shot Slick a daring glare.

"I could name a few thousand things I'd rather be doing than talking to you!" she said coldly. Slick's lip curled into that malicious grin as he crossed his arms.

"Please," he said with a roll of the eyes. "That's just your defence mechanisms kickin' in, because *I* know you really want nothin' more than a night of passion with me."

"You're more disgusting than the rot growin' on these walls." Lexi turned her back to him, heading for the Tube.

She didn't make it that far.

Slick lunged, caught hold of Lexi's wrist, and whipped her around so they were face to face. She clamped down on her tongue so she wouldn't cry out; he'd grabbed her sprained wrist and was squeezing it so tight that she thought he might snap it, right then and there.

With his free hand, he shoved her hard into the wall, just like he had with Sapphire. She could feel the wall's jagged corners stabbing into her back, tearing her sweater.

Just as quickly, Slick darted forward, swallowing the space between them until his body was pressed up against hers. His face was so close to her own, she could feel his hot breath on her face. She felt her throat constricting.

No, she never cried, and she refused to give him the satisfaction of knowing he was hurting her. Instead, she met his cold glare, biting harder on her tongue to ignore the pain, ignore the fear.

"Don't you *ever* talk back to me again," Slick said in a harsh whisper, his face pressed up against her cheek. "Maybe you don't understand how things work down here, but *nobody*, especially a girl, gives me attitude, unless I *let* them. You're *nothing!*"

Lexi swallowed. She was *not* going to stand here and take it like Sapphire had. She wasn't anything like Sapphire.

"Then, if I'm nothing, you can just quit talkin' to me! Do everyone a favour," she said evenly, steadying her voice to some semblance of calm. Her heart was hammering away like crazy, and he was so close to her that she wondered if he could feel it, but she wouldn't let herself seem afraid. She couldn't let him believe that.

Slick didn't say anything, but he wouldn't let her go, either. His grip on her wrist got tighter, and his eyes never left hers. He took another step in, squashing her against the wall. The rocks dug into her back, but she still glared up at him with as much defiance as she could muster.

"Sapphire may be scared of you, but I'm not!" she hissed through clenched teeth. This *had* to end. "So if you think you can scare me, you're an idiot!"

She waited for the blow. After all, he'd hit Sapphire... but nothing came. Just silence, as he stared down at her with those dark, empty eyes.

He let go of her wrist.

But he didn't move.

"You may walk away from this and think I'm lettin' you off the hook, but I'm not done with you yet," he said in a hard voice.

"You'll learn just as fast as everyone else in this place. *Nobody*, especially a girl, talks down to me."

Lexi lifted her right hand and pushed him off her. "If anyone else in this place actually buys that," she said, "they're deluded."

She left the Pit, conscious of keeping a steady pace, ignoring the urge to run until her legs couldn't carry her anymore, ignoring the urge to glance back for fear he would jump her again. No, she had to keep her guard up, her mask on. She *couldn't* let him see her fear. Anybody who could read your emotions like that could prey on you. It was too risky.

Especially with someone like Slick.

Reaching the surface, she took hold of her wrist. Sure enough, four deep purple bruises the size of Slick's fingers were beginning to form in a circle around it. The pain was almost blinding, and on top of her stomach ache... well, maybe that was why she still felt fresh tears prickling her eyes.

She forced them down.

Numb.

She had to be numb.

The pain in her stomach didn't matter.

The dizziness didn't matter.

The dull throbbing in her wrist didn't matter.

Slick didn't matter.

Nothing mattered.

At least that way, in her mind, she was safe.

CHAPTER 41

L I Z

Wednesday, October 21
2:39 p.m.

The girl was found in a park the previous night, unconscious. A heroin overdose.

Now, the seventeen-year-old was stable, hooked up to an IV to keep her hydrated and oxygen to stabilize her breathing.

And it was part of Liz's rounds to check in on her.

Upon entering the tiny room, Liz found a frail girl with stringy black hair, a pinched nose, and chapped lips, lying very still in the hospital bed. Her face was as white as a sheet, and her skin was almost transparent. It was like looking at a ghost.

According to the other doctors, this girl, Abby, had drifted in and out of consciousness all night and all morning. They hadn't been able to get any information out of her yet.

That was Liz's job.

She couldn't help but notice that the girl looked so young, so childlike.

Like Lexi...

"Hi, Abby," Liz greeted quietly. The girl would no doubt be sporting a massive headache. "I'm Dr. Swavier. I came to see how you're doing."

Well, Liz hardly needed Abby to tell her anything. The girl was a mess, and rightly so. A heroin overdose was never pretty. A psychiatrist was scheduled to assess her that afternoon to check if any suicidal ideation was involved, but heroin attacked the central nervous system; the girl would be out of sorts for days.

"I... feel... sick," Abby groaned as her eyes fluttered, unable to focus on Liz. Or anything else, it seemed.

"I know you do," Liz said. "We've given you some drugs to help with that, but unfortunately, it won't take away all the discomfort."

Liz went about all the standard checks. She made sure the IV was still properly attached; she checked for air bubbles, felt Abby's pulse, adjusted the tubes around her nose. Still, she felt somewhat detached. She couldn't even *look* at Abby, because she couldn't help but wonder.

What if this had been Lexi?

No. Keep your focus!

"Honey, is there anyone we can call for you?" she asked, pulling out her chart. "Your parents?"

Part of her expected the same response she had received from Lexi that first day. No parents.

A street kid.

Did Abby know Lexi? Were they friends?

"Yes," Abby replied quietly. "C–call my mom."

No. Not a street kid.

It took some time. Abby was hardly coherent enough to dictate a phone number, but Liz got it, eventually. After making sure Abby was as comfortable as she could be, Liz headed out to the main desk.

"Abby's mother," Liz explained, handing Jill the number.

"Who?" Jill asked, and after a pause, "Oh, the heroin addict?"

Liz nodded, stealing a peek toward the room where Abby was probably losing consciousness again.

She sighed. What if it *had* been Lexi? Would she ever see Lexi in here for something like that? Was her mother right? Was Lexi into drugs?

Well, she didn't seem to be, but Liz couldn't help but wonder how long it would be until street life caught up with the young girl.

How long until life became too painful to deal with on her own? How long before Lexi caved under the pressure and dabbled with things she might never get out of?

It made Liz sick with worry. Lexi was just a kid!

"Geez, Liz, you're pale!" Jenn interrupted Liz's train of thought. "You okay?"

"Fine," Liz lied. "Just had a kid who OD'd on heroin."

Jenn hardly seemed convinced. "That's not a reason to be upset, Liz," she pointed out. "I mean, as terrible as it is, you treat situations like that all the time."

Liz couldn't argue that. "Yeah, I guess."

But everything's so different now...

"Hey, Liz?" Jenn grew solemn. "Does this have anything to do with that kid you met a couple of weeks ago? That street kid?"

Liz exhaled. "What gave me away?" she asked, lips curling into a meek smile.

"Just something I've noticed. You seem... I don't know, *different* since that kid. It's like you've got this new look about you whenever teenagers come in." Jenn looked down. "Sorry, I know I notice the weirdest things, but that's me. So, what's up, Liz? You worried about her?"

Worried? That was an understatement, but still, Liz nodded. "You know, Jenn, I don't get it. You're right. I mean, since when have I ever been this concerned over a kid? We're trained to detach ourselves from patients, so I don't get why I'm so worried about some random girl. She seems independent enough."

Who was she trying to convince anyway?

"I don't know, Liz. It's not necessarily a bad thing. Those street kids have it rough. But honey," Jenn offered a small smile, "you know you can't fix the problem."

It was like a broken record. First Kathryn, now Jenn.

You can't fix the problem.

Jenn patted Liz's arm. "I think it's nice, you caring about this kid. I mean, maybe it's a good sign. Maybe it means you're ready to let go."

Liz looked up quickly. "Let *what* go?" she asked.

"Look, Liz, it doesn't take a minor in psychology to see that since Kurt died, you've shut yourself off emotionally," Jenn said, a sort of sadness glazing her eyes. "You work hard, you hardly laugh, you hardly cry, you hardly *feel*. Then, out of nowhere, this kid comes along, and suddenly you're a mother hen."

Liz bit her lip, looking away. Why did it feel like everybody was making this about *her*?

"Look, all I'm saying is maybe your heart is telling you it's time. That it's okay to *feel* again. It's been two years, kiddo." Jenn tried to smile. "Maybe it's time to move on. Maybe—"

"Jenn, I appreciate the concern, but it's ungrounded." Liz faked a smile, even laughed a little. "She's a kid who's living on the streets by herself. I doubt I'm the first person who's been upset about that."

"Liz, you're not hearing me," Jenn said. "You *feel* concerned for her! You don't have to believe me, but I see this as a gigantic stepping stone toward healing."

Healing.

As Jenn moved on to finish her rounds, Liz stood frozen, her thoughts everywhere but here.

She didn't get it. Kathryn had told her the same thing, and even, to some degree, her mother! Why was everybody under the impression that she didn't feel things, that she wasn't dealing with things? She was dealing with things just fine. Besides, how could they know? They weren't the ones who'd lost a husband at the age of thirty-four, so what did they know about *dealing*?

No, she couldn't do this. She wouldn't feel angry, not toward them. It wasn't their fault. They just didn't understand.

But then again, did she?

Dear Journal,

I can't get Jenn's words out of my head. Sometimes it bugs me that she has psych training. I know she's been trained to dig deep, get beneath the surface, but she's got it all wrong. I'm dealing just fine with Kurt's death. Shutting myself off emotionally? That's ridiculous!

It *is* ridiculous.

Isn't it?

Maybe she's right.

Maybe that's exactly why this thing with Lexi feels so weird.

So foreign.

But no, that doesn't make any sense. If Jenn is right and this sudden compassion for Lexi is some weird way of opening up my heart again, then why Lexi?

A stranger?

Why a *kid*? I mean, why not someone a little closer to home? Kathy? Jenn? My family?

God is in control, so I know He's in control of all this. Did God ordain this whole thing with Lexi for *my* sake, or am I meant to do something for *her*?

While reading my Bible tonight, I came across this passage in James: "Religion that God our Father accepts as pure and faultless is this: to look after orphans and widows in their distress..."

Is that what this is all about? Is God bringing Lexi to my attention, to my heart, in order to do something about it? I've always liked the idea of being called to something, some divine purpose.

Is that what this is?

Or is this nothing more than some kind of emotional breakdown?

I feel so helpless, and all I can do is pray. For Lexi, and maybe for me, too.

I guess if God wants this to develop into something, it will.

But I don't get what Jenn is saying.

I don't understand what any of this has to do with Kurt.

—Liz

CHAPTER 42

L E X I

Thursday, October 22
10:19 a.m.

Her arm was still a mess Thursday morning.

Great, Lexi thought as she circled the block for the seventh time that morning. *Stupid thing's never gonna heal.*

Those purple welts were a daunting reminder of her encounter with Slick two days earlier. Could bruises become permanent, just like that small circle on the inside of her wrist was permanent?

Why does everything bad always happen to the same arm?

DV was right. It was a good thing she wasn't a lefty.

The smell of greasy food wafted under her nose as she passed by the hotdog stand again. It made her want to hurl. She'd been starving since Monday, hadn't had a bite since that doughnut Barney had split with her.

That seemed like a thousand and one years ago. The only real thing now was the pain in her stomach that was slowly melting into a constant state of nausea. She felt like she was going to puke.

It was almost laughable—what exactly would she puke up anyway?

As she circled the block for the eighth time, hoping the exercise would liven her up a little, she couldn't help but wonder if she'd made the right decision.

Maybe she should have stayed at Everidge.

At Everidge, people left her alone. Nobody gave her a second glance.

Down here, she had Slick slamming her into walls, Star fussing over her diet, and DV calling her a shell.

At Everidge, they fed her three times a day.

Here, she had to sift through rotting garbage for food.

At Everidge, she could shower when she wanted.

Here, she had to walk sixteen blocks, and they could only use the shower if Barney's buddy was gone.

Weighing her options like this, she wondered if she should go back.

But then the truth settled in.

Sure, she'd have the luxury of being left alone, of having food and clean water, but at what cost? It wouldn't be long before they'd stick her in another foster home. That was how the state worked, and nobody cared where the kids ended up, as long as they were placed. They figured being placed equalled being safe.

Showed how much they knew; only one of her four foster homes had turned out to be safe.

Social Services made no sense. After pulling her out of a place where Des called the shots, knowing *exactly* what he'd done to her, how could they even *consider* placing her again? What if it happened again? What if the next foster father was just like Des? What if there weren't two other foster kids to rotate? What if Lexi was the plaything *every* night?

The vivid nightmare of that place lashed at her. No, she could never forget, no matter how badly she wanted to.

And she wouldn't go back. Even though it meant sacrificing daily comforts, she refused to be carted around to deeper levels of foster hell until she was eighteen. Four homes was enough; she wouldn't take it anymore.

The tunnels would have to do, for now.

Ready to circle the block for the ninth time, she came to a halt when an odd sensation pulsed through her body. Everything around her seemed suspended as her constant dizziness suddenly doubled in intensity. Her ears started ringing, her limbs tingling. Her head became a rock, her body detached itself, and her vision was going, fast.

What's going on?...

Blackness overtook her. She reached out to grab something, but her hand wasn't her own; she couldn't even see it.

Before everything disappeared, she felt herself hit the concrete—hard.

Then she heard her name.

CHAPTER 43

L I Z

Thursday, October 22
10:15 a.m.

Liz had to get out of the house!

She'd gone and done it again—wandered into that art studio. Why? She didn't know, but as soon as she stepped into that room, she knew it was a mistake.

It was only seconds before the hurricane of memories nearly crippled her.

So much for being shut off emotionally.

She wasn't due at work until noon, but she *had* to get out of here.

Maybe she'd stop by the Patio. They served great brunch, and she had enough time to spare. Just enough time to distract her from images of half-painted canvases and Kurt's smiling face.

***

Agitation crawled through her bones as she drove through town. Exhaling harshly, she thought, *I never should have gone into the art studio. What was I thinking?* Honestly, what was she hoping to accomplish by going in there? It wasn't like she'd decided to take up painting again. Right now, that was the farthest thing from her mind.

So why else would she go in there?

Was it because of what Jenn had said, about being ready to let go?

Well, that was where she felt closest to Kurt, in that art studio. Maybe it was all part of this healing process.

Then why did she run away?

No, Jenn was wrong. She wasn't ready for anything.

Right now, she needed to clear her mind, push away all those unwanted thoughts, find a distraction.

I wouldn't have to distract myself from anything if I hadn't gone in there in the first place.

As Liz cruised down the street, she spotted a familiar red sweater floating along, a familiar mop of messy brown hair.

Was it Lexi?

Liz slowed a little, trying to catch a glimpse of the girl's face.

There it was. Yes! It *was* Lexi.

In that exact moment, Lexi buckled and fell to the ground.

"Lexi!"

Liz's heart fired up as she stomped on the brakes. Whoever was driving behind her slammed on his own brakes, wailing on the horn. Muscles tensing, Liz mouthed an apology into her rearview and pulled over to the side of the road, ignoring the strings of unwholesome language coming from the passing elder.

Let him think whatever he wants.

Right now, Lexi was her priority.

Car parked, Liz jumped out, her body trembling as she sprinted toward the girl who lay in a heap, unconscious and white as a sheet.

"Lexi?"

Liz dropped to her knees as she rested her hand on Lexi's forehead. She was so warm. "Come on, sweetie, talk to me."

Liz's insides were tumbling, but she had to stay calm. Still, panic clawed its way in with all its unanswered questions. What was Lexi doing here? What had caused her to collapse like that?

Why did it happen exactly as Liz *happened* to drive by?

Liz felt for a pulse, then heaved a sigh of relief when she found it. Lexi's air passage was clear. Her vitals were all fine; she just had to wake up.

"Come on, kiddo." Liz smoothed Lexi's damp hair away from her clammy face. "Wake up."

Very gently, Liz patted the girl's cheeks.

Slowly, Lexi's eyes fluttered.

"Lexi?"

When Lexi opened up her eyes, she looked everywhere but at Liz, seemingly disoriented.

"Can you hear me?" Liz asked again, squeezing Lexi's hand in her own, hoping to pull her back to consciousness a little faster.

Lexi's wide eyes finally found Liz's, squinting. "What..." the girl tried, but Liz shushed her.

"It's okay, Lexi. You passed out."

No, that *wasn't* okay, but she hardly wanted to scare the poor girl. She'd just passed out in the middle of the sidewalk, and she was clearly out of sorts. The last thing Liz wanted was to make this any worse.

"Just lie still, okay?"

Lexi hardly moved for a few seconds, only to crane her neck to sneak a glance left, and then right. Liz noticed a rosy hue slowly returning to Lexi's cheeks. That was a good sign.

Liz waited a bit longer before asking Lexi if she felt okay to sit up.

She did, and Liz helped her, easing her up against the brick wall along the sidewalk. Liz wouldn't take her eyes away, not even for a second. She needed to be ready for any relapse.

"You doing okay?" Liz asked, kneeling in front of Lexi, thankful to see the girl had stopped swaying.

Lexi met Liz's eyes again, and this time recognition flashed behind them.

"You again," she said in a tired voice. "Why does it always seem like you're around when I do somethin' stupid?"

Liz smiled. She had been wondering the same thing. "Well,"

she said, "Maybe Somebody up there is looking out for you."

So maybe it was a God thing after all, because this was too weird to be a coincidence.

Lexi rolled her eyes a little in response. "Yeah, sure."

Well, they could debate all that later. Now that Lexi was conscious, Liz needed to find out what would had made Lexi pass out like that.

But she had a feeling she already knew.

"Lexi?" Liz eyed the girl seriously. "When was the last time you ate?"

Lexi hesitated a moment before shrugging indifferently. "I don't know. A couple of hours ago?"

Liz didn't buy it, and she raised an eyebrow for good measure.

The teen only bit her lip and looked away. That was another one of the things Liz noticed about Lexi: when she didn't want to talk about something, she wouldn't look you in the eye.

"Look, you don't have to tell me anything. I'm not going to force you to." Liz paused, checked her watch quickly. Yes, she had time. "But will you at least let me buy you some brunch?"

Lexi peered up, narrowing her eyebrows. She was being careful, and why shouldn't she? She was a fifteen-year-old living on the streets with nobody to take care of her. Of *course* she wouldn't trust anybody.

But, oh, Liz wanted to be the one she could trust.

"No, thanks," Lexi replied. "I'm not really hungry."

Liz only smiled. "I don't believe you."

Again, Lexi looked away.

Yes, she was a stubborn one.

"I understand that you don't want to talk to people. I get it; you're just keeping yourself safe. That's good, but like I told you before, I'm not telling anyone. So if it's against the rules, you don't have to worry." Liz nodded toward the Patio, only a few blocks down. "Just a quick brunch. Trust me, having something to eat will help you feel better."

215

Lexi was silent for the longest time, and Liz decided not to push. This had to be Lexi's decision; if Liz was too pushy, the girl would only push back, which wouldn't solve anything.

Lexi opened her mouth, then closed it again, as though struggling with what to say.

"How do I know you haven't already called the cops?" she finally asked in that quiet little voice.

Well, it was a fair question.

"Because if I was going to do that," Liz replied, "I would have done it two weeks ago."

***

Convincing Lexi to go for brunch was like pulling teeth, but somehow she managed, and soon they were seated outside at the Patio, perusing the menu.

"Order whatever you want, okay?" Liz peered over her menu at Lexi, who shifted in her seat. She seemed so uncomfortable, so out of place. "Anything. You're probably famished."

Lexi didn't speak as she scanned the menu. Well, at least her cheeks were back to their pinkish tint. Lexi might be feeling better, but Liz's own nerves were shot. Watching Lexi collapse had sparked something in her she hadn't felt in ages. And now, even with the girl conscious and coherent, Liz felt an overwhelming need to play the protector. She had to resist every urge to order Lexi vegetables or something with protein because she would need her strength.

Maybe some chicken soup would do her good.

Maybe not. Baby steps.

Their waiter returned with ice water and asked for their orders.

Liz caught Lexi's eye and mouthed, "Anything."

"Can I just have a ham sandwich?" Lexi asked the waiter, handing him the menu.

Liz was crushed. A ham sandwich would hardly tide her over.

Well, what could she do? She ordered the same.

Once the waiter moved on, Liz raised a disapproving eyebrow.

"Is that all you're going to eat?"

Lexi, who was playing with her straw, stopped to shoot Liz an icy glare.

Liz couldn't help but chuckle.

"Okay, fair enough," Liz replied. "So, how have things been since the last time I saw you?"

Lexi shrugged. Liz guessed that was her staple: the shrug. Perhaps an outward expression of how much she supposedly didn't care.

"Alright," Lexi replied in a flat voice. "Street life's nothin' to brag about, but it's fine."

Liz wanted to ask exactly *what* street life was like, but she decided against it.

Besides, maybe she didn't want to know.

"How's your arm?" Liz asked, keeping the conversation casual.

"Still hurts."

That caught Liz slightly off-guard.

"Still?" she asked. "That arm should be better by now."

Lexi didn't say anything. She only returned to stirring the ice cubes in her water.

Liz watched, her own mind reeling. The last time Liz had seen her, her arm was still in pain because somebody had hurt her. Was somebody *still* hurting her? What exactly was going on down there? Was Lexi safe?

Of course she's not safe—she has no one taking care of her!

"Cool necklace," the quiet voice spoke up from across the table.

Brought back to present reality, Liz looked up and found Lexi gazing at the golden cross fastened around Liz's neck.

"Oh, thank you," Liz replied, her fingers instinctively touching the necklace she hardly ever took off. "My good friend Kathy gave it to me five years ago."

"Oh." Lexi paused. "So, like, does that mean you believe in God, and Jesus, and all that?"

Liz smiled. "I get the feeling you don't."

"Nope," Lexi said. "It's pointless."

Well, Liz wasn't sure why God had caused the two of them to cross paths on more than one occasion, but if Lexi brought it up, Liz wasn't about to pass up a chance to tell somebody about God.

"Yeah, I believe in God, and Jesus, and *all that.*" Liz paused. "But I didn't always. In fact, I never really believed in anything. I guess you could say I was agnostic. I suppose I didn't care either way, but God's funny that way. He can grab hold of you and reveal Himself in ways you never thought possible."

Lexi responded with a barely audible scoff. "Sorry," she said as she peered into her glass. "No offense, but I just don't get this God thing. Like, if there actually is a God, why do so many bad things happen?"

Liz got the impression Lexi wasn't exactly searching for an answer. She was bitter, simple as that, and why shouldn't she be? She'd experienced true horrors. Lexi didn't have to tell her anything; Liz could see it in her eyes.

Her heart shattered for the girl all over again.

"You've had a rough life," Liz said softly. "Haven't you, Lexi?"

Lexi held her tongue. This was obviously a conversation she wasn't interested in having. That was abundantly clear when she sipped away at her water, distant again, as she gazed at the passing cars.

Try as she might, Liz couldn't even guess at Lexi's past, and that bothered her. Why, she didn't know. There was so much pain in those eyes, and Liz wasn't allowed in. All she knew was that the girl's parents were dead. Wasn't that enough to make anybody question the love of God?

Still, Liz had a strong feeling there was more to Lexi's past than that. She wished she knew, but even if she could catch a glimpse into Lexi's life, there wasn't anything she could do. How do you protect a stranger from a pain even she isn't willing to face?

"You're married?" Lexi asked, suddenly changing the subject after a painful silence.

218

Liz's stomach plunged to her knees.

Married…

That was always a touchy issue. Technically, she *was* still married, wasn't she? She still had the marriage certificate.

But then, she had no husband.

"What makes you ask that?" Liz wanted to know, clearing away the lump in her throat.

"You're wearing a ring."

"Of course." Liz sighed, catching the glimmer of the diamond on her left hand. "Uh, yeah, I am, well, I mean I *was*. But… my husband passed away two years ago."

Lexi lowered her head, her eyes shifting uncomfortably. Liz was quiet too; it still felt like acid on her tongue to actually use the words "husband" and "passed away" in the same sentence.

She wondered if Lexi had felt the same way when her parents died.

"Sorry," Lexi muttered, breaking the silence. "I shouldn't have said anything."

How could Liz fault the girl for something she couldn't have known? Still, she was eager to change the subject. "You seem to ask a lot of questions about jewellery," Liz pointed out.

Well, there was that shrug again.

"I guess," Lexi mumbled. "I mean, I never owned any."

Liz looked up, surprised by this. "Never?"

Lexi met her eyes then and smiled, ever so slightly.

It was the first time Liz had seen the girl smile.

"I'm a street kid, remember?" Lexi asked.

"Yes, but you haven't always been. You told me you've only been here a few weeks." Liz folded her hands in her lap. "So where were you *before* all this?"

"All over," Lexi replied.

Well, at least she was answering questions, albeit evasively. *I guess I'll have to be a little more specific.*

"Where were you right before you came here, to Jacksonville?"

"Just a group home."

"Where was that?"

Lexi shook her head, an expression on her face that seemed to say *"Come on, Liz, you know better than to ask that."*

"It's bad enough you know my name," Lexi replied tightly.

Liz had to give her that.

The waiter came back with their food, and when Lexi reached up to take her sandwich, Liz caught sight of her wrist—and the dark purple bruises circling it.

They were fresh!

"What happened?" Liz asked sharply, pointing at Lexi's wrist.

Lexi swallowed her first bite, looked to her wrist, and shrugged. "I already told you. Somebody wasn't happy when I had that bandage on a couple of weeks ago."

Liz caught the lie before it was even out of the girl's mouth. "Sorry, kiddo, I don't buy it." Liz leaned forward, trying to catch a closer glimpse of the wrist, but Lexi pulled it under the table. "I saw your arm last week, remember? I would have seen bruises like that, and besides, those bruises are fresh. So why don't you try telling me what *really* happened?"

Lexi leaned back in her seat with an exasperated huff, and Liz wondered whether she'd get the story at all. Part of her expected Lexi to jump up and run off, leaving her uneaten sandwich in a forgotten lump.

But that wasn't what happened.

"It's no big deal," Lexi said stiffly. Liz didn't believe that either, because to Lexi, *nothing* was a big deal.

"Maybe not to you, but it is to me," Liz tried.

"Why?"

"Because if someone's hurting you, you need to know how dangerous that is!"

Lexi laughed a little. "It's not dangerous. There's just this guy who's kind of power hungry. I guess we had a bit of a misunderstanding."

No, a misunderstanding didn't end in bruises.

"Tell me about this guy," Liz said, her insides churning with anger.

"Why? He's an idiot." Lexi paused. "He's just your typical guy. You know, he thinks guys are better than girls. He mostly says all these stupid things to me, but the other day, I told him off. So, he got ticked and slammed me into a wall." She shrugged again. "No big deal."

Maybe not to Lexi, but Liz wanted to kill the guy.

What kind of horrible person threw kids into walls? And what in the world had he done to her poor wrist?

She sucked in a long breath to calm herself. She needed to keep her head if she was going to keep asking questions. She *needed* to know what was going on down in those tunnels.

"What kinds of things does he say to you?" Liz asked carefully.

"I don't know, the usual stuff guys say." Lexi cleared her throat. "He's always telling me to come to his place for... well, you know. He calls me stupid things like 'sexy' or 'baby.' And, well, he likes to look at girls."

Lexi shrugged it off with a quiet laugh.

Liz felt sick to her stomach, imagining this poor defenceless girl down in some dark tunnel with a sex-craved male who was control-freakish enough to think he had the power to hurt her. She swallowed. "That's not good, Lexi."

Lexi shrugged again, and it made Liz want to shake some sense into the girl. Didn't she even care how she was being treated?

"It's not a huge deal," Lexi said. "It's not the worst thing that's happened to me."

Liz wanted to ask what was, but she recognized the look on Lexi's face; she was wishing she'd just kept her mouth shut.

"I don't like that people are hurting you, Lexi," Liz said, her blood boiling as Lexi nibbled away at her sandwich like nothing was wrong.

"I can take care of myself," Lexi replied with a mouthful of food.

"Please promise you will."

Lexi's whole demeanour changed. She seemed to shift from disinterested to perplexed. Liz wished she could see what was going through Lexi's head at that moment, but there wasn't any time to ask, because Lexi gulped back the last of her sandwich and sipped up the rest of her water in a hurry.

"Yeah, I will," she said passively, rising. "Um, thanks. You know, for lunch and everything."

Liz looked up at her, resisting every temptation to pull her back down and refuse to let her go anywhere without coming up with a solution that would suit them both.

"You're welcome," was all she could manage.

Lexi turned to leave, but before she did, she looked back, shuffling her feet.

"So, maybe I'll see you around sometime."

That was all Liz needed.

That was all it took to melt the icy rock that had formed in the pit of her stomach. No matter how much she wanted to protect Lexi, pull her out, save her from a terrible fate, she couldn't, and the helplessness bit her like a snake.

But Lexi's words gave her hope. *Maybe I'll see you around sometime.* That wasn't something that would have come out of the cold Lexi of two weeks ago. Something was changing; something was different.

And that was new.

"I hope so," Liz replied with a smile.

And just like that, Lexi was gone.

Liz glanced heavenward and pondered. None of this was any clearer than it had been two days ago, a week ago, two weeks ago, but the smallest bit of peace settled into her. Yes, there was still a tear inching down her cheek for what Lexi would be returning to, but Lexi's words rang in her ears like a symphony.

Maybe I'll see you around sometime.

Liz had no doubt in the world that her path would cross Lexi's once again.

CHAPTER 44

L E X I

Thursday, October 22
11:19 a.m.

Lexi took the long way back, but even that wouldn't give her enough time to sort everything out.

First, she couldn't get out of her head how weird it was that Liz just *happened* to find her when she fainted. How often did things like that happen? Of all the people in the city who could have found her, what were the odds of it being that doctor?

It was definitely strange, some kind of bizarre coincidence.

Then there was the whole brunch thing. Now that she was thinking, she shouldn't have let Liz buy her food. Nobody did things like that without wanting something in return.

So, what exactly did Liz want? Information? Was she trying to gain Lexi's trust only to gather enough facts to turn her in?

Hilary had once told her that people existed in the world who were genuinely good. She said that even though Lexi had been through a terrible ordeal, it wasn't good to let bitterness consume her. Not *everybody* was out to get her.

Yeah, well, that was before Hilary kicked her to the curb, wasn't it?

Sure, Liz seemed legit. They'd crossed paths three times now, and the doctor was still promising to keep her mouth shut. So far, she'd made good on those promises. Lexi didn't know what to think. There had to be more going on here.

If Star were here, she'd tell her to trust Liz, let her in, allow herself to become vulnerable and *feel* something.

Well, Star was a little too optimistic. The world didn't work like that, not the *real* world. Maybe it did in Star's world, where God was real.

God.

That was what Lexi remembered most from brunch: Liz's belief in God.

What had Liz said? *"God's funny that way. He can grab hold of you and reveal Himself in ways you never thought possible."*

Lexi imagined God as a tall green alien in a complicated spaceship, coming down to earth and beaming up Liz, taking her to some heavenly world where He probed and prodded before spitting her back out with a sudden belief in God.

Well, Lexi knew Liz meant it metaphorically, but she just didn't get it. What had Liz meant by God "revealing" Himself? Even the alien theory made more sense to her. But imagining God coming down and changing what she believed just like that, like some kind of magical formula... well, Lexi didn't buy it. That just seemed crazy.

What she *really* didn't get was how Liz could believe in God, even after her husband died.

So Liz knew what it was like to have bad things happen.

Where was the logic in that? The same logic that kept Lexi from even considering an all-loving God was flawed, because Liz had a rough time too, and she still believed in God.

Star's father had abandoned her, and her mother killed herself, but Star still believed in God.

What part of this equation was Lexi missing?

***

"Dude, where you *been?*" Barney was wide-eyed, arms flailing, a cheesy grin etched across his face.

She'd been in the Pit all of ten seconds, and Barney was his usual self.

"I told you, Barn, I was lookin' for food."

Sure, it wasn't the whole truth, but he hadn't *asked* for the whole truth.

"What's the matter, anyway?" Lexi paused. "Are you high?"

"No," Barney said with a chuckle. "But I found something really cool, and I have to show you! So, come on!"

So much for hiding out in her space to dwell on things that didn't matter anyway.

***

Lexi followed Barney down to the outskirts, where they came to an old landfill. The place was covered with dry dirt and piles of garbage. A distinct stench rolled across the forgotten plain.

"You brought me here to show off a pile of *trash*?" Lexi asked, unimpressed.

"Come on, man, I got better taste than that." He hopped the wire fence. "Just trust me."

Curiosity sparked, she jumped the fence after him.

"Careful you don't break your wrist again," Barney warned.

"It was a sprain!"

"Okay, close your eyes."

"Why?"

"Would you just *do* it?"

Hardly in the mood to argue, she did as she was told, feeling Barney's sticky fingers twining around her arm, slowly easing her forward.

"If you make me walk into something…"

"You won't," Barney said, and Lexi could almost sense his eyes rolling. "I thought you trusted me."

"Yeah, yeah, just hurry up."

Barney was careful, she had to give him that, and he was good about warning her when to step over something gross or sidestep something sharp.

"Don't you dare open your eyes!" he warned every five seconds or so.

"I won't!" Lexi would yell back.

Finally, after what seemed an eternity, Barney stopped and rotated her slightly.

"Okay." His voice was bursting with excitement, like a little kid's at Christmas. "Open!"

Lexi opened her eyes, squinting for a second to adjust to the blinding sunlight.

It didn't take long before she saw it.

A piano.

A forgotten piano, surrounded by heaps of rank trash, but a *piano*.

She suddenly forgot how to breathe.

"I come here every now and then. You can find some pretty sweet stuff sometimes, but today, I found this!" He circled the piano once, patting it on the top. "Anyway, I already tried it, and it still works! Isn't that awesome? I mean, you told me you used to play, so I thought..."

He couldn't even finish his sentence, he was so excited.

Lexi opened her mouth, but nothing came out.

"Come on!" Barney exclaimed. "Play me something."

Something was welling up inside of her, but she wasn't even sure what it was.

Whatever it was, it didn't feel good.

Mechanically she stepped toward the foreign instrument, eyes transfixed upon it. She gazed at the ivory keys; they were caked with dirt, but in her eyes they were still perfect.

She couldn't even swallow as she lowered herself onto a stool Barney found.

She couldn't move.

She stared hungrily at the keys, music just *waiting* to happen.

Then the music splashed through her mind like a wave, distant memories of pieces she'd played, wanted to learn, all locked away in a part of her she hardly remembered.

Until now.

Suddenly, there were flashes: the sound of Hilary's laughter, the smell of clean bed sheets, the taste of the chocolate cake Hilary had baked to celebrate Lexi's straight-A report card, the first-place trophy next to her bed from the best recital she'd ever played.

Then came Hilary's voice:

"Lexi, you're a natural."

"Don't give up; come on now."

"You're the next Mozart."

"Will you play for me again? Hearing you play always puts my mind at ease."

"Of course you should keep taking lessons. Why let all that talent go to waste?"

"You have no idea how proud I am of you."

Lexi's hands shook as she reached out and rested them on the keys. It was magnetic, how quickly her fingers found their places.

But no matter how much she longed to play, it wasn't happening.

"I..." she stumbled, realizing how shaky her voice was. Were those tears stinging her eyes? "I can't do it."

She could feel Barney staring at her.

"Why not?" he asked quietly.

"I don't remember how," she managed in a quiet whisper, shutting her eyes, ignoring the moist droplets beginnings in the corners. Reluctantly, she let her fingers slip away from the keys.

Glancing up, she caught the disappointment on Barney's face. She offered him a consoling smile.

She punched him playfully. "It's the thought that counts."

Barney shrugged, and, slowly, his lips curled into a smile. "Well, as long as we're here..."

He took Lexi's place and began to run his fingers across the piano, filling the landfill with the most broken noise Lexi had ever heard.

Well, at least it made her laugh, Barney making up words to some song that didn't exist.

But it would only distract her for a little while. She was still plagued by memories, like some distant tune of their own. No amount of noise or laughter could block out the music of her past.

Dear Journal,

If God isn't working in this whole thing with Lexi, then I'm going to have to start believing in coincidences. How else could you explain me leaving the house early to grab some brunch before work, only to see Lexi on the side of the street right before she collapses!

And I just happen to be there.

She was okay, but it was obvious she hadn't eaten in a while. Somehow I convinced her to let me buy her brunch.

Something was different about her this time. She was far more open with me than she's been the last two times I saw her. Sure, she's still evasive, but I doubt that will *ever* go away. She's been through too much to trust anyone, I guess.

I can't even begin to imagine what she's been through, and it scares me when I let my imagination wander. What could have been so horrible that she decided to stop feeling? When did she become so cold? I can't help but wonder if she's always been like this, or if there was ever a time when she was a happy, wholesome little girl. How badly has she been hurt? She's already told me her parents are dead, and today she told me she was in a group home before coming here, but is that all there is? Is there more to the story?

I'm sure there is. I bet I've only just scratched the surface of Lexi.

It was everything I could do to let her go today. I didn't want to let her go back to those tunnels, especially after seeing the bruises on her wrist. She told me about this boy who lives down there who makes all these derogatory comments toward her.

He was the one who hurt her wrist, all because she talked back to him! She's so vulnerable down there, and it kills me! She's just a kid, there's hardly anything to her, and she's got this guy roughing her up. The thought of him makes me more worried about Lexi than I've ever been. He wants to be in control, and that kind of power can be dangerous, and the worst part about it is that Lexi just doesn't care!

That scares me more than anything else. She needs to be careful, but I don't think she sees that.

It was so hard to watch her go, but I'll never forget what she said as she was walking away.

She said, "Maybe I'll see you around sometime."

I don't know where God is taking this, or if He is at all, but hearing Lexi say that gave me a bit of hope. I can't explain it, but to me it's a great step forward. She doesn't seem as willing to hide behind her mask anymore.

And that's huge!

—Liz

CHAPTER 45

L I Z

Friday, October 23
11:57 a.m.

Kathryn was already waiting for her when Liz arrived at the mall.

Only half an hour ago, Kathryn had called her up just as Liz was leaving the house. Kathryn was eager to get together, but Liz already had plans to go to the mall. There was something she needed to get, and it couldn't wait.

But as usual, Kathryn wasn't backing down.

"Well, that's perfect. You know me, I *love* shopping! Where can I meet you?"

And sure enough, there was Kathryn, waiting outside the mall with a grin on her face.

"Hey, Liz!" She smiled up at the sky. "I was just soaking up some sun while I waited for you. The other day, I decided I need a tan."

"Shut up," Liz said playfully. "You have more of a tan than I do, but you don't see me complaining."

"You don't have a tan because you never see the sun, little Miss Workaholic." Kathryn smirked. "Speaking of which, it's nice you actually have a day off."

"Well, maybe." Liz led the way into the mall. "I told them if there was an emergency and they're short-staffed, they can call me."

"See? Like I said—workaholic."

"Oh, don't start."

It didn't take long before Kathryn was pointing out all the stores she wanted to visit.

"What? I'm in desperate need of a new pair of shoes!" Kathryn defended herself.

"Do you know how much you sound like a teenager?" Liz asked when Kathryn actually squealed at a pair of stilettoes.

When was the last time Lexi had been shopping for new shoes?

"Um, listen, Kathy, I have to head over to the sporting goods store," Liz said as Kathryn ogled a pair of suede sandals. "Should I meet you back here?"

"No, I'll come with you," Kathryn replied, distancing herself from those sandals. "These are too expensive anyway."

Darn it. Liz had hoped to embark on this part of the shopping trip alone. That one thing she had to buy... well, she highly doubted Kathryn would understand.

But she'd have to deal with it. Kathryn was tagging along, whether she liked it or not.

"So, what do you need here?" Kathryn asked once they stepped into Sonka's Sports. "You taking up skiing or something?"

"In *Jacksonville*?"

"You *could* travel, you know." Kathryn followed her to the back of the store. "So, what are you looking for?"

"Just something I thought of yesterday," Liz answered as evasively as possible. Eventually she'd have to spill, but she'd rather put that off as long as possible.

Liz moved through the aisles blindly, having no idea where she was even supposed to find what she was looking for. It wasn't something she regularly kept on her shopping list.

Then again, it wasn't something most people kept on their shopping lists.

It took some time, but she found it, enclosed in a glass case.

Just what she was looking for.

"Pepper spray?" Kathryn asked incredulously. "What, are you planning on attacking your patients if they don't co-operate?"

Liz only smiled as she flagged down a nearby associate. "Excuse me," she called. "Can you open up this display for me?"

The middle-aged associate obliged and had his keys out in seconds, jiggling one of them into the lock, opening the case. As he stood by, Liz reached inside and perused the labels on the different canisters. Some were large and some small, and as she read through the chemical ingredients, she only sank deeper into her own confusion. How was she supposed to know what would do the trick?

Clearly, this wasn't her field of expertise. She turned to the sales associate.

"I don't know anything about this stuff," she admitted. "I need something that's easy to conceal, but it *has* to be powerful. Powerful enough to incapacitate a person."

She ignored the look of surprise Kathryn shot her way.

"Okay, your best bet is this product." The man pulled out a tiny tube-like canister, no bigger than a pen. "This is our most popular pick for girls, mostly because of its size. It's easy to hide and easy to use."

"How easy?"

"See this?" The associate tapped the top of the pen-like contraption. "This is the release valve. You just press it down, simple as pie, and here's where the spray is emitted."

Liz took note of its location. "And the spray itself," she continued. "How effective is it?"

She could almost feel Kathryn's curiosity getting ready to explode.

"Very. This has enough chemical to severely mess up your perp's eyesight for hours." He nodded at the product. "It's the number-one recommended product for young women by police. But it's only for emergencies!"

Liz nodded, then held out her hand. "I understand. I'll take it."

While the associate locked up the case, Liz beelined for the checkout, Kathryn following on her heels with a thousand questions.

"Is there something you need to tell me?" Kathryn asked in a worried voice. "Do you have a stalker? A pervert doctor who's messin' with you? Should we call the cops?"

Liz shook her head with a smile. "No, I'm fine," she replied simply as she paid for the pepper spray.

Liz only made it about ten steps from the sports store before Kathryn tugged on her arm, stopping her in the middle of the mall. Her eyes raged with impatience. "Tell me what this is for!"

Liz sighed. She had known she wouldn't be able to get away with buying pepper spray without having to explain it to Kathryn.

"It's for Lexi," she explained quietly.

"Who in the world is Lexi?"

"You know, that girl I found who'd sprained her wrist."

Kathryn's face dropped. "Oh, the street kid. Why are you buying her pepper spray?"

"Look, I ran into her yesterday, totally by chance." Chance? Oh yeah, she didn't believe in chance. "She passed out on the sidewalk while I was driving by. I stopped, checked on her. Anyway, long story short, I bought her some brunch. I'm pretty sure—"

"Oh Lizzie, please be careful! That kid's gonna expect food every time she sees you now. It's like when a stray cat comes to your door and you put out a bowl of milk because you feel bad for it. That cat will *always* come back," Kathryn warned. "Seriously, Liz, you don't want this kid getting too attached."

Liz shook her head, a heavy lump forming in her throat. "She's not the one getting attached, Kathryn." She paused. "But that's beside the point. She told me about this guy down in those tunnels who's been throwing her around, checking her out! I just hated the idea of her going back to that without any kind of protection. They're creeps, and I don't trust them."

234

"But you trust *her*," Kathryn pointed out. "What makes her different from the rest of them?"

Liz searched for a decent answer, something that would sound convincing, but she failed. "I don't know," she admitted. "But I'm scared for her. I don't know why we keep crossing paths, but I do know all I want is to go down to those tunnels, take her hand, and pull her out!"

"And then what, Liz?" Kathryn asked. "Say you *do* go down, pull her out, rescue her. You know where she'll end up? Back into Social Services where she probably came from, and how long do you think it's going to be before she just runs away again, comes back here, or goes somewhere worse? I think it's great you feel so strongly about wanting to help that poor girl, but maybe saving her is the *worst* thing you can do. She probably doesn't even want to leave."

Liz considered her friend's words in silence. Kathryn had always been her voice of reason, even before Kurt died. She'd never led her astray, never given her a word of advice that was damaging or harmful, and even now, Liz's brain told her Kathryn was right. All the facts were legit; it all added up.

But her heart contradicted her head.

Liz swallowed. "I had to at least buy her the pepper spray, Kathryn. I had to do something."

I may not be able to save her, but I can't just sit around and do nothing. Not anymore.

CHAPTER 46

L E X I

Sunday, October 25
10:49 a.m.

Lexi's life had become an awful lot like a television rerun. Every day was the same story, over and over—the same characters, the same setting, the same *everything.* Lost in the same crowd in the Pit, who did the same drugs, made out with the same people, painted the same murals. Struggling to sleep in the same dingy space, hearing the same fights, smelling the same smoke, seeing the same mould. Picking clothes from the same donation bin, having the same issues finding something that actually fit. Wandering around the same streets, checking the same cracks and corners for loose coins, and feeling the same sense of despair when another few hours passed and you only managed to scrounge up thirty cents.

Story of my life.

That was where Lexi found herself once again on Sunday morning, as the billowing clouds threatened rain. She'd ditched the tunnels early, feeling hungry, cranky, and sleep-deprived... desperate to be alone. She didn't even stop on her way out to yell a good morning to DV, like every other morning. She did, however, notice him working on a new part of his mural.

The baby birds were walking.

Well, good for them. At least *their* lives were progressing!

It had been almost a month—a month of circling these familiar streets and scrounging up loose change for survival. A month of being too good to steal.

Maybe Barney was right. This whole scene was about survival, wasn't it? She could easily starve to death out here if she wasn't careful. Would she be too good to steal *then*? Maybe it was time to accept that this was it, the end of the road, that her life was destined to be nothing more this.

Kicking at the same stone, hopelessness sucking the life out of her, she hardly heard the distant sound of a strumming guitar being played somewhere.

Somewhere.

She circled, wondering where the music was coming from this time.

And there it was.

A church.

She slowed, staring up the building with growing curiosity. It was huge, for one thing, towering majestically above its neighbours. Lexi took in its white stone walls, its high turrets and bright stained-glass windows. It felt so surreal; she hadn't seen a lot of churches in her lifetime, and she wasn't in the habit of stopping to take in their architecture, but this one grabbed her attention for whatever reason. The sheer size of it alone made her gawk.

Just like clockwork, it brought her back to the idea of God. It made her remember the passion in Liz's voice when she talked about Him. That woman spoke of God like He was the best thing in the world.

But why? Wasn't it *His* fault Liz had lost her husband?

Bitterness swept her up in its clutches again. She was about to move on when she spotted a figure on the steps of that church. A familiar figure, just sitting there, eyes closed, swaying back and forth, her dark red hair dancing with the steady music.

Star.

Well, Lexi figured, she should at least say hello. That was the polite thing to do, wasn't it?

She shuffled toward the church, feeling awkward. She'd never been inside a church—even *near* a church, really. Somehow it felt all wrong, like her foot touching that first step was some kind of hellish act. No, she didn't believe in God, but if He did exist, would He be ticked that she dared come near His building?

She swallowed a heavy lump and eased herself next to Star, whose eyes shot open when she heard her.

Her mouth relaxed into that peaceful smile she always wore, that smile that never seemed to change, even though the world around her was falling apart.

"Hi, CJ!" Star exclaimed, flashing her off-white teeth.

"What are you doing here?" Lexi gazed up at the church again, noticing something she hadn't noticed before—the image of a man stuck on some kind of wooden board in one of those stained-glass windows. Was the red supposed to be blood?

She shivered.

"I like going to church," Star replied simply.

"But... you're out here." Lexi couldn't help but notice. "Why aren't you inside?"

Star didn't answer, not right away. Though her smile never faltered, her eyes, Lexi noticed, looked sad.

"Well... I'm afraid to go inside," Star replied in a low voice. "But I like to hear the music."

Lexi's attention drifted back to the music that echoed within the church loud enough to reach their ears. It sounded like something new had started, and if Lexi listened hard enough, she could make out almost all the words.

"Amazing grace, how sweet the sound that saved a wretch like me. I once was lost, but now am found. Was blind, but now I see."

It was familiar. She'd heard it before. Where? Where had she—oh yes, it was from one of her mother's old records.

But that didn't make any sense. Her mother hadn't been religious. In fact, Lexi was pretty sure the song had come from an Elvis Presley record.

"Why're they singing Elvis songs in church?" Lexi asked, furrowing her eyebrows as the song continued.

Star laughed softly. "It's not an Elvis song. He *covered* it, but he didn't write it."

"Well, it doesn't make any sense."

"What doesn't?"

"The song. I *once* was lost, but *now* am found. What's it even talkin' about?" The anger floated off her tongue all too easily. Well, whatever. If God was the one responsible for where she'd ended up, she wasn't interested in sugar-coating what she said around Christians.

"Salvation," Star replied, nodding up at the image of the man on the wood. "The song's talking about salvation."

"Huh?" Lexi followed her gaze to that glass depiction of... whoever it was.

"That guy up there?" Star gestured. "That's Jesus. See how He's nailed to that cross? That's what He did for us all, for everyone. We're all screwed up, sinners, separated from God. I mean, think about it. God is completely holy and infinite. We're only human, making all kinds of mistakes and nowhere near holy. We couldn't *be* any more incompatible with God. That's why God sent Jesus, His Son. When He died on that cross, He died for our sins. He took our punishment, because that's exactly what we deserved— death. What I mean by salvation is accepting that as truth. You know, believing Jesus is the Son of God, that He came to die for our sins, being sorry, and letting Him be Lord of your life."

Lexi arched an eyebrow. "And that's what *you* did?"

"Yep. I accepted Jesus into my life not long after my mom died."

"Right." The music ended. Silence. "Well, it doesn't make any sense. Why would somebody willingly die like that if we're so screwed up?"

"That's the beauty of it!" Star exclaimed with the same passion Liz had spoken with. "It's because He loves us!"

"Love?" Lexi asked skeptically. "Nobody loves that much."

"But God isn't just anybody," Star said with a smile. "He's *God!*"

Lexi stared off down the street, struggling to understand it all. What was she missing in this search to figure out why people believed in God? What was it about Him that was so appealing?

Love?

Maybe that was it, but it didn't seem to fit. Nobody could love like *that*.

Could they?

"So what does it mean for Him—you know, *God*—to 'grab hold of you and reveal Himself'?" Lexi asked, going back to that conversation she'd had with Liz only a few days earlier.

"Why do you ask?"

Lexi shrugged. "Someone I know was talkin' about it. I didn't get it."

"Well, I can tell you how it happened with me," Star said. "I had a friend who believed in God, you know. She talked about Him all the time—"

"Like you do."

"Yeah." Star laughed a bit. "I guess so. Anyway, I was completely against the idea. I wasn't interested in believing in something that didn't make any sense to me. So instead, I decided to do things my way, because at least then I was in control of my own life. But... well, the night my mom killed herself, things definitely couldn't get any worse. Everything that ever mattered in my life was gone, and nothing made sense.

"Some time passed, and I can't explain it, CJ, but there was this *burden* on my heart. It's like my heart was saying there was still something there. I was asking all kinds of questions, looking for answers. What I kept coming back to was this: there was one Person who hadn't left me, and even though it was the one thing that made the least amount of sense to me, suddenly it made the most sense. He revealed Himself to me, and I broke down like crazy. I asked Jesus to come into my life and be in control when everything else felt like crap.

240

"And before you ask—no, CJ, my life didn't magically get better. I ended up *here*, didn't I? But I believe in the promises of the Bible, and Jesus said, 'I will not leave you as orphans. I will come to you.' I know I'm His child, and even though my mom's gone and I've got nobody to take care of me, *He's* taking care of me."

Lexi swallowed, trying to wrap her mind around all of it, all this new information, all these things she'd never heard about God before. She'd never heard about a *Son* of God. She'd never heard about Him dying on a cross for sins. She'd never heard about God being holy. It was all new to her, but she still didn't get it... if you couldn't *see* God, how could He reveal Himself without *showing* up?

She exhaled, frustrated. "It doesn't make sense," she muttered, feeling a headache coming on.

"Yeah, but that's what makes God so great. He's a mystery, but His love doesn't change." Star tilted her head. "Hey, just out of curiosity, what's got you so interested in this stuff all of a sudden?"

Lexi laughed, because really, she was just as surprised as Star. "I was talkin' to that doctor, you know, the one who fixed my arm. Anyway, I saw her on Thursday, and we ended up talking. She believes in God too, and she was going on about Him revealing Himself to her. I didn't get what she was saying, so I thought maybe you could explain it."

Star was silent for a moment, considering Lexi. "This doctor... Liz, right?"

Lexi couldn't believe Star actually remembered the name. "Yeah," she replied.

"I like her," Star confessed.

"Why? You haven't even *met* her!"

"I know. But I like her, because it means you're actually talking to someone."

"Okay, no!" Lexi exclaimed defensively. "She told me she believes in God, but that doesn't mean we *talk*."

Star smiled with a casual shrug. "If you say so, but at least you're talking to someone, since you don't talk to anybody down in the tunnels."

"I'm not talking to anyone! Not *anyone*, not Liz! You can even ask her!" she shouted, jumping to her feet. Her irritation had reached its boiling point. "I didn't want to find her! I didn't want to talk to her! It was all random, coincidence, whatever! It didn't mean *anything!*"

Star still had that smile on her face. "I don't believe in coincidence," she said quietly.

That was about all Lexi could take. She stormed down the steps and up the street, anger searing through her blood like a virus. She shouldn't have stopped to say hi to Star, she shouldn't have told her anything about Liz, she should have kept it all to herself, like she was so good at doing. "Curiosity killed the cat," wasn't that the expression? Her curiosity about what Liz said was responsible for this, and for what? Now she was ticked off and even more confused.

The tension was killing her, and the worst part about it all was that she didn't even know why she cared so much in the first place.

CHAPTER 47

L I Z

////////////////////////////////

Sunday, October 25
12:02 p.m.

Liz waited with the impatience of a child.

Church was over. The organ instrumental that had drifted through the church at the end of service had come to a close, and congregants slowly filed their way out, pausing to shake their pastor's hand.

She waited alone, seeing as Kathryn and her family had already taken off. They'd invited her over for lunch, but Liz opted for a rain check. She had to speak to Pastor Reid.

This was one conversation she didn't want under a spotlight.

I just hope he's not too busy. Liz sighed, fiddling with her purse's strap. *But I have to talk to somebody, and soon.*

Finally, after what seemed an eternity, the last of the stragglers vacated the small building, leaving only Liz and Pastor Reid. When he noticed her, he smiled warmly, and Liz already felt her nerves settling. The man was so full of God's light, so wise, so peaceful about everything. His kindly smile creased dimples in his cheeks, and his brown hair with flecks of grey emanated a fatherly air. Maybe that was why everyone felt so comfortable around him.

"Hello, Liz!" He took her hand in his own. "It's so good to see you again this Sunday. You've been awfully busy, haven't you? We miss you at Thursday Bible studies."

Wow. When was the last time she had attended *that* class?

"Yes, I know; I miss you all, too. You gotta love the hectic schedules, but I've been happy it allowed me to get to church these past few Sundays."

"Me too." Reid paused. "So, what can I do for you? I couldn't help but notice you were waiting for everybody else to leave."

That was another thing about Pastor Reid. He was intuitive. He could see past any walls you tried building around yourself.

Sometimes it was terrifying!

"Well, I understand if you're busy, but I wondered if you had a few minutes," Liz replied, clearing her throat. "I'd like to talk to you about something."

Did she sound as nervous as she felt?

She wasn't surprised when Pastor Reid agreed and joined her in the pew.

"What's going on, Liz?" Reid asked, straight to the point.

Liz caught hold of his deep green eyes, focussed intently on her. He was like that—a great listener. That was why she had chosen him. She just hoped he responded a little better than everyone else in her life had.

Starting from the beginning, Liz recounted her Lexi story, from the first time she spotted her across the street from Micky Jo's to stumbling across the same girl with a sprained wrist only days later. She felt her heart kindling all over again when she spoke of Lexi's return the next week, of the chance encounter on the sidewalk, and of her hesitant acceptance to have brunch with Liz. She shared with her pastor all of what Lexi had confided, being careful to leave out anything that might identify her specifically. She wouldn't even tell him Lexi's name. Though Liz doubted she had anything to worry about with Reid, she'd promised Lexi she wouldn't say anything. She wouldn't break a promise to that girl, not for anything.

Regardless, Lexi needed help.

Reid listened with ferocious intensity, his eyes sparkling when Liz spoke of the coincidental meetings and even misting up when she shared what she knew of Lexi's past.

"I don't know, pastor. I don't understand why I feel this way. It certainly came out of left field, and I'm not making much sense of it, even now. It's like I have this strange protective drive toward her. All I want to do is pull her out, protect her, keep her safe, but that's not my job, is it?" Liz exhaled. "It just breaks my heart to know she's down there, all alone, maybe scared, maybe in pain, and maybe even in danger. I don't like anything about this situation. It's not right! Nobody should have to live there, away from people. And what doesn't make any sense is my sudden desire to fix it, to fix her life. I've never given a second thought to these kids, so why does this one girl break my heart?"

Pastor Reid waited, his silence encouraging her to go on.

"She's just so cold. She doesn't seem to care about anything, and certainly not about the boy who's throwing her into walls. How can she even sleep at night? Isn't she terrified? I know I am. I went to the mall yesterday and bought her pepper spray, but I don't even know if she'll *take* it from me, because she doesn't seem to think she's in danger. She shrugs it all off like it's nothing." Liz gripped her hair. "I mean, listen to me! I know how I sound, but I don't know what to do. I don't know whether this burden has been placed on my heart by God, and if it has been, is He just calling me to pray for her? I've been praying for her every day, but is it possible God keeps letting our paths cross because I'm meant to do something more for her? I really want to help her, but what can you do for someone who doesn't want help?"

Liz tried to swallow the lump in her throat, those darn tears threatening again. "I just... all I want is to hug all her pain away, but she won't even let me in."

She was staring down at her clasped hands, afraid to meet her pastor's eyes. Jenn, Kathryn, and her mother all disapproved of Liz's sudden interest in this Tunnel Kid, claiming everything from her being too involved to being emotionally shut down to being in *danger*. All she wanted was affirmation, but if her pastor agreed with everyone else... well, she'd have to let this go, wouldn't she?

But like the great guy that he was, he didn't let her down. "Liz, what you're feeling is good, and nowhere *near* wrong. Those children living in the tunnels are hurting greatly. They are God's children just as much as you or me, but they feel so forgotten. Think about where these kids come from. Most of them have been abandoned, betrayed, abused, hurt by the adults in their lives. This is exactly what drove them to this place, but they're still children, and it's heartbreaking that something as simple as trust has been shattered, betrayed by their parents, foster parents, family members, whomever.

"Whatever the case, it's no surprise those kids stay away from us. They don't trust us. It's why they're all so cold. You've already noticed this girl has a cold attitude toward life. Well, that's probably why. Somebody in her life really let her down, and the only way she knows how to cope is to shut down, emotionally speaking. I suppose it's a defence mechanism."

Pastor Reid smiled knowingly. "They need to see that they *aren't* forgotten by God, but how difficult must that be for them when they've been forgotten by everyone else?"

A blanket of peace settled upon Liz's heart. So it wasn't just her. Kathryn, Jenn, her mother... they just didn't understand. But neither did Liz, not really. She didn't know what it was like to feel forgotten, sentenced to a life on the streets because there wasn't a single person left who cared.

"But why *just* this one girl?" Liz asked, still conflicted. "There are hundreds of kids like her. Why don't I feel overwhelmed by any of the other street kids?"

Something sparkled behind Pastor Reid's eyes, a look that said he was using his X-ray vision to see past one of her walls. Liz was worried before he even opened his mouth.

"Have you considered, Liz, that perhaps the reason you're so drawn to this young lady is because you see a piece of yourself in her?" Reid asked, a small smile curling his lip as though he'd uncovered a hidden mystery.

Liz, however, had no idea what he was talking about.

246

"That's silly. How could I? Her and I, we're so different. For one thing, I'm twenty years older. I've never been poor. We always lived well, went to private schools. I've never known what it's like to be without money. I've never been abused, hurt, betrayed, or anything like what you were talking about." She was rambling now, and her heart pounded. Why? What did she have to be nervous about?

"Maybe not." Reid shrugged casually. "But, there is *one* similarity I can see."

That's what Liz was nervous about; she was afraid to find out.

"You refuse to acknowledge your pain over losing Kurt. No, let me finish. You *know* it hurts, but you don't let yourself hurt. Instead, you throw yourself into work. There, you can numb yourself from reality." Reid leaned back with a raised eyebrow. "Isn't that what your girl does, numbs herself to the pain? You said she seems so cold about everything. Well, that's her way of surviving. Maybe the reason you feel so connected with her is because both of you have no idea where to begin in terms of dealing with your feelings."

Liz's chest felt like it was caving in on itself.

No. He was wrong. He *had* to be. It didn't matter that Jenn had told her almost the same thing, it didn't matter that Kathryn had attested to it more than once, it didn't matter that even her *mother* thought so. Just because four people believed something, that didn't make it true.

Then why was she feeling so deeply convicted?

She opened her mouth but found herself speechless.

Pastor Reid jumped in. "I know. It's hard to accept, but somewhere deep down, you know it's true. You're just not quite ready to believe it. That's okay. It's a lot to consider, but know this: I do not believe it was accidental, your path crossing this girl's. I believe God will show you why you feel so drawn to her, in time." He smiled warmly. "Or perhaps He already has. You just can't see it yet."

Somehow, Liz managed a nod, but her mind was buzzing with uncertainties, confusion, fear, sadness, anger. She wished she could ask her pastor to figure it all out for her, but even she knew better than that. This was between her and God now. Maybe Pastor Reid was just there to point her to the truth.

Was it truth?

She felt so lost.

"Your presence in this girl's life has been good, and will continue to be good. If nothing else, you are showing her that we're not all harmful people who betray trust." Pastor Reid winked at her. "That's a step in the right direction."

Dear Journal,

I met with Pastor Reid today, to talk about Lexi.

He affirmed my feelings but left me more confused than ever.

He said the reason I feel drawn to her is because I also numb myself from the pain I feel over Kurt's death.

And that's what Lexi does, to protect herself.

Is this true? Is this what's happening? Do I freeze myself emotionally, shut down, become numb because I don't want to face it?

Is that what I've been doing all this time?

I just don't know how to take all of this.

—Liz

CHAPTER 48

L E X I

Monday, October 26
10:17 a.m.

She woke up to Barney poking at her face.

"Dude, what is it with you sleepin' in all the time?"

Lexi's groaned. *What a wakeup call.*

"I didn't get much sleep," she admitted, slowly easing herself up into a sitting position. Oh, it felt good to stretch out her back. "I swear, this floor gets harder every night."

"Yeah." Barney nodded knowingly. "It don't matter how long you've been here, that's the one thing that don't grow on you."

Lexi yawned. "Anyway, what're you wakin' me up for? I could have used a couple more hours."

"Yeah, sorry." Barney scratched the back of his neck. "I have a favour to ask."

Yeah, she figured as much.

"What?" she asked, expecting the worst. "You need me to go with you to Slick's again?"

"No, but it kinda has somethin' to do with him. I have to get some money today so I can grab my stash, but the thing is, I owe Slick for the last two batches, and he won't give me nothin' else until I pay him."

Lexi sighed, rubbing her eyes. "See? This is why you need to quit smoking that crap."

250

"If you smoked it, you wouldn't wanna quit, either," Barney said irritably.

"Okay, okay, whatever." Lexi wished the fog in her head would clear. "What do you need me to do? It better not be anything stupid."

"Nah, all you gotta do is back me up."

He uncoiled a gold chain from his palm, a gold chain attached to a pearl. Lexi didn't know much about jewellery, but the thing looked really cheap.

"I found this in the dump yard," he said. "It's a piece of crap, I mean, just *look* at it, but I thought I could pawn it off, get some money. I figure if we come up with the right story, we can get something decent for it. That's where you come in."

Barney's lips curled into a sneaky smile.

"See, nobody will believe it's mine. I mean, why would I have some old piece of jewellery? But if you say it's *yours*, it's more legit, you know, 'cause girls own jewellery. Just tell 'em it belonged to, like, your great-grandmother or something. Say she got it during the war. You can lie pretty good, right? Anyway, if they believe it, they'll pay us for it, and I swear, if we get a *lot*, I'll split it with you."

"So you want me to lie for you." Lexi crossed her arms, unimpressed.

Barney nodded with a desperate grin.

"And what makes you think I'd be so convincing?" Lexi asked. "I've never even *owned* a piece of jewellery. What would I know about it?"

"Come on, CJ, please?" He stuck out his lower lip for good measure. "I'd do it for you."

Lexi groaned. He looked so pathetic.

But it was true: he would do it for her. In fact, wasn't that what he'd been doing? No doubt about it, she owed him big for everything he'd done for her, but that was what made Barney so great. He never *expected* anything in return.

How could she say no?

"Fine," Lexi obliged, standing up. "But don't come crying to me if they chase us out just 'cause I can't tell them what year the war was."

***

"Are you serious?" Barney asked with a sarcastic scoff. "As if you can even compare them!"

"There's nothing to compare," Lexi replied as the two wandered toward the pawn shop. "I'm just right, and you're wrong."

Barney raised his voice a little. "Yeah, well, you're nuts if you think that!"

"*I'm* nuts?" Lexi laughed. "If you're saying Barney Rubble wins for best cartoon character, you're the one who's crazy!"

"Come on, he's hilarious! He's short, his kid could beat up anyone in the neighbourhood, and his wife is *hot!*" Barney shot up an eyebrow. "How can you even think Tweety Bird could compare to that?"

"Being short isn't funny!" Lexi spat. "And anyway, Tweety is way more hilarious. First of all, he's a talking *bird.* That should be enough of an argument right there! Everyone expects Barney to talk, 'cause he's human, but a talking bird is actually creative. Besides, Tweety is smart. How many birds do you know who can outwit a cat every time?"

"Oh yeah? Well, Barney's environmentally friendly. His car doesn't use gas."

"Except he doesn't even have his own car. Fred always drives him around. So, he's a mooch."

"Whatever!" Barney said. "Tweety looks like a girl, and he does the same thing every episode—escape Sylvester. Big whoop."

"Barney doesn't know anything about fashion! All he wears is a sack!"

"Tweety walks around *naked!*"

"He's a *bird!*"

"Hello, Lexi."

It was another voice.

Not Barney's.

Lexi's insides turned to ice when she heard it. Her real name. *Lexi.*

Barney was still bickering, as though nothing was amiss. He probably hadn't even heard it. Lexi, on the other hand, turned, and sure enough, there was Liz, the only person in this entire city who knew her real name.

Barney, finally figuring out Lexi wasn't fighting back on the Barney vs. Tweety debate, turned and realized they had company.

Lexi couldn't breathe. This was it. Her cover was blown.

"Hi, Lexi; how are you?" Liz asked, acknowledging Barney with a smile and nod.

But Barney didn't nod back. In fact, he wasn't even looking at Liz. No, he was staring at Lexi. Staring hard.

"Lexi?" Barney whispered, his eyes boring a hole into her.

Lexi swallowed. No doubt he wanted an explanation, and why shouldn't he? He'd never heard that name before. He wasn't *supposed* to hear it.

"I'm fine," Lexi said quickly to Liz, seizing a firm grip of Barney's arm. "But I gotta go."

She didn't stick around long enough for anything else. She imagined Liz still standing there, shell-shocked by Lexi's disappearing act, but right now she couldn't care less. She had to get out of there before Liz brought up brunch or anything else Lexi had failed to mention to Barney.

As soon as she and Barney rounded a corner, Barney yanked his arm from her grasp and glared, his arms crossed.

"Okay, *first* of all, who was that?" he asked, narrowing his bushy eyebrows.

Lexi fought the urge to laugh. If he was trying to be intimidating, he was failing miserably. But eager to leave this whole thing behind them, she shrugged like it didn't matter. "That was the doctor who wrapped my arm," she replied.

"Oh! So you guys are all, like, buddy-buddy now?" His voice was laced with a hint of sarcasm.

Lexi rolled her eyes. "Come on, Barn."

Barney unravelled his arms after a few seconds and succumbed to a fit of giggles. "I'm just messin' with ya." He paused. "Seriously, she seems nice."

"I guess."

"So... Lexi. Another code name, I presume? Why didn't you just tell her 'CJ' like you told the rest of us? Why remember different names for different people?"

Lexi felt her cheeks warming. So, he figured Lexi was another code name. He had *that* much faith in her. It would be easy to keep up the lie, to go on about how she thought it would be better to make up different names to make sure she was safe.

But guilt ate away at her conscience. This was *Barney*, one of the closest friends she'd ever had. Even in her head, before it was on her tongue, the lie weighed heavy.

She heaved a sigh, hesitating. "Lexi's my real name, okay?"

Barney stopped, glanced at her sideways. "What? But... how did Lynn know it?"

"It's Liz."

"Whatever." He didn't sound impressed.

"Look, when I fell and hurt my wrist that day, I said my name. Not on purpose, just, you know, 'Way to go, Lexi.' That doctor heard me say it when she came over. I know it was stupid, but I didn't tell her 'cause I *wanted* to. I didn't even know she heard it, not until she used it."

Barney didn't say anything at first, and Lexi felt her throat closing up. She'd gone and done it now. She'd broken the unwritten rule: *never* tell anyone your real name. Anyone who knew your real name was an enemy. Sure, Liz didn't seem like the enemy type, but that was the second unwritten rule: never trust *anyone*.

Finally, after a painful silence, Barney let out a long whistle. "Man, Sapph's gonna *kill* you!"

"She won't be killing anyone," Lexi said as she took a menacing step toward him. "Because you're gonna keep your mouth shut!"

Barney shook his head, laughing. "Relax, Ceej, I'm not tellin' anyone."

His smile was just enough to reassure her.

Well, at least that was out of the way.

Or not...

"So," Barney said, "this is a little weird. I mean, knowing your real name. I don't know *anybody's* real name down there."

"Yeah, I guess," Lexi said noncommittally.

"Lexi, Lexi..." Barney said it a couple more times, letting it roll off his tongue. "It's nice. Short for Alexandra?"

"Alexis, actually."

"So what does it mean?"

"What does *what* mean?"

"Your name, idiot. What does your *name* mean?"

Lexi rolled her eyes. "Mean? How should I know? My parents never wanted me. It's not like they were studying up on baby names. When I was born, all my folks did was use the name that was on the crib next to mine in the nursery, wrote it up for my birth certificate. So yeah, somewhere out there, there's another girl with the same first name *and* middle names as me." She managed a smile. "Talk about creativity, huh?"

Barney wasn't laughing.

"My name's Patrick," he said after a pause. "My real name, I mean."

Lexi's breath caught in her throat, and she shot him a look. Now *he'd* broken the rule. If Sapphire ever got wind of this conversation, they'd both be skinned alive!

"You didn't have to tell me that," she said quietly.

"I know." Barney shrugged. "But hey, we're buds right?"

"Yeah, we are."

"Awesome. But we need to do some damage control here. We should pinky swear on it. You know, swear we'll never reveal each other's real name, anytime, life or death. Deal?" Barney thrust out his pinky finger with a corny grin plastered on his face.

"What is this, fifth grade?" Lexi scoffed.

But she twined her own pinky around Barney's anyway. Once linked, she couldn't help but giggle.

"So," she said as they reached the pawn shop. "What does Patrick mean?"

"I dunno," Barney said with an awkward shrug. "It's Irish. I think it means 'noble' or something."

"That's pretty fitting."

"Yeah, yeah. Very funny," Barney said, punching her playfully.

"No, I'm serious." Still, she punched him back. "You're a good guy."

Barney's cheeks turned red, and Lexi snickered to herself as something welled up inside of her. It wasn't romantic—nothing like that—but Barney was the closest thing to a friend Lexi had had in a long time. He saw her like nobody *ever* had. He saw her for who she was, and accepted her. It was clear to her: he'd never hurt her, he never *had*, and he stuck by her, even though she hadn't asked him to.

Lying for him at a pawn shop didn't seem so horrible anymore.

Dear Journal,

I'm pretty sure I did something really stupid today.

I was heading over to get some coffee, and there she was again.

Lexi.

I was so happy to see her, overjoyed she was safe for another day. When she passed me, I couldn't help but say, "Hello, Lexi."

That was obviously a mistake, because she wasn't alone. I can't even express the look on her face. Betrayal, fear, a deer caught in headlights. I clued in that I'd messed up right away. Kathryn once told me that they don't use their real names down there. Well, she must have been right, because Lexi's friend looked at her like she was growing a third arm. He'd never heard it before.

Well, she took off like the devil was chasing her.

I feel *horrible!* If they have street names, they must have them for a reason! I shouldn't have said it, but it just came out.

Idiot, I'm such an idiot! I just hope it doesn't mean any kind of danger for her. That scares me.

I wanted to give her the pepper spray, but she ran off so quickly, and after saying her name like that, I wasn't about to chase her down. I did enough damage for one day. I hope I'll see her again. To give her the pepper spray, and to apologize.

—Liz

CHAPTER 49

L I Z

Wednesday, October 28
2:15 p.m.

She could hardly keep her eyes open.

Liz hated night shifts. That was when you got all the binge-drinkers, victims of gang fights, drug abusers.

Everything bad seemed to happen at night.

It was midafternoon now. Her shift should have ended at 10:00 that morning, but with the ER as packed as it was, she stayed longer, rushing around while her body strained to keep up. She pressed on, ignoring the dull aches of fatigue until 2:00, when Jenn ordered her to go home and get some sleep. Liz was reluctant, but she finally agreed—only after making Jenn promise to call her if it got busy again. Jenn promised, though judging by the look on her face, she wouldn't call.

Maybe that was okay.

Liz fought off an erupting yawn as she turned down Main Street, on her way home. Maybe she would make herself another cup of coffee, lounge in front of the television for a while, catch a soap opera, maybe drift off. Maybe she could do a workout. Or she could call Kathryn. No, she'd still be at work.

Not a lot to do on a Wednesday afternoon.

I miss work already. How sad is that?

Liz occasionally turned her attention to the crowd, scanning those unfamiliar faces for the one that stood out. Lexi. She was *always* searching for Lexi, praying for another encounter. Especially after Monday, after Lexi ran away.

Guilt had plagued her ever since, and, of course, she imagined the worst—some powerful gang member in charge, some power-hungry guy, maybe even the same one who'd bashed Lexi against a wall. Maybe he had found out about Lexi's real name. What kinds of horrible things would he do to the poor girl? Beat her, spit on her, banish her from the tunnels to fend for herself?

Or worse?

Then, like some kind of magic mind trick, as though thinking about her was enough to make it happen, Liz spotted Lexi dawdling along, hands stuffed into her pockets.

That was when it hit Liz like a ton of bricks.

Oh no. The pepper spray!

Her stomach knotted.

She'd left it at home.

That was twice now. *Twice* she'd seen Lexi since she bought the pepper spray, and *twice* she'd failed. Sure, she could always drive on and hope she'd pass by Lexi again later when she actually had the pepper spray... but who was to say that would actually happen? Besides, by then it could be too late.

She didn't want to think about it. No, she needed to give it to Lexi now.

She pulled over, parked by the library, and rolled down her window just as Lexi was passing.

"Hey," Liz called out, careful not to use her name this time. She had to call a couple of times before Lexi finally cocked her head.

Liz's stomach dropped when Lexi looked less than impressed. Well, what had Liz expected? A beautiful smile, an eager recognition? *"Oh Liz, I'm so happy to see you!"*

Maybe one day, but not today.

Lexi stole a hurried glance up and down the street before hesitantly approaching the car window. Liz felt terrible. How much trouble had Lexi been in for the name thing? Did anybody even know about it, besides that other kid? Was she even *allowed*

259

to talk to anybody? If someone saw her talking to Liz, would it be frowned upon?

"Listen, I'm sorry about the other day," Liz said quietly, staring up at Lexi, who wouldn't meet her eyes. "You know, when I said your name. I didn't really know... you guys don't use your real names down there, do you?"

Lexi only had to shake her head, and Liz felt the guilt virus hit again. If only she could travel back in time and leave out Lexi's name. She would have, in a heartbeat, if it meant protecting the young girl.

Lexi was still watching down the street. It made Liz nervous. Any minute now, she expected someone to pounce out of some alleyway and grab Lexi. What would Liz do then?

She kept her cell phone in hand, just in case.

"I'm sorry," Liz said, trying to smile, hoping to case the tension.

Lexi only shrugged. Well, Liz hadn't really expected much else, but at least Lexi wasn't running off.

"So, what do they call you down there?" Liz asked before she could think about it. Why did she want to know that? Why did she even care?

It hardly mattered, because she *did* want to know, and she *did* care. She wanted so much to cross over into Lexi's world, get inside her head, to understand why she was the way she was. Any glimpse into the girl's life would be welcome, even if it was something as simple as a code name.

"CJ," Lexi said quietly, her head down, hair falling over her face. Maybe she was trying to hide herself, in case someone passed.

"Why CJ?" Liz asked curiously. "Does it stand for something?"

"Yeah, my middle names." Lexi paused, clearing her throat. "Carolyna Jade."

Liz felt her heart warming inside of her. She had never even asked what her middle names were, but Lexi told her anyway.

Progress. That was progress.

"They're beautiful," she said, meaning it.

Lexi shrugged.

Well, Liz couldn't keep the poor girl standing here any longer. She was a sitting duck. Any one of these teens walking by could be a Tunnel Kid, could recognize Lexi, could already be sprinting down to the tunnels to report Lexi's crime.

Now was the time, if there would ever be one.

"Listen, I know this is probably going to sound really weird, and I understand if you'd rather not, but I have something for you. Typical me, though, I left it at home. I know how it sounds, but I have the memory span of a goldfish sometimes." Liz smiled. "What do you say? Will you come with me to get it?"

She waited, nervous. Did she actually expect Lexi to say *yes?* Every kid on the planet knew better than to get into cars with strangers.

But... Lexi wasn't just any kid.

Lexi chewed on her lip as she considered Liz's request, bouncing from one foot to the other. What thoughts were reeling through the girl's head? If they were anything like Liz's, then Lexi was paranoid someone would jump out from the shadows and catch Lexi getting into a car with the enemy, an adult.

Well, whatever Lexi was thinking, she still managed a small nod. "Okay," she said so quietly Liz could hardly hear her. "I'll come."

Liz was shocked. She hadn't expected a yes. She'd imagined the thousand and one ways Lexi could say no, but she'd said yes.

Yes.

Nodding at Lexi, Liz stretched over to unlock the passenger side door, and Lexi hesitantly lowered herself into the car. Merging back into traffic, Liz felt blown away. Did this mean Lexi was finally trusting her?

Maybe, but there was still a small part of Liz that worried over Lexi's motives. What if some stranger had pulled over instead, told her he had something for her at his house? Would she have gotten in the car with him? Did she really trust Liz, or had she just stopped caring about what happened to her?

Just thinking about it made her stomach drop.

***

They drove in silence, but as they turned onto Liz's street, she noticed the expression on Lexi's face completely transform as she ogled the passing houses, mouth agape. She seemed... fascinated, sizing those houses up like she'd never seen anything like them, like they were castles.

It broke Liz's heart. She lived in a decent neighbourhood. Most of the real estate here wasn't cheap, and it showed. The houses were fairly large, with spacious backyards and modern landscaping. Still, Liz never thought of her own house as huge, at least not in comparison to her parents', but when she pulled into her driveway, Lexi gazed at her house wide-eyed, brown eyes sparkling.

Liz swallowed. *What kind of house did Lexi live in before?* Did she have her own room? Was it painted her favourite colour? Was it filled to the brim with toys and books? Was there someone who tucked her in at night?

Lexi never shared much of anything about her life, but Liz was learning more about her all the time.

L E X I

Wednesday, October 28
2:34 p.m.

Her place was a freaking mansion!

Lexi knew Liz was a doctor, but still.

Almost forgetting why she was here in the first place, Lexi hopped out of the car and went back to gawking at the massive yellow house. The high windows had white trim with shutters, and red flower pots with sunflowers rested on a few of the sills. There was a chimney, which meant there was a fireplace. There was a porch—an actual *porch*—and a cobblestone walkway. It was all so... well, it was pretty awesome.

While Liz locked her car, Lexi wondered to herself how only one person could live here. She knew Liz had been married, but her husband was gone now. Why would Liz want to keep living in such a huge house, all alone?

I mean, it would take forever to clean.

The house made her reflect on the biggest house she'd ever lived in. She backtracked, remembered all the foster homes, all the times she'd moved, and came to one conclusion. She guessed it would have to be the brick house on Morgan and Third: the Norwoods'.

Theirs was a four-bedroom house, which sucked, because there were seven people living in it. Ray and Shelley had their own room, of course, and Caleb had his own room, but Melanie and

Suzie had to share, and the two foster kids, Lexi and Kyla, shared the smallest room, hardly spacious enough for their two beds.

But even that house was nothing in comparison with Liz's. The Norwoods only had one bathroom, and the house used to only have three bedrooms, but a wall had been built in the one bedroom to make a second room for the foster kids. That wall was so thin that Lexi always heard Caleb crying himself to sleep next door.

I bet Liz doesn't have problems with thin walls. She probably has seven *bathrooms.*

"You coming?" Liz called from up on the porch.

Lexi reeled herself back to the present. She hadn't even realized Liz was already at the front door. She slowly walked up the front steps.

Being here felt so strange.

Maybe that's 'cause I'm not supposed to be here.

If she thought about it, how well did she really know this woman? Was it really such a smart idea to come out here without anybody knowing where she was?

Oh, who was she kidding? Lexi was nothing, garbage, the lowest of the low, forgotten, reduced to nothing more than another statistic in some research about runaways. Did it really matter whether or not this was a smart idea? Did she even care anymore?

Besides, Liz didn't seem like a threat, and Lexi's curiosity was sparked. What was it Liz had for her?

"Your house is really nice," Lexi finally said. It seemed like a polite thing to say.

What else do you say to someone who invites you to their house? It wasn't like Lexi had been invited to a lot of places. She was usually forced into them.

"Thank you," Liz replied, holding the door open to let Lexi through first.

Lexi was floored all over again! The inside of Liz's house was fifty times nicer than the outside. The walls were painted a calming cream colour, the stairs leading to another floor were plushly carpeted, and above her, in the front foyer, hung a crystal chandelier, which came to life when Liz turned the hall lights on, dropping her keys on an oak end table.

"I..." Lexi swallowed, catching sight of Liz's kitchen in her periphery; it was even bigger than the kitchen at Everidge! "I've never seen a house this big."

Liz sighed, looking around. "Would you believe me if I said my parents' house, the one I grew up in, was bigger?" She laughed when Lexi widened her eyes. "Honestly, I don't understand why anyone needs this much space. I would be happy with just a bedroom and a coffeemaker."

Lexi found herself wanting to laugh but resisted. No, she couldn't let herself get sucked in too far. She was only here to get whatever Liz wanted to give her, then get out.

As Liz led the way deeper into the house, Lexi took in every detail—the paintings hanging on the walls, the beautifully finished furniture, the way everything matched, like something out of an old TV sitcom. It was like the kind of house Lexi always dreamed of as a little girl. They were all gigantic, with matching furniture and families that didn't hurt each other. Yeah, they had it made.

But that was TV. Families like that didn't exist in real life.

They stopped in what Lexi guessed was the living room, a thick white carpet squishing under her feet. She distantly wondered if this was what it felt like to walk on the moon.

"Wait here; I'll be right back," Liz said suddenly, and Lexi turned in time to watch the woman scurry from the room.

Lexi swallowed. She'd left her alone. Why? Wasn't she afraid that Lexi, a good-for-nothing street kid, would do something wrong? Vandalize? Steal something? There was a forgotten gold watch laid out on the coffee table. It would be so quick and easy for Lexi to swipe it. Liz would never know any different.

Lexi would never do it, but how did Liz know that? Street kids had a bad reputation. Why would Liz trust her enough to leave her alone in such a high-class place?

It was enough to make Lexi's head spin. Nobody had ever trusted her before.

Well, maybe Hilary, but Hilary ended badly, so it didn't really count.

Lexi moved through the living room, slowly, so she could enjoy the plushy sensation under her feet with every step. When she came to the fireplace, a smile touched her lips; there was an actual *log* inside. She pictured Liz lounging on the sofa, the fire burning away while she read a book and sipped hot chocolate. Maybe there would be some classical music playing. Some Debussy, maybe some Bach.

How perfect...

And just like the houses on TV, Liz's mantelpiece held pictures. Simple black frames were homes to four school pictures, the kind they took on picture day.

Lexi had hated those days; it hurt to fake a smile. But the kids in these pictures, they weren't faking anything.

Lexi stood frozen, hardly budging as Liz's footsteps fast approached. Swallowing, Lexi continued to gaze into each of those kids' eyes, seeing a slight resemblance in all of them to Liz.

"Are they your kids?" she asked.

"No." Liz sighed beside Lexi, staring at the same pictures. "I don't have any kids. Kurt and I... my husband... well, we always wanted to have children, but..."

Lexi bowed her head. Why did she have to bring it up? Why couldn't she just learn to keep her big mouth shut?

"Anyway, they *are* related to me. They're my nieces and nephews," Liz said after a short silence, pointing at the frames. "The two boys belong to my older brother. That's Liam. He's twelve now and big into sports, nothing like his little brother, Ricky. That's him there. He's ten, and he likes the girls. Now, he'd never tell any of the girls in his class this, but he really likes piano. He just started taking lessons this year. He thinks if the girls knew, they'd think he was a sissy."

Lexi took in the photograph of the kid with long shaggy hair staring out at her with bright blue eyes. A stab of jealousy hit her; *he* got to take piano lessons.

"These are my nieces. They belong to my little brother. That's Erica. She's seven and the girliest girl you've ever met. Princesses, tea parties, the works. And it's hard for her, because her little sister, Lissy, hates *all* of that. She's only five, but she's already like her mom, a tomboy, playing sports, getting dirty."

Lexi peeked sideways and caught Liz smiling at the pictures, but something didn't add up. The woman bragged about these four kids like they were the sun, the moon, and the stars, but none of that took away the emptiness Lexi could see in Liz's eyes. Hadn't Liz just finished telling her that she and her husband had wanted kids? Wasn't it hard for her not to have any of her own?

"They look happy," Lexi said quietly, feeling something brewing inside her, the same as when Barney had brought her to that piano.

Not again!

No, she was *not* going to get all emotional about something so stupid! They were just pictures of kids, for crying out loud. So what if Liz was sad she couldn't have her own kids? Why should she care?

Lexi felt guilty for even thinking it and was relieved when Liz killed the awkwardness by placing something in Lexi's hand.

"This is for you," she said quietly.

Lexi turned the small tube over in her hand. At first, Lexi thought it was a thick pen, but there was no tip.

"What is it?" she asked, feeling like an idiot for asking. Was she supposed to know what it was?

"It's pepper spray," Liz replied, taking the canister from Lexi long enough to show her where the trigger was, where the spray came out.

Lexi stared at it, stared at Liz like she was crazy. Why in the world would she want to give Lexi pepper spray? Why would she even *think* to?

"Listen, after what you said about that guy, the one who threw you into a wall, the one who's been saying nasty things to you—"

"Slick?" Lexi inquired.

"That's his name? Oh, great. Well, I don't like the idea of you being down there, alone and unprotected, while this *Slick* character is around. He sounds dangerous, and you're young, and you're down there without any kind of protection. I don't like it, and I don't trust him."

Liz handed the pepper spray back to Lexi, who couldn't help but laugh a little.

"It's not a big deal. Slick's all talk; he—"

"Please, just take it." Liz actually looked desperate. "And promise you'll keep it in your pocket all the time. If not for yourself, then at least for my own peace of mind."

Lexi's breath caught in her throat. Her safety was rattling Liz's peace of mind? That was weird.

"People exist in this world who are genuinely good, Lexi. Even though you've been through a terrible ordeal, it isn't good to let bitterness consume you. Not everybody is out to get you."

Maybe, just *maybe*, Hilary was right, and maybe Liz was one of them—someone who did nice things without expecting anything in return, someone who actually *cared*, someone who wouldn't hurt you.

That thought lasted all of three seconds.

Yeah right. People like that belonged on television, taunting a hurting world.

But for whatever reason, Liz was desperate for Lexi to have the pepper spray, in case something happened. Well, Liz didn't know what she was talking about; nothing was going to happen. Slick might try throwing her into a wall again, but no big deal. Next time, she'd kick him where it hurt. She wasn't about to let anybody treat her like that.

But she took the pepper spray anyway. "Okay," she said, pocketing the odd gift. "I'll keep it with me."

This seemed to make Liz happy, for whatever reason.

With that out of the way, Liz clapped her hands together, lightening the mood. "Would you like a tour of the house?" she asked.

Lexi's stomach knotted. A tour of the house? Liz had already given her what she came here to get. Why was she still being nice to her? Didn't people only give tours to people who mattered? People they were friends with?

Swallowing, Lexi managed a nod. The truth was, she *did* want to see the rest of the house. She wanted to see the thick walls separating bedrooms. She wanted to see more than one bathroom. She wanted to see it because maybe she'd been wrong all along; maybe the houses on TV actually *did* exist.

And then came a nagging thought in the back of her mind. If the houses existed, did that mean all the wonderful people who lived inside them existed too?

CHAPTER 51

L I Z

Wednesday, October 28
2:42 p.m.

The art studio.

Lexi wanted to see the art studio.

Up until now, the tour of her house had been going well. Liz still chuckled whenever Lexi's jaw would drop even further at the sight of a new room. It was so strange; the girl seemed in complete shock over the house Liz never thought much of. Liz couldn't stop herself from pondering what kind of house Lexi must have grown up in. Granted, children didn't *need* large houses, but Lexi was acting like she'd never even seen a house this big, and she'd already admitted to never owning any jewellery either.

The more Liz learned about this child, the more she believed Lexi couldn't have had a decent upbringing.

And that cut to her core.

But there wasn't time to dwell on it, because when they tackled the second floor, even though Liz skipped over the art studio without a second thought, Lexi noticed.

"What about that room?" she asked, jerking her thumb toward the door that was slightly ajar.

Liz swallowed. To her, that room was no longer a part of this house. It wasn't a room anymore; it was a crypt.

But Lexi didn't know that. How could she?

"Oh," Liz mumbled. "That used to be my art studio."

Used to be...

"Art?" Lexi asked. "Can... can I see?"

So this was what it felt like to be stuck between a rock and a hard place.

The fact that Liz had somehow been able to convince Lexi to come here in the first place was a breakthrough. Add the fact that the girl was actually letting Liz give her a *tour*... well, the Lexi from three weeks ago would have bolted, no questions asked.

The Lexi from three weeks ago wouldn't have even gotten in the car.

So Liz had to be careful. Unchartered waters had to be treaded carefully. Oh, how she wanted Lexi to feel comfortable with her. She longed for Lexi's trust, but for that to happen, for that to happen *naturally*, she would have to be open.

Which meant letting her see the art studio.

Liz sucked in a breath.

"Sure," she said after a short pause, tilting her head toward the door. "Go ahead."

Lexi smiled, actually smiled, and pushed the door open, letting herself into the forgotten art studio. Liz held back, only for a moment, mustering up the energy for this. Going into that room felt like stepping into the first level of hell, for all the pain it caused.

So Liz focussed on Lexi, her distraction, who gawked around the studio with as much awe and admiration glimmering behind her eyes as she had in the other rooms. She considered each canvas carefully, studied it, accepted it.

Liz wouldn't look at the paintings. This was nothing more than a brief detour, and she found herself hoping Lexi wouldn't want to stay here long. She was already beginning to feel that icy feeling in the bottom of her stomach. The memories were too overwhelming, even if she tried to ignore them. They avalanched on top of her without mercy.

"Did you paint *all* of these?" Lexi asked, venturing a little further.

Liz could only nod.

"They're really good," Lexi said quietly, her eyes transfixed by all the art.

The spell of this room momentarily lost its hold on Liz, and she felt her lips curling. Lexi had been through so much in her short life, and even though Liz didn't know the specifics, it wasn't difficult to see years of torment beyond those brown eyes.

Despite all of that, Lexi *still* thought to compliment Liz's art.

This kid was one of a kind.

"Thank you," Liz said.

"When did you learn how to paint?"

"Oh." Liz strained to remember, but it was like reaching into a blurred abyss. Those memories were held prisoner somewhere deep down inside her. All memories of art brought her to a memory of Kurt. It was all related; what could she do but bury it?

But somehow, she conjured up the memory of herself as a young child with her first paintbrush.

"A long time ago," she finally said.

"Who taught you?" Lexi asked.

"Um, I don't think anybody taught me. I believe I just started one day."

"And you painted all of these?" Lexi asked, arching her arm to include all the paintings.

Liz nodded again.

"Is there anyone else in your family who can paint, or is it just you?" Lexi asked.

Liz smiled, shaking her head a little. This was hardly the same kid she'd met three weeks ago.

"You're asking me so many questions, but how come you never tell me much about yourself?" she asked, genuinely curious. This was the most Lexi had ever spoken, but still, Liz wasn't learning anything.

"You already know my name," Lexi pointed out, crossing her arms tight. "What more do you want?"

272

Well, she asked.

Time to get my feet wet.

But everyone knew it was better to wade into the shallow end before diving into the deep.

"Alright," Liz made a show of thinking hard. "What's your favourite subject?"

"Seriously?" Lexi almost laughed. It was like she couldn't believe that of all the questions Liz could ask, she'd picked *that*.

But Liz simply nodded. *Baby steps, remember?*

"Um." Lexi shook her head, no doubt still in disbelief. "I guess music."

"Why music?"

"Well, I mean, I used to play."

"Play what?"

Lexi swallowed. Her eyes dropped to the dusty floor.

Somehow Liz had struck a chord.

"Piano," Lexi muttered, eyes floating back to the paintings on the wall. A defence mechanism was taking over, and Liz could see it. The girl was avoiding something, some *feeling*, and Liz wasn't about to let that go, not that easily. She was finally catching a broader glimpse into Lexi's life. Somehow she'd managed to dig past yet another layer of the girl's cold exterior.

Liz couldn't ignore that.

"What do you mean, you *used* to play?" she asked gently, but Lexi had already built her wall. Her body language said it all; her hands went back in those pockets, her face froze up like a statue, and a casual demeanour took over. She was acting as though it had never come up. She'd already moved on through the room, perusing the details of each painting until she paused at that old cabinet, the one that was home to Liz's old art supplies.

The one that the forgotten *Lion Cubs* painting was leaning against.

Lexi saw it.

"Why's this one on the ground?" she asked suddenly, squatting down to get a better look. "It's... not finished."

273

The walls in Liz's throat were closing in, the eruption of emotion bubbling to the surface. She swallowed, looked up at the ceiling, a trick she'd learned a long time ago. It helped dissolve unwanted tears.

Not now. Not now.

Liz was sure Lexi had caught sight of her ceiling trick before she met her gaze again, trying to smile. It must have looked faked, because Lexi rose to her feet and stared at the ground while shuffling her feet awkwardly.

"Sorry," Lexi muttered.

Liz sighed to herself. No, this was all wrong.

She wanted Lexi to release the deepest, darkest secrets of her soul, to trust her, but there Liz stood, pretending like *she* was okay, pretending like it didn't tear her apart her to stand in this room, pretending like the ghosts of her past didn't haunt her.

Who was the cold one now?

Maybe… just maybe it took a vulnerable person to help someone else *become* vulnerable.

"No, it's okay," Liz said, piercing the hollow silence. "It's just… well, I haven't actually painted anything… in two years."

Lexi tilted her head to one side, furrowing her eyebrows a little, as though trying to unravel the mystery.

"Why not?"

God, give me strength.

This was so hard, so unexpected. She couldn't even talk about this with her best friend. Truth be told, she'd never really admitted this to *anybody*. Nobody had really asked why she gave up painting, and most people accepted the lie that she was simply too busy. Except Kathryn, who already knew the truth, but Liz had never come right out and said anything. Kathryn was just intuitive.

But here was this fifteen-year-old girl, who, asking harmless questions, had reached into the depths of Liz's soul, pulled out all the stuff she'd been refusing to acknowledge. Liz had known she could never touch another brush, knew from the moment Kurt had been taken from this world. She'd packed away the last of her brushes the next day. Over the years she'd become an expert at denying the truth, but now, how could she bring herself to lie to Lexi?

But why can't I? Why can't I just lie? She didn't know. It certainly didn't make sense that she could lie to her best friend, lie to *herself*, but feel convicted to be honest with a teenage girl.

Was Pastor Reid right? Did she somehow resonate with Lexi? The girl had been through something terrible, experienced sorrow to some degree.

So Lexi knew what heartbreak felt like.

"I..." Liz swallowed. Weren't adults supposed to be the strong ones? "I stopped painting when my husband... passed away."

She waited for the "why?"

But it never came.

Instead, Lexi nodded to herself, like she didn't need Liz to explain. Somehow, it already made sense to her.

"They're cool," Lexi said after a pause, nodding at the unfinished canvas. "Why did you want to paint baby lions?"

Kurt had asked the same thing.

"Baby lions are born blind," Liz explained. Oh, this was all too familiar. "The cubs have to depend on their mother for survival until they get their sight. I painted them because that's how I was when I found God. I had no idea what I was doing, but God did. I relied on Him for survival."

No argument, no eye roll, no resistance. Instead, Lexi continued to stare at the scratchy pencil lines that were meant to become lion cubs.

That was different. The last time Liz had mentioned God, Lexi had practically flat-out denied any belief in Him.

"But," Lexi started, "if it's about *your* life, why are there two cubs?"

Liz felt her heart swelling. "Well, everybody needs a friend."

It was then that Liz wished there was some kind of magical technology that could read Lexi's thoughts. The girl was perplexed—her mind was running a marathon, that much Liz could see—but what could possibly be going through her young mind? Why was she so interested in the unfinished painting? Why did it matter to her?

After a long silence, Liz opened her mouth, ready to suggest they move on with the tour, but Lexi spoke first.

"I think you should finish it."

Liz felt as though a bolt of electricity had surged through her body.

"W–what?" she asked.

"Finish it," Lexi replied, pointing to the forgotten canvas. "I think you should finish this painting."

Liz forced herself to look at it, her stomach doing flip-flops.

"Why?" she inquired. "Why do you think I should?"

Lexi shrugged. "I dunno." But she did. "Closure maybe?"

Closure.

Letting go.

Liz felt her throat constricting as Lexi went on.

"I just mean... well, life sucks when someone... you know, leaves you." Lexi awkwardly scratched her nose. "But maybe finishing your painting would be, like, your way of saying it's time to move on."

Somehow, this was no longer about Liz. Sure, Lexi had meant it to be, but Liz was reading between the lines now.

This was the closest Lexi had ever come to opening up. Somehow, she was saying she *also* knew what it was like for someone to leave. Her parents had died, but was there more?

Suddenly Liz's concern for Lexi won out. She forgot the painting, forgot her own heartache when Lexi's pain seemed somehow illuminated. All Liz wanted was wrap her arms around the girl and protect her from the world, from herself, from her past.

But she couldn't, not now. Instead, she stared hard at Lexi, ready to dive into the deep end. "You seem to know an awful lot about feelings for someone who doesn't seem to care," she said quietly, managing a sympathetic smile. She didn't say it to be mean but as truth, because that was how Lexi was—anytime things became personal, emotional, or close to her heart, she'd lock herself away somewhere. As long as it had nothing to do with her... well, that was the easy stuff.

Liz understood it all too well.

It was always so easy to ask Kathryn how work was going, discuss the auto business with her father, review a patient's medical history with her colleagues, but if anybody crossed the line, asked how *she* was doing, that's when life became a challenge.

Maybe that was how Lexi saw it, too. Maybe that was why Liz felt so connected to her.

Oh my gosh, Pastor Reid was right!

Her head began to throb.

Lexi didn't say a word. She only stood very still, as though shell-shocked by Liz's revelation, but then she shrugged it off like it didn't matter, turned her back to Liz, feigning interest in the paintings on the other wall.

Liz sensed this was the closest she would come to getting through to Lexi, helping her see reason, maybe even getting her off the streets.

She wasn't about to let her go without a fight.

"You don't belong there, Lexi," she said, knowing it was a risk to say anything. It was like tiptoeing on eggshells, waiting for the explosion, waiting for Lexi to freak out, run away, but she'd already come this far.

And Lexi was still here.

"Maybe it's not my place, but you shouldn't be in those tunnels. It's not right; you don't *belong* there," Liz said again, stepping forward, closing the gap between them.

Lexi just shook her head, transfixed on an island landscape. "I don't belong anywhere else."

Liz opened her mouth to argue, but Lexi whirled around and interrupted. "And before you say that's *not* true, try living in four—that's right, *four*—different foster homes!" Lexi yelled out, taking a step back. "You'd know you didn't belong anywhere if that's what happened."

So that was it. Lexi's parents passed away, and Lexi was thrown into the system. She had said her parents died two years ago, so that meant four foster homes in two years.

Liz felt sick to her stomach. What had gone wrong?

She wanted to ask, but the ball was in Lexi's court now. It was huge that Lexi had shared *anything*; she wasn't going to try forcing anything else.

"That sounds rough," Liz said quietly, wanting to reach out, place a hand on Lexi's shoulder, console her, but she held back.

Lexi was silent; she didn't say anything else about foster homes, group homes, or even the paintings on the wall. Now she just seemed anxious for a way out.

"Listen, I know you don't believe in God, but hear me out. No matter how strongly you feel about not belonging anywhere, He loves you so much, and you belong to Him." Liz managed a small smile. "I know it doesn't always seem like it, but He's always there, ready for you when you need to cry out to Him."

Oh, if only Lexi would believe in God. If only she knew how much He cared about her, was looking out for her. If only she had some kind of reminder when things got rough.

And then, a thought floated into her mind.

A strange thought.

No, Lexi wouldn't—

Would she?

It seemed crazy, like something out of left field. Was it God who wanted her to do it? Would He use something that, to Liz, seemed so small? Well, she wasn't sure what prompted her, but somehow it felt right.

Slowly, she reached around her neck, unclasped the gold cross necklace she'd worn for five years, and, carefully taking Lexi's hand, placed it in her palm.

"I want you to have this," Liz said quietly, putting a hand up as Lexi tried to protest. "Look, you're fifteen, and you told me you've never had any jewellery, so... here's your first. Will you wear it? Look, maybe you don't want anything to do with God right now, but I just want you to know He's there."

Lexi was her usual silent self. She opened her mouth as though she wanted to say something, but nothing came out. Instead, she stared at the cross in her hand, eyes flickering across its every detail.

What was the girl thinking about? She gazed upon that necklace like it was some kind of treasure.

Swallowing, Lexi finally nodded and struggled with the clasp. Liz told herself not to smile. It wasn't Lexi's fault; she'd never owned jewellery—how was she supposed to know how a necklace worked?

"Here." Liz put out her hand, but Lexi held back. Liz didn't back down, didn't pull her hand away, not until she was sure.

Lexi finally handed over the gold chain. Her hands were shaking.

What's going through her head?

Lexi turned around while Liz brought the necklace down around the girl's neck, clasping it gently at the back, keeping herself from fixing Lexi's hair that was caught up in the chain. Lexi did that herself.

Lexi took hold of that miniature version of the cross in her fingers and held it out, craning her neck to have a look. For a long time, she just stared at it.

Liz held back and let her.

Finally, Lexi peered up, her eyebrows narrowing. She didn't seem angry. Just... confused. "I don't get it," she said quietly. "Why aren't *you* angry at Him?"

"Why aren't I angry at *whom*?" Liz asked, curious.

"God! How can you talk about Him like that, about love and Him being there and stuff, like He's really great? How can you say things like that when... when your husband died?" Lexi swallowed, fingering the cross carefully. "Aren't you *angry?*"

Liz felt the dam breaking loose. What was it about this kid

that brought all of this to the surface?

No, she had to keep herself together, for Lexi's sake. The girl standing in front of her was hurt and confused. She needed to hear the truth.

"Don't misunderstand this, because sometimes I am *very* angry at God for taking my husband." Liz swallowed back the tears. These were feelings she hadn't shared with anybody. "I have been *really* angry with Him, but that doesn't mean I stop loving Him. It doesn't mean He stops loving me."

Lexi seemed even more confused, so Liz went on.

"That's what makes a relationship work, especially with God," she said simply. "You can be angry at someone and still love them."

Lexi dropped her gaze, her face all squished up like she was trying to figure it out. Sure, it didn't make sense to Lexi, and Liz knew why.

"But you've never had that," she said quietly. "Have you, Lexi?"

That was when Liz was sure she saw something in the corner of Lexi's dark brown eyes, something she'd never seen before. The start of what looked like a tear.

Emotion.

Liz moved toward her, opening her mouth to say something, but Lexi backed away, clearing her throat and eyeing the door. She suddenly looked panic-stricken.

"I have to go," she said, her voice aquiver. "I've been gone too long. They'll be wondering where I am."

Lexi made for the door, but Liz reached out and took hold of Lexi's arm, gently pulling her back to face her.

"Don't leave like this, Lexi," she said, for lack of anything better to say, but Lexi pulled away, shaking her head.

"I have to go," she said again, stronger.

Liz exhaled. What could she do but respect Lexi's space?

She would have to let her go.

"Alright, but do me a favour." Liz searched her work table, scoped out a scrap piece of paper and a forgotten pen. She scribbled down a number. "This is my number at work. Please keep it with you, just in case, and call me anytime."

Never once looking at her, Lexi took the piece of paper and shoved it into her pocket without a word. She passed Liz, headed for the door.

"Thanks for the necklace," Lexi said in that quiet, flat voice, the one she used when she tried not to care.

And then, just like that, she was gone.

Liz stood alone, left in the tomb her studio had become. She stood frozen until she heard the front door distantly open and then close.

Lexi was gone.

Liz was alone.

That was when she crumbled to her knees and sobbed.

CHAPTER 52

L E X I

Wednesday, October 28
4:14 p.m.

Lexi's fingers were glued to that cross around her neck. She couldn't stop staring at it, either... its shimmery gold finish, the tiny white diamond in its centre, its smooth edges. She also couldn't stop thinking about it, but it didn't matter how many different ways Lexi tried to wrap her mind around everything that had happened, it still didn't make sense.

Why? Why would Liz just *give* her a piece of jewellery? Why would she part with something so special, just for Lexi?

Lexi remembered the time Liz had first told her about this necklace. She said it had been a gift from her best friend, so why, just like that, did she want Lexi—*Lexi*, of all people—to have it?

The weirdest part was that Liz hadn't asked for anything in return, except that she wear it.

Lexi bit her lip, fingering the gold, committing to memory the feel of its edges.

Was Liz really that nice?

Tears tickled Lexi's eyes. *Tears.* When was the last time she'd actually cried?

Crying makes you weak! Stop it, Lexi, stop it, stop it, stop it!

She was on her way back toward the tunnels, away from Liz's house, away from it all. What had she been thinking, going there? It was a mistake, all of it. And what was with all the questions? It was weird, but being in that house had somehow sparked Lexi's curiosity about Liz. The more time she spent there, catching small glimpses into the doctor's life, she couldn't help but ask questions.

But why? Why did she care?

No, I don't care.

Still, something strange was definitely going on. It was like being inside that house had broken something inside of Lexi, some kind of emotional barrier, because even as she dawdled down the street, she felt ready to fall apart. But all it would take was one tear, and she'd never be able to stop. Every memory, every past hurt, every sleepless night, every bruise, every touch, every word... it would all pour into her and tear her to pieces if she let it.

But she wouldn't. She *couldn't!* What was it about Liz's place that had gotten her all worked up in the first place? Was it because Liz had started talking about her husband being dead? Was it because Liz couldn't paint? Was it because Lexi somehow got it? Was it because it made Lexi think about things she didn't want to deal with? Things she *couldn't* deal with, not if she wanted to survive?

She remembered that forgotten painting in Liz's art studio, the one she hadn't been able to pry her eyes from, the one she would always remember, even if she never saw Liz again.

It wasn't even the painting itself. They were just shadows of lion cubs, after all, but it wasn't that; it was what it stood for. Liz confided that she hadn't been able to paint since her husband had passed away, and Lexi got that. That was why she hadn't said anything back at the house. She knew *exactly* why Liz couldn't touch it, why it would hurt too much if she even tried.

That was why Lexi couldn't play piano. Because the last time Lexi had played was when she'd been happy, back during a time when Hilary would stop everything just to be there for her.

But that had fallen apart at the seams before it even had a chance to become something great. Any dreams Lexi ever had about being part of a family were shattered that year.

Playing the piano would only bring her back to that place, would only cut another hole into her heart, a sharp reminder of how good things never lasted.

But what was it she had told Liz? Hadn't she told her that she should finish the painting, for closure, so she could move on? Was that what Lexi needed to do? Did she need closure to move on too?

Just like Liz needed to start painting again, maybe Lexi needed to play to let go of that time in her life when she'd been genuinely happy, the short chapter in her pathetic existence that actually *meant* something.

Maybe it was time to let go of Hilary.

That's when Lexi realized, as she dawdled toward the tunnels, that she was close to the landfill—the same one Barney had brought her to a few days ago.

She pressed her lips tightly together, a looming emptiness churning in her stomach as she glanced toward the dump yard.

Was it still there?

Lexi moved forward, driven by something unseen, like there was a chain around her waist, reeling her toward the dump, because it didn't feel like she was going willingly.

It didn't feel like she was being forced, either.

She jumped the fence, blindly stumbling around. How was she supposed to know where it was? Barney had made her close her eyes the first time.

It didn't take long to spot the piano. Something that beautiful in a place of trash was bound to attract attention.

The piano had a dreamlike ambience to it. She felt like she was floating above herself, watching the shell of a girl beneath her drift toward the piano and nervously place her fingers on the ivory keys.

It came quickly, just like last time... the music of laughter, love, and trust.

Of family. A family that had been nothing more than a lie.

Lexi recoiled her fingers from the piano as though it had burned her.

284

No, just do it!

She drew a deep breath, placed her fingers back on the keys, and closed her eyes, recalling a distant piece of music she'd spent hours practising, once upon a time. Learning this piece had been about proving her music teacher wrong. Mrs. Mooney had been under the impression that Mozart's *Fantasia* in D Minor was a very complex piece, too complex for Lexi to attempt at her level.

But it was too late; Lexi had already fallen in love with the piece, was intrigued by its irregularity, its uniqueness. It was different, and Lexi delved in, learned it, and blew her teacher away.

It helped that she'd always been a fast learner.

And now, in that landfill, alone with the music in her heart, it came back to her as naturally as riding a bike. Her fingers danced across the keys, finding all the right notes, filling the forgotten place with a sad ballad, one that Lexi thought she'd forgotten. The piece was her life, each irregular leap in tempo another horror Lexi had been through, each note a terrorizing memory.

Still, she played, feeling the surge of emotion welling up inside of her as she leaned in and played like never before. She forgot where her fingers ended and the keys began; she was one with the piano.

It felt like she was home.

But where was home?

She *had* no home.

Lexi yanked her fingers away from the piano, breathing in sharply, and she became conscious of the tears stinging her eyes. She blinked quickly, jumping away from the piano as though it was going to explode.

No, no, no, I don't care, I don't care, it's stupid, it doesn't hurt, it's dumb, it's just a piano, Hilary meant nothing, it's all stupid, I don't care, I don't care, it doesn't matter!

She repeated it again and again as she fled from the landfill without looking back, ignoring the melody of Mozart's piece echoing in her head.

This had been a mistake—a moment of weakness, a serious lapse in judgment. She'd gone and let herself become vulnerable, even if it was only for a second. Now look where she was, running like she'd committed some kind of heinous crime.

No, this would *never* happen again. She hated herself for getting in Liz's car, for letting herself grow curious about Liz's life enough to hear about that stupid painting and be reminded of all the crap in her own life. Liz had said too many things that got Lexi thinking, got her *feeling*, but she had to forget it all. She couldn't let herself feel again. She knew she couldn't survive another heartbreak.

Hearts were like that. They could only take so much.

But that was the problem; how could you shut off a heart but still let it beat?

CHAPTER 53

L I Z

Wednesday, October 28
7:10 p.m.

Could there be any tears left?

Liz was quickly losing all track of time, buckled on the floor of her art studio, alone. She hadn't so much as moved since Lexi left, but that had to be hours ago now.

She was pressed up against the wall, hugging her knees tight, staring fixedly at the unfinished lion cubs. For however long Liz had been stuck here, she kept circling back to what Lexi had said about needing to finish that painting.

How was it that a fifteen-year-old girl who'd been through more in her young life than anyone Liz had ever met could nail things so precisely? All this time, Liz had been positive that if God was the One divinely orchestrating this relationship, it was because Liz somehow had to help the girl, maybe to get her off the streets, help her find safety, be a confidante, or at least introduce her to God.

So why did it feel more like Lexi was helping her?

Lexi was right. The teenage girl had it all figured out, Liz couldn't deny it, not anymore, not even if she tried. Her mother had said it, Jenn had said it, Kathryn had said it, Pastor Reid had said it, and now a fifteen-year-old street kid had said it.

Liz had to face her grief, deal with her emotions, seek the closure she'd been running from for so long.

287

But it didn't quite feel real. For two years now, had she really been avoiding the pain? Had she really thrown herself into work so she'd be so busy that there would be no time left to remember her husband, no time to acknowledge that gaping hole inside her? Had she really chosen not to deal with her loss?

"Instead, you throw yourself into work. There, you can numb yourself from reality. Isn't that what your girl does, numbs herself to the pain?"

Was Pastor Reid right after all?

Retrospectively, it all seemed to make sense. Yes, the last two years had certainly seen a doubling—or even tripling—of shifts at St. Marcus. She'd withdrawn from the Bible study she'd once attended with Kurt, she managed to always change the subject whenever Kurt's name popped up, and she was in the habit of always claiming to be totally fine.

Well, she *wasn't* totally fine.

How could I be?

Her smile to the rest of the world was like Lexi's shrug: an outward expression of how "fine" she was, while inside she was just screaming!

Ever since Liz had first met Lexi, her heart had been in shambles, knowing this was a girl who shouldered so much pain, and the only way she knew how to deal, knew how to *survive*, was to shut herself off from it, numb herself.

It was exactly what Liz did. *That* was why she couldn't even go into that art studio without falling apart. *That* was why she felt her defences rise every time her mother suggested moving on. *That* was why she feared time with Kathryn; there was always a chance Kurt's name would come up.

When was the last time she'd even gone to the cemetery?

Fresh droplets burned the corners of her eyes, and soon steady rivers streamed down her face.

For two years, she'd shut him out.

For two years, she'd pretended.

For two years, she'd functioned no better than a robot.

Kurt deserved more than that.

It was time.

***

She ended up cross-legged on her bedroom floor, cautiously eyeing the dark underworld below her bed. That was where he was, where she'd put him, thinking perhaps by hiding him everything would be easier.

Out of sight, out of mind.

Aware of her hurried breaths, and ignoring the sick feeling in her stomach, she finally ventured under that bed and felt for the edges of the cardboard box she'd pushed under it two years ago.

Two years, three months, and eight days ago...

And now, here it was.

It rested in her lap like a concrete block. The layer of dust on its lid brought fresh tears to Liz's eyes; how could she have thought she could just forget?

She leaned up against her dresser and for a long while, absorbed in the suffocating silence, held the box in her lap, her throat tightening whenever she thought of opening it.

Maybe she wasn't ready for this. Maybe it was all a mistake.

No. It was no mistake; this was just her way of coping, of pretending it didn't hurt.

If she wanted to come to terms with all this, she'd have to *let* it hurt.

God, be my strength.

She opened the box.

One... two... three.

That was exactly how long it took before the floodgates opened up.

Now her vision was so obstructed with pools of water that she hardly saw the contents of the box. But it was all there, just as she'd left it.

She first reached for the stack of photographs, sifted through them one by one with trembling hands, a fresh tear squeezed out for each moment frozen in time, a moment captured, a moment she had once taken for granted.

Each photo stung her deeply, cut a fresh longing into her heart for those days to once again become her reality.

There she was with Kurt in Vermont, both garbed in thick coats, scarfs, and mitts, donning skis. That was the weekend Kurt had taught her to ski. They were only dating back then.

The Halloween they dressed up as Mickey and Minnie Mouse; the neighbourhood kids had a good laugh at their costumes. Their first Christmas morning as a married couple. The wrapping paper was strewn about the living room like they didn't have a care in the world.

Then came the wedding pictures. Kurt in his handsome tuxedo, his dirty-blond hair slicked back, his smile as wide as ever, and Liz, her flowing white gown beaded at the waist, her long blonde hair tucked back with a lace veil, and the glimmer in her eye all marking the happiest day of her life.

There were so many others: Kurt cradling Liam as a baby, Kurt and Liz lounging on the beach, Kurt and Liz in her mother's pool, Kurt and Liz roasting marshmallows over Kathy's fire pit.

Liz went through them more than once, all the while craving just one more picture, one last moment they could capture and cling to forever, but it wouldn't happen.

He was gone.

Hands still rattling, she placed the photographs beside her and stared deeper into the box, the vortex of memories.

All that was left were his letters.

His letters...

Kurt was always writing her letters or little notes, hiding them in her lunch bag, sticking them on the fridge, leaving them on her pillow.

And she'd kept them, every last one. How could she have known they would one day cease? If only she had known that one morning she would wake up and there would be no Post-it note on her bedside table with the simple words "I love you."

The pictures were hard, but the letters would be harder. Choking on a sob, she reached in and began to read.

Good morning, lovely lady.

I wanted my love for you to be the first thing you thought of this beautiful morning. Enjoy your day, see you at 5. Kurt.

My dearest Buttercup,

I wanted you to know that I really enjoyed our trip up to Vermont last weekend. You've really come a long way since I first taught you to ski. Remember when you slid down the bunny hill on your bum that first time? It was so hard not to laugh! Those days are gone, now that you're a pro! Keep it up and you could be the next Olympic champion!

Except I would miss you too much if you had to travel the world every four years. Then again, I could just quit my job and travel to the ends of the earth with you, because being apart from you for even a moment breaks my heart in pieces. You are my other half, you complete me, and all those other wonderful clichés.

I love you more than the stars that number the sky. Always and forever. Your Prince Charming.

Don't forget to buy cream today.

PS: You made me proud last night when you finished the painting of the mountain range. It's your best work yet. Kurt.

My sweetest and only Liz,

I can't describe the agony I felt today when I saw the pain in your eyes after we received the news from my doctor. Finding out I have cancer was hard, but what was even harder was seeing how hurt you were, and knowing there was nothing I could do to relieve your fears, encourage you, comfort you.

We are going to fight this, and overcome it. God is in control, and I praise Him for that truth, because things would fall apart so easily in this world if we tried to do it ourselves.

There is nothing in this world that can ever tear me from your arms. I couldn't bear it, so keep that truth close. Together, we are strong, and our hearts beat as one. This is just another hurdle, and we have overcome hurdles in the past. You need never fear when God is on our side. Love you. Kurt.

Lizzie-bean,

The doctors have not given me much longer, and I trust with all my heart that when it is my time, God will be waiting at the gates with arms open wide, ready with a promise to take care of my lovely wife, whom I will no longer be able to protect.

When I imagine life without you, I feel a worse pain than anything this disease has done to me. I can't imagine a morning when I'm not there to turn over and see you breathing, reminding me why I'm alive. But God is in control, His plan is perfect, and I thank God I will be able to watch over you from

Heaven. For you it will be harder, because you won't see me.

But know that death cannot separate us, not now, not ever. Know there will be a day when we are together again. Know this, hold tight to this, and do not forget. Do not ever forget how much I love you.

I love everything about you, and I pray that everything I love about you will live on, even after I go. Your precious smile, your infectious laughter, your intense and eager willingness to help others through their sorrows. Don't ever lose that, Lizzie.

There will be times when you'll feel alone, forgotten, sad, angry, confused, and that's okay, but never forget who you are. Your identity is not wrapped up in me but in the Father, and so when I am no longer there to hold you when you cry, you will never be alone. Don't forget who you are, what you love to do. Be a light to others, as you have been a light to me since the day I truly came to life—the day I met you.

I will never forget you as I move from this world into the next, because you are etched on my heart, embedded there forever.

I love you, but words can never express the depths of that.

Kurt

That was the last letter Kurt had written. He died a week later.

Liz let the letters slip from her fingers and lost control. Her sobs erupted in hurried gasps as she clutched at her hair, wailing into her knees. This was why she kept it all under her bed! It hurt, it hurt so much, it hurt worse than the worst form of torture! Once upon a time, she'd had it all. The love of her life had been within her reach, and now he was gone!

There was no hurt like it, and now that the floodgates had opened, Liz didn't think she could ever stop crying.

She ached for him, ached for his touch, his deep voice, his laugh, his smile. She ached for the little things too, the way he would forget to put the lid back on the toothpaste, the way he would try and fool Liz with decaf because he thought she was drinking too much caffeine, the way he would sneak up behind her, lean in close just to whisper the sweetest things into her ear. *I love you...*

"Oh God, I don't want to be angry," Liz found herself saying out loud, her trembling voice sounding so foreign in the silence of her empty home. "I don't blame You for taking him from me. I know You're in control, but... but..." She tried to catch her breath. "He said he'd never forget me, but... oh God, that's what I've been *trying* to do, isn't it? Oh Lord, please know I never did it because I didn't love him. I loved him more than life itself, more than *breathing*, and that's why I wanted to forget. That's why I buried all the memories in this box, tried to bury them in my heart. It was too hard.

"I loved him so much, and I... I... I didn't want to face it, I didn't... want... to... face... losing him forever. I thought pretending would be easier. Putting on a smile, acting like I was dealing with it. It was all a lie! How do you deal with life when half of you disappears? How do you ever become whole again? Oh God, I don't understand why Kurt had to die! I don't understand why it had to happen, but You're good, and I try to remember that. I just... I just... oh God, I don't know what to do!"

She hugged her knees to her chest like a small child, inconsolable. She missed him; oh how she missed Kurt. She wanted him here, she longed for his arms around her. How would she overcome this? How would she be able to deal with it? How could she ever find closure?

Sniffling loudly, she glanced around at the scattered contexts of her box, letters and photographs, and swallowed hard as silence buzzed through the room.

What would Kurt want?

The question popped into her mind as though it wasn't her own.

God, what would Kurt want? If he was here, here right now, what would he want for me?

Would he want her to keep pretending?

No.

Would he want her to forget?

No.

Would he want to see her crying like this?

No.

Would he want to see her happy?

Yes.

Liz reached out and picked up his last letter again.

I love everything about you, and I pray that everything I love about you will live on, even after I go. Your precious smile, your infectious laughter, your intense and eager willingness to help others through their sorrows. Don't ever lose that, Lizzie.

But I have, Liz thought, biting her lip. *I've lost my zest for life, my will to keep going. I have no passion to help anyone anymore. I've lost that spirit.*

But in the silent void encamping around her, Liz heard a voice echo through her mind. It wasn't audible, but she knew where it was coming from, and He only had to give her one little name.

Lexi.

There was Lexi.

So she *hadn't* lost her zeal to help others, not completely, because she wanted to help Lexi.

And that was something to go on.

CHAPTER 54

L E X I

Wednesday, October 28
7:20 p.m.

She didn't go back, not right away. For a while, Lexi just circled the same few blocks, wandering aimlessly, but this time she wasn't on the prowl for loose change or food. The only thing she wanted was for the world to make sense.

Yeah, good luck with that.

Why should things start making sense now?

Eventually she made it to the tunnels, after what seemed like an eternity of mindless meandering. She knew Barney would be waiting for her. Anytime she disappeared for more than an hour, he worried. She figured he was just being protective. He wasn't anything like the control freak Slick was.

And predictably, there was Barney, lounging with his back up against the stone wall, springing to life when he spotted Lexi.

"Man, I gotta get you a beeper or something," he said. "You've been gone a long time. Where you been?"

She could lie, but she was too exhausted, even for that. "Liz found me. She told me she had something for me at her house," Lexi said, lowering her voice. "So I went."

She expected Barney to ream her out, but he didn't. Instead, he had a curious sparkle in his eye.

"What was it?" he asked, but before Lexi could answer, Barney's eyes travelled down to her neck, his wide eyes fixing on the cross there. "Where'd you get that?"

Lexi looked down, took the cross in her fingers again.

"Oh," Lexi replied. "She gave me this too. I mean, it was kind of random, and it wasn't what she brought me there for, but she said—"

"Oh man, that's *bad* news, CJ!" Barney hissed, panic flashing in his eyes. "Seriously, you might wanna hide that. Sapph's a stickler for expensive stuff! Well, *you* know how she is! She thinks it's everyone's responsibility to contribute to our little society. Anyone who has something expensive is supposed to give it to her so she can pawn it off and buy more stuff—lights, blankets, candles, you know? She figures we're all in this together. Besides, you know how she's been lately. She seems... angrier."

Lexi clung to her necklace defensively, feeling her blood sizzling. She thought of Sapphire; yes, she *had* been acting weird lately, bullying kids more than usual, but Lexi didn't care.

"So what? I should be allowed to have nice things!" She was fuming. "I told you, I never had any jewellery before, and *this* was given to me. I didn't steal it or nothing!"

Barney put his hand up, trying to silence her. "Hey, I'm on your side, Ceej. I'm just sayin' you might wanna hide it before—"

"Hide what?"

There was Sapphire, hovering as always. Lexi didn't budge, not even when Sapphire's line of vision centred in on that necklace, her eyes locking on it like a missile ready to fire.

"Where did you get that?" she asked, stepping forward.

Lexi glowered. She didn't care what had set Sapphire off these past two weeks; she wasn't giving the necklace up, not for *anything*.

"From someone I know," Lexi said snottily. "What's it to you?"

She ignored the sharp nudge from Barney. Always the peacemaker. He was probably trying to shut her up before Sapphire got mad.

Well, *let* Sapphire get mad. Lexi was tired of being ordered around like a child.

"What's it to *me?*" Sapphire raised her voice. "Do you have any idea what something like that is worth?"

Lexi shrugged. "I don't care. It was a gift, and it's *mine*. Besides, Star has a necklace. Why shouldn't I get to have one?"

"Star's necklace is a fake. *Anyone* can see that. Yours is real gold!" Sapphire was freaking out now. "Maybe you've forgotten how things work down here, but let me spell it out for you! Down here, you don't get to own things. You don't get to keep things just because you think they're nice, sentimental, whatever. Down here, you share the wealth."

Lexi crossed her arms, stuck out her chin. "Too bad."

Well, that ignited a wicked fuse. If there was anything Sapphire couldn't stand, it was people like Lexi.

It all happened so fast. Sapphire sprang, snatching Lexi's arm, driving her long fingernails into her skin. Lexi howled and threw a fist forward, but Sapphire ducked it, using her hold on Lexi's arm to twist it backwards, which sent Lexi to the ground, hard.

The sprained wrist, again!

The pain made her ears ring.

Lexi tried to roll away, but Sapphire was like a cheetah and drove her knee into Lexi's stomach before she could even move.

Feeling the wind knocked out of her, Lexi threw fists in a blind frenzy, her hands the only weapon she had left, trapped under Sapphire's knee like some weak animal, but her enemy was on the ball tonight; she dodged every single blow.

Lexi still fired away, barely hearing Sapphire yelling out for something, but quickly realized she'd called for backup, because someone's cold hands trapped Lexi's wrists, held them still. Fury unleashing the rage inside, she tried kicking Sapphire off her, but Sapphire dove forward, her hands closing themselves around Lexi's neck, those hard blue eyes staring down at her.

"Next time I tell you what to do," Sapphire whispered, pressing harder against Lexi's neck, "you *do* it."

She let go but grabbed hold of the cross, yanking it off with ease before stomping off, her accomplice glued to her hip.

Lexi jumped to her feet, staggered for a second, caught her breath.

She headed after Sapphire, but Barney stopped her.

"Leave it alone, CJ," he warned, holding her back. "It's gone."

Lexi glared after Sapphire, eyes burning, hands shaking, heart racing. That girl had just stolen the *one* thing that made Lexi feel important, if even for a second! Liz had given up a necklace from her best friend to give to her. It meant something. It was worth something, and not financially. *Nobody* could understand that. *Nobody* could replace that.

Lexi pulled away from Barney fiercely, seeing red dots everywhere.

"CJ, I'm sorry. I know it was impor—"

"No," Lexi said through gritted teeth. "It doesn't matter. It's not that big a deal. Who even cares?"

Barney would have said more, but she didn't give him the chance. Instead, she headed for the Combs, craving nothing more than solitude.

It doesn't hurt. It doesn't hurt. Who cares? It was just a necklace.

She had to say it again and again, but it didn't matter how many times she repeated it, she couldn't fight off the anger inside, the injustice of it all.

Relieved that Barney hadn't followed her, she examined her arm. Sapphire had drawn blood: four crescent-shaped scars indented the bruises Slick had left earlier. Lexi wiped her arm on her sweater, leaving a small trail of blood behind.

It was all too familiar, because this wasn't the first time some psycho's fingernails had made her bleed.

CHAPTER 55

L E X I

////////////////////////////////

Tuesday, December 11
11:43 p.m.

One Year, Ten Months Ago

Lexi couldn't sleep.

But that wasn't new. For five months now, she'd been sentenced to staring at ceilings, watching the sunrise, nodding off in class. Sleep was a luxury she wasn't permitted, not anymore.

Not since the night her parents died.

But that was how life was. It sucked, simple as that. It was hard enough being thirteen, but being thirteen and having to readjust your entire life?

Brutal.

When they first took her away, they stuck her in a group home, dropped her off without a word, no disclaimers as to what the next few months would hold. All she knew was that, with no living relatives, this was the only place left for her.

Great.

She only lived there for a month, which was just as well. The six older girls who set out to make Lexi's life miserable wouldn't be missed, not by a long shot. She'd lost count of how many times they'd cornered her in the girls' bathroom, pushed her around, taunted her in ways she would rather forget.

It was easier when you could just forget.

So it wasn't so bad when Bridget showed up and had her pack her things. Lexi didn't even know where she was going, but once you fell into hell, you knew nothing would be pleasant.

On the drive, Bridget told her about foster care.

Oh, she'd made it out to be this wonderful experience for kids like her with no families, but Lexi didn't buy it. Maybe she was only thirteen, but she'd known kids who'd gone through foster care, and it was the farthest thing from wonderful there was.

Not like Bridget cared; not like any of them cared. She still dumped Lexi on Janet Stevens' doormat, and just like that, Lexi had a new home.

Now, four months later, it didn't matter what Lexi tried; she'd never get used to her new bed, her new room, her new life.

That's because it was too weird, living in a house with people you weren't related to. It was different with parents; you got stuck with them. It was a simple law of nature. When you shared the same genetics with someone, you were tied to them for life, like it or not. Sure, Lexi had hated it, hated every minute of it, dreamed of running as far away from them as was humanly possible, but she couldn't, because that wasn't how it worked. The laws of nature forbade it.

Well, apparently the laws of nature were wrong. Now, Lexi was housing with people she'd never met before, people who shared no genetic makeup with her, but she was as stuck with them as she had been with her parents.

She'd learned an important lesson these past few months: life wasn't fair.

Lexi guessed it wasn't all bad. She'd heard all the horror stories about kids in foster care, kids who'd been beaten, kids who'd been chosen for the sole purpose of being some sick pervert's play toy, kids who'd been starved, tortured, raped.

She guessed it could always be worse.

For the most part, Janet hardly said two words to her, and that was fine by Lexi. She had absolutely nothing in common with her foster mother, the hairstylist who grew her nails to a ridiculous length, painted them a different colour each day. The woman used half a can of hairspray a day to poof out her bleached blonde hair, and she plastered on so much makeup, Lexi barely even recognized her on the rare occasions she forgot to wear any.

When Janet wasn't at work, she was on the phone, pacing through the house with the cordless glued to her ear. Every day, it was someone new, another schmuck she'd met at the bar the night before, only worthy of a one-night stand. "You were a good time, but I'm just not ready to commit," she'd tell them. That was the secret, she told Lexi. Never commit.

If Janet wasn't talking to her flings, she was chitchatting with Georgiana, an old friend from high school who must have had an extra dose of patience, because all Janet ever went on about were the amazing happenings of her life.

Which never included Lexi—or even Bruce, for that matter.

Bruce was Janet's sixteen-year-old son, and he was weird. In fact, weird didn't even begin to describe Bruce. Lexi had known from her first day here that she didn't like him. She couldn't explain it; he just gave her the creeps. He never said anything to her, but he always stared at her. It was like the kid didn't know how to blink!

So Lexi did her best to ignore him, but he still freaked her out. Just what did he think he was looking at, anyway? Hadn't he ever seen a foster kid before?

Come on, sleep, come on!

Lexi tossed and turned. School would be so much easier if she could just get some sleep! Mrs. Harnelson had warned her that if she fell asleep in class one more time, she'd call Janet.

That was the last thing Lexi wanted to happen.

As she rolled over onto her side, she spotted the shadow by her door, again. It was the same lurking shadow she'd seen more than once since coming here, but it always seemed to disappear into the night as soon as she noticed it.

Like a ghost.

And she wondered why she couldn't sleep.

Sure, she'd tried telling Janet about it over breakfast one

morning, but Janet just shrugged it off as a nightmare.

"It's no surprise, is it? Come on, you're a smart girl, ain't ya? You're having nightmares because of what your daddy did, the psycho. You'll probably have nightmares for the rest of your life."

That was how it was, living with Janet Stevens.

***

Mornings always took forever to show up, but Lexi guessed that was how it was when you didn't sleep.

So there she was, alone in the kitchen, pouring herself a bowl of cereal. It wasn't like Janet ever made breakfast, or packed lunches, or anything else normal moms did.

As if Lexi was an expert on "normal" moms.

Making her own breakfast didn't bother her. For the most part, she fended for herself, which was fine by her. In fact, Lexi preferred to avoid Janet.

She still had an hour before the bus came, so she munched her Cheerios in the silent hum, glancing into the living room where the fake Christmas tree took up half the room. Lexi sighed. Christmas, what a stupid holiday! Wasn't it supposed to be all about families and quality time together, and all that mushy stuff?

A bunch of bull!

Still, with Christmas only two weeks away, Lexi distantly wondered if there were going to be any presents under the tree with her name on them.

She wasn't holding her breath.

Breaking through the bubble of silence, Janet was suddenly shrieking her head off upstairs. Lexi came close to spilling her juice, she startled so bad.

Most of it was incoherent, but Lexi picked out a few phrases.

"How long has this been going on, Bruce?"

"You're nothin' but a little pervert!"

"Has that little slut been makin' passes at you?"

Sighing, Lexi dropped her empty bowl into the sink, trying to tune it all out. Well, at least this time Janet was freaking out at

Bruce. It had nothing to do with her. That was how Janet rolled; if she wasn't at the bar picking up men or bragging to Georgiana, she was hollering about something. Pick up this or clean up that, but it didn't phase Lexi.

She'd heard worse.

A door slammed, rattling the house, and before Lexi even knew what was happening, Janet stormed down the stairs, set on destruction.

Lexi paled. Janet was heading right for her.

There wasn't even time to blink. Janet darted forward and grabbed Lexi's arm so tight, she actually yelled out.

"Shut up!" Janet screamed as she dragged Lexi back up the stairs. Lexi slipped a couple of times trying to keep up with the maniac, feeling the carpet rubbing her knees raw. Her eyes filled as Janet's claws stabbed her arm, piercing her skin.

"You're nothin' but a little tramp, ain't ya? Well, your days are numbered here! How dare you take advantage of my trust like that? I give you a home, and this is how you repay me? Comin' in here, actin' all innocent, but you can't pull the wool over my eyes! I'm no idiot!"

When they reached the top of the stairs, Janet seized a fistful of Lexi's hair, hauling her along like an old doll.

"You're hurting me; please stop!"

Warm tears trickled down Lexi's face as Janet shoved her into Bruce's bedroom, of all places.

And there was Bruce, lounging on his bed with his stupid guitar like nothing was going on. He strummed a few chords—tuning out all the screaming, no doubt.

But now that Lexi was in the room, Bruce stopped strumming and stared instead.

Stared at Lexi.

Well, let him stare. That's the last thing on my mind.

But not Janet's.

"Bruce! Quit lustin' after her! You're done, boy! You're done lookin' at her!"

What was she talking about? Done looking at who? Lexi? Was

304

Janet this angry because Bruce had looked at Lexi? Hadn't she known this all along? Bruce wasn't exactly subtle.

Before she even had the chance to ask, Janet snagged Lexi's arm again, forced her down in Bruce's swivel chair, the one that faced his computer.

"See these?" Janet screeched, flicking her finger at Bruce's computer screen.

Lexi was frozen, trapped like a rabbit. Janet was high-strung; if Lexi tried to leave, it would be bad. So she had no choice but to look at the pictures Janet was already scrolling through.

Lexi's head swam.

They were all of her.

There had to be hundreds of them.

There were several pictures of her just lying in bed, eyes fixated on the ceiling. There were pictures of her sprawled out on her bedroom floor, doing homework. There were pictures of her jogging from the bus stop. Some of the shots were close-ups of her budding chest!

The worst ones were near the end, pictures of her in the bathroom, getting out of the shower. Close-ups.

Tearfully, she turned away, but Janet had her hair again, jerked her back so she had no choice but to live out the nightmare in front of her.

Lexi felt sick. How... how did he get all of these?

"You little tramp! You come into my home and you seduce my kid!" Janet screamed. "If you get pregnant—"

"I didn't do anything!" Lexi nearly tripped over the chair as she jumped up, backed away from Janet, who looked ready to strike. "I never even talked to him!"

"Do you expect me to believe you?" Janet laughed like a psycho. "Wearing your little tank tops, showing off your scrawny little legs, spraying yourself with your pretty body spray, all so you could get your hands on my kid."

Lexi swallowed. Tank tops? She didn't even own a tank top. The group home had a strict dress code, and it wasn't like Janet had ever taken her shopping.

But Janet wouldn't hear it.

"Nothin' but your slutty behaviour is responsible for this!" Janet gestured to the screen again, where a still of Lexi brushing her teeth lingered. "He can't keep his eyes off you!"

"I didn't do anything!" Lexi said again, feeling icky. Her mind circled back to those pictures of her in the bathroom. How had she not known he was there, especially with a camera?

"You're done!" Janet said, her eyes afire. Lexi stumbled back, but only until she found the wall. "I have worked too long and too hard on raising that boy to let a brat like you turn him into some kind of sex-crazed maniac that lusts after little girls!"

Trapping Lexi's wrist in her vice, Janet yanked her from Bruce's room, down the hall.

"You're through. Consider this your ticket out of here!"

Once in Lexi's room, Janet shoved her down hard, driving her to her hands and knees.

"Do not *move!" Janet glared with a violent rage.*

Then she slammed the door behind her, rattling the house again.

Lexi was alone.

Carefully, quietly, Lexi inched toward her door, hearing the explosions of Janet's stomping as the woman stormed into her own room, picking up the phone.

Lexi heard everything; Janet had called her caseworker, Bridget.

So that was how it was going to be. She'd be kicked out, sent back to the group home, put on the market for another foster home. That was how the system worked.

Well, good. Bruce had been snapping secret pictures of her, naked *pictures of her. The whole thing made her want to throw up.*

No, she didn't want to stay here.

All this time, four months, she'd been stalked, watched, and now it dawned on her that all those nights she thought she was imagining moving shadows by her door, it had actually been Bruce.

Bruce with his camera.

The thought was unnerving.

She hoped it wouldn't take long for Bridget to come and get her. She didn't know what her next foster home would be like, but nothing could be worse than this.

CHAPTER 56

L E X I

Wednesday, October 28
9:01 p.m.

Lexi didn't even bother lighting her candle. Why shed light on the disgusting truth that this, these cave-like walls, this underground prison, would be her life until the day she died?

Besides, she found it fitting, sitting alone in the dark. At least this way, nobody could see her, nobody would notice her. She was invisible; she didn't matter. That was how it always had been.

That was how it always would be. Why expect anything different?

Her fingers grazed along her neck, already feeling so naked without that necklace around it.

Why did she even care? When was the last time she'd even let herself care? About anything? Caring was stupid; nothing ever worked out anyway, not the way you wanted it to.

Besides, it wasn't like she really knew Liz that well. It wasn't like they had some kind of deep friendship that went back for years. So why did it matter? Why should Lexi care whether she had the necklace or Sapphire had it? It was just a *thing*, after all.

Just a thing...

She could tell herself it was no big deal until she was blue in the face, but she still wasn't convinced.

Even she couldn't deny that the necklace meant something.

It wasn't that it was the first and only piece of jewellery she'd ever owned. Sure, that was cool, but that wasn't why it was important. It was important because Liz had given it to her after only knowing her for three weeks. Liz had given away a piece of her life without even really *knowing* Lexi. And the weird part was, somehow, Liz actually remembered Lexi saying she'd never had any jewellery.

"Look, you're fifteen, and you told me you've never had any jewellery, so... here's your first."

That meant she'd been listening.

That was why it meant something.

But it didn't matter anymore. It was gone, just like everything else in her life that had ever been good.

Whatever.

If it didn't matter, why was she still sulking in the dark?

Well then, quit sulking!

Easy as pie.

Yeah right.

As she tried to empty her mind, make it as black as the darkness around her, she was aware of light footsteps echoing closer and closer.

Great. Company. Well, maybe whoever it is will pass right by, ignore the loner in the dark.

But whoever it was had a candle with them, a dancing light breaking through the blackness, and it was heading right for Lexi's space.

Star.

"You're still bleeding," she said, kneeling in front of Lexi, pointing out her arm.

Oh, right. Courtesy of Sapphire's monster fingernails.

"Who cares?"

Star, typical Star, wasted no time reaching into her pocket, bringing out a handkerchief. She scooted closer, motioning with it, like she was asking for permission to play nurse.

Lexi didn't care. She didn't care about anything anymore, so she only shrugged.

Star went to work, gently dabbing her handkerchief along the craters Sapphire had dug into Lexi's skin. Frig, it hurt! It was still fresh, and it stung bitterly. Lexi clamped down on her tongue, didn't say a word. If she spoke, Star would start a conversation, and Lexi wasn't feeling like much of a conversationalist. The sooner Star was finished, the sooner she'd leave Lexi to wallow in the darkness again.

But that wasn't how Star worked.

"What made Sapphire angry this time?" she asked quietly, dabbing away methodically.

Lexi huffed. The last thing she felt like doing was talking, to *anybody*. Today, of all days, Lexi was not in the mood.

But it was rude not to answer.

"She was mad 'cause of my necklace!" she snapped.

"But… you don't have a necklace," Star pointed out. "At least, not that *I've* ever seen."

"I just got it today, okay?"

"From where?" Star inquired, naive to Lexi's irritation.

"From Liz," Lexi replied, straining to keep her voice steady. She wanted to yell, she wanted to scream, she wanted to lash out at something, but it wouldn't be fair to freak out on Star. It wasn't Star's fault her life sucked so bad. "Liz gave it to me."

Star met Lexi's eyes and flashed that smile of hers.

"That's so nice!" Her eyes glittered above the glow of her candle. "That Liz sounds like such a wonderful person. Why did she give you a necklace?"

Even Lexi didn't know the answer to that.

"I don't know," she replied honestly, exhaustion sweeping through her entire body. "She said she wanted me to look at it and think of God or something."

"That's really nice," Star said quietly, pulling her handkerchief away. No more blood.

"Yeah, she wanted me to look at it and remember that, like, God will be there whenever I'm ready to call out to Him, or something stupid like that!" Lexi shook her head, angry, hardly realizing how sarcastic and bitter she actually sounded.

But Star noticed. "Does that make you angry?" she asked.

"Yeah, it makes me angry! In fact, it ticks me right off! Why should I call out to a God who's done nothing but make my life miserable since the day I was born?" Lexi crossed her arms. "No offense, Star, but your God, He doesn't know what He's doing."

Instead of getting upset or defensive, Star only smiled. "He *does* know what He's doing, CJ. You just don't understand *why* He does what He does." She leaned up against the wall. "God may allow bad things to happen, but He doesn't cause them to happen. Look around you; this world is a horrible place. I mean, look at what they did to Jesus, and He was the Son of God! Humans have free will, and people in your life have truly hurt you. I get that, CJ, I really do, but that doesn't change the truth that God loves you like *crazy*, and He's working in your life. I can see it.

"I believe even Liz's presence is a blessing from God, and you've got friends here, too. I care about you a lot, DV likes hanging out with you, and Barney... well, he's crazy about you. All I'm saying is that God hasn't forgotten about you, whether you feel that way or not."

Lexi wanted to argue, wanted to fight Star on how wrong she thought she was, but she didn't have the energy, not anymore. Silence required less energy, and she'd already maxed out.

"Anyway, CJ, I think it's great you're asking questions. It means you're curious. It means you're not closing the door on the idea of God." Star found her feet. "And I'm sorry your necklace got stolen, but even without it, God is still with you, and He'll still be there when you're ready. I hope one day you'll know that's true."

Star left her candle behind, leaving Lexi a little more in the light than when she'd arrived.

Curious. Was that true? Was Lexi actually curious about God? Was that why she was asking so many questions?

She thought about what Star had said about free will, about God not being the One to cause bad things.

That was new.

But Lexi still didn't believe it.

With nothing left but her own thoughts and an emptiness she'd known since she was little, she curled up, faced the wall, and waited for sleep.

But it never came.

CHAPTER 57

L I Z

Thursday, October 29
2:17 p.m.

The day was perfect. Not a single cloud floated across the pale blue sky, the breeze was gentle, the sun beamed down. Even the temperature was exactly right.

A good day for a trip out to Arlington, and Liz was already on her way.

Yes, she still had to work later, but this was important.

Her thoughts were all over the place, scattered. Her eyes were raw from all the tears she'd shed since yesterday, her cheeks still blotchy. She hadn't slept a single wink last night, and the heavy bags under her eyes were hard evidence of this. Sleep was useless, after all. When you avoided something for two years, then unleashed its power in the blink of an eye, why should you expect to sleep?

All through the night, Liz had clung to the photographs of Kurt, longing to feel close to him again. Anytime she touched the side of the bed that used to be his, she felt her heart splitting all over again.

It was so surreal. He'd been gone for two years, but since she'd pulled out that box, it was like travelling through time, back to that first day, the day she'd found out her husband was gone. The sting of grief was just as painful two years later.

Liz wondered how long it would take the pain to go away, how long it would take before she felt whole again, but maybe Kathryn was right. Maybe it was something that would never go away.

Then again, maybe it would get easier with time.

Too many maybes.

Nothing absolute.

That was the hard part.

***

Liz puttered up the familiar driveway and noticed her father's car was gone.

It was just as well.

She'd come to see her mother.

God, strengthen me…

Donning her sunglasses, Liz dawdled up the driveway, each step like dragging a heavy load. Fear snuck in more and more until she reached the front door.

By then she was panicking.

Maybe this wasn't such a good idea. Sure, it seemed right when she'd planned it last night, but thinking about doing something and actually doing it were two very different things.

But no, she would have to fight it, fight the urge to run away. Running away would be the easy way out.

Liz was done with taking the easy way out.

She rang the doorbell.

God, give me strength, she prayed again.

She heard scrambling on the other side of the door, and Liz imagined her mother stealing one last glance in her hall mirror, obsessing over whether or not she was presentable for whoever could be paying her a surprise visit.

That was Anne Deston, always concerned with outward appearances.

The door swung open, and there was her mother, layers of makeup and hair primped.

Leave it to Mrs. Deston to look fantastic on a day she wasn't expecting company.

"Elizabeth!" Anne exclaimed, her bright red lips curling into a smile, showing her sparkling white teeth and age lines. "Why, what are you doing here?"

Anne stepped out onto the porch and engulfed her only daughter in a hug, squeezing a little too tight.

"I mean, pardon my surprise. I'm very glad to see you, but I haven't seen you since Kevin's birthday." Anne rested her hand on the doorknob. "What brings you by?"

Strength, God, please give me strength.

"I know, Mom, and I can't stay long. I still have to work this afternoon." Liz swallowed. *No more running.* "But I need to talk to you."

***

Anne insisted it was too beautiful a day to waste indoors, so Liz found herself sitting on the edge of one of the lounge chairs by the pool, while her mother, garbed in a fancy sunhat and sunglasses, leaned right back, already soaking up the sun.

"Elizabeth, relax, dear. Are you sure you don't want any lemonade? It's fresh. I squeezed the lemons this morning."

"I'm fine, Mother." That was far from true.

"Suit yourself, dear." Anne sighed contently. "What did you want to talk to me about? Are you feeling guilty for missing my pool party?"

Yes, Mother, it's all about you. Liz sucked in a breath as pressure built up behind her eyes. Thankfully, her mother was too preoccupied with her tan to notice.

"You know what I did last night, Mother?" Liz asked, concentrating on steadying her voice.

"What?" Anne asked passively, sipping her lemonade.

"I sat on my bedroom floor, and..." Liz gulped down a salty lump as a tear drizzled down her cheek. "And I looked at pictures of Kurt for the first time since... since he died. I looked at them;

I read his letters. I allowed myself—no, *forced* myself—to do it!"

She heard the creaking, her mother sitting up in her lounger, but Liz couldn't bring herself to look over. It was easier if eye contact was avoided, for now.

"Do you know why I did it, Mom? Because a fifteen-year-old street girl who's been through more in her life than I could ever imagine told *me* I needed closure!" Liz knew she was raising her voice, but she didn't care anymore. This had to be said. "Why, of all people, did it take a *child* to convince me of this?"

"Honey," Anne started in her singsong voice, probably ready to chastise her about the dangers of fraternizing with street scum.

"No, let me finish," Liz said through clenched teeth, gazing into the pool's deep end. "That's why I felt so drawn to her, the one I told you about. It's because that girl has dealt with her pain by numbing herself, by walking around in a stupor, by pretending she doesn't care. I didn't understand it at first, but now I do. Mother, I've been avoiding the truth, but it's exactly what *I've* been doing—pretending like I don't care. But I can't pretend anymore, because I *do* care!"

She lost count of how many tears zipped down her face. She knew her mother saw them, and she knew that meant she'd become vulnerable, but there was no turning back now.

"Kurt meant more to me than life itself, more than anything this world had to offer, and he died! What could I do but hide myself from that, shield myself from it?"

Liz drew in a breath. She became aware of her thudding heart. She knew her mother wasn't going to like what was coming next. It didn't matter how many times Liz had rehearsed this in her mind, she *still* dreaded her mother's reaction.

Okay, Liz, no turning back.

It was now or never.

"Mother," Liz said, lowering her voice to a sound calm. "That's why I stay away. That's why I avoid visits, why I avoid calling, because you keep bringing him up. When you tell me we should have had children, when you tell me I should move on, when you tell me I still have a chance to have my own children, it hurts! Mother, I can't *stand* hearing it, because, to me, it's a constant reminder of what I can't have! And it kills me to see Craig and Kevin with their beautiful wives and their fantastic children. Then there's me—a childless widow! Yes, Mother, I wanted children, I *want* children! It's what I've *always* wanted, and I will never have them. You may think it's easy for me, that I can just turn on a switch and leave all the grief behind, move on, meet somebody new and create a family for myself, but Mother, you don't understand. How can I move on when I haven't let go of Kurt? I'm not ready, and I don't want to hear you telling me anymore. It hurts too much."

Well, there it was, bottled up for over two years, out in the open.

All she could do now was wait for the reaction.

Once, when Liz was twelve, she had bravely asked her mother not to volunteer as a chaperone for the junior high dance the country club was hosting. It was hard enough trying to find a date, but how embarrassing was it to have your mother watching your every move at the most important social event of the year?

But the look in her mother's eyes that day spoke louder than any words she could have said. It was like Liz's request had stung somewhere deep inside her soul. For days, her mother gave her the cold shoulder, stayed out of Liz's way, spoke to her only when she had to. The rest of the time, she trudged around the house, her face all ice. She didn't chaperone the dance, but Liz learned an important lesson that year.

She had to be very careful what she said to her mother.

So it came as no surprise, as she tensed up in the lounge chair, that Liz anticipated the worst.

She didn't even dare to look. To say her mother was sensitive was an understatement; she took everything personally, always made it about herself. Her mother was probably sitting there with crocodile tears in her eyes, ready to fire a rant about how hard this whole ordeal had been on *her*, because that was how it always was with her mother. She could turn anything into her own personal tragedy.

"Well," her mother started after a painfully long silence. "Elizabeth, I'm not going to sit here and pretend like the things you said didn't hurt…"

Here it comes…

"But honey, didn't it feel good to let that all *out?*"

Liz's heart stopped.

She must have heard wrong.

But when she looked up, there were no tears running down her mother's cheeks. Nothing in her body language indicated that she was ready to strike. Instead, Anne took off her sunglasses and smiled at Liz—an encouraging smile, like she actually accepted what Liz was saying.

Liz managed a nod. Yes, it felt good—*more* than good—to let all that out, and what made her feel even better was that her mother was supporting her and not condemning her.

That was an answer to prayer.

"Honey, everyone deals with their pain in different ways," Anne said gently. "You chose to deal with it by clamming up. I knew from the beginning what you were trying to do. I could see it. You can't know how painful it is for a mother to see her child struggling so fiercely and not being able to kiss it better, make it go away."

Now a layer of tears formed in her mother's eyes, but suddenly they didn't seem so repelling.

"Darling, bringing up Kurt was just my subtle way of trying to help you deal with your pain. Elizabeth, you don't have children, and perhaps you don't want to hear this, but a mother *knows* when her child is hurting, and it's the worst feeling in the world to be totally and utterly helpless. All I wanted to do was help you, but there was just no practical way of doing so. So, I suggested you move on. I… I thought it would help, but… well, I suppose I failed to think of you, and where your heart was at.

"Sweetheart, please know my motives were pure. I don't like to see you so closed off to love, darling. You always wanted children. Ever since you were a little girl, you had big dreams for your future, and now all you do is work." Anne even looked elegant brushing a tear away. "Maybe now isn't the time, but it's never too late, Elizabeth. You can still have the family you've always wanted, one day. But before that can happen, you need to open up. You don't have to close the door on love, not anymore."

Love.

Don't close yourself to love.

"I haven't, Mom," Liz said quietly, meeting her mother's eyes. "Not entirely."

Lexi.

She thought of how deeply moved she'd been whenever she saw those chocolate brown eyes filled to the brim with a pain she couldn't share in, a pain she couldn't take away. She thought of how happy it made her whenever she spotted Lexi walking down the street, praising God she was safe for another day. She thought of the fear that consumed her when she didn't know where Lexi was or what she was doing. She thought of how helpless she felt when she knew how hurt Lexi was and couldn't do a darn thing to fix it.

Helpless...

Wasn't that what her mother was talking about?

"That's love, isn't it?" Liz asked. Suddenly, things were starting to make sense. "That's what you feel for me, Mother. You see me hurting and you want to fix it, because you love me." She swallowed. "That's what I want to do for this girl. She's hurting, and all I want to do is take it away, fix it."

Lexi had been tugging on Liz's heartstrings since the first day she saw her, and her heart broke every time they'd bumped into each other since. It killed her how helpless she was. She wanted nothing more than for Lexi to be happy, safe, healthy, whole.

That was love.

"But darling." Anne cleared her throat. "She lives on the streets."

"It doesn't matter, Mom. She still has feelings." Oh, it all felt so easy now. "And she means the *world* to me."

319

As Anne pondered in silence, Liz was aware of something new, something she'd never seen in her mother before. Maybe it was compassion, reconciliation, or maybe it was understanding. She wasn't sure, but something had changed.

And maybe, for the first time, Liz's mother would keep her two cents to herself and respect her daughter's feelings.

It was a cathartic feeling. Liz suddenly felt freer than she ever had visiting her mother. Would things be different now? Better? Easier?

Only time would tell, she supposed.

"So tell me, Elizabeth." Anne's lip curled into a small smile. "What is it that *you* want?"

CHAPTER 58

L I Z

Thursday, October 29
3:42 p.m.

Liz had one more stop to make.

She'd debated all through the night whether or not she'd go, but if she was serious about all this, about healing, about closure, she'd have to do it right. And that meant doing it all. She'd already succeeded in confronting her mother, something she'd wanted to do for two years now.

Well, even that seemed tame compared to what was next.

Liz glanced at her watch. Would there even be time for this?

Oh yes; in fact, there was plenty of time.

Driving along, the scenery hardly seemed recognizable. She was out of the city now. No high-rise buildings lining the busy streets, no traffic—just Liz, the open road, and her thoughts. She still couldn't believe it, couldn't believe what had just transpired at her mother's house. It all seemed so unlikely, but there it was.

Two years. For two years, Liz had kept those feelings buried in a locked-up chest inside, contained them, hidden them. For two years she'd kept her mouth shut, chosen silence whenever her mother spoke out of turn. For two years she'd resisted this confrontation with her mother, resisted out of fear.

Now, two years later, Liz had broken her unwritten contract with herself. She'd told her mother the truth. And it hadn't ended up the way she'd always imagined it would. There were no explosions, no falling apart, no "poor old me."

That *had* to be thanks to God.

Now, Liz's mind buzzed with the changes it might mean, the pressure it might take off family visits, the fact that she might even *enjoy* trips out to Arlington... but right now, there was still so much to think about, so much else to deal with.

It was much like a baby taking her first steps, only these steps would lead her toward healing.

At least, that was her prayer.

Liz slowed as she merged onto a road she'd only ever travelled once before. Once had been enough; she'd never been able to return. It was like some giant force field kept her away, a force field she had built. Now, that field had somehow dissolved.

She parked the car.

It was quiet. Liz could hear her shoes crunching the dead grass beneath her as she passed through the tall wire gates. They opened with ease, as though encouraging her to go on, whispering with the gentle wind, *You can do this, Liz.*

Breath held, she crossed the mowed lawn, the silence deafening. Had it been this quiet the first time she'd been here?

She came to a small hill, the hill she'd visited in so many of her dreams those first few months.

But this wasn't a dream. This was as real as it could get.

Fear threatened to paralyze her.

Should she go back home, forget all of this? Maybe now wasn't the right time after all.

No. This was the right time. She *had* to move on.

She trekked on a little further, until she came to a set of stones.

Gravestones.

None of it felt real, not until she saw his name engraved into a marble slab.

Kurt's gravestone.

Liz froze up, staring at the stone, the stone she hadn't laid eyes on since the burial. Still, she remembered it all so well, that rainy day in July two years before.

Reminding herself to breathe, Liz sank to her knees, felt the cushion of the soft dirt below her, and read the name on the polished slab of stone several times, as though she could erase its truth by doing so.

Kurtis Joseph Swavier
Born: February 9, 1972
Died: July 6, 2007
Beloved Son and Husband

A cold tear trickled out of Liz's eye as she reached out, let her fingers graze the stone, tracing out his name.

She exhaled, long and low.

"I'm sorry I didn't bring any flowers, love."

***

She was lost in the feel of this place. She didn't know how long she knelt in the stillness. She didn't know how many cars rolled by. She didn't even know if she was late for work, but none of that mattered. She was in a place that wasn't constrained by time.

Liz gazed upon his name, touched the blades of grass that had the privilege to live so near her husband. It all came back to her, that day. Now it was easy to remember the thousand knives that pierced through to the centre of her heart as she watched those men lower her dead husband into the ground that awful Thursday morning.

Here she was again, those same knives digging in.

"I..." She struggled to speak. "I would give *anything* to hear you say... say something to me again, to hear your voice."

The emptiness inside was a deep chasm, bottomless, pulling her down. She'd never felt so lost. This was the closest to Kurt she'd come since his death, and yet she wasn't allowed to have his arms engulf her, his gentle fingers brush her hair out of her face like he had a habit of doing, his lips grazing hers, his hand twined with hers.

The longing came close to consuming her.

At least she could talk to him, but it felt so strange.

Could he hear her? If he couldn't, would God pass along a message to him? She didn't know how it worked, only that she had to do it.

"Kurt." His name felt foreign on her lips. "I'm... I'm sorry I haven't come to visit. I... I just couldn't face it. You being gone, I... I just couldn't face it."

Distantly, she could hear a sparrow. She ignored its song.

"I've been... I thought it would be easier to forget the pain, but... yesterday... I realized... I... I haven't been able to accept that you're—"

Everything came into focus. This *was* real.

"—gone."

Shaking, she pulled a tissue from her purse, wiped the tears from her eyes. It hurt. Oh, how it hurt.

"I don't *want* to accept it, Kurt. Don't you see? I'm miserable without you!" Her body trembled rhythmically with her sobs. "You were the love of my life, my heart, my reason to live. My waking, my sleeping, my breathing, my *everything*."

She struggled to catch her breath, wrapped her arms around her body.

"I can't do this, Kurt." A tear landed on the green grass. "I can't bury it anymore. It's not right, it's not fair. I can't pretend like it didn't matter."

And suddenly, another day flashed vividly in her mind. The day she had found out.

She'd just finished picking fresh daisies for Kurt's hospital room. He always liked her to brighten up his drab room with fresh flowers from her garden.

But she never made it that far.

She remembered collapsing to her knees when the doctor told her. She remembered feeling like the walls were closing in on her, like all the oxygen had been sucked from the room. She was crippled in every sense of the word; she couldn't breathe, couldn't move, couldn't speak. Her life was gone.

It felt just as debilitating now, two years later.

"I thought I could... I thought I could just, you know, throw myself into work, not have to deal with it, but... I realized... with some help, it's not good to do that, not for me, or for anyone else." Her vision blurred. "Especially you. All you ever wanted was for me to be happy, and... and I haven't been. The thing is, Kurt, I... I just don't know *how* to be happy without you."

Her stomach felt like a rock as she sat for the longest time, shivering. She heard nothing but that sparrow's whistling. Its song filled the empty cemetery.

Slowly, strangely, that song brought Liz comfort, a sense of peace. As the gentle breeze touched her skin, the simple sparrow's notes touched the depths of her soul. She remembered Kurt, how he had liked to whistle—while he made breakfast, while he showered, while he drove, even while he watched television. The funny thing was, he would never whistle any particular song; it was always something new, something made up, his own creation.

That was one of the things Liz had loved about him, even though she teased him endlessly about being terribly off-key.

"How can you know I'm off-key," he'd say, *"if only I know the song?"*

***

For however long she sat there, that sparrow never left. It continued its song, and Liz felt her insides melting from the ice they had become. It was only a small feeling, hardly enough to make all the pain go away, but she knew she wouldn't feel completely whole—not for a long time, maybe never. Right now, though, she felt such a peace and comfort in knowing she was taking the right steps.

Maybe she had Lexi to thank for that.

Liz bent back her head, looked up toward the sky, toward the place where Kurt was waiting for her, watching over her.

"I bet it's beautiful, isn't it, honey?" she asked, eyes glistening anew. "Heaven?"

A tear squeezed out from her eye, imagining Kurt with that big grin on his face.

"Make sure you save me a place, okay?"

She could almost hear him whispering her a promise.

And as she realized she'd been away for two years, a small smile crossed her lips; they had a lot to catch up on.

"Well, I guess I'll let you in on what's been happening down here," she said quietly, moving so she could lean up against the tombstone. "I've been working a lot, and most people give me a hard time about it. I guess it's only fair. They just care about me."

They just care about me. I have to let them back in.

Suddenly, it didn't seem so impossible.

"I still see Kathryn, and Brian, too. You should see Nancy; she's growing up so fast. She's becoming more like her mother every day, so you can imagine what a little spitfire she is."

Kurt had always been big on teasing Kathryn about the handful Nancy would become. If he could see her now, he'd be in stitches.

"I have to admit, I haven't really visited my family an awful lot. Mom, well, she brought you up a lot, and it was hard to deal with. I talked to her about it today, though, so maybe things will be different. Craig and Meghan, Kevin and Lisa are all great, and the kids... well, they're growing, too. Lissy's already in school, if you can believe that!"

She even laughed a little, feeling, if only for a fraction of a second, a semblance of normality.

It was as though Kurt were sitting right here, listening.

"Speaking of kids, I have to tell you about this girl I met." A smile touched her lips, just thinking of her. "Her name is Lexi."

As the sparrow belted out a new song, Liz told Kurt all about Lexi—about how they'd met, about how she'd wrapped the girl's arm, about how she'd learned her name. She told him about her sleepless nights because of how worried she'd been over this stranger. She told him about how she hoped Lexi would come back to have her arm looked at and about the sheer joy she'd felt when she actually did.

She told Kurt about her daily frustrations in wondering if praying was enough, about all the times their paths crossed, about her fears in letting Lexi return to the tunnels, especially after knowing the girl had been beaten up, thrown into a wall, and watched by some kind of teenage predator.

She told Kurt about the pepper spray, about Lexi coming to her house, *their* house, about her seeing the art studio, about it being Lexi's suggestion that Liz should finish the *Lion Cubs* painting.

"She's a sweetheart, Kurt. You really would have liked her. But she's been through so much, and I've only caught a glimpse into her life. I feel so helpless, so unsure what I'm supposed to do. But here's the thing: I think she's done more for me than I've done for her. I can't help but wonder if there's more to this than I'm seeing. I worry about her all the time, and I would give up everything just to know she's safe. I would risk my own life to see her happy."

She sighed, smiling a little. "I guess that's just crazy, huh?"

Crazy...

But was it? She'd tied off her heart to love, shut herself away from feeling anything, and a stranger had torn through all those walls in a second. Liz had never *chosen* to care about Lexi. It had just... happened.

The fog she'd been weathering for weeks was finally starting to clear.

Maybe her path *was* crossing with Lexi's for a reason. Maybe none of this—dealing with Kurt's death, meeting Lexi—was accidental. Things didn't just happen by accident. Maybe her heart opened up again for a reason. Yes, to learn closure, but maybe there was more to it than that.

"*So tell me, Elizabeth,*" her mother had said, "*what is it that you want?*"

Was this all God's way of helping her answer that question? Or was coming here the wake-up call she needed to clear away the mess in her thick skull, to see what God had been trying to show her all along?

She didn't know, but suddenly she felt a peace in knowing what it was she wanted.

She knew *exactly* what she wanted. No more doubts.

Liz looked up toward Heaven, toward her husband.

"Kurt, I know what I want, and it doesn't make a lot of sense right now." She paused. Yes, this was right. "I think I want to adopt Lexi."

CHAPTER 59

L E X I

Thursday, October 29
7:25 p.m.

Lexi was bored. No surprises there. It wasn't like she was bombarded with options in a place like the tunnels.

So she strayed through the Pit, scanning the downcast faces she'd become so familiar with the past month. They were all too caught up in their own worlds to notice her, but it didn't matter. She didn't *want* them to notice her, but she was looking for Barney. He was always good for an idea or two. The last time she'd been bored, he took her to the beach, and they chased after seagulls for a while. Sure, it was simple, but it passed the time.

But Barney wasn't anywhere in the Pit. He wasn't in his space; he wasn't wandering through the Combs like he sometimes did when he was high. If he wasn't down here, it probably meant he was still up on the streets, panhandling, maybe digging through trashcans.

Well, Lexi had already spent her afternoon on the streets, and all she had to show for it was fifty lousy cents. No, she wasn't going back up there, and besides, she didn't feel like looking for Barney. She'd just have to wait down here until he decided to show up.

Lexi trudged on over to DV's corner, where the live-in artist was still working hard on the same mural he'd been painting on the day she arrived.

Only now, it looked so much more alive.

The birds were flying! You couldn't help but smile. Lexi could still remember the infancy of this mural, when it was nothing more than a nest under a tree. Now the mural was nearly finished.

"Hey, girl." DV noticed the cuts on Lexi's arm. "I hear Sapph swiped your necklace. Left you some nasty scars, too."

She felt acid boiling in the pit of her stomach. If it was left uncontrolled, it would erupt like some kind of emotional volcano. She couldn't let that happen.

"It's not the worst thing I've had," she said flatly, meaning her arm. She took in the cavorting birds in the spotless sky.

I bet they feel so free...

"Man, you are *so* cryptic," DV said, rising to his feet so he could reach the birds in flight. "I never know what to think of you. I mean, I don't know if there's actually a human being in there somewhere, or if you seriously just don't care about *anything*."

"That's not true!" Lexi snapped. "I care that my necklace got taken!"

"Oh, I hear ya, girl." DV swirled his brush in a brown blob of paint. "When I first got here, Sapph took my watch. Gold-plated, ya know? I was ticked at first, but you gotta understand where she's comin' from. I mean, she's doin' a good thing, takin' us all in, givin' us a place to chill, a place to sleep."

"No, she's not! It's not like she *owns* these tunnels! They were probably here before she ever even thought about running away. They're fair game. Anybody should get to decide if they stay or go!"

Lexi didn't care who heard her. She didn't even care if Sapphire heard her. Why should she care about anything anymore?

"Maybe you're right, but that's just how the world works, I guess." DV paused. "Seriously, though, don't worry so much about the necklace. I mean, it's just a *thing*, right?"

Right.

Just a thing.

Just a gift.

330

Just the first piece of jewellery she'd ever owned.

That's all.

Sighing, Lexi leaned up against the wall, staring mindlessly at those birds, when out of the corner of her eye she saw Barney barrelling through the Pit.

Finally!

He flew right past her.

"Hey!" Lexi yelled, irritated.

He stopped, looked at her impatiently. What was *his* problem?

"Dude, where you been?" Lexi asked. "I've been looking for you. I'm bored; we should—"

"Yeah, yeah, in a bit, Ceej. I just need to get stuff from Slick, okay?"

Lexi hadn't noticed it before, but she noticed it now. Something was different about him, something she couldn't quite put her finger on. It was like there was something... missing. There was no cheesy grin, no witty comeback, no animated limbs.

He wasn't his usual goofy self; *that's* what was different. He seemed like a completely different person.

It was weird. Was it because he wanted his weed? She'd seen him desperate for a hit before, but he'd never been like this.

"I just... I just need to see Slick, okay? Sorry, man, just, like... just give me a few minutes. I'll meet you at your place, okay?" Barney managed a small wave. "Okay? I'm good; just meet me there. Gotta get it."

That was the other thing. Barney's eyes were moist.

Almost like he's been... crying.

Barney didn't cry. At least, Lexi had never *seen* him cry.

What was going on? Was he really that upset about needing his stupid fix, or was there more to the picture than just that?

Barney disappeared into the Combs, and Lexi rolled her eyes. He was probably playing it up, being a little melodramatic. He didn't need his drugs... he was just being a drama queen.

She said goodbye to DV and headed to her space to wait for

Barney. As much as she hated him smoking the junk, she hoped it would at least take the edge off tonight.

He was acting too weird.

CHAPTER 60

L I Z

Thursday, October 29
7:53 p.m.

For the first time in a long time, Liz was beginning to feel more like herself.

She'd been at work for a few hours now and looked terrible. Having spent most of the last day in tears... well, that definitely didn't do much for one's looks, but Liz didn't mind. There were too many other things to think about.

Between patients, Liz's mind flickered back to the cemetery, to when she'd sat by Kurt's final resting place and told him about Lexi.

About *adopting* Lexi.

Had that really only happened a few hours ago?

It had felt so strange, speaking to Kurt for the first time in two years. Even now, working the rounds in the ER, she still felt like she was floating on a cloud, like she was drifting through some distant dream. Surely she shouldn't take anything she'd said in that cemetery seriously.

Should she?

After all, she *was* still thinking about it, imagining it.

What if... it *could* work?

Lexi said she'd spent time in a group home, gone through foster care. Did that mean she was eligible for adoption? What kinds of people would Liz have to contact about something like this? Was it even realistic?

Still, Liz couldn't stop herself from picturing a future where Liz helped Lexi with her math homework, took her out for brunch every weekend, let her cry on her shoulder as she poured out her heart and soul. Maybe one day, Liz would send a smiling, healthy, and happy Lexi off to some Ivy League school; she'd be top of her class!

Liz imagined all the simple things, too, like decorating her spare bedroom to house a teenager. She imagined letting Lexi pick her favourite colour, painting it together.

It all brought a smile to her face. Warm feelings brewed inside her, but there was still a part of the equation missing—and that was Lexi.

Would Lexi even be interested?

That girl had been through too much for someone her age— her parents passing away only two years ago, thrown into four foster homes, living the life of a runaway... it was enough to bring *anyone* to tears. Pastor Reid was right. It was no wonder these kids didn't trust adults. Lexi had been moved around so much, how could she believe she belonged anywhere?

But Liz wanted to be the one to change all that. She *longed* to help Lexi believe she was valuable, important, deeply cared for. She wanted to protect her from anything bad for the rest of her life.

Liz sighed. It seemed so simple, constructing it all in her mind's eye, but making it a reality? Well, that was another story.

God, I don't know what I'm doing. I don't know if it's possible, or even right, but I know You're in control of this. You have been since the beginning. Am I just crazy, Lord? Adoption... is it right, could I even be a good mother, am I ready for something like this? Is Lexi?

I trust You're in control, but I could really use some kind of affirmation. I want to be sure.

***

After sending home a twenty-seven-year-old man who'd waited in the ER for five hours only to find out he had an inner ear infection, Liz traded in charts at reception and bumped into Jenn.

"Hey, stranger!" Jenn greeted. "I didn't know you were working tonight. How long have you been here?"

Nightshifts were like that. Sometimes you had no idea who you were working with until hours into your shift.

"A few hours now," Liz said, confirming with her watch. "You?"

"Since noon. I'm off in twenty minutes, though." Jenn grinned. "What's your story? You look like hell."

Leave it to Jenn to state the blatantly obvious. "Long day. Listen, do you have a sec?"

"Sure! You know, there *is* this room filled with impatient people, and they're all waiting on us, but no rush," Jenn said with a smile.

"What do you know about adoption?"

"Uh." Jenn stared. "What?"

Well, Liz wasn't surprised. After all, it had come out of nowhere.

"Adoption." Liz said again. "Do you know where I would go to find out what I'd need to be able to adopt?"

Jenn seemed at a loss for words. For a while, Liz didn't think she was going to say anything at all.

"Honey, it's really neat that you're interested in adoption, and I can definitely help you look into it, but I know there are waiting lists. I mean, babies are hard to get. *Everybody* wants to adopt nowadays, and—"

"Not a baby," Liz interrupted. "A teenager, one who's probably already in the system. I know she's been in foster care, so I'm guessing she's represented by some kind of social service."

Jenn was silent, pensive. Liz could almost hear the gears whirring away.

Then, something flashed behind Jenn's eyes; she'd already figured it out. Sometimes Jenn was too smart for her own good.

335

"Oh Liz," Jenn finally said, her voice ringing with disapproval. "You're talking about that street kid, aren't you? The one you helped with the sprained wrist?"

"Is that so wrong?" Liz asked. No, it didn't *feel* wrong, but it was no secret how everyone felt about the Tunnel Kids. *Bad news, dangerous, avoid them at all costs.* Why should she expect Jenn's support?

Truth be told, she wasn't really expecting anyone's support.

"Well," Jenn shrugged, "you *have* only seen her a few times, haven't you?"

"I know," Liz started, "but there's so much more to it than that. Jenn, I know you don't believe in God, and I'm not asking you to, but you have to understand. He's put that girl on my heart. This isn't just some random encounter; I know it isn't. I don't believe in chance. There's so much I just can't explain, Jenn, but I'm telling you this is more than just some crazy idea I conjured up."

It was useless. Nobody would understand.

"Listen, Liz, we need to get back to work, but I don't want to leave this hanging." Jenn pointed her chin toward the overcrowded waiting room. "I still want to talk about this, okay? We'll make time."

Liz nodded, but knew it didn't matter how many times she and Jenn had this conversation; Jenn wouldn't understand.

As Liz delved back into work, discouragement wedged itself into her thoughts. Maybe this *was* wrong. Maybe Jenn was right. Maybe it was silly to think she could adopt a girl after only knowing her a few weeks.

But then, God's plan didn't always have to make sense, did it?

She supposed that, for now, all she could do was leave it in His hands.

CHAPTER 61

L E X I

////////////////////////////////

Thursday, October 29
8:04 p.m.

"It's about time," Lexi said in her best annoyed voice when Barney finally sauntered into her space half an hour later. "I thought you said you were just gettin' your stash from Slick. Did you get attacked by tunnel ninjas or something?"

Barney didn't laugh. In fact, he just stood there.

Lexi frowned. What was his problem? Sure, her jokes were a little lame, but Barney always laughed, even if it was just to humour her. What had happened to the Barney she knew?

"Barn!"

He startled, then crawled out of whatever funk he was in long enough to catch Lexi's eye. Weird. He looked at her like he was seeing her for the first time.

"What?" he asked flatly, finally sitting.

"Get your hearing checked, bud." Lexi rolled her eyes. "Did you get your stash from Slick?"

"Um, no, not exactly." Barney pinched the bridge of his nose, his eyes shut tight. Did he have a headache?

Lexi noticed that his hand was all clenched up, like whatever he was holding required the utmost protection.

Everything felt wrong...off. Barney wasn't himself at all. He'd barely uttered a full sentence, and usually he was a run-on chatterbox. And what was with the space-cadet demeanour? Sure, he was a stoner, but for the most part he was pretty with it.

No, something sat like a rock in her gut. She couldn't explain it, but she suddenly had a bad feeling.

"What do you mean, 'not exactly'?" she asked warily.

What had happened in Slick's cove? Why wasn't Barney hunched over his new stash, rolling up his joints like usual? And *why* was Barney hesitating to answer Lexi's question? Since when did he have anything to hide?

Defeated, Barney let out a puff of air before leaning forward. "Don't judge, okay?"

Judge? Judge what?

But before Lexi could ask, Barney opened up his hand.

Lexi stared.

There were two little pills resting on his palm, bright yellow ones with tiny smiley faces inked on, grinning up at her like everything was fine.

If everything was fine, then why did that bad feeling just get worse?

"What are those?" Lexi asked. *Please tell me they're just aspirin.*

But she wasn't stupid; she already knew they weren't aspirin. Aspirin didn't smile at you.

"Just something new," he replied. "Slick sold 'em to me."

"Something new?" Lexi yelled out. "What happened to your normal stash? The weed?"

Barney met her gaze. He glared—*actually* glared; his thick eyebrows narrowed, and his cheeks had just a touch of red in them.

Something was definitely weird. Barney never got angry, not about *anything*.

"CJ, don't get like that. You don't know what it's like for me! Weed only goes so far, you know! It used to take the edge off, but it don't anymore." Barney exhaled, fingering the pills. "Anyway, Slick told me these'll help."

"The edge off?" Lexi shook her head. "Barn, you don't *have* any edge to take off."

"Shows how much you know," Barney muttered. "I had a bad day. Besides, you don't know the baggage I carry."

Lexi crossed her arms. "Is that my fault? It's not like you tell me anything."

"Neither do you." He cracked a tiny smile. "I guess that makes us even."

Lexi wanted to say something, something that would stop him from taking those pills, but nothing came to her. For weeks, she'd given him heck for smoking the weed, and he never listened. Why would he listen to her about the pills?

Even if he would listen, it was too late. When Lexi looked up, Barney was already tipping back his head, downing those stupid pills.

"You're an idiot," Lexi muttered. "The weed was bad enough, man. Now you're getting into the hard-core crap?"

"I'm not getting into anything, CJ!" She'd never seen him so irritable. "Geez, they're just a couple of pills. Relax! Why do you always gotta give me a hard time? You sound like an old bag who's got nothing better to do than nag."

So apparently it's nagging—not caring.

"Whatever," Lexi muttered, lifting her eyes to the rafters above. A black spider was spinning its web.

"Don't get all mad, okay? I'm fine." Barney flashed a grin. Sure, *now* he was acting like himself. "By the way, your arm's lookin' a lot better."

"Gee, thanks for noticing," Lexi replied with a snort. Leave it to Barney to point out the most random things.

Before Lexi could spew out another witty remark, lighten the mood, Barney went all serious again.

"Look, I, uh, I know that necklace meant something to you." He was rocking on his heels. "But things will look up, right?"

"Things will look up? Really? Do you actually believe that?"

Barney shrugged. "I don't know. Things can't stay bad forever, can they?"

"You're the one who needs to take the edge off, so you tell me." Lexi paused. "Anyway, all this talk about things looking up, you're almost starting to sound religious."

Barney's eyes fluttered closed. Seriously? Was he going to fall asleep on her? His dumb drugs were probably starting to work. What an idiot. She would *never* ease up on him for this.

"Who knows?" he said, his words slurring together. He sounded like a different person. "Maybe there's more to this God thing than we realize. You're nice to me, maybe one of the only ones who has been in a long time. I figure that means the world's gotta be kinda good, and if that's true, maybe someone up there is *making* it good."

"I don't know about that, Barn," Lexi replied. "I think those drugs are just messin' with your head."

Barney opened his eyes, squinted them like he was trying to get her into focus.

"Yeah." He took a few deep breaths. "Maybe."

"I wish you wouldn't take crap like that," Lexi said quietly with a shake of her head. No, she wasn't trying to be a nag, but she had to say something. "Can't you just stick with the weed?"

But Barney didn't reply. Well, he was probably as sick of this argument as she was. It felt like they were running around in circles. Why couldn't he just listen to her?

"I mean, I hate the weed, too, but at least—"

She was cut off by a strange sound, something like a gurgle. When she looked up, she found Barney gulping back air, coughing hard, pounding at his chest like he was giving himself CPR.

"What are you doing?" Lexi asked, her heart skipping a beat. "What's wrong?"

This had to be one of his practical jokes. Had to be!

But Barney wasn't laughing.

Why wasn't he laughing?

His eyes closed, he rocked on the spot, still beating his chest.

He was gasping for air like he was drowning!

It chilled Lexi to the bone.

"Barney, you okay?" she asked quietly. This wasn't like him. Sure, there was joking, but there were lines that shouldn't be crossed for a good joke.

This was one of them.

When he put up a hand and nodded his head, meeting Lexi's worried gaze, she felt relief wash over her. He must have swallowed his spit the wrong way. Everything was fine.

"S'okay, CJ, I'm... f—"

And Barney collapsed.

At first, Lexi thought he was trying to be funny, freak her out a little, but then his body went rigid, jolted as though some electrical current was pulsing through him.

Her heart stopped. "Barney!" she cried, crawling over quickly.

His face was as white as a sheet.

His eyes were closed.

Low grunts bubbled from his throat.

And his body wouldn't stop jerking like that!

"Barney!" Lexi grabbed his shoulders, tried to stop him from shaking like that. "Barney, stop it!"

Her heart threatened to explode. Her throat went dry, and she couldn't catch her own breath. Fear took hold of her ankles, threatened to pull her under.

This was no joke.

"Barney!"

As quickly as it had all started, Barney let out one last struggled gasp before his body went still, a heap on the concrete.

Silence.

But Lexi was sure she could hear her own heart racing.

"B–Barn?"

Her fingers shook as she touched his arm.

It was so clammy.

His eyes were still closed.

He was so... still.

Lexi stopped breathing.

But *he* hadn't.

She hovered her trembling hand over Barney's mouth and nose, felt the smallest air current brush against her fingers, felt the smallest ounce of hope creeping in.

"Barney!" She tried shaking him, to no avail.

He was out cold, but at least he was breathing. It sounded weird, like nothing she'd ever heard before. It was slow, screechy, like something was stuck in his throat.

Something was seriously wrong. It didn't matter how many times she shook him, whapped him across the face, and pinched his arm… he wouldn't wake up.

Okay, don't panic! Think, Lexi, fast!

She was out of options. She'd tried everything she knew; there was nothing she could do for him, not by herself.

What he needed was a hospital.

How am I gonna get him to the hosp–

Then she remembered the phone number Liz had given her. There was no other choice.

Lexi scrambled over to her backpack, the knees in her jeans ripping on a loose stone. She hardly felt the sting as she fidgeted with her zipper, but her hands wouldn't stop shaking!

Finally, she got the bag open and plunged her hand inside. She found the paper quick, recognized Liz's handwriting.

Lightheaded and terrified, she slid back over to Barney. *Oh, please still be breathing!*

He was.

"Okay," she said, her voice trembling. "I swear I'll be back, Barney. Just… please be okay."

The terror was so real, the reality weighing heavily on her. This was happening, this was *actually* happening, to her best friend, and she couldn't stop it!

She hesitated, knowing she needed to get to a phone, but she couldn't pry her eyes from Barney. His body was still as the dead.

Her body shook, and fear seized her. *What if…*

No, she couldn't think like that. As long as she hurried, he was going to be okay!

"I'll be back, Barney."

She tore out of there as fast as her legs could carry her, through the Combs, through the Pit, out the Tube, onto the streets. She didn't even know if anyone had noticed her fleeing from the tunnels like something was chasing her. She didn't care. She didn't stop, she *wouldn't* stop, not for anything! She didn't care about the burning sensation in her chest, she didn't care that her legs were on fire, she didn't care that her heart was ready to leap into her throat and jump out of her mouth, because she wouldn't stop, not until she reached the first payphone she could find.

That terrible scene unfolded again and again in her mind as she sped through the streets, eyes peeled. It was still so vivid, a vicious loop in her head—Barney swallowing the pills, Barney saying things would look up, Barney collapsing, Barney swallowing the pills, Barney saying things would look up, Barney collapsing...

What had happened? Was it the drugs? What exactly *were* they, anyway? Why would he take something he wasn't sure about?

And why hadn't she stopped him?

She should have stopped him.

What have I done?

Before guilt could wedge its way too deep, she spotted a payphone, a beacon of hope.

As dizziness exploded in her head, she skidded to a stop. Without bothering to catch her breath, her trembling hand found her pocket, grabbed those two quarters she'd found earlier, plunged them into the phone.

Good thing she still had them. What would have happened if she didn't?

She swallowed seven times, the lump in her throat stinging. She couldn't breathe but focussed her attention on steadying her shaking hand to dial the number Liz had given her.

Barney, be okay. Please be okay!

343

"St. Marcus' Hospital, Emergency Department."

It wasn't Liz.

Panic suffocated her. What now?

"I—I... I need to talk to Liz!" she stammered, resting her head up against the glass cubicle.

Whoever answered the phone huffed impatiently; Lexi could hear her.

"Liz?" the voice asked. "Liz who?"

"I don't know her last name!" Lexi screamed. "Just... Liz. I... I think, I mean, it's probably short for Elizabeth or something!"

Silence.

Lexi didn't have time for silence!

"Look, she's a doctor there, okay? She's the one who gave me this number! So get her! This is *important!*" She was freaking out now. Every second that ticked by could mean Barney getting worse!

How much worse could he get?

Could he die? She paled. *No, you can't die!*

There was rustling, a little bit of static. It sounded like whoever answered had put the phone down.

Please be getting Liz. Please be getting Liz. Please.

Lexi clenched her eyes tight, her head spinning out of control.

It has to be alright. It has to be! Be okay, Barney, be okay!

A minute or two passed—an eternity—before someone finally picked up the phone.

"Hello?"

It was Liz. She sounded worried.

"It's... it's L—Lexi," she stammered, a sob strangling her. No, she would not cry! Barney would be fine!

"Lexi," Liz said into the phone. "What happened? Are you okay?"

Lexi shook her head, but Liz couldn't see that.

"It—it's not me; it's... it's my friend." She was trying to be calm, but it wasn't working. How could she be calm when Barney was down in the Combs, all alone, out cold? "It's B…Barney. Something is—is really wrong with him. He's, like, p…passed out or something, he won't t…talk to me, and he won't wake up. He was, sh…shaking really bad, and, his breathing sounds… wrong. I d…don't know what to do!"

She wanted to sit, to buckle to her knees, to let herself relax for only a second. Her whole body threatened to shut down, it was so exhausted, but she couldn't let it. She had to pull herself together, or she'd be no help to anybody.

"Okay, honey, I know this is scary, but you need to listen to me, okay? We're going to help your friend," Liz said in a calm voice. How could she be *calm*? "Lexi, you need to tell me where you and Barney are so I can send an ambulance."

Lexi's heart skipped a beat.

People coming into the tunnels.

Adults.

"I…" She couldn't breathe again. "I don't think—"

"Listen, I know you're scared," Liz said, speaking slow and clear, "but we need to get to Barney if we're going to help him, and that means you have to tell me where you are."

Tell me where you are.

If Lexi brought adults into the tunnels, Sapphire would fly off the handle! If bringing back a gold necklace was bad, how would she react to Lexi bringing in paramedics?

Well, what other choice did she have? Lexi didn't care if Sapphire beat her up so bad that she couldn't remember her own *name!* She would do whatever she had to do if it meant helping Barney.

"He's in the tunnels," Lexi said, tears prickling her eyes.

That was it. She'd broken the tunnel law, committed the unforgivable sin. She'd just earned herself a one-way ticket out of that place, but if it meant saving his life…

"The… the entrance is on Water Street, b—by the market."

"Okay, I'm sending an ambulance, but I need you to wait by the entrance so the paramedics can find you. You need to be able to show them where Barney is. Can you do that for me?" Liz asked quietly.

Lexi imagined the worst. She'd already left him alone too long.

"I—I don't... I don't want to leave him... down there," she said.

"I know, honey, but you have to do this for him, okay? The paramedics won't know where to go. You have to show them."

Lexi took a deep breath. There was no other choice, no other way out of this.

"Okay," she whispered, clenching her eyes. This was a dream, just a really vivid nightmare. Maybe if she kept her eyes closed long enough, her body would realize it was dreaming, and she'd wake up.

Right?

Wake up, wake up, wake up...

"Hang in there, sweetie, okay?" Liz said quietly.

Lexi barely heard her.

Who was she kidding? This was no dream.

Arms tingling, she hung up the phone.

Gotta get back to the tunnels. Gotta get back to Barney.

With the little strength she had left, she raced back to the tunnel entrance, frantically pacing in a tight circle as she scanned the streets for signs of flashing lights. That was what they did in emergencies, wasn't it?

An emergency...

It was a struggle to think positively. Too much time had passed.

No, it was going to be alright. It *had* to be alright.

That's what Barney had said, wasn't it?

"Things will look up, right?"

Lexi bit her lip.

Don't you dare die, Barney, she warned him, ignoring the tear that threatened to break the barrier. *Just... please be okay.*

346

CHAPTER 62

L E X I

Thursday, October 29
8:29 p.m.

Lexi was shivering, but it was seventy-five degrees outside. She wasn't cold. That wasn't the issue—and even if it *was* cold, she doubted she'd even feel it.

Her eyelids were so heavy. How could her body even consider sleep at a time like this?

Her stomach bubbled, and she thought she would throw up all over the sidewalk any minute now. This was the worst feeling in the world: helplessness. There was absolutely nothing she could do, not right now. She was sentenced to waiting while Barney...

Where are they?

Where were those paramedics? What if they'd gotten lost? Or what if they just didn't care? Was Barney okay? Had anyone found him? Had he woken up? Was he still breathing? Or was he down there, wide awake and drawing Daffy Duck on her wall?

She'd kill him...

Finally, up ahead, Lexi spotted the blinding flashing lights.

A smile barely touched her lips; help had come. Barney was going to be okay.

Climbing up on a bench, she flailed her arms like an idiot, shouted, bounced up and down!

They saw her. How could they not?

After the ambulance parked, two paramedics hopped out, a middle-aged man with a bad comb-over and a younger woman with long jet-black hair pulled back in a tight ponytail.

Lexi could feel the woman looking right at her, but Lexi was more concerned with watching the man pull a stretcher from the back of the vehicle.

"You the kid who called Liz?" Jet-Black asked.

Lexi nodded, still watching that stretcher.

"Uh." Her lips felt like rubber. "That... that thing won't fit... down there."

She was surprised she even considered the narrow entrance, especially now.

Jet-Black glanced over her shoulder, shook her head, and Comb-Over rolled his eyes, muttered a curse as he lifted the stretcher back in the ambulance.

Deal with it.

"Alright," Jet-Black said with a nod. "Where's your friend?"

Sucking in a breath, reminding herself there was no other choice, Lexi led them down through the Tube, through the dark chasm that led to the Pit, ignoring the bellowing curses coming from Comb-Over, who along with Jet-Black was trying to manoeuver his way through the dark.

Right, Lexi reasoned. She'd been freaked out her first time through here too.

"Can't believe these kids actually *live* down here," Jet-Black whispered to Comb-Over. "It reeks!"

Did they honestly think she couldn't hear them?

Lexi wished they would just shut up. Didn't they realize somebody could be *dying*?

He's not dying!

"Through here," Lexi said, squeezing through the entranceway to the Pit.

Every eye shot up, met hers with expressions of sheer panic, while whispers rose up all around her. They saw the paramedics; she'd broken the rules; she'd never be allowed back. Their silence screamed "Traitor!"

She didn't care.

She broke into a jog, checking behind her to make sure the paramedics were following.

Sapphire would have her head on a silver platter when she found out, but none of it mattered anymore. If Lexi had to sleep under a bridge for the rest of her life in exchange for knowing Barney was safe, that Barney was *breathing*, she would. She would even go back to Everidge, another foster home, back to *Des* if it meant Barney was okay.

Barney, you gotta be okay!

They came to the Combs and wove their way through the seemingly endless tunnels until they reached her space.

Her breath caught in her throat.

Barney was still lying there, her shadow cast upon his limp body.

If it was possible, he looked even *whiter*.

She stood frozen, staring at Barney, her head as heavy as a house, while Jet-Black and Comb-Over shouldered past her, dropped to their knees, and went to work.

Okay, Barney, I brought help. You'll be okay now.

Comb-Over started touching Barney—his neck, his forehead... then he brought his ear to Barney's mouth. He didn't say anything.

Was that good? Was silence good? Did that mean Barney was still breathing? If the paramedic wasn't freaking out, did it mean everything was okay?

Jet-Black was talking.

"I need you to tell me what happened," she said quickly, motioning toward Barney.

Lexi swallowed, feeling herself sway on the spot. She couldn't tear her eyes away from Barney.

"He..." Words. She needed words. "I... I don't know. We were j...just sitting here, t...talking and then he just... he just starting shaking really bad. Then he stopped and he p...passed out."

Was it right to leave out the drugs?

By now, a small crowd had gathered around her, watching, whispering. Obviously, the unconscious boy in the Combs was news to them.

"Can you think of anything your friend could have been doing that might have caused this?" Jet-Black asked. "Was he drinking? Did he take any drugs?"

Lexi swallowed. Her mouth felt like paste.

Drugs.

"Uh..."

Drugs were illegal; that much she knew. If she said anything, would Barney go to jail?

He'd never speak to me again if I sent him to juvie.

Jet-Black read her mind. "Look, nobody's in trouble right now, but we need to know so we can help him," she explained, nodding toward Barney, who looked worse than ever, his lips purple. He sounded like an old man, wheezing like that.

"He... he took something. I, I don't know what it was, but they were new. T...two pills. They were y...yellow. He swallowed them, and a little while later..." She looked at Barney. "This."

She should have stopped him. She should have tackled him, pried the pills from his hand, stomped on them, hid them, *something.*

This was her fault.

This was all her fault!

"Can you tell us his name?" Jet-Black asked.

Patrick.

"B...Barney."

Jet-Black wasn't stupid.

"His *real* name," she said, with a roll of her eyes.

Pinky swear.

"Barney," she said again, flatly. They could think what they wanted about her; she didn't care. She wasn't giving up his name, not after she had sworn.

"We have to get him to the hospital," Comb-Over said from his spot next to Barney. Lexi's stomach lurched. The guy's voice

350

sounded hurried, almost panicked. Something was really wrong! If the paramedic was worried, *that* was bad.

"I'm coming with you," Lexi said, stepping toward Barney. A gasp erupted from her throat as she stepped into the light. His face looked *blue!*

Her heart forgot how to beat; she was sure of it.

Jet-Black shot her a look then, one that said, *"Why would we take you?"*

"He's my brother," Lexi said quickly, catching how unbelievable the lie sounded. Well, whatever! Even if she had to be dragged by a rope behind the ambulance, she was going with him.

It didn't come to that; they agreed to take her along.

Lexi held back while Comb-Over carefully lifted the scrawny Barney into his arms, while Jet-Black yelled at all the kids to clear out.

Lexi's knees felt like they were about to buckle, but she followed them.

As they hurried through the Pit, she felt an icy hand catch her arm.

Not now! Not now!

Lexi met Sapphire's hard eyes.

"You shouldn't have brought them down here," Sapphire said through clenched teeth. "You should have found me first."

Lexi wanted to yell, wanted to scream, wanted to punch her between the eyes!

But she was needed somewhere else, so she just pulled away.

"You can kill me later," she said quietly. "But right now, I'm going with Barney."

***

The ride was bumpy, and all Lexi could think about was whether or not Barney could feel it.

Hey Barn, don't worry, the bumps aren't forever. We just gotta get you to the hospital. She thought of his corny grin, his impish laugh. *This chick needs a few driving lessons, doesn't she, Barney?*

351

Was he aware of anything? Was it like sleeping? Would he remember all of this like he'd remember a dream?

We'll laugh about this in the morning.

The paramedics were talking medical mumbo-jumbo to each other through the screen that separated the driver from the back. Comb-Over kept checking Barney's pulse and doing other things, but Lexi wasn't really watching. All she could do was stare at Barney's white face, willing him to wake up, trying to send along some kind of message that she needed him to stick around, that she would never tease him again.

Barney, I swear I'll never give you heck about your weed again. I really don't care that you do it. I just... I won't bug you anymore.

She tried asking Comb-Over what was wrong, why Barney was breathing weird like that, why he wouldn't wake up, why they were taking him to the hospital, but all he kept telling her was "Let me do my job, okay?"

She wanted to take Barney's hand in hers, but she was too afraid. Of what, she wasn't sure. It felt like she was looking at someone else, because this pale, choking Barney wasn't the Barney she knew. Her Barney would jump up any minute now and yell, "Just kidding!"

But that wasn't happening.

They turned a corner, and she glanced up just in time to see Comb-Over saying something into some kind of walkie-talkie.

"We're just pulling in now; get some doctors out here, stat!" he yelled. "This kid can't wait!"

This kid can't wait.

Wait for what?

Barney!

His eyes fluttered, and his body trembled all over again. All the colour had drained from his face. Lexi watched him, so struck with fear that she didn't even notice when the ambulance came to a stop.

Everything happened so fast. The back doors of the ambulance flew open, and a team of doctors stood waiting, all reaching out to grab a part of the stretcher they'd strapped him on.

Lexi was left forgotten in the ambulance.

She stumbled out, chased after the action, a knot tightening in her stomach when she couldn't see Barney through all the white jackets.

"Barney? Wait!"

One of the doctors was Liz. She was talking to Jet-Black in a hurried voice. "Status?"

"Ingestion of unknown substance," Jet-Black reported. "Airway clear, reported seizure before he lost consciousness, breathing irregular."

Liz looked scared. Why did she look so scared? Why did everyone *sound* so scared?

Barney.

They barrelled into the hospital, and they started wheeling Barney faster.

Away from her.

They ran Barney through a set of double doors. Lexi tried to follow, but Liz caught her hand.

"Honey, you have to stay out here, okay?"

Lexi's heart dropped as she stared at the doors. Barney was out of sight. She couldn't see him anymore. Now she felt like she really would collapse.

"But..." She tried to find her voice, but it sounded so distant. She couldn't swallow. "I have to... I have to be with him."

She couldn't stop staring at those doors, still swinging. Barney had only been gone seconds.

She couldn't feel her legs. She couldn't feel her arms. None of this felt real.

"I understand, Lexi, but right now you have to wait out here." Liz put a hand on Lexi's shoulder. "We're going to do everything we can, okay?"

Liz didn't wait for a response, and she, too, disappeared through those doors.

Lexi watched them swing.

She couldn't do anything, again.
Helpless.

CHAPTER 63

L I Z

Thursday, October 29
8:42 p.m.

Liz lost no time rushing into the room where three doctors were already working on the boy.

Dr. Gustave strapped an oxygen mask around Barney's pale face.

Dr. Eleve started an IV drip, hooked him up to a heart monitor.

Dr. Narobi extracted a vial of blood from his arm.

They're testing to see what drug did this, Liz thought as she approached the examination table. Barney still wasn't breathing properly, his fingernails were purple, his eyes concaved.

Whatever he had taken, his body was rejecting it, fast!

Liz swallowed as she stared at him, her mind floating to the young girl waiting outside those doors. The look in her poor eyes had been sheer panic.

Liz remembered all the times Lexi had confided stories about her "buddy." Was that Barney? Was this the boy who'd drawn on Lexi's cast?

"Come on, Barney, pull through," Liz said quietly as she adjusted the mask around Barney's head and checked his pupils. "Pull through. For Lexi."

CHAPTER 64

L E X I

Thursday, October 29
8:44 p.m.

Lexi couldn't stay still.

How could she be *expected* to stay still?

She paced back and forth, chewed on her knuckles, tasted blood. Her gaze never left the operating room doors.

Once, she even ran up to them and peered through the wire window for even just a glimpse of her friend.

She couldn't see anything but a long white hallway.

CHAPTER 65

L I Z

////////////////////////////////

Thursday, October 29
8:49 p.m.

Moments later, Narobi darted through the doors, carrying the results from Barney's blood test.

"MDMA!" He exhaled.

Nothing more needed to be said. As Liz felt her heart plummet, she launched toward the supply drawer, scavenging for a fresh syringe.

Ecstasy, she thought to herself as a bead of sweat drizzled from her forehead.

After plunging the syringe into a vial, she tapped at the needle quickly before administering the shot. It all took less than a minute.

"Cyproheptadine?" Gustave asked.

Liz nodded. Standard procedure. He hadn't overdosed, but his body was treating the drugs as though he had.

This wasn't the first time Liz had been forced to administer the drug, but somehow this felt different. Closer to home.

"Come on, Barney!" Liz whispered, removing the needle from his arm. "Come on."

But he wasn't responding. Liz paled as the heart monitor's steady beeping became rapid blips echoing off the walls.

No...

"We'd better do something fast," Eleve shouted. "He's crashing!"

CHAPTER 66

L E X I

Thursday, October 29
8:53 p.m.

Lexi finally decided to sit down. She didn't want to, because sitting felt too much like defeat, and she *wasn't* giving up!

But her body told her otherwise; she was exhausted, spent, done like dinner. Every part of her body felt weighed down. Would she even be able to get back up? As exhausted as her body was, her mind made up for it by tripling the speed of her racing thoughts. Her heart was thrashing as she stared up at the clock on the wall.

Fourteen minutes.

That was when she'd last seen Barney.

How long did it take to fix something like this? Doctors knew what they were doing, right? Why was this taking so long?

Tapping her foot, she leaned back against the seat, the cold metal burning her skin. Did anybody else in this waiting room notice how cold these seats were? Did anybody care?

Whatever; they weren't important. She should be concentrating on Barney, about how he was going to be alright, about how they'd walk out of here like nothing was wrong. Maybe, just maybe, all of this was just some sick joke of Barney's, something he'd conjured up in a moment of boredom.

Lexi smiled as she pictured the two of them laughing about it later. *Yeah, he just wanted some attention after everything that had happened with my arm.*

Barney? Needy for attention? No, that wasn't like him at all! That theory was shot to sunshine.

Besides, it didn't take doctors fourteen minutes to realize some stupid kid was playing a prank on his best friend. Doctors were smarter than that.

Lexi drummed her fingers on the arm of her chair, focussed on the linoleum floor, felt sick.

Fear. Anxiety. Panic. They all clung to her, refused to let go, and she didn't like it, not one second of it. This was what she'd spent her whole life fighting against, fighting to crawl into that place where she didn't have to care about anything. It had taken her years and years to finally find it, a place where feelings didn't drag you down and make you vulnerable.

Now here she was in some stupid hospital, terrified for her best friend's life.

That made her vulnerable.

After this, she would have to learn to control herself all over again.

***

Seconds ticked by, and each second felt like a minute, each minute an hour. Was that clock still working? Was time still moving forward? Were they suspended in some alternate universe where time didn't exist?

Waiting was agony.

Finally, the doors, those double doors that had taunted her for sixteen minutes, swung open.

Lexi popped up, dizziness threatening her balance as Liz came toward her.

Everything around Lexi became invisible; everything else disappeared. All she could see, all she could focus on, was Liz.

She gulped back a lump of air, struggling to read Liz's expression. Once upon a time, she'd been so good at reading people, at figuring out what they were thinking, what they were feeling.

That had all died when she shut herself off.

She didn't know much, but she did know that Liz wasn't smiling. Wouldn't she be smiling if she was coming to tell Lexi that Barney was alright?

Lexi felt walls crumbling inside her, her heart collapsing in on itself. Liz was standing in front of her now, and she *still* wasn't smiling.

Maybe she's just tired. Maybe she's just in a bad mood. Maybe she's just mad at Barney for taking those stupid pills. Maybe—

None of it sounded right; none of it matched up with the wetness in Liz's eyes.

Lexi struggled to find her voice, but it had taken off, hidden itself, because the question she wanted to ask was a question she knew she didn't want answered.

Her hands were still trembling when she looked past Liz to the double doors.

She *had* to ask.

"W...where's Barney?" she asked. Her mouth tasted like sawdust.

Liz hesitated.

Lexi stopped breathing. You only hesitated like that when something was wrong. When everything was all right, there was *never* hesitation.

Liz blinked, and Lexi was sure she caught a glimmer of a tear in the corner of the doctor's eye.

Suddenly, the room spun.

"We took a blood sample from Barney," Liz started, clasping her hands together, her eyes never leaving Lexi's. "He had high levels of MDMA in his blood. Those pills were ecstasy, Lexi."

Lexi wanted to pummel him. He was such an idiot for taking drugs he knew nothing about. Boy, would he hear an earful from her!

Liz wasn't finished.

"He had a dangerous amount."

Dangerous... but they were only two pills.

361

"We did everything we could," Liz said, her voice breaking. "I'm... I'm sorry, Lexi."

No.

Why was she sorry?

No, no, no!

"What do you mean, you did everything you could?" Lexi asked, backing away, away from the truth that was burning a hole through her heart. "He's... he's *okay*, right?"

Liz was silent, like she didn't want to say the words.

She didn't need to say anything; Lexi knew before those words were ever spoken.

"I'm sorry, Lexi." Liz swallowed. "Barney didn't make it."

Lexi stared.

Just stared.

Then came the tidal waves, the dark walls of water that crashed in from either side, sucked her under into the deep abyss, down, down, down, filling her lungs with blackness, devouring her, killing her.

Was she still breathing? She couldn't tell.

Was she still standing? Was she still in the hospital?

Lexi could sense Liz watching her, waiting for some kind of reaction, waiting for words.

But all Lexi could see was Barney—flashes of his smile, visions of him laughing, memories of him teasing her, his drawings, his weed, his bushy eyebrows, the pinky swear, Barney Rubble vs. Tweety Bird, Barney the Noble, Barney the Brave.

Gone.

"Barney didn't make it."

Didn't make it.

Didn't. Make. It.

She would never have Barney beside her again.

She would never hear his laugh again.

She would never give him heck again.

Her stomach was churning, her lungs were shattering, her heart was exploding.

Barney was dead.

Dead.

She was coming undone. The truth grabbed her wrists, her ankles, threatened to drag her down into some deep pit she'd never crawl out of. Tears stung at her eyes, her breath caught, her knees wobbled. She was going to collapse. It was too much, it was all too much.

Barney…

No. She couldn't let herself feel it. She couldn't.

It doesn't hurt, it doesn't hurt, it doesn't hurt…

Lexi plunged deep inside herself, fervently digging to find that place she needed so desperately to survive.

That numb centre.

And there it was, waiting for her.

Lexi swallowed, cleared the lump in her throat, worked on freezing her face, voiding her mind, burying all the feelings that were hell-bent on destroying her.

"Lexi," Liz said quietly, stepping forward. "I'm… I'm so sorry."

Lexi could only shake her head, the only part of her body she remembered to move. Her eyes were locked on those double doors.

This was crazy. This was happening to someone else. Not her. It couldn't be true.

"I know this is hard," Liz said suddenly. Lexi had almost forgotten she was here. "Do you want to see him?"

"See who?" Lexi's voice didn't sound like her own anymore.

"Barney," Liz said quietly. "Would you like to see him, before we—"

Lexi shook her head again. Why would she want to see him? He was dead.

He wasn't Barney.

"Sweetie, you can talk to me," Liz cooed. "I know this hurts."

All Lexi could do was shake her head, faster and faster, like it would take off in flight any second now.

"No, it doesn't," she stammered. "I'm fine."

Lexi had to get out of here. This place was suffocating.

When she turned to leave, she was caught off-guard when Liz reached out and grabbed hold of her arms, crouching a little until she was face to face with her.

"Lexi, you are *not* fine!" Liz exclaimed.

Lexi dropped her eyes. She couldn't even bring herself to look at her.

"You *have* to let yourself feel this, Lexi," Liz said firmly, seriously, as if she knew what she was talking about. "It's okay to be hurt. He was your friend! Don't shut yourself away from this, too."

Too?

Lexi glared at her. What did she know about shutting herself off?

Lexi pulled away hard, scrambling backwards.

"I *said*," Lexi said through clenched teeth as the outline of Liz grew smaller and smaller, "I'm *fine!*"

She said it loud enough that some stranger walking past her actually turned and stared.

But Lexi wasn't sticking around.

She sprinted toward the exit as fast as her jelly legs would carry her.

CHAPTER 67

L I Z

////////////////////////////
Thursday, October 29
9:02 p.m.

Liz felt tears dissolving on her cheeks as she stared after Lexi, chased by a reality she was refusing to face. All Liz wanted to do was to run after her, stop her, force her to cry, force her to let the pain in.

But that would be hypocritical, wouldn't it?

Wasn't that exactly what *she* had done when Kurt died?

Maybe that was why Liz wanted to stop Lexi so badly. Maybe she wanted to save the girl from making the same mistakes, to keep her from spiralling down the same path, to protect her from ending up in the same place Liz had.

No, she wouldn't wish that on anyone, especially not Lexi.

That girl's face had been a stone—no tears, not one, no expression whatsoever—but Liz could see past it all, past the front. Lexi was struggling.

Liz remembered that inner battle all too well.

How could Lexi not be hurting? This was her friend. He'd meant something to her. Liz still recalled quite vividly the terror blazing in Lexi's eyes when they'd first wheeled Barney away. Of course his death would hurt.

But what about now? Where would Lexi go? Didn't she know it didn't matter where she ran? That it didn't matter how *fast* she ran? She'd never be able to outrun the truth.

No. Lexi hadn't learned that hard truth, yet.

Liz became aware of someone joining her.

"Did you get the kid's name?" Narobi asked. "From that girl?"

Liz slowly shook her head. Barney would have been his street name, just a code name. Did Lexi even know his real name, like he knew hers?

"No," she replied, her thoughts still on Lexi. Who would comfort her where she was going?

Narobi exhaled. "Then who should we contact?"

Standard protocol was to call the parents, but in this case Lexi was the closest thing to a family Barney had. And she already knew.

"He lived on the streets," Liz said in a low voice. "I don't think there's anyone we *can* contact."

Narobi nodded and left Liz to ponder the severity of such a situation: code names masking one's true identity, marking them as nameless and faceless children—just a number, a statistic. Yes, somewhere out there, Barney might have a family, but they would never know his fate.

Worse, they probably wouldn't care.

Liz swallowed.

What if it had been Lexi? What if Lexi had been the one to swallow those pills? What if it had been Lexi who ended up in a hospital, nameless and faceless, nothing but a number? What if she had been the one to die?

Nobody would ever know.

CHAPTER 68

L E X I

//////////////////////////////////
Thursday, October 29
9:11 p.m.

The Pit looked different somehow. Like it was missing something.

Some*one*.

The whole place seemed empty without him.

It doesn't hurt, it doesn't hurt, it doesn't hurt!

No matter how much Lexi willed it to go away, no matter how much she tried to slink away to that place where it didn't matter, no matter how much she tried to shrug it off, she couldn't help but replay the evening, over and over again. She couldn't get the image out of her head of Barney collapsing, convulsing. It was forever etched in her memory.

Worse, she couldn't stop hearing Liz's words, again and again, reverberating inside her skull.

Didn't make it...

Barney didn't make it.

This had to be a nightmare.

But then, that was what life was, wasn't it? Just one long nightmare you couldn't ever wake up from.

Lexi was hardly conscious of the looming shadow hovering over her.

"You and I need to get some things straight!" Sapphire

shouted. "I get that Barney was sick and all, but bringing people down here? Do you realize what this *means?* You're sending out a message that we're okay with them being down here. Get a brain, CJ. Those are the kinds of people we fight every day, just trying to keep them *out!*"

Lexi stared at the ground, at the way hers and Sapphire's shadows merged together under the dim glow of the Christmas lights. It seemed so... abstract, so dreamlike.

Maybe this was all an illusion. Maybe she wasn't even really here.

Maybe that was wishful thinking.

"Barney's dead," she said simply, surprised at how easily the words slipped off her tongue. It shouldn't be that easy. *Nothing* was ever that easy. But they were just words. It was the swirling vortex of unending heartache *inside* that was the hard part.

Sapphire was quiet. For the first time since Lexi had known her, she'd finally said something that shut Sapphire right up.

Lexi didn't even look at her, didn't care how Sapphire took the news. Sapphire never cared an ounce for Barney, and if she had, she'd never shown it.

No, she didn't deserve Lexi's sympathy. Shouldering past Sapphire, she lifted her eyes just high enough to spot Star standing there, staring hard.

The expression on her face said it all: she'd heard.

"What did you say?" Star asked in a low whisper.

If she already knew the answer, why was she asking?

"Barney's dead," Lexi replied monotonously, the words tasting like acid. They may be easy to say, but they were still so wrong. "They couldn't save him."

Her insides were ice, her face a stone. She felt so empty, she was nothing but a husk.

"CJ." Star moved forward. "Are you—"

"Yeah," Lexi replied, sidestepping her.

"CJ, stop," Star called.

Lexi stopped, but she didn't turn around.

"Where are you going?"

"Bed," Lexi replied flatly, staring off toward the Combs.

"But don't you... don't you want to talk about this?" Star asked, moving up beside Lexi, glancing at her sideways, her own eyes sparkling with tears. "I mean, he was your best friend."

Was...

Lexi met Star's gaze, blinked.

"No, I just want to sleep," she said quietly. "I'm fine, Star. It's not the worst thing that's happened to me."

Leaving Star behind, Lexi dragged herself through the Combs toward her own space, where her candle was still burning.

Lexi's eyes trailed over to the spot where, only an hour ago, Barney had sat with his back pressed up against the wall and swallowed those stupid pills... the pills she should have stopped him from taking.

He'd only wanted to feel better. He said he'd had a bad day, that the weed wasn't strong enough to help him anymore.

Would... would things be different if I'd just... asked why he had a bad day?

What kind of a friend am I?

She paused.

It's not the worst thing that's happened to me.

"What is?" she found herself asking.

I always say that, Lexi realized. *It's not the worst thing that's happened to me.*

But what if the worst thing hadn't happened yet? Or what if it had happened in a hospital only moments ago?

Barney was wrong.

Things wouldn't look up.

They wouldn't look up, because life sucked.

Desperate for a distraction, anything that would tear her away from the guilt, the torture of trying to forget, she grabbed her backpack and busied herself with digging through its compartments, searching for something to keep her from remembering the night, from remembering Barney.

Loose coins. How long had she kept those for? Why hadn't she spent them?

A ripped sweater.

"Things can't stay bad forever, can they?"

Extra underwear.

A hair tie.

A toothbrush.

"You're nice to me, maybe one of the only ones who has been in a long time."

Had that really only been an hour ago?

She swallowed. No, it had never really happened.

She unzipped the front pocket of her pack, the one she'd pulled Liz's number from.

Only there was something else there, something she hadn't noticed earlier.

A rolled-up napkin.

When had she put that there? Why would she have kept a piece of garbage?

Lexi pulled it out, feeling a bump in the middle of the roll.

What the...

Curiously, she unrolled the napkin, catching what seemed to be the beginnings of a scrawled-out message in black Sharpie. Before she had a chance to read what it said, something tiny and shimmering fell from the napkin into Lexi's lap.

Her breath caught.

It was the necklace, the necklace Liz had given to her.

Lexi gawked at it, wide-eyed. It couldn't be. How... ?

The note.

The note would tell her.

She scooted over to her candle, held the napkin close to its flame where she could make out the messy writing.

I no this ment sumthing to you. And don't ask how I got it, cuz it wasnt easy. Don't show SaFF, she don't know I took it. I hop this maks you happy, you deswrv it. Barney.

Lexi stared at the napkin, at the scrawled penmanship, at the bad spelling, at the way the marker leaked through the napkin, smearing all the letters together. She clung to the necklace, her hand shaking as she felt the coolness of its chain against her palm, its edges touching her fingertips.

A tear rolled down her cheek.

A tear? Was she actually crying? When was the last time she'd cried?

She couldn't believe it, couldn't believe what it meant; Barney had gone behind Sapphire's back and somehow gotten the necklace back, all because it meant something to Lexi, all because he thought she deserved happiness.

Lexi held it tightly. She would never let it out of her sight again. *Never!* It was the first piece of jewellery she'd ever owned, yes, but it meant so much more now.

The truth was a stark reality, and it lay right in front of her. She couldn't numb herself from it. Not anymore.

Barney had cared enough about her to steal the necklace from Sapphire just so she could have it back.

How many friends would do that?

Friend...

Lexi hastily brushed away a tear, unclasped the necklace, and wound it around her neck. She hid it under her sweater.

Sniffling, she thought of Barney, of all he'd done for her, of all the things he would miss out on, all because his life had been too hard to deal with.

All because the weed wasn't helping him chill anymore.

All because someone had told him ecstasy would make things better.

Slick.
All because of Slick.
Slick had sold Barney the pills that killed him!
Barney's dead because of Slick.
This was Slick's fault!

Without a moment's hesitation, without spending a few seconds to think up a plan, she scrambled to her feet and began to tread a warpath toward Slick's space.

CHAPTER 69

L E X I

//////////////////////////////////
Thursday, October 29
9:29 p.m.

She had no idea what she was going to say or do. Right now, the only thing Lexi could concentrate on was the startling memory of Barney collapsing in front her, falling into a fit of convulsions, *dying,* all because he had trusted Slick to deliver the good stuff.

Yes, she still should have stopped Barney from taking the pills in the first place. She shouldn't have just sat there and watched. She should have *done* something.

This was her fault too, but she had to yell at somebody.

Her whole body felt like it was on fire as she half-walked, half-jogged through the winding tunnels that spiralled down to the place where Slick had sold Barney those yellow pills, the place where Slick had inadvertently sentenced him to death.

Lexi imagined Barney, hours ago, treading this same path. Back then, he'd only wanted his weed. He'd only wanted the weed to calm him down. How had Slick convinced him to buy something else instead? Barney was smarter than that; why would he have tried something else? What exactly had Slick said to him?

"Oh, it's nothing, Cartoon Boy. You'll just feel good. It ain't gonna hurt you."

Yeah, Lexi could hear the smooth talk now.

Well, he'd hear an earful from her! Barney's blood was on his hands, and he was going to know it!

The air seemed to thin the closer she got to Slick's space, like his presence alone was enough to scare off oxygen.

As she hurried along on her endless journey, she remembered the only other time she'd been down these parts of the Combs. She'd gone with Barney because Slick freaked him out. So why hadn't Barney asked Lexi to go with him tonight? If she'd been there, she could have talked Barney out of buying those pills.

This is my fault! His blood is on my hands, too!

She picked up the pace, pushing those thoughts to the farthest crevice of her mind. Right now, she had to ream out Slick.

Strange, how things panned out. Barney didn't like going to Slick's alone, because Slick was a creep, sketchy, all things bad news, but here was Lexi, heading right for the viper's pit.

She came to that familiar sliver of light in the wall, the one that crept along the stone like some architectural mistake.

Slick's hiding place.

She shimmied her way through the hole, and there he was, the creature from the black lagoon himself, lounging on his shag carpet, just *lounging*, drumming his fingertips against his stomach like he didn't have a care in the world.

Lexi hated him, hated everything about him, every movement, every inch. How unfair was it that he was still breathing when Barney wasn't?

She stomped deeper into his cave, wanting him to hear her.

Slick caught her eye. He looked surprised to see her.

Good!

"Well, hey there, Sexy," Slick said, smoothly gliding to his feet. His eyes did a quick scan down her body. "Come for a good time?"

Lexi lost all control.

"You don't deserve to be alive, Slick! You don't deserve to be sitting here, thinking you're all high and mighty, not after what you did!" she shrieked, her hands shaking from the pent-up rage. "You sold Barney ecstasy, and his body couldn't handle it!"

She sucked in a sharp breath. Now, the words were hard. "He's dead! Barney's dead, because of *you!*"

If Slick felt any remorse, he didn't show it. He just gazed at her, considering the news.

Then he shrugged.

"Hey baby, don't blame me, 'cause it ain't my fault. I don't *make* the drugs; I get my merchandise elsewhere. Does it look like I'm set up for that?" Slick motioned around his empty nook. "I have a buddy who prepares it all. He makes it, I sell it, we split the cash, fifty-fifty, you know? It's sweet, baby, a win-win, what with me livin' down here surrounded by all the crackheads and hard-core druggies. I only gave Cartoon Boy something to help him feel better. Besides, he was practically *begging* for it."

"How *dare* you talk about him like that!" Lexi screamed. "He's dead!"

His sick smile disappeared into a thin line. "I thought I warned you about talkin' back to me," he said in a low voice, glaring at her with those empty eyes.

Lexi didn't care. If he wanted to shove her into another wall, let him. Lexi wasn't finished!

But neither was Slick.

"Hey, baby, this is street life. You can't expect everyone to survive, can ya? People die; that's how life rolls!" He was back to his casual, smooth self. "Barney's time was comin'. What did *he* know about life?"

Lexi narrowed her eyes, exhaled through clenched teeth, fisted her hands so tight that she could feel her fingernails digging into her palms.

"Barney knew more about life than anyone I've ever known, especially you!" she snapped. "He actually cared! And now he's dead, all because you could only think about your stupid money!"

Slick swallowed the space between them until he hovered only inches from her. She could smell his breath; it reeked of smoke, and he clearly hadn't brushed his teeth in ages.

"I told you to watch your tongue, girl! I don't like it when girls give me tongue!" He stared at her mouth, smiled slyly. "Not like that, anyway."

Lexi didn't move. She wasn't backing down, not until she was good and ready.

She returned his gaze, glared hard. "I'll say whatever I *want* to say," she said with edge. "Because you *killed* him!"

Slick breathed in long and hard as he cracked his neck, his eyes never dropping.

"I *told* you not to talk to me like that!"

Now Slick was yelling. Well, let him yell.

"Screw you," Lexi hissed. The words felt good rolling off her tongue.

But Slick didn't like it. Ice cold hands tightened around her upper arms in a flash, and a maniacal glimmer flashed across Slick's eyes as he yanked her farther into the depths of his dungeon.

Lexi wrestled against his hold, but his fingers dug deep. She couldn't pull away... he was too strong. Instinctively, she let out a yell.

Slick only laughed, like it was the greatest joke anyone had ever pulled. His hands tightened like vises around her arms, whipping her forward until their noses touched.

"Scream all you want, baby. Nobody will hear ya." She felt his moist breath on her lips. "Why do you think I live so far in?"

In one swift movement, Slick swung her around like a doll and pushed her to the concrete floor. The impact knocked the wind out of her, but there wasn't time to catch her breath. She scrambled to her knees, fought to crawl away, but Slick was one step ahead of her.

With all his weight, he hurled himself at her and collided with her on the ground. They scrambled for a while, Slick trying to grab her, Lexi trying to push him off, but he was so much stronger than she'd guessed.

She fought him with a wild vengeance, elbowed him in the ribs, ripped out some hair, but he handled her with ease, like she was nothing more than a wild animal that needed to be tamed.

In a moment of frustration, Slick backhanded her, filling her vision with stars. He grabbed the opportunity, manoeuvring himself on top of her, straddling her, positioning himself to sit on her stomach.

Lexi scratched, kicked, and twined her body in the hopes of knocking him off, but he expertly cuffed her wrists in his hands, choking them in his hold and forcing them above her head.

She called upon all the strength she had left, made use of every muscle, but it all seemed a futile effort. It didn't matter how viciously she fought him; she couldn't move an inch.

Slick watched her, a smile curling his lips as he considered the dire position his victim was in. He seemed satisfied, because his laughter bounced off the stone walls.

"I like it when girls struggle," he said breathily. His trap was foolproof; he held Lexi down with ease, even while she twisted around madly. "You know, sometimes girls think they can just talk to me however they want. They think they can get away with it. Sometimes they just need a little lesson in submission. They need to learn that *I'm* the one in control, and that's the way I like it!"

Panic filled her gut and terror pulsed through her blood, sending along a message of horror. She knew what he was doing, what he was *going* to do. She could sense it, sense it in his voice, in his iron hold, even in the way he was breathing. That same sick feeling that rose up inside of her whenever Des had pinned her plagued her now. She could almost *hear* Des in Slick's laugh, *see* him behind Slick's black eyes.

She had to keep fighting! She had to stop him! She couldn't let him!

She kicked, she squirmed, she tried to buck him off, but all it did was egg him on.

"Why don't you just quit strugglin'? Just enjoy yourself." Slick bent over her. "And even if *you* don't, *I* will."

Lexi's throat closed up when he inched his face closer, his weight pressing down on her like a boulder. His eyes traced the contours of her lips, just for a second, before he brought his own down to connect with hers.

Lexi gagged when he expertly parted her lips with his tongue, explored the insides of her mouth. She tried to scream. She swung her head from side to side, escaping him for seconds at a time, but he followed her lead, his tongue sliding his way back into her mouth, like he'd done this before.

She wouldn't let him. No, she wouldn't! She would *not* let him do this to her! She would *not* be powerless like she had been with Des.

"Stop moving!" Slick yelled out, releasing his iron grip on one of her wrists, using his free hand to push her head down against the floor, gripping her temples with his skeletal fingers, trapping her.

He came back down and met her lips again. Only this time, she couldn't pull away.

Using her free arm to her advantage, she pounded mercilessly into Slick's side, his back, wherever she could, as hard as she could to make him stop, but he continued kissing her, kissing her like he couldn't even feel the blows.

He must have gotten fed up, because he caught her wrist in midflight, tsking at her.

"Shouldn't keep trying to get away," Slick said in a low murmur. "It only turns me on more."

He smiled.

Actually smiled.

Lexi's insides turned to rocks.

"See, I like it when they fight back. You know, Sapphire tried fighting back too." He leaned in close, like he had a secret to tell, his hot breath like magma against her skin. "But I think I'm gonna have more fun with you than her."

It all came back to her, that day Slick had hit Sapphire and threw her into the wall. What was it he'd said to her?

"And you of all people don't tell me what to do; I'll make sure you learn this very quickly."

So that's what he'd done. That's why Sapphire was acting so weird.

378

He'd raped her. He'd dragged her down here and raped her!

And now, he was going to do it to Lexi.

That had been his plan all along.

A surge of fear and energy jolted through her as she conjured up all the strength she had left, squirming like an animal, yelling, struggling… but Slick wasn't budging.

"Get off!"

He was busy plastering wet kisses on the nape of her neck, breathing heavily.

"Stop it! Get *off!*"

"Quit fightin' back," Slick warned, his lips finding her cheek, her lips, her neck.

Her tears were traitors, each one of them. Vulnerable. She was in the hands of a rapist, and she was *vulnerable!*

There wasn't a thing she could do to stop him!

When he let go of her wrist again, she hurled a clenched fist at his ribs, barrelled into him with all the energy she had left, but Slick snatched it every time and knocked it hard against the concrete. After a few times, she was sure she heard a bone shatter. Pain shot through every limb. Her arm was like putty.

She couldn't move it anymore.

She couldn't hit him, because she couldn't move it.

She was stuck. The fight was over. He'd won.

And he knew it.

He went in for the kill.

He went for her sweater, fumbled with the zipper, stripped it off, one arm at a time, his wild eyes glaring hard when he realized she was still wearing a T-shirt.

"You just gotta make it hard on me, don't ya?"

He tried to rip it, tried to rip it right down its middle, but he couldn't do it, not with one hand.

Lexi wasn't going to let herself lie there like a slug and take it. No, she would use whatever means she could, no matter how pointless it seemed. Her arms were no longer an option, with one probably broken and the other trapped above her. Still, she wiggled, she kicked, she twisted. If he somehow managed to get her shirt off, it would be over.

"Stop it!" she shrieked, a tear leaking down her cheek into her ear. "Just stop!"

He didn't stop. Frustrated with the shirt, he went back to kissing her instead.

Oh, she wanted to float away. She fought to numb herself from this moment, struggled to think of something nice, anything so she wouldn't have to be here. She couldn't fight him anymore. Her limbs were filled with sand, heavy and useless. Floating away was her last defence.

She floated back to that day at Liz's house; she remembered the paintings, the smiling faces of her nieces and nephews, the matching furniture, the fireplace, the pepper spray.

The pepper spray!

"Please just take it. And promise you'll keep it in your pocket all the time. If not for yourself, then at least for my own peace of mind.'

Lexi's eyes widened. It was still in her jeans pocket!

Right here. Right now.

She had to get to that pocket.

With her good arm still pinned above her, she'd have to use the one lying limp at her side, the one that was only inches from her pocket.

The one that felt like a million shards of glass piercing through her skin.

But there was no other choice. If she could just get it without him noticing... her breath caught in her throat.

Slick ripped at her shirt again, trying to tear it in half, grumbling under his breath. He was distracted. Now was her chance.

Biting her lip, she shifted her arm, felt a sharp pain that made her eyes water, but forced herself to keep moving. She could deal with the pain later. She carefully slid her hand into her pocket.

She felt the cylinder in her hand.

Slick was too busy with her shirt to notice.

380

Lexi pulled out the pepper spray, rolled it over in her palm, positioned her finger on top of the release button.

She'd never before felt fear like the breathtaking terror of that long moment.

Seconds passed, and Slick let go of her other wrist, deciding to go for her jeans instead—her zipper.

He forgot all about restraining his victim.

This was Lexi's only chance. It was now or never!

Shaking, she raised the pepper spray, pressed down the release button.

The mist shot into the air, right at Slick's face.

It took about two seconds before he started to scream, clawing at his face in a panic, eyes clenched tight, leaking.

The enemy was down.

Lexi rolled over, scrambled to her knees, then her feet. She felt her knees threaten to give out. Strong, she had to be strong. She had to concentrate on getting out.

She didn't look back. She propelled forward, barrelling out of his cave, stumbling every few steps. Her fear was like gravity, threatening to take her down.

I can't fall, I can't fall!

"Hey!" Slick was screaming.

She heard rumbling stones, echoing footsteps.

He was coming after her!

A frenzied panic seized Lexi, pulled on her like chains around her ankles, but she couldn't let it immobilize her. Not now. Not when she'd come this far.

She stumbled through the darkness, tears blinding her from navigating the tunnels properly. She launched down the winding paths without really seeing where she was going.

Bad idea.

When she scrubbed the tears from her eyes, she recognized nothing.

Nothing at all.

No!

She knew what she'd done. She'd made a mistake she couldn't reverse, a mistake that would cost her *everything!*

She'd never make it to the Pit.

"You're gonna pay!" Slick screamed. His voice was dangerously close. He couldn't be too far behind her.

So, he knew she'd gone down the wrong tunnel. The ball was in his court now. This was *his* playground, his stomping grounds. Lexi was a fly caught in the web of a deadly spider.

She tripped over a rock, scraped her knee, felt the warm blood ooze down her leg. She hastily collected herself, kept moving. She didn't know where she was going, but moving forward had to be better than standing still, waiting for the enemy to catch his prey.

"I'm not *done* with you yet!"

Slick's screams echoed against the cave-like walls, way too close for comfort. Any second now, he would sneak up on her! Any second now, he would whip around a corner and grab her.

He can't! He can't!

Lexi scurried down another unfamiliar bend in the road, fighting to control her breathy sobs. This was a fight for survival; she couldn't let him hear her.

Reality confronted her, shook her to her core. She'd never make it, not when she was already lost. But she had to *try!* What good would she be if she didn't at least *try?*

She shimmied along the rock wall, tiptoeing lightly so she wouldn't disturb any loose rocks, make any noise. If he heard her...

She came to a tunnel that curved slightly, and she slunk around its bend, pressed her back up against the sharp wall, and held her breath.

"Come on, doll, you don't wanna do this," the monster sang out.

Lexi bit her lip—bit *hard* to keep her from whimpering like an idiot.

She heard his footsteps.

He was getting closer. *So* close!

Lexi was trapped, completely trapped.

He was too close for her to run now, and she'd never be able to fight him off. She'd never be able to scream loud enough for anyone to hear her. She'd never outrun him.

These truths swarmed her, taunted her. There was nothing left to do. There was no hope left.

Tears pooled in her eyes as defeat immobilized her. Lexi brought her hand up and placed it against her heart. Did she think she could drown out its heavy beat? What was she thinking?

Then her finger touched the edge of something cool. Something familiar.

The cross.

"Look, maybe you don't want anything to do with God right now, but I just want you to know He's there."

Lexi swallowed.

Are... are You there?

Slick was getting closer, was seconds away from finding her. She couldn't be in any more of a dire situation. There was nothing else to do.

Except for one thing. Just like Star, it felt like the only thing left... and it was the one thing she thought she'd never do.

God, if You're there, she said in her mind, *You gotta help me. Liz said You'd be there if I needed You. So did Star. If they're right, then help me. He wants to rape me, that's why he's chasing me, but don't let him. Please, don't let him. I don't want him to touch me, I don't want anyone ever touching me again, I don't want to go through that again.*

The tears were uncontrollable. This truly was the end of her rope.

Please get me out of here.

It seemed so useless, her own voice inside her head, crying out to a God she wasn't even sure she believed in.

But it was all she had left. It was the only thing left to do.

Slick's footsteps were getting closer, so close she could almost feel the ground below her trembling.

So much for praying.

But then she turned her head and saw it.

Light.

Four pinholes of light up ahead, beaming down on the dirt floor.

Distantly, she heard the sounds of cars passing.

She stared, the floating dust in the beams of light like glitter.

Could it be?

Had God really heard her prayer?

That fast?

A way out of the tunnels? If she could just get out of the tunnels, up to the streets, she would be safe, because Slick would never draw attention to himself—not if he could help it. He was only in control down here. Up there, he'd be the one who was vulnerable.

That was it. Lexi just had to get up there, and she'd be safe.

"Where are you?" Slick called out, his voice so close. Lexi knew he was in the same tunnel as she was, was in her line of vision. She was sure she could make out a moving shadow down the way. It was dark, so he couldn't see her, not yet.

But he would once his eyes adjusted, once he spotted her shadow like she'd spotted his.

Lexi watched the dancing glitter in the pools of light and bit her lip. Was it what she hoped it was? Was it a way out?

Slick was gaining on her. There was no other choice. She'd have to make a run for it. She'd have to have faith that those lights really were a way out, that they were God's answer to her prayer.

Otherwise, she'd be trapped, and he'd rape her right here on the stone debris.

God, please help me!

Her legs came back to life... and she made a run for it.

"Hey!" Slick yelled down the tunnel, the echo deafening her.

He'd heard her, and now he was stumbling down the tunnel, right toward her.

Lexi's breath came in strangled gasps, pelting at her chest. Her legs didn't feel like her own anymore. Every part of her was focussed on those lights, her goal.

She wouldn't stop, not for *anything*.

She screeched to a halt at the end of the tunnel, the streams of light coming to life around her. Above her was a sewer grate, and before her a metal ladder climbing the wall.

That was it! Somehow, the tunnels were connected to a sewage system, or had been once.

She didn't need any explanation. It was a way out, and that was all that mattered. Would there be enough time?

Trembling, Lexi clawed at the metal rungs, climbed fiercely, her foot slipping once.

"Hey!" Slick was seconds behind her.

God, please!

She reached the top, and with all the strength she had left, she rammed her fist up against the sewer lid, felt it give.

Lexi felt the ladder shaking; Slick was on the bottom rung!

She was so close, she wouldn't let fear take her now.

Knocking the lid aside, she hoisted herself up through the hole, feeling a blinding pulse of pain through her arm until her knees scraped the surface above her.

Light. Streetlights. Buildings, shops, people!

Slick darted up through the hole like a snake, grabbed her foot, but he only got her shoe.

She stumbled to her feet, forgetting the shoe, and darted down the alleyway. Pretty soon, she emerged onto the main street and was engulfed with the sounds of life, activity, and freedom.

A quick glance over her shoulder confirmed what she already knew; Slick wasn't coming after her. He'd lost the war.

Still, Lexi ran.

Tears flew from her face, stones stabbed the bottom of her foot, and she hugged her crushed arm to her stomach. She hardly felt its pain anymore. She couldn't breath, and her sobs smothered her.

Everything was a blur, hazy, and all she knew was to keep running, away from that place, away from the enemy. She silently vowed never to go back.

She couldn't take it anymore. She couldn't *do* this anymore, not any of it!

Grief clung to her heart as tears blinded her, pooling down her hot cheeks. She'd never cried like this.

Never.

Except once.

CHAPTER 70

L E X I

Friday, August 24
11:17 p.m.

Two Years, Two Months Ago

Lexi was afraid to move. Movement equalled pain. The fresh bruises speckling her legs stung whenever she shifted in her bed, and the soles of her feet still felt like a thousand tiny needles were stabbing her, even though she was sure she'd pulled out every last tiny shard of glass.

Yes, it was better if you didn't move. If you lay perfectly still, it was almost like there was no pain at all. If you couldn't feel the pain, it was easy to pretend nothing had happened.

But even now, lying in bed hours later, it didn't matter how much she wished she could pretend it hadn't happened... she still remembered it all so vividly.

It happened at dinnertime. In a moment of carelessness, Lexi had knocked over her glass of tap water, sending it hurtling to the ground, where it smashed into a thousand little beads of glass.

Her dad tackled her faster than a tiger chasing down its prey.

He was drunk, so it was no surprise when he went off, using her body as a punching bag. It was no surprise when he stripped her of her socks and shoes and forced her to walk over the sea of shards before hurling her to the ground to pick up the broken pieces by hand. It was no surprise when he went after her mother, started blaming her for the horrible excuse they called a daughter. It was no surprise when he beat her mother, too, right there in front of her, just for the heck of it.

But it wasn't until later, when Lexi sat on the side of the tub, using tweezers to remove the bits of glass from her feet, that her mother came after her, seething in anger because she had set her father off.

That was how Lexi got the bloody lip.

Plus, it didn't help that her mom was high.

Like that was a decent excuse.

But as brutal as it all seemed, even this *wasn't the worst pain she'd felt. No, there'd been worse, she'd heard worse, she'd felt worse, so maybe she should be counting her blessings that it was only glass this time.*

It was all part of her routine now. Her father would get drunk, find something to get mad about, take it out on Lexi and then on her mom, who later came after Lexi because she was always the one responsible for "instigating" the whole thing.

That was her mother's favourite word: instigate.

Well, that was life. That was how Lexi lived and what she'd come to accept. The worst part was that she'd never get out. Nobody would believe her. The Vogans were loved by everyone. They were perfect in everyone's eyes—the perfect neighbours, the perfect couple, the perfect parents.

Nobody had a clue what went on behind closed doors.

She couldn't escape the beatings. There was never a break, because she was an only child. She had no brothers or sisters to protect her, nobody else to take it in her place.

No, she took it all.

Just like she'd taken it tonight.

Wide awake, Lexi's eyes fixed upon the circular scar on her wrist, illuminated under the pale light of the moon through her window.

That came from her dad too, but a couple of years ago.

Still, she remembered.

He had been drunk, as usual, and when he complained that Lexi had the volume too high on the television, he pounced on her, drove her to the ground, and held her still while he pressed his lit cigarette into her wrist, watching with glowing eyes to see how fast it would take to burn through the flesh.

And there was her mother, hand pressed against Lexi's mouth to silence her screams.

They couldn't let the neighbours hear.

That had been the worst of it. She'd never be able to forget the feeling of fire singeing her skin. Sometimes Lexi wondered if her parents would ever do something like that again. At least the bruises would go away with time, but that scar wouldn't.

And neither would the scars on the inside.

As Lexi rolled over onto her back, realizing it was going to be another long night, she felt her ears prickle. The screaming had begun.

Like it always did when her dad ran out of beer.

"What did you do with it?" her father shrieked at her mother, who Lexi imagined was glowering back at him, arms crossed at chest level. It was weird. He beat her nearly as savagely as he beat Lexi, but she wasn't afraid of him.

Her dad wasn't finished. "There's no more beer!"

"I don't drink, Phil. That's your thing!" her mother shot back.

"Well, give me some of your stash then. I need something!"

"I got no stash left, because you forgot to buy more!" Her mom sounded like a banshee with all that high-pitched shrieking, and it sounded like she was throwing something. Lexi heard whatever it was shatter. "We got no money because you spent it all on your booze! You haven't been working, because you're a sorry excuse of a man! You're nothin' but lazy!"

If there was one thing that set her father off more than anything else, it was when he was talked back to.

Lexi held her breath.

All hell broke loose. Everything jumbled together—the crashing, the screaming, the thumping, the yelling, the shrieking. Lexi couldn't hear any of their words. That was bad news; when you couldn't hear words anymore, you knew it had reached the potential for an explosion.

She wanted to float away from it all, find a cloud somewhere and drift away. She'd heard enough for one day.

The sounds were easy to pick out. There was the slap, there was her mother wailing, there was her mother shrieking through her tears, there were her father's booming threats.

Lexi swallowed as the screaming escalated. It seemed like they couldn't possibly scream any louder, but they did.

She shivered, felt her arms tingling. Things were getting really bad down there. Had they ever battled each other this *bad? Their fights were always bad, but Lexi had never heard anything like this.*

And then her mother shrieked, high-pitched, terrified.

The shriek echoed off every wall, pulsed through every room.

Lexi's eyes widened.

She'd never heard her mom scream like—

BANG!

Lexi jumped, nearly screamed out.

She knew that sound. She wished she could pretend like she'd never heard it before, but no; she'd know that sound anywhere. Her dad had his hobbies. He enjoyed hunting in the woods, bagging a deer every few weeks. Lexi had never gone with him on a hunt, but she'd watch from her bedroom window when he practiced on soup cans in the backyard, his prized shotgun resting on his shoulder.

BANG! There went the soup can.

That was the sound that ricocheted off every surface in their tiny house.

Now, it was quiet.

Too quiet.

Her mother wasn't screaming. Why wasn't she screaming anymore? Her mother never buckled that easily, not even after she'd been beaten.

Lexi couldn't move. It was like her limbs forgot they were alive.

Still, that heavy silence.

Lexi didn't even blink.

"Mary?" *her father yelled out, his tone desperate.* "Mary, Mary! Oh, what did I do?"

It almost sounded like he was sobbing now. No, that couldn't be right. Her dad didn't cry. He'd never cried a day in his life. He hadn't even shed a single tear when his own father had passed away, seven months ago. Everyone else at that funeral had cried, everyone but him.

So, why would he cry now? And why was it so quiet? Why wasn't her mother fighting back? Why wasn't her father bellowing?

His sobs carried to Lexi's ears, sounding so foreign, so wrong. Why was he crying like that? What would—

BANG!

The same echo that had sparked her memory, brought back those images of the lined-up soup cans. Yes, she'd know that sound anywhere.

But no. It couldn't be that sound—not here, not in this house, not tonight.

A silence deader than anything she knew of floated in the balance, hovered even in her room, where she lay as still as a corpse.

She waited, waited for the eruption of her parents to start all over again, but there was nothing but silence. After a while, she told herself to go downstairs, to solve this mystery, to figure out why it was so quiet—but she didn't dare.

She was terrified of what she would find.

Lexi had no idea how long she lay there, wide-eyed, staring at the ceiling, waiting for the screaming to begin again. It could have been hours. It could have been minutes. It could have been days. She didn't know. The only thing that was real right now, right this second, was the paralyzing terror of the unknown.

It was like she was trapped in a nightmare, like she couldn't wake up. Those couldn't have been gunshots, not like the gunshots that killed all those deer, not like the gunshots that pelted holes through those old soup cans. Not actual *gunshots. Not in her house, not right downstairs. That was only something that happened in nightmares.*

Right?

If she was right, then why weren't they fighting anymore? If everything was normal, why weren't they bellowing at each other like always?

The answer tried to creep its way into her mind, the truth, but denial was so much easier. There hadn't been gunshots. Her parents were probably passed out on the sofa, too drunk or high to fight anymore.

Except, wasn't that why they'd been fighting in the first place, because they'd been out of beer, they'd been out of drugs?

Lexi's thoughts were frozen, her heart a wild animal in her chest. She wanted to wake up from this prison of a nightmare.

Then she heard the sirens, just like the sirens she always heard at night, especially in this part of town. These sirens rang louder and louder, breaking through the silent void.

Those sirens weren't going to pass her house. They were coming *to her house.*

Tires screeched to a halt; the gravel in her driveway turned. Car doors opened up, slammed shut. Lexi heard muffled voices floating up to her bedroom window.

She trembled, crawled out of her stupor long enough to rise up on knees that threatened to buckle underneath her. She stole a careful peek out her window.

Her front lawn looked like a scene from a movie: there were cop cars, an ambulance, and a crowd of nosy neighbours speckling the sidewalk, all whispering to each other. Everyone looked so panicked. Why? Even the police officers seemed unsettled as they stepped onto her front porch and came through the door.

Her *door!*

They were in the house.

A gasp caught in her throat as she backed away from the window, heavy breaths exploding from her chest. Why would the cops be here?

She knew. She knew why the cops were here, but she couldn't bring herself to admit it. The longer you floated in the balance of denial, the longer you could go without having to deal with truth.

But even now, she couldn't find that place, and in a fit of panic she drew her knees to her chest, breathing fast, clinging hard.

Go away. Go away. Go away.

She squeezed her eyes shut tight.

This. Wasn't. Real.

But if it wasn't real, why could she make out the voices from downstairs?

"You know these people long, ma'am?" a deep voice asked.

"Yes, ever since I moved in, seven years ago," came the response.

It was Mrs. Shoeing, their busybody neighbour who had to make everything her business. She was just a big snoop.

She must have been the one who called the cops.

Why can't you just mind your own business?

"Would there be anyone else in the house, ma'am?" that deep voice asked.

Lexi froze. No, no there isn't anybody else, just go away, please go away!

"Why yes, they had a daughter," Mrs. Shoeing replied, the traitor. "She's about twelve or so."

Frig, she couldn't even get her age right! She was actually thirteen this year.

As if Mrs. Shoeing cared.

It didn't matter, because right now the reality was the thumping footsteps ascending the hardwood stairs that creaked loudly with every step.

Someone was coming.

Mrs. Shoeing had told the police there was a daughter. If her parents were still downstairs, that could only mean one thing: they were looking for her.

Why were they looking for her? Why were they here?

You know why they're here!

No, no, no.

Go away. Go away!

It all happened so quickly that there wasn't any time to come up with a plan, a way out. Her doorknob jiggled, and just like that her door was open.

They'd found her.

Two figures stepped into the room. One of them fumbled for a light switch, and found it.

Lexi squinted, temporarily blinded. After her eyes adjusted, she made out the two police officers with her in the room, a man and a woman.

The woman was looking right at her. Her eyes were as big as saucers, her mouth a thin line. Her presence didn't help Lexi's denial. How could she deny it anymore? The reality of the situation was settling on her.

The gunshots.

Now the police.

It all had to be connected.

Does that mean…?

For some stupid reason, the policewoman thought to offer a small smile.

"Hey, honey," she said quietly. "Can you tell me your name?"

She was speaking to Lexi like she was five.

"Lexi," *Lexi replied, hugging her knees tightly.*

"Do you think you can you tell me what happened tonight?" *the woman asked.*

Lexi's mind buzzed with all that had gone down tonight. No, how could she tell them what had happened? She didn't know. She'd been up here the whole time.

"Mary, oh, what did I do?"

And that hum of silence.

"I—I don't know," *Lexi replied, noticing her fingers trembling against her legs.* "I was just… I was just in bed and, and I… I heard, I thought I heard… gunshots… What happened?"

As if she didn't already know.

The woman's face dropped.

It didn't matter. Lexi knew before the words left her mouth.

"Honey, your parents are dead." She said it bluntly. "There was a struggle. It looks like your dad shot your mother, then shot himself."

Just like that.

Lexi stared at the police officer, repeating her words in her head again and again.

Dead.

Her parents were dead.

She heard it, but she couldn't believe it.

It didn't make sense.

Her parents were dead.

Dead.

Why was she crying?

They'd never loved her.

They'd never wanted her.

They'd only kept her because it would look bad if they didn't.

She had been a mistake. Nothing but a mistake, so why should she care if they were dead?

Stop crying!

She couldn't, no matter how wrong it felt.

"We're going to have to take you to the station, Lexi," the woman said, breaking through the wall of silence. "Can you put on a sweater?"

Mechanically, like someone else was in control of her body, Lexi crawled out of bed and drifted to her closet. She couldn't even feel the pain in her legs, the cuts on her feet. She was floating, this wasn't real. But tears still leaked down her cheeks as she imagined the scene downstairs.

Would there be blood?

She shivered as she pulled on a zip-up hoodie.

"Come on, let's go," the policewoman said.

Sniffling, tears attacking her eyes, Lexi followed the two officers from her room, through the hall and down the creaking stairs.

That was when Lexi noticed the other police officer, a bulky guy, nonchalantly trying to position himself next her.

He was trying to shield her from the scene. They didn't want her to see her parents.

But as Lexi came to the bottom of the stairs, passed through the living room, it didn't matter how hard the officer tried; Lexi still caught a glimpse.

Just a small one... just enough to haunt her for the rest of her life.

She saw the thick blood staining the carpet.

She saw their lifeless faces staring at the ceiling.

Their hands were almost touching. It was the closest they'd ever been.

The forgotten shotgun lay between them.

Panic swept Lexi up.

This. Was. Real.

Lexi began to choke on her sobs, to feel sick, to shake all over. She barely felt the policewoman's arms around her, pulling her away from the crime scene.

"I'm getting her out of here," the woman said. "She doesn't need to see this."

As the cop led her away from the house, her *house, Lexi was overcome by tears and terror. Still, she distantly heard the cop answer a question from Mrs. Shoeing, a question Lexi hadn't heard.*

"Well, we'll find out if she has any relatives," the woman answered, trapping Lexi in her hold. "If she doesn't, we'll contact Social Services."

So it began.

CHAPTER 71

L I Z

Thursday, October 29
10:12 p.m.

Liz was finishing up with a patient when she heard the commotion from the waiting room.

Someone was *shouting*.

"You're all set to go, Mrs. Monroe," Liz told her patient, excusing herself from the room, furrowing her eyebrows.

What was going on? Was it an unruly patient who was tired of waiting? Was it a frustrated parent who was demanding their child be seen next?

No, none of that. As the voice grew louder, Liz recognized it as Lexi's before she even saw her.

"I need to see her! Liz, Elizabeth, Dr. Liz, *whatever*... where is she?" Lexi was screaming at the front desk. Poor Jill's eyes were wide with bewilderment.

"Look, she's working," Jill managed. "You can't just come in here and expect everyone to stop what they're doing just for you!"

"But this is important! Call her, tell me where she is, *anything*! Please!"

That was when Liz realized the girl was crying.

Her heart stopped; Lexi *never* cried. Something was very wrong.

Liz jogged toward her and placed her hand on the small of Lexi's back, hoping to calm her down. She recoiled when Lexi flinched, swinging around to see who had touched her.

Oh, Lexi.

The girl was a mess! Her hair was everywhere, her shirt was ripped, bruises had formed around her temples, one of her shoes was gone, she clung to her arm like it hurt, and her face was red and blotchy; tear streaks stained every part of it.

This was *not* the same Lexi who had left an hour ago.

"It's okay, Jill, I got this," Liz told the lost-for-words receptionist, turning back to Lexi. "Come with me."

What had the girl been through in an hour? What had brought her back in this state?

Heart thumping, Liz led the way to an empty room, ushered Lexi inside, and closed the door behind them.

Lexi's sobs sounded like they were strangling her. Her tiny body shook from head to toe.

Liz couldn't even find words. What was going on? Surely Lexi had to be upset about Barney's death, but that didn't explain the bruises, the rips in her clothes, the missing shoe. Liz was sick with worry, but she calmed herself enough to ease Lexi into a chair.

"Hey, you're okay," she tried soothingly, carefully moving stray strands of hair off Lexi's face. "Try and calm down, sweetie; it's going to be all right."

Was it? She didn't even know what had happened. How could she make promises like that?

Lost for words, lost for what she should do next, Liz jumped up to get a glass of water while Lexi bent over, hiding her face in her knees.

Water seemed a good place to start; the girl was in hysterics!

Then Liz noticed that the sweater Lexi had been wearing earlier was gone. Where was it?

Her hands trembled as she poured the water.

God, please help us.

398

Resuming her place in front of Lexi, she took the girl's hand in her own, pressed the cold glass into it, and motioned for her to take a sip.

Lexi didn't. She could barely hold the glass.

"Okay, maybe in a bit." Liz took the glass away and concentrated on Lexi, her heart snapping in two seeing all those tears, seeing the *terror* behind those eyes.

What had happened?

Lexi was trembling, and her sobs were more like gasps. No, Liz couldn't wait any longer. Lexi wasn't going to calm down anytime soon.

"Lexi, what happened?" she asked finally, trying to catch Lexi's eyes. She had to know.

Lexi's voice trembled as she tried to speak. "I'm n–not going b–back there," she said, trying to catch her breath. "I'm n...not, I c...can't, I'm n...not ever g...going back!"

"It's okay, Lexi. I'm not going to make you." She took Lexi's hand in her own, needing to send a message that she wasn't alone.

Lexi didn't pull away, but she squeezed her eyes shut.

Liz swallowed; this had to be more than Barney's death. Something else had happened. Something that had torn her from the inside-out.

"Talk to me, Lexi," Liz tried, squeezing Lexi's hand for support, finding her own hand trembling along with the girl's. As much as Liz needed to know the truth, she was scared to find out what it was. What could have rattled the girl to this point?

"It was S...Slick. He attacked me." Lexi covered her eyes with her hand, released a convulsive sigh. "I...it was h...his fault B... Barney took the pills. I...I went to him, I wanted t...to y...yell at him for what he did, but, h...h...he j...jumped me, and..."

She couldn't even finish. She was bordering on hyperventilating.

Liz's heart was clawing at her chest, her blood reaching a boiling point, fear terrorizing every corner of her mind as she imagined the worst.

Be strong! Be strong for her!

Sucking in a breath, she squeezed Lexi's hand again, prompting her. "Lexi, keep going. I need to know."

Lexi shook. "He held me down, he t...tried to kiss me, he held me there, he... he t...tried to g...get m...my shirt off, he..."

Lost for words, again.

Bitter tears burned the corners of Liz's eyes, her next question resting on the tip of her tongue. A big part of her didn't want to know the answer, didn't want to hear about anything else Lexi had been through.

It hurt too much.

But she had to know, for Lexi's sake.

"Lexi," Liz started, placing her other hand on top of her own, with Lexi's. "Did he rape you?"

Lexi was quiet for a moment, a long moment. Fresh tears leaked from the corners of her eyes.

Liz's breath hovered in the quiet space, waiting.

The girl shook her head, and gentle relief washed over Liz.

"N...no, but h...he wanted to. I...I c...couldn't get away, he... he held me there, I...I t...tried, but he held me there. But... the p... pepper spray... I got away. H...he ch...chased me and..." Lexi was hysterical. "I can't go back there! I can't! I *can't!* I'm sorry! I'm sorry! I didn't know... I didn't know where else to g...go!"

Liz couldn't believe what she was hearing, couldn't believe what had happened. She was terrified for Lexi but thankful to God a million times over for that pepper spray. To think what could have happened...

Oh, Lexi. All Liz wanted was to pull the girl close, to tell her it would be okay, but what could she ever say that would make it all better?

Then Liz felt a nudge. A nudge at her heart.

That was it—she could speak from her heart.

"Lexi, you don't have to go back there. I'm not going to make you." Liz reached out to smooth Lexi's hair back. "We'll figure this out."

But Lexi pulled away, glared at Liz with fire in her eyes.

"Figure this out?" she yelled. "Figure *what* out? Where I'm gonna live, where I'm gonna go? Don't you get it? I've got nowhere to run this time!"

Lexi's body was still shaking, but now she was angry.

"Nobody ever wanted me! My mom and my dad only kept me 'cause they had to. They were always drunk or stoned out of their faces, and they always got angry. At *me!*" Lexi stuck out her wrist, the one with that purple scar, the cigarette burn Liz remembered so well.

Liz opened her mouth, but Lexi wasn't finished.

"My parents hated me, but it doesn't matter, because they died anyway! Nobody's ever wanted me! I was nothing but a slut to the others, a replacement for the baby they'd always wanted, shoved out the door as soon as a baby came along, treated like an object for men's pleasure, beaten like an animal! Nobody ever wanted me, not for anything good! The only place left for me was the streets, and I can't even go there anymore!" Bitter tears rolled down her face. "So don't tell me we'll figure this out! I'm not going back to Tampa! I'm not going back into foster care! I'd rather *die!*"

Liz watched Lexi unravelling at the seams. A very real pain cut Liz to her deepest core as she finally learned what Lexi had been through.

It was worse than anything she'd imagined.

Physical abuse.

Sexual abuse.

Emotional abuse.

Neglect. She had no one in the world to call her own, no one in the world who cared.

It was no wonder she'd run away. It was no wonder she'd shut down.

It wasn't fair.

Liz was seeing poor Lexi through a whole new lens. Yes, it all made sense now. It all came together.

"Oh Lexi," Liz said. "I'm so sorry. You have every right to be angry, upset, frustrated. You've been through more in your life than anyone your age should *ever* have to go through."

She gently placed her hand on Lexi's, waiting for her to pull away, but she didn't, not this time.

"And it's not true, Lexi." Liz took a breath, mouthed a silent prayer. "You *are* wanted."

But Lexi could only shake her head. "Yeah, I know what you're gonna say: *God* wants me."

It wasn't said out of malice or anger. She was just saying it.

"Well yes, that's very true, but there's more than that." Liz managed a small smile. "*I* want you."

There it was. Out in the open.

Lexi stopped, then froze up like an ice sculpture and met Liz's eyes. Her brown eyes glowed with uncertainty.

"W...what?" she asked, skepticism lacing her voice.

Liz couldn't blame her. It was foreign to her, too.

"I care about you, Lexi." She felt stronger with every word, as though God was affirming this more with every passing second. "I want to take you home with me. I want you to be healthy and happy, and I want you to know you are loved, *every* day."

Her own tears streamed down her cheeks as she squeezed Lexi's hand tight.

"Lexi, I know this is new to you, but I care about you more than I've cared about anything for a long time. Honey, we've both been through so much, but I know we can get through it. Together."

Lexi didn't move, she didn't pull away, and she didn't say anything. She just listened.

"I know how this sounds. You're scared, and that's okay." Liz paused, feeling the stone walls around her heart tumbling. "I want to keep you safe. I want to take care of you. I... I want you to be my daughter."

Terror pulsed through her, but also peace. It was a strange balance.

True, she had no way of knowing how Lexi would react, how she was going to take it. How could she know if the girl would ever trust Liz enough to know she was telling the truth? It was frightening place to be.

At the same time, an overwhelming sense of assurance rested upon her like a warm blanket. She almost thought she could hear words in her heart, words from her loving Father.

"Well done, good and faithful servant."

Suddenly, Lexi was crying again.

She wasn't angry.

She wasn't freaking out.

She was just... crying.

Like a little girl who needed her mother.

In the quiet hum of that hospital room, she spoke. "Nobody," Lexi whispered, shuddering with her sobs, "nobody could ever love *me!*"

Instinctively, Liz grabbed hold of Lexi's arms, stared at her with all the authenticity she had.

"Lexi, that's not true! *I* love you! So much. More than that, *God* loves you." A tear touched her lip. "You don't have to be alone ever again! I know that a lot of people have hurt you, and it makes me so angry to imagine what you've been through, but Lexi, you are a wonderful girl who didn't deserve any of it. I know you've been hurt, but I promise you, from the bottom of my heart, that I will do my best to keep you safe, and I will *never* hurt you."

Lexi looked like she couldn't speak, couldn't frame any response. She only shook her head, slowly, like she wanted desperately to reach out and grab the opportunity but was terrified to let herself become this vulnerable, scared to death of being hurt again. How could Liz blame her for that?

But Liz also knew, with all her heart, that she could *never* hurt Lexi. She was too precious.

Lexi's silent weeping seeped through to the inner chambers of Liz's heart.

She couldn't take it anymore. She rose to her knees and carefully gathered Lexi in her arms, pulled her close and held her snug.

Lexi's body went rigid against Liz, but she didn't push away. For that, Liz refused to let her go. Lexi had to know... she *needed* to know... that this was safe.

"It's okay, Lexi," Liz whispered, her hand smoothing Lexi's hair. "I'm right here."

It took three seconds. Only three.

Liz knew, because she would remember this moment for the rest of her life.

Lexi's body collapsed, all the tension melted, and her arms flung around Liz's neck, holding on as though the world would fall apart if she ever let go. She cried, and Liz joined right in as she rocked the girl back and forth.

"It's okay, Lexi. I'm right here; I'm not going anywhere," she whispered. "You're safe."

Liz held Lexi close, and for the first time since she'd known Lexi, she knew why their paths had crossed. God had been watching from the very beginning, orchestrating the whole thing. Yes, it had all been for a reason.

And this was it.

You turned my wailing into dancing;
you removed my sackcloth and clothed me with joy,
that my heart may sing to you and not be silent.
O LORD my God, I will give you thanks forever.

~Psalm 30:11–12

||||||||||||||||||||||||||||||||||||||||||||

L I Z and L E X I

It was a rough start, those first few months.

That night, after Lexi's broken arm was casted, Liz took her home. She brought her up to the guest room and put her to bed, lending her a pair of pajamas. There wasn't much more needing to be said that night, so Liz left Lexi to try and find sleep. Lexi was exhausted, emotionally savaged, and so was Liz.

Poor Lexi was a wreck and couldn't sleep for several nights. Nightmares plagued her.

Liz prayed for her every night. How long would it take for a lifetime of terror to disappear?

Eventually, Liz sat down with Lexi to discuss adoption, to discuss keeping her here on a permanent basis. Lexi was hesitant and unsure at first, scared to death that the whole thing would turn out to be another bad experience to tack onto her growing list of bad experiences.

But Lexi also knew there was nowhere else to go.

So she finally told Liz about Everidge, about Bridget, and together Liz and Lexi made the trip down to Tampa.

They met with Bridget, who was less than pleased at the sight of Lexi. The caseworker chastised her for running away, for making her worried sick. Lexi didn't buy it, not a single word— Bridget probably hadn't even noticed her absence. How many kids was she responsible for? No, Lexi was nothing more than a number.

Either way, Liz and Lexi recounted their story, about how they had met and all that Lexi had been through. Mostly important, they talked about Liz's interest in adopting Lexi.

It took some time, a lot of paper work, and night classes for Liz to attend, but it wasn't long before Liz was signed on as a temporary foster mother to Lexi, on the right track toward adoption.

Oh, the paperwork was endless, the interviews intrusive, the home visits uncomfortable, but it was all worth the effort, because six months later, the official papers came in the mail. Liz signed them, and it was official: Lexi was adopted.

The name on the certificate took some getting used to: Alexis Carolyna Jade Swavier.

It was a long time before Lexi came to trust Liz. A lifetime of bad memories stood in the way, so there were struggles, hurdles to overcome. It wasn't always easy, for either Liz or Lexi, but Liz refused to give up. It took time for Lexi to feel safe, to feel wanted, but eventually, after several months of safe experiences and happy memories, Lexi knew and believed Liz would *never* hurt her.

She genuinely did care for her—and *love* her.

At first, Lexi was reluctant to go to church with Liz, still unsure about the whole God thing, but a few months passed and Lexi accepted Jesus into her life. She remembered what Star had said about life not magically becoming better because of it, but Lexi did *feel* different. The best word to describe it, for Lexi, was peace, like an inner knowledge that Someone was *always* there, loving on you no matter what you did, no matter where you went. For Lexi, it was a hope she'd never experienced, a hope that there was always something more—something better—no matter what crap this life could hurl at you. It was a love like nothing she'd ever experienced. It changed her life.

To Liz's surprise and great joy, and despite all the negative feedback she'd received from Kathryn, Jenn, and her mother, everyone fell in love with Lexi almost instantly. Her parents, her brothers, and her nieces and nephews took to Lexi like glue. Anne was teaching Lexi how to crochet, Erica somehow managed to drag Lexi into her doll haven *every* visit, and Lexi even helped Ricky out with his piano lessons. Lexi was great with kids, and it wasn't long before even Kathryn enlisted Lexi to babysit Nancy every other Saturday evening.

Lexi still kept in touch with her friends from the tunnels. She even managed to convince Star to come to church with her and Liz every Sunday, which floored Star, but she was even *more* excited to hear that Lexi had found Jesus. She had Lexi repeat her story almost every week.

Not long after she moved in with Liz, Lexi saw DV, and he brought her down to the Pit, covered up her eyes so he could show her his finished mural, a beautiful landscape with all those amazing birds progressing through life.

Now, they were soaring through the air, happy, free.

DV told Lexi she ended up being his number-one inspiration for the way it all turned out. He said that once he found out about Liz, and about Lexi's adoption, he finished those birds playing together in the sky as a tribute to Lexi's happy ending. Sometimes Lexi wished she could take that mural home with her. There were so many memories in that corner with DV, with Barney.

Lexi always held a very special place in her heart for the Tunnel Kids. She could never forget how hard it had been to survive through hunger and extreme poverty. She even started up a food drive with the help of the youth group at Liz's church—*her* church—to collect money and make sandwiches once a week for her to take down to the Pit.

Lexi was the only one who could bring the sandwiches, of course. The street kids would never let anyone else in; the Tunnel Kids were an exclusive club, but they still saw Lexi as one of their own.

Even though she went down into the Pit, she was asked by Liz to carry her cellphone with her at all times and to stay in places where there were eyes everywhere. Liz was terrified of even letting her down here in the first place but understood why Lexi needed to do it.

Still, Liz couldn't help herself. She was overprotective of Lexi and was thankful that Lexi didn't rebel against her for it. After everything Slick had done, Liz was hesitant to even let her go *downtown* alone.

But Lexi never saw Slick again. Sure, they'd called the cops, reported him, but somehow Slick vanished from the tunnels. Nobody had seen him since.

Lexi knew he was out there, somewhere.

Lexi visited Barney a lot. He was buried in the same cemetery as Kurt, and Liz and Lexi made an effort to go as often as they could. With the help of Star and DV, Lexi managed to track down the name of Barney's mother and sent her a letter, telling her that Patrick had passed away. It didn't matter how bad of a mother she may have been to Barney, she still deserved to know.

Liz cut back her hours at the hospital. She still worked full-time, but she limited herself to days as much as possible, so she could spend her evenings at home with Lexi.

It took a while for Lexi to catch up on all the schoolwork she'd missed during her absence, but she started at a new school, and with Liz's constant encouragement and help, Lexi pulled her average back up to the straight-As she was used to, excelling in music and classical piano.

Liz took up painting again and bought Lexi a piano, saying that they both needed their creative outlets. The first thing Liz did after she cleaned up the art studio was finish *The Lion Cubs*. Even though it was painful, she knew it needed to be done. It helped that Lexi was almost as encouraging as Kurt had been.

Now *The Lion Cubs* hung over their fireplace, finished at last.

They had their highs, and they had their lows. Life wasn't a fairy tale, but at least it became easier. Liz and Lexi moved forward, taking each day as it came. Though there were many bumps along the way, they travelled the road together.

***

Ten Months Later

"Lexi, for goodness sake, would you hurry up?" Liz called up the stairs. "We're going to be late, and you know how my mother is about being late."

She checked her watch for the third time since she'd first called Lexi down.

"I'm coming!"

Liz rolled her eyes with a grin. *Sure, that's what you told me ten minutes ago.*

But then came the thunderous footsteps, and there was Lexi at the top of the stairs, gazing down at Liz.

"Is this shirt appropriate?" Lexi asked, spinning around to model a new tank top with wide straps. It covered her belly completely. "Or will your mom think it's too revealing?"

Liz sighed, glancing at the shirt she'd never seen before. "When did you get that?"

Lexi shrugged.

That was one habit she hadn't broken.

"I bought it last week when I went shopping with Ginger," Lexi replied. "Don't you like it?"

"It's nice, and it's not revealing at all, but," Liz made a face, "it's pink."

Lexi laughed, coming down the stairs. "You and pink, seriously! Anyway, you should embrace pink a little more. It would go really well with a lot of your paintings."

"You sound like Kurt," Liz said with a smile. "He used to tease me because I never used pink."

Lexi grinned, looking at her shirt. "You sure it's okay?"

Liz nodded. "Yeah it's great. It's just pink."

"Well, I'm not changing," she said with a groan.

"You don't have to." Liz grabbed her purse. "Do you have your swimsuit?"

"Yeah, I'm wearing it underneath."

410

"Good, because you know Lissy. She'd have a hissy fit if you didn't swim with her."

Lexi laughed. "Believe me, I won't make that mistake again. I felt so bad for making her cry."

"Okay, we'd better get going. The car's unlocked," Liz said, reaching for her keys.

"Did you get the brownies I made last night? I left them on the table," Lexi asked, stopping at the door.

"Yes, sweetheart, they're in the car." Liz raised an eyebrow with a grin. "Everything's ready. We're just waiting on a certain slowpoke."

Lexi smiled back.

"Yeah, whatever."